I0785685

B. M. Bower

The Trail of the White Mule & Casey Ryan
(Western Adventure Classics)

OK Publishing 2021

B. M. Bower

The Trail of the White Mule & Casey Ryan

(Western Adventure Classics)

Wild West Adventure Novels

Published by

Books

- Advanced Digital Solutions & High-Quality book Formatting -

musaicumbooks@okpublishing.info

2021 OK Publishing

ISBN 978-80-272-7567-0

Contents

Casey Ryan

Chapter I

From Denver to Spokane, from El Paso to Fort Benton, men talk of Casey Ryan and smile when they speak his name. Old men with the flat tone of coming senility in their voices will suck at their pipes and cackle reminiscently while they tell you of Casey's tumultuous youth-when he drove the six fastest horses in Colorado on the stage out from Cripple Creek, and whooped past would-be holdups with a grin of derision on his face and bullets whining after him and passengers praying disjointed prayers and clinging white-knuckled to the seats.

They say that once a flat, lanky man climbed bareheaded out at the stage station below the mountain and met Casey coming springily off the box with whip and six reins in his hand. The lanky man was still pale from his ride, and he spluttered when he spoke:

"Sa-ay! N-next time you're held up and I'm r-ridin' with yuh, b-by gosh, you s-*stop*. I-I'd ruther be shot t-than p-pitched off into a c-canyon, s-somewhere a-and busted up!"

Casey is a little man. When he was young he was slim, but he always has owned a pale blue, unwinking squint which he uses with effect. He halted where he was and squinted up at the man, and spat fluid tobacco and grinned.

"You're here, and you're able to kick about my drivin'. That's purty good luck, I'd say. You *ain't* shot, an' you ain't layin' busted in no canyon. Any time a man gits shot outa Casey Ryan's stage, he'll have to jump out an' wait for the bullet to ketch up. And there ain't any passengers offn' this stage layin' busted in no canyon, neither. I bring in what I start out with."

The other man snorted and reached under his coat tail for the solacing plug of chewing tobacco. Opposition and ridicule had brought a little color into his face.

"Why, hell, man! You-you come around that ha-hairpin turn up there on two wheels! It's a miracle we wasn't —"

"Miracles is what happens once and lets it go at that. Say! Casey Ryan *always* saves wear on a coupla wheels, on that turn. I've made it on one; but the leaders wasn't runnin' right to-day. That nigh one's cast a shoe. I gotta have that looked after." He gave up the reins to the waiting hostler and went off, heading straight for the station porch where waited a red-haired girl with freckles and a warm smile for Casey.

That was Casey's youth; part of it. The rest was made up of fighting, gambling, drinking hilariously with the crowd and always with his temper on hair trigger. Along the years behind him he left a straggling procession of men, women and events. The men and women would always know the color of his eyes and would recognize the Casey laugh in a crowd, years after they had last heard it; the events were full of the true Casey flavor, —and as I say, when men told of them and mentioned Casey, they laughed.

From the time when his daily drives were likely to be interrupted by holdups, and once by a grizzly that reared up in the road fairly under the nose of his leaders and sent the stage off at an acute angle, blazing a trail by itself amongst the timber, Casey drifted from mountain to desert, from desert to plain and back again, blithely meeting hard luck face to face and giving it good day as if it were a friend. For Casey was born an optimist, and misfortune never quite got him down and kept him there, though it tried hard and often, as you will presently see. Some called him gritty. Some said he hadn't the sense to know when he was licked. Either way, it made a rare little Irishman of Casey Ryan, and kept his name from becoming blurred in the memories of those who once knew him.

So in time it happened that Casey was driving a stage of his own from Pinnacle down to Lund, in Nevada, and making boast that his four horses could beat the record-the month's record, mind-of any dog-gone auty-*mo*-bile that ever infested the trail. Infest is a word that Casey would have used often had he known its dictionary reputation. Having been deprived of close acquaintance with dictionaries, but having a facile imagination and some creative ability, Casey kept pace with progress and invented words of his own which he applied lavishly to all automobiles; but particularly and emphatically he applied the spiciest, most colorful ones to Fords.

Put yourself in Casey's place, and you will understand. Imagine yourself with a thirty-mile trip to make down a twisty, rough mountain road built in the days when men hauled ore down the mountain on wagons built to bump over rocks without damage to anything but human bones. You are Casey Ryan, remember; you never stopped for stage robbers or grizzlies in the past, and you have your record to maintain as the hardest driver in the West. You are proud of that record, because you know how you have driven to earn it.

You pop the lash over the ears of your leaders and go whooping down a long, straight bit of road where you count on making time. When you are about halfway down and the four horses are running even and tugging pleasantly at the reins, and you are happy enough to sing your favorite song, which begins,

"Hey, ole Bill! Can-n yuh play the fiddle-o?   Yes, by gosh! I —I —kin play a liddle-o —"

and never gets beyond that one flat statement, around the turn below you comes a Ford, rattling all its joints trying to make the hill on "high." The driver honks wildly at you to give him the road-you, Casey Ryan! Wouldn't you writhe and invent words and apply them viciously to all Fords and the man who invented them? But the driver comes at you honking, squawking, —and you turn out.

You have to, unless the Ford does; and Fords don't. A Ford will send a twin-six swerving sharply to the edge of a ditch, and even Casey Ryan must swing his leaders to the right in obedience to that raucous command.

Once Casey didn't. He had the patience of the good-natured, and for awhile he had contented himself with his vocabulary and his reputation as a driver and a fighter, and the record he held of making the thirty miles from Pinnacle to Lund in an hour and thirty-five minutes, twenty-six days in the month. (He did not publish his running expenses, by the way, nor did he mention the fact that his passengers were mostly strangers picked up at the railway station at Lund because they liked the look of the picturesque four-horses-and-Casey stagecoach.)

Once Casey refused to turn out. That morning he had been compelled to wait and whip a heavy man who berated Casey because the heavy man's wife had ridden from Pinnacle to Lund the day before and had fainted at the last sharp turn in the road and had not revived in time to board the train for Salt Lake which she had been anxious to catch. Casey had known she was anxious to catch the train, and he had made the trip in an hour and twenty-nine minutes in spite of the fact that he had driven the last mile with a completely unconscious lady leaning heavily against his left shoulder. She made much better time with Casey than she would have made on the narrow-gauge train which carried ore and passengers and mail to Lund, arriving when most convenient to the train crew. That it took half an hour to restore her to consciousness was not Casey's fault.

Casey had succeeded in whipping the heavy man till he hollered, but the effort had been noticeable. Casey wondered uneasily whether by any chance he, Casey Ryan, was growing old with the rest of the world. That possibility had never before occurred to him, and the thought was disquieting. Casey Ryan too old to lick any man who gave him cause, too old to hold the fickle esteem of those who met him in the road? Casey squinted belligerently at the Old-man-with-the-scythe and snorted. "I licked him good. You ask anybody. And he's twice as big as I am. I guess they's a good many years left in Casey Ryan yet! Giddap, you-thus-and-so! We're ten minutes late and we got our record!"

At that moment a Ford touring car popped around the turn below him and squawked presumptuously for a clear passage ahead. Casey pulled his lash off the nigh leader, yelled and charged straight down the road. Did they think they could honk him off the road? Hunh! Casey Ryan was still Casey Ryan. Never again would he turn out for man or devil.

Wherefore Casey was presently extricating his leaders from the harness of his wheelers ten feet below the grade. On the road above him the driver of the Ford inspected bent parts and a smashed headlight and cranked and cranked ineffectively, and swore down at Casey Ryan, who squinted unblinkingly up under his hatbrim at the man he likewise cussed.

They were a long while there exchanging disagreeable opinions of one another, and Casey was even obliged to climb the steep bank and whip the driver of the Ford because he had applied a word to Casey which had never failed as automatic prelude to a Casey Ryan combat. Casey was frankly winded when he finally mounted one of his horses and led the other three, and so proceeded to Lund as mad as he had ever been in his life.

"That there settles it final," he snorted, when the town came into view in the flat below. "They've pushed Casey off'n the grade for the first time and the last time. What pushin' and crowdin' and squawkin' is done from now on, it'll be Casey Ryan doin' it! Faint! I'll learn 'em something to faint about. If it's Fords goin' to run horses off'n the trail, you watch how Casey Ryan'll drive the livin' tar outa one. Dog-gone 'em, there ain't no Ford livin' that can drive Casey off'n the road. I'll drive 'em till their tongues hang out. I'll make 'em bawl like a calf, and I'll pound 'em on the back and make 'em fan it faster."

So talking to himself and his team he rode into town and up to one of those ubiquitous Ford agencies that write their curly-tailed blue lettering across the continent from the high nose of Maine to the shoulder of Cape Flattery.

"Gimme one of them dog-goned blankety bing-bing Ford auty-*mo*-biles," he commanded the garage owner who came to meet Casey amiably in his shirt sleeves. "Here's four horses I'll trade yuh, with what's left of the harness. And up at the third turn you'll find a good wheel off'n the stage." He slid down from the sweaty back of his nigh leader and stood slightly bow-legged and very determined before the garage owner, Bill Masters.

"Wel-l—there ain't much sale for horses, Casey. I ain't got any place to keep 'em, nor any feed. I'll sell yuh a Ford on time, and—"

Casey glanced over his shoulder to make sure the horses were standing quiet, dropped the reins and advanced upon Bill.

"You *trade*," he stated flatly.

Bill backed a little. "Oh, all right, if that's the way yuh feel. What yuh askin' for the four just as they stand?"

"Me? A Ford auty-*mo*-bile. I told yuh that, Bill. And I want you to put on the biggest horn that's made; one that can be heard from here to Pinnacle and back when I turn 'er loose. And run the damn thing out here right away and show me how it works, and how often you gotta wind it and when. Lucky I didn't bring no passengers down—I was runnin' empty. But I gotta take back a load of Bohunks to the Bluebird this afternoon, and my stage, she's a total wreck. I'll sign papers to-night if you got any to sign."

Thus was the trade effected with much speed and few preliminaries, because Bill knew Casey Ryan very intimately and had seen him in action when his temper was up. Bill adjusted an extra horn which he happened to have in stock. One of those terrific things that go far toward making the life of a pedestrian a nerve-racking succession of startles. Casey tried it out on himself before he would accept it. He walked several doors down the street with the understanding that Bill would honk at him when he was some little distance away. Bill waited until Casey's attention was drawn to a lady with thick ankles who was crossing the street in a hurry and a stiff breeze. Bill came down on the metal plunger of the horn with all his might, and Casey jumped perceptibly and came back grinning.

"She'll do. What'll put a crimp in Casey Ryan's spine is good enough for anybody. Bring her out here and show me how yuh work the damn thing. Guess she'll hold six Bohunks, won't she-with sideboards on? I'll run 'er around a coupla times b'fore I start out-and that's all I will do."

Naturally the garage man was somewhat perturbed at this nonchalant manner of getting acquainted with a Ford. He knew the road from Lund to Pinnacle. He had driven it himself, with a conscious sigh of relief when he had safely negotiated the last hair-pin curve; and Bill was counted a good driver. He suggested an insurance policy to Casey, not half so jokingly as he tried to sound.

Casey turned and gave him a pale blue, unwinking stare. "Say! Never you mind gettin' out insurance on *this* auty-*mo*-bile. What you wanta do is insure the cars that's liable to meet up with me in the trail."

Bill saw the sense of that, too, and said no more about insuring Casey. He drove down the canyon where the road is walled in on both sides by cliffs, and proceeded to give Casey a lesson in driving. Casey did not think that he needed to be taught how to drive. All he wanted to know, he said, was how to stop 'er and how to start 'er. Bill needn't worry about the rest of it.

"She's darn tender-bitted," he commented, after two round trips over the straight half-mile stretch, —and fourteen narrow escapes. "And the man that made 'er sure oughta known better than to make 'er neck rein in harness. And I don't like this windin' 'er up every time you wanta start. But she can sure *go* —and that's what Casey Ryan's after every day in the week.

"All right, Bill. I'll go gather up the Bohunks and start. You better 'phone up to Pinnacle that Casey's on the road-and tell 'em he says it's his road's long's he's on it. They'll know what I mean."

Pinnacle did know, and waited on the sidewalk that afforded a view of the long hill where the road curled down around the head of the gulch and into town. Much sooner than his most optimistic backers had a right to expect-for there were bets laid on the outcome there in Pinnacle-on the brow of the hill a swirl of red dust grew rapidly to a cloud. Like a desert whirlwind it swept down the road, crossed the narrow bridge over the deep cut at the head of the gulch where the famous Youbet mine belched black smoke, and rolled on down the steep, narrow little street.

Out of the whirlwind poked the pugnacious little brass-rimmed nose of a new Ford, and behind the windshield Casey Ryan grinned widely as he swung up to the postoffice and stopped as he had always stopped his four-horse stage, —with a flourish. Stopping with a flourish is fine and spectacular when you are driving horses accustomed to that method and on the lookout for it. Horses have a way of stiffening their forelegs and sliding their hind feet and giving a lot of dramatic finish to the performance. But there is no dramatic sense at all in the tin brain of a Ford. It just stopped. And the insecure fourth Bohunk in the tonneau went hurtling forward into the front seat straight on his way through the windshield. Casey threw up an elbow instinctively and caught him in the collar button and so avoided breakage and blood spattered around. Three other foreigners were scrambling to get out when Casey stopped them with a yell that froze them quiet where they were.

"Hey! You stay right where y'are! I gotta deliver yuh up to the Bluebird in a minute."

There were chatterings and gesticulations in the tonneau. Out of the gabble a shrill voice rose be-seechingly in English. "We will *walk*, meester'. If you *pleese*, meester! We are 'fraid for ride wit' dees may_chine_, meester!"

Casey was nettled by the cackling and the thigh-slapping of the audience on the sidewalk. He reached for his stage whip, and missing it used his ready Irish fists. So the Bohunks crawled unhappily back into the car and subsided shivering and with tears in their eyes.

"Dammit, when I take on passengers to ride, they're goin' to *ride* till they git there. You shut up, back there!"

A friend of Casey's stepped forward and cranked the machine, and Casey pulled down the gas lever until the motor howled, turned in the shortest possible radius and went lunging up the crooked steep trail to the Bluebird mine on top of the hill, his engine racing and screaming in low.

Thereafter Pinnacle and Lund had a new standard by which to measure the courage of a man. Had he made the trip with Casey Ryan and his new Ford? He *had*? By golly, he sure had nerve. One man passed the peak for sheer bravery and rode twice with Casey, but certain others were inclined to disparage the feat, on the ground that on the second trip he was drunk.

Casey did not like that. He admitted that he was a hard driver; he had always been proud because men called him the hardest driver in the West. But he argued that he was also a safe driver, and that they had no business to make such a fuss over riding with him. Didn't he ride after his own driving every day of his life? Had he ever got killed? Had he ever killed anybody else? Well! What were they all yawping about, then? Pinnacle and Lund made him tired.

"If you fellers think I can't bounce that there tin can down the road fast as any man in the country, why don't yuh pass me on the road? You're welcome. Just try it."

No one cared to try, however. Meeting him was sufficiently hazardous. There were those who secretly timed their traveling so that they would not see Casey Ryan at all, and I don't think you can really call them cowards, either. A good many had families, you know.

Casey had an accident now and then; and his tire expense was such as to keep him up nights playing poker for money to support his Ford. You simply can't whirl into town at a thirty-mile gait —I am speaking now of Pinnacle, whose street was a gravelly creek bed quite dry and ridgy between rains-and stop in twice the car's length without scouring more rubber off your tires than a capacity load of passengers will pay for. Besides, you run short of passengers if you persist in doing it. Even the strangers who came in on the Salt Lake line were quite likely to look once at the cute little narrow-gauge train with its cunning little day coach hitched behind a string of ore cars, glance at Casey's Ford stage with indifference and climb into the cunning day coach for the trip to Pinnacle. The psychology of it passed quite over Casey's head, but his pocket felt the change.

In two weeks-perhaps it was less, though I want to be perfectly just — Casey was back, afoot and standing bow-legged in the doorway of Bill Master's garage at Lund.

"Gimme another one of them Ford auty-*mo*-biles," he requested, grinning a little. "I guess mebby I oughta take two or three-but I'm a little short right now, Bill. I ain't been gitting any good luck at poker, lately."

Bill asked a question or two while he led Casey to the latest model of Fords, just in from the factory.

Casey took a chew of tobacco and explained. "Well, I had a bet up, y'see. That red-headed bartender in Pinnacle bet me a hundred dollars I couldn't beat my own record ten minutes on the trip down. I knowed I could, so I took him up on it. A man would be a fool if he didn't grab any easy money like that. And so I pounded 'er on the tail, coming down. And I had eight minutes peeled off my best time, and then Jim Black he had to go git in the road on that last turn up there. We rammed our noses together and I pushed him on ahead of me for fifty rods, Bill-and him yelling at me to quit-but something busted in the insides of my car,

I guess. She give a grunt and quit. All right, I'll take this one. Grease her up, Bill. I'll eat a bite before I take her up."

You've no doubt suspected before now that not even poker, played industriously o' nights, could keep Casey's head above the financial waters that threatened to drown him and his Ford and his reputation. Casey did not mind repair bills, so long as he achieved the speed he wanted. But he did mind not being able to pay the repair bills when they were presented to him. Whatever else were his faults, Casey Ryan had always gone cheerfully into his pocket and paid what he owed. Now he was haunted by a growing fear that an unlucky game or two would send him under, and that he might not come up again.

He began to think seriously of selling his car and going back to horses which, in spite of the high cost of feeding them, had paid their way and his, and left him a pleasant jingle in his pockets. But then he bumped hard into one of those queer little psychological facts which men never take into account until it is too late. Casey Ryan, who had driven horses since he could stand on his toes and fling harness on their backs, could not go back to driving horses. The speed fiend of progress had him by the neck. Horses were too slow for Casey. Moreover, when he began to think about it, he knew that the thirty-mile stretch between Pinnacle and Lund had become too tame for him, too monotonous. He knew in the dark every twist in the road, every sharp turn, and he could tell you offhand what every sharp turn had cost him in the past month, either in repairs to his own car or to the car that had unluckily met him without warning. For Casey, I must tell you, habitually forgot all about that earsplitting klaxon at his left elbow. He was always in too much of a hurry to blow it; and anyway, by the time he reached a turn, he was around it; there either was no car in the road or Casey had scraped paint off it or worse and gone on. So why honk?

Far distances called Casey. In one day, he meditated, he could cover more desert with his Ford than horses could travel in a week. An old, half-buried passion stirred, lifted its head and smiled at him seductively, —a dream he had dreamed of finding some of that wealth which Nature holds so miser-like in her hills. A gold mine, or perhaps silver or copper, —what matter which mineral he found, so long as it spelled wealth for him? Then he would buy a bigger car and a faster car, and he would bore farther and farther into yonder. In his past were tucked away months on end of tramping across deserts and up mountain defiles with a packed burro nipping patiently along in front of him and this same, seductive dream beckoning him over the next horizon. Burros had been slow. While he hurtled down the road from Pinnacle to Lund, Casey pictured himself plodding through sand and sage and over malapai and up dry canyons, hazing a burro before him.

"No, sir, the time for that is gone by. I could do in a week now what it took me a month to do then. I could get into country a man'd hate to tackle afoot, not knowing the water holes. I'll git me a radiator that don't boil like a teakettle over a pitch fire, and load up with water and grub and gas, and I'll find the Injun Jim mine, mebby. Or some other darn mine that'll put me in the clear the rest of my life. Couldn't before, because I had to travel too slow. But shucks! A Ford can go anywhere a mountain goat can go. You ask anybody."

So Casey sold his stage line and the hypothetical good will that went with it, and Pinnacle and Lund breathed long and deep and planned trips they had refrained from taking heretofore, and wished Casey luck. Bill Masters laid a friendly hand on his shoulder and made a suggestion so wise that not even Casey could shut his mind against it.

"You're starting out where there won't be no Bill handy to fix what you bust," he pointed out. "You wait over a day or two, Casey, and let me show yuh a few things about that car. If you bust down on the desert you'll want to know what's wrong, and how to fix it. It's easy, but you got to know where to look for the trouble."

"Me? Say, Bill, I never had to go lookin' for trouble," Casey grinned. "What do I need to learn how for?"

Nevertheless he remained all of that day with Bill and crammed on mechanics. He was amazed to discover how many and how different were the ailments that might afflict a Ford.

That he had boldly-albeit unconsciously-driven a thing filled with timers, high-tension plugs that may become fouled and fail to "spark," carburetors that could get out of adjustment (whatever that was) spark plugs that burned out and had to be replaced, a transmission that absolutely *must* have grease or something happened, bearings that were prone to burn out if they went dry of oil, and a multitude of other mishaps that could happen and did happen if one did not watch out, would have filled Casey with foreboding if that were possible. Being an optimist to the middle of his bones, he merely felt a growing pride in himself. He had actually driven all this aggregation of potential internal grief! Whenever anything had happened to his Ford auty-*mo*-bile between Pinnacle and Lund, Casey never failed to trace the direct cause, which had always been external rather than internal, save that time when he had walked in and bought a new car without out probing into the vitals of the other.

"I'd ruther have a horse down with glanders," he sighed, when Bill finally washed the grease off his hands and forearms and rolled down his sleeves. "But Casey Ryan's game to try anything once, and most things the second and third time. You ask anybody. Gimme all the hootin'-annies that's liable to wear out, Bill, and a load uh tires and patches, and Casey'll come back and hand yuh a diamond big as your fist, some day. Ole Lady Trouble's always tryin' to take a fall outa me, but she's never got me down so't I had to holler 'nough. You ask anybody. Casey Ryan's goin' out to see what he can see. If he meets up with Miss Fortune, he'll tame her, Bill. And this little Ford auty-*mo*-bile is goin' to eat outa my hand. I don't give a cuss if she does git sore and ram her spark plugs into her carburetor now and agin. She'll know who's boss, Bill. I learnt it to the burros, and what you can learn a burro you can learn a Ford, take time enough."

Taking that point of view and keeping it, Casey managed very well. Whenever anything went wrong that his vocabulary and a monkey wrench could not mend, Casey sat down on the shadiest running board and conned the Instruction Book which Bill handed him at the last minute. Other times he treated the Ford exactly as he would treat a burro, with satisfactory results.

Chapter III

Away out on the high mesas that are much like the desert below, except that the nights are cool and the wind is not fanned out of a furnace, Casey fought sand and brush and rocks and found a trail now and then which he followed thankfully, and so came at last to a short range of mountains whose name matched well their inhospitable stare. The Starvation Mountains had always been reputed rich in mineral and malevolent in their attitude toward man and beast. Even the Joshua trees stood afar off and lifted grotesque arms defensively against them. But Casey was not easily daunted, and eerie places held for him no meaning save the purely material one. If he could find water and the rich vein of ore some one had told him was there, then Casey would be happy in spite of snakes, tarantulas and sinister stories of the place.

Water he found, not too far up a gulch. So he pitched his tent within carrying distance from the spring, thanked the god of mechanics that an automobile neither eats nor drinks when it does not work, and set out to find his fortune.

Casey knew there was a mining camp on the high slope of Barren Butte. He knew the name of the camp, which was Lucky Lode, and he knew the foreman there-knew him from long ago in the days when Casey was what he himself confessed to be wild. In reaching Starvation Mountains, Casey had driven for fifteen miles within plain sight of Lucky Lode. But gas is precious when you are a hundred miles from a garage, and since business did not take him there Casey did not drive up the five-mile hill to the Lucky Lode just to shake hands with the foreman and swap a yarn or two. Instead, he headed down on to the bleached, bleak oval of Furnace Lake and forged across it as straight as he could drive toward Starvation Mountains.

But the next time Casey made the trip-needing supplies, powder, fuse, caps and so on-Fate took him by the ear and led him to a lady. This is how Fate did it, —and I will say it was an original idea:

Casey had a gallon syrup can in the car which he used for extra oil for the engine. Having an appetite for sour-dough biscuits and syrup, he had also a gallon can of syrup in the car. It was a terrifically hot day, and the wind that blew full against Casey's left cheek as he drove burned even his leather skin where it struck. Casey was afraid he was running short of water, and a Ford's comfort comes first, —as every man knows; so that Casey was parched pretty thoroughly, inside and out. Within a mile of Furnace Lake he stopped, took an unsatisfying sip from his big canteen and emptied the rest of the water into the radiator. Then he replenished the oil in the motor generously, cranked and went bumping along down the trail worn rough with the trucks from Lucky Lode.

For a little way he jounced along the trail; then the motor began to labor; and although Casey pulled the gas lever down as far as it would go, the car slowed and stopped dead in the road. After an hour of fruitless monkey-wrenching and swearing and sweating, Casey began to suspect something. He examined both cans, "hefted" them, smelt and even tasted the one half-empty, and decided that Ford auty-*mo*-biles do not require two quarts of syrup at one dose. He thought that a little syrup ought not to make much difference, but half a gallon was probably too much.

He put in more oil on top of the syrup, but he could not even move the crank, much less "turn 'er over." So long as a man can wind the crank of a Ford he seems able to keep alive his hopes. Casey could not crank, wherefore he knew himself beaten even while he heaved and lifted and swore, and strained every muscle in his back lifting again. He got so desperately wrathful that he lifted the car perceptibly off its right front wheel with every heave, but he felt as if he were trying to lift a boulder.

It was past supper time at Lucky Lode when Casey arrived, staggering a little with exhaustion, both mental and physical. His eyes were bloodshot with the hot wind, his face was purple from the same wind, his lips were dry and rough. I cannot blame the men at Lucky Lode for a sudden thirst when they saw him coming, and a hope that he still had a little left. And when he told them that he had filled his engine with syrup instead of oil, what would any one think?

Their unjust suspicions would not have worried Casey in the least, had Lucky Lode not possessed a lady cook who was a lady. She was a widow with two children, and she had the children with her and held herself aloof from the men in a manner befitting a lady. Casey was hungry and thirsty and tired, and, as much as was possible to his nature, disgusted, with life in general. The widow gave him a smile of sympathy which went straight to his heart, and hot biscuits and coffee and beans cooked the way he liked them best. These went straight to ease the gnawing emptiness of his stomach, and being a man who took his emotions at their face value, he jumped to the conclusion that it was the lady whose presence gave him the glow.

Casey stayed that night and the next day and the next at Lucky Lode. The foreman helped him tow the syruppy car up the hill to the machine shop where he could get at it, and Casey worked until night trying to remove the dingbats from the hootin'annies, —otherwise, the pistons from the cylinders. The foreman showed him what to do, and Casey did it, using a "double-jack" and a lot of energy.

Before he left the Lucky Lode, Casey knew exactly what syrup will do to a Ford if applied internally, and the widow had promised to marry him if he would stop drinking and smoking and swearing. Since Casey had not been drunk in ten years on account of having seen a big yellow snake with a green head on the occasion of his last carouse, he took the drinking pledge quite cheerfully for her sake. He promised to stop smoking, glad that the widow neglected to mention chewing tobacco, which was his everyday comfort. As for the swearing, he told her he would do his best under the circumstances, and that he would taste the oil hereafter, and try and think up some new names for the Ford.

"But Casey, if you leave whisky alone, you won't need to taste the oil," the widow told him. Whereat Casey grinned feebly and explained for the tenth time that he had not been drinking. She did not contradict him. She seemed a wise woman, after a fashion.

Casey drove back to his camp at Starvation Mountain happy and a little scared. Why, after all these years of careless freedom, he should precipitate himself into matrimony with a woman he had known casually for two days puzzled him a little.

"Well, a man gits to feelin' like he wants to settle down when he's crowdin' fifty," he explained his recklessness to the Ford as it hummed away over Furnace Lake which was flat as a floor and dry as a bleached bone, —and much the same color. "Any man feels the want of a home as he gits older. And Casey's the man that will try anything once, you ask anybody." He took out his pipe, looked at it, bethought himself of his promise and put it away again, substituting a chew of tobacco as large as his cheek would hold without prying his mouth open. "G'long, there-can't you? You got your belly full of oil-shake a wheel and show you're alive."

After that, Casey spent every Sunday at Lucky Lode. He liked the widow better and better. Especially after dinner, with the delicious flavor of pie still caressing his palate. Only he wished she would take it for granted that when Casey Ryan made a promise, Casey Ryan would keep it.

"I've got so now I can bark a knuckle with m'single-jack when I'm puttin' down a hole, and say, 'Oh, dear!' and let it go at that," he boasted to her on the second Sunday. "I'll bet there ain't another man in the state of Nevada could do that."

"Yes. But Casey dear, if *only* you will never touch another drop of liquor. You'll keep your promise, won't you, dear boy?"

"Hell, yes!" Casey assured her headily. It had been close to twenty years since he had been called dear boy, at least to his face. He kissed the widow full on the lips before he saw that a frown sat upon her forehead like a section of that ridgy cardboard they wrap bottles in.

"Casey, you swore!"

"Swore? Me?"

"I only hope," sighed the widow, "that your other promise won't be broken as easily as that one. Remember, Casey, I cannot and I will not marry a drinking man!"

Casey looked at her dubiously. "If you mean that syrup —"

"Oh, I've heard awful tales of you, Casey dear! The boys talk at the table, and they seem to think it's awful funny to tell about your fighting and drinking and playing cards for money. But

I think it's perfectly awful. You *must* stop drinking, Casey dear. I could never forgive myself if I set before my innocent little ones the example of a husband who drank."

"You won't," said Casey. "Not if you marry me, you won't." Then he changed the subject, beginning to talk of his prospect over on Starvation. The widow liked to hear him tell about finding a pocket of ore that went seventy ounces in silver and one and seven tenths ounces in gold, and how he expected any day to get down into the main body of ore and find it a "contact" vein. It all sounded very convincing and as if Casey Ryan were in a fair way to become a rich man.

The next time Casey saw the widow he was on his way to town for more powder, his whole box of "giant" having gone off with a tremendous bang the night before in one of those abrupt hailstorms that come so unexpectedly in the mountain country. Casey had worked until dark, and was dog-tired and had left the box standing uncovered beside the dugout where he kept it. He suspected that a hailstone had played a joke on him, but his chief emotion was one of self-congratulation because he had prudently stored the dynamite around a shoulder of the canyon from where he camped.

When he told the widow about it as one relates the details of a narrow escape, and pointed out how lucky he was, she looked very grave. It was a very careless thing to do, she said. Casey admitted it was. A man who handled dynamite ought to shun liquor above all things, she went on; and Casey agreed restively. He had not felt any inclination, to imbibe until that minute, when the Irish rose up hotly within him.

"Casey dear, are you *sure* you have nothing in camp?"

Casey assured her solemnly that he had not and drove off down the hill, vaguely aware that he was not so content with life as he had been.

"Damn that syrup!" he exploded once, quite as abruptly as had the giant powder. After that he chewed tobacco and drove in broody silence.

Chapter IV

Being Casey Ryan, tough as hickory and wont to drive headlong to his destination, Casey did not remain in town to loiter a half a day and sleep a night and drive back the next day, as most desert dwellers did. He hurried through with his business, filled up with gas and oil, loaded on an extra can of each, strapped his box of dynamite upon the seat beside him where he could keep an eye on it-just as if that would do any good if the tricky stuff meant to blow up! —and started back at three in the afternoon. He would be half the night getting to camp, even though he was Casey Ryan and drove a mean Ford. But he would be there, ready to start work at sunrise. A man who is going to marry a widow with two children had best hurry up and strike every streak of rich ore he has in his claim, thought Casey.

All that afternoon, though the wind blew hot in his face, Casey drilled across the desert, meeting never a living thing, overtaking none. All that afternoon a yellow dust cloud swirled rapidly along the rough desert road, vainly trying to keep up with Casey who made it. In Yucca Pass he had to stop and fill motor and radiator with oil and water, and just as he topped the summit a front tire popped like a pistol.

Casey killed the engine and got out a bit stiffly, pried off a chew of tobacco and gazed pensively at Barren Butte that held Lucky Lode, where the widow was cooking supper at that moment. Casey wished practically that he was there and could sit down to some of her culinary achievements.

"I sure would like to flop m'lip over one of her biscuits right now," he said aloud. "If I do strike it, I wonder will she git too high-toned to cook?"

His eyes went to Furnace Lake, lying smooth and pale yellow in the saucerlike basin between Barren Butte and the foothills of Starvation. In the soft light of the afterglow it seemed to smile at him with a glint of malice, like the treacherous thing it was. For Furnace Lake is treacherous. The Big Earthquake (America knows only one Big Earthquake, that which rocked San Francisco so disastrously) had split Furnace Lake halfway across, leaving an ugly crevice ten feet wide at the narrowest point and eighty feet deep, men said. Time and passing storms had partly filled the gash, but it was there, ugly, ominous, a warning to all men to trust the lake not at all. Little cracks radiated from the big gash here and there, and the cattle men rode often that way, though not often enough to save their cattle from falling in.

By day the lake shimmered deceptively with mirages that painted it blue with the likeness of water, Then a lone clump of greasewood stood up tall and proclaimed itself a ship lying idle on a glassy expanse of water so blue, so cool, so clear, one could not wonder that thirsty travelers went mad sometimes with the false lure of it.

Just now the lake looked exactly like any lake at dusk, with the far shore line reflected along its edge; and Casey's thought went beyond, to his claim on Starvation. Being tired and hungry, he pictured wistfully a cabin there, and a light in the window when he went chuckling up the long mesa in the dark, and the widow inside with hot coffee and supper waiting for him. Just as soon as he struck "shipping values" that picture would be real, said Casey to himself; and he opened his tool box and set to work changing the tire.

By the time he had finished it was dark, and Casey had yet a long forty miles between himself and his sour-dough can. He cranked the engine, switched on the electric headlights, and went tearing down the fifteen-mile incline to the lake.

"She c'n see the lights, and she'll know I ain't hangin' out in town lappin' up whisky," he told himself as he drove. "She'll know it's Casey Ryan comin' home-know it the way them lights are slippin' over the country. Ain't another man on the desert can put a car over the trail like this! You ask anybody."

Pleased with himself and his reputation, urged by hunger and the desire to make good on his claim so that he might have the little home he instinctively craved, Casey pulled the gas lever down another eighth of an inch-when he was already using more than he should-and nearly bounced his dynamite off the seat when he lurched over a sandy hummock and down on to the smooth floor of the lake.

It was five miles across that lake from rim to rim and taking a straight line, as Casey did, well above the crevice. In all that distance there is not a stick, or a stone, or a bush to mark the way. Not even a trail, since Casey was the only man who traveled it, and Casey never made tracks twice in the same place, but drove down upon it, picked himself a landmark on the opposite side and steered for it exactly as one steers a boat. The marks he left behind him were no more than pencil marks drawn upon a sheet of buff wrapping paper. Unless the lake was wet with one of those sporadic desert rains, you couldn't make any impression on the cement-like surface.

And when the lake was wet, you stuck where you were until wind and sun dried it for you. Wherefore Casey plunged out upon five miles of blank, baked clay with neither road, chart nor compass to guide him. It was the first time he had ever crossed at night, and a blanket of thin, high clouds hid the stars.

Casey thought nothing much of that, —being Casey Ryan. He had before him the dim-very dim-outline of Starvation, and being perfectly sober, he steered a straight course, and made sure he was well away from the upper end of the crevice, and pulled the gas lever down another notch.

The little handful of engine roared beautifully and shook the car with the vibration. Casey heaved a sigh of weariness mingled with content that the way was smooth and he need not look for chuck holes for a few minutes, at any rate. He settled back, and his fingers relaxed on the wheel. I think he dozed, though Casey swears he did not.

Suddenly he leaned forward, stared hard, leaned out and stared, listened with an ear cocked toward the engine. He turned and looked behind, then stared ahead again.

"By *gosh*, I bet both hubs is busted!" he ejaculated under his breath, —Furnace Lake subdues one somehow. "She's runnin' like a wolf-but she ain't goin'!"

He waited for a minute longer, trifling with the gas, staring and listening. The car was shaking with the throb of the motor, but Casey could feel no forward motion. "Settin' here burnin' gas like a 'lection bonfire-she sure *would* think I'm drunk if she knowed it," Casey muttered, and straddled over the side of the car to the running board.

"I wish-to —*hell* I hadn't promised her not to cuss!" he gritted, and with one hand still on the wheel, Casey shut off the gas and stepped down.

He stepped down upon a surface sliding beneath him at the rate of close to forty miles an hour. The Ford went on, spinning away from him in a wide circle, since Casey had unconsciously turned the wheel to the left as he let go. The blow of meeting the hard clay stunned him just at first, and he had rolled over a couple of times before he began to regain his senses.

He lifted himself groggily to his knees and looked for the car, saw it bearing down upon him from the direction whence he had come. Before he had time to wonder much at the phenomenon, it was upon him, over with a lurch, and gone again.

Casey was tough, and he never knew when he was whipped. He crawled up to his knees again, saw the same Ford coming at him with dimming headlights from the same direction it had taken before, made a wild grab for it, was knocked down and run over again. You may not believe that, but Casey had the bruises to prove it.

On the third round the Ford had slowed to a walk, figuratively speaking. Casey was pretty dizzy, and he thought his back was broken, but he was mad clear through. He caught the Ford by its fender, hung on, clutching frantically for a better hold, was dragged a little distance so and then, as its speed slackened to a gentle forward roll, he made shift to get aboard and give the engine gas before it had quite stopped. Which he told himself was lucky, because he couldn't have cranked the thing to save his life.

By sheer dogged nerve he drove to camp, drank cold coffee left from his early breakfast, and decided that the bite of a Ford, while it is poisonous, is not necessarily fatal unless it attacks one in a vital spot.

Casey could not drill a hole, he could not swing a pick; for two days he limped groaning around camp and confined his activities to cooking his meals. Frequently he would look at the Ford and shake his head. There was something uncanny about it.

"She sure has got it in for me," he mused. "You can't blame her for runnin' off when I dropped the reins and stepped out. But that don't account for the way she come *at* me, and the way she *got* me every circle she made. That's human. It's dog-*gone* human! I've cussed her a lot, and I've done things to her-like that syrup I poured into her-and dog-gone her, she's been layin' low and watchin' her chance all this while. Fords, I believe, are about as human as horses, and I've knowed horses I believe coulda talked if their tongues was split. Ask anybody. That there car *knowed*!"

The third day after the attack Casey was still too sore to work, but he managed to crank the Ford-eyeing it curiously the while, and with respect, too-and started down the mesa and up over the ridge and on down to the lake. He was still studying the matter incredulously, still wondering if Fords can think. He wanted to tell the widow about it and get her opinion. The widow was a smart woman. A little touchy on the liquor question, maybe, but smart. You ask anybody.

Lucky Lode greeted him with dropped jaws and wide staring eyes, which puzzled Casey until the foreman, grasping his shoulder-which made Casey wince and break a promise-explained their astonishment. They had, as Casey expected, seen his lights when he came off the summit from Yucca Pass. By the speed they traveled, Lucky Lode knew that Casey and no other was at the steering wheel, even before he took to the lake.

"And then," said the foreman, "we saw your lights go round and round in a circle, and disappear —"

"They didn't," Casey cut in trenchantly. "They went dim because I was taking her slow, being about all in."

The foreman grinned. "We thought you'd drove into the crevice, and we went down with lanterns and hunted the full length of it. We never found a sign of you or the car —"

"'Cause I was over in camp, or thereabouts," interpolated Casey drily. "I wish you'd of come on over. I sure needed help."

"We figured you was pretty well lit up, to circle around like that. I've been down since, by daylight, and so have some of the boys, looking into that crevice. But we gave it up, finally."

Then Casey, because he liked a joke even when it was on himself, told the foreman and his men what had happened to him. He did not exaggerate the mishap; the truth was sufficiently wild.

They whooped with glee. Every one laughs at the unusual misfortunes of others, and this was unusual. They stood around the Ford and talked to it, and whooped again. "You sure must have had so-ome jag, Casey," they told him exuberantly.

"I was sober," Casey testified earnestly. "I'll swear I hadn't a drop of anything worse than lemon soda, and that was before I left town." Whereupon they whooped the louder, bent double, some of them with mirth.

"Say! If I was drunk that night, I'd say so," Casey exploded finally. "What the hell-what's the matter with you rabbits? You think Casey Ryan has got to the point where he's scared to tell what he done and all he done? Lemme tell yuh, anything Casey does he ain't afraid to *tell* about! Lyin' is something I never was scared bad enough to do. You ask anybody."

"There's the widow," said the foreman, wiping his eyes.

Casey turned and looked, but the widow was not in sight. The foreman, he judged, was speaking figuratively. He swung back glaring.

"You think I'm scared to tell her what happened? She'll know I was sober if I say I was sober. She ain't as big a fool —" He did not want to fight, although he was aching to lick every man of them. But for one thing, he was too sore and lame, and then, the widow would not like it.

With his neck very stiff, Casey limped down to the house and tried to tell the widow. But the widow was a woman, and she was hurt because Casey, since he was alive and not in the crevice, had not come straight to comfort her, but had lingered up there talking and laughing with the men. The widow had taken Casey's part when the others said he must have been drunk. She had maintained, red-lidded and trembly of voice, that something had gone wrong with Casey's car so that he couldn't steer it. Such things happened, she knew.

Well, Casey told the widow the truth, and the widow's face hardened while she listened. She had permitted him to kiss her when he came in, but now she moved away from him. She did not call him dear boy, nor even Casey dear. She waited until he had reached the point that puzzled him, the point of a Ford's degree of intelligence. Then her lips thinned before she opened them.

"And what," she asked coldly, "had you been drinking, Mr. Ryan?"

"Me? One bottle of lemon soda before I left town, and I left town at three o'clock in the afternoon. I swear —"

"You need not swear, Mr. Ryan." The widow folded her hands and regarded him sternly, though her voice was still politely soft. "After I had told you repeatedly that my little ones should ever be guarded from a drinking father; after you had solemnly promised me that you would never again put glass to your lips, or swallow a drop of whisky; after that very morning renewing your pledge —"

"Well, I kept it," Casey said, his face a shade paler under its usual frank red. "I swear to Gawd I was sober."

"You need not lie," said the widow, "and add to your misdeeds. You were drunk. No man in his senses would imagine what you imagine, or do what you did. I wish you to understand, Mr. Ryan, that I shall not marry you. I could not trust you out of my sight."

"I —was —*sober!*" cried Casey, measuring his words. Very nearly shouting them, in fact.

The widow turned pointedly away and began to stir something on the stove, and did not look at him.

Casey went out, climbed the hill to his Ford, cranked it and went larruping down the hill, out on the lake and, when he had traversed half its length, turned and steered a straight course across it. Where tracings of wheels described a wide circle he stopped and regarded them intently. Then he began to swear, at nothing in particular, but with a hearty enjoyment of the phrases he intoned.

"Casey, you sure as hell have had one close call," he remarked, when he could think of nothing new and devilish to say. "You mighta run along, and run along, till you got *married* to her. Whadda I want a wife for, anyway? Sour-dough biscuits tastes pretty good, and Casey sure can make 'em!" He got out his pipe, filled it and crammed down the tobacco, found a match and leaned back, smoking with relish, one leg thrown over the wheel.

"A man's best friend is his Ford," he exclaimed. "You can ask anybody." He grinned, and blew a lot of smoke, and gave the wheel an affectionate little twist.

Chapter V

Some months later Casey waved good-by to the men from Tonopah, squinted up at the sun and got a coal-oil can of water, with which he filled the radiator of his Ford. He rolled his bed in the tarp and tied it securely, put flour, bacon, coffee, salt and various other small necessities of life into a box, inspected his sour-dough can, and decided to empty it and start over again if hard fate drove him to sourdough.

"Might bust down and have to sleep out," he meditated. "Then, agin, I ain't liable to; and if I do, I'll be goin' so fast I'll git somewhere before she stops. I'm —sure-goin' to go!"

He cranked the battered car, straddled in over the edge on the driver's side and set his feet against the pedals with the air of a man who had urgent business elsewhere. The men from Tonopah were not yet out of sight around the butte scarred with rhyolite ledges before Casey was under way, rattling down the rough trail from Starvation Mountain and bouncing clear of the seat as the car lurched over certain rough spots.

Pinned with a safety pin to the inside pocket of the vest he wore only when he felt need of a safe and secret pocket, Casey Ryan carried a check for twenty-five thousand dollars, made payable to himself. A check for twenty-five thousand dollars in Casey's pocket was like a wildcat clawing at his imagination and spitting at every moment's delay. Casey had endured solitude and some hardship while he coaxed Starvation Mountain to reveal a little of its secret treasure. Now he wanted action, light, life and plenty of it. While he drove he dreamed, and his dreams beckoned, urged him faster and faster.

Up over the summit of the ridge that lay between Starvation and Furnace Lake he surged, with radiator bubbling. Down the long slope to the lake, lying there smiling sardonically at a world it loved to trick with its moods, Casey drove as if he were winning a bet. Across that five miles of baked, yellow-white clay he raced, his Ford a-creak in every joint.

"Go it, you tin lizard!" chortled Casey. "I'll have me a real wagon when I git to Los. She'll be white, with red stripes along her sides and red wheels, and she'll lay 'er belly to the ground and eat up the road and lick her chops for more. Sixty miles under her belt every time the clock strikes, or she ain't good enough fer Casey! Mebby they think they got some drivers in Californy. Mebby they *think* they have. They ain't, though, because Casey Ryan ain't there yet. I'll catch that night train. Oughta be in by morning, and then you keep your eye on Casey. There's goin' to be a stir around Los, about to-morrow noon. I'll have to buy some clothes, I guess. And I'll git acquainted with some nice girl with yella hair that likes pleasure, and take her out ridin'. Yeah, I'll have to git me a swell outfit uh clothes. I'll look the part, all right —-"

Up a long, winding trail and over another summit to Yucca Pass Casey dreamed, while the stark, scarred buttes on either side regarded him with enigmatic calm. Since the first wagon train had worried over the rough deserts on their way to California, the bleak hills of Nevada had listened while prospectors dreamed aloud and cackled over their dreaming; had listened, too, while they raved in thirst and heat and madness. Inscrutably they watched Casey as he hurried by with his twenty-five thousand dollars and his pleasant pictures of soft ease.

At a dim fork in the trail Casey slowed and stopped. A boiling radiator will not forever brook neglect, and Casey brought his mind down to practical things for a space. "I can just as well take the train from Lund," he mused, while he poured in more water. "Then I can leave this bleatin' burro with Bill. He oughta give me a coupla hundred for her, anyway. No use wasting money just because you happen to have a few thousand in your pants." He filled his pipe at that sensible idea and turned the nose of his Ford down the dim trail to Lund.

Eighty miles more or less straight away across the mountainous waste lay Lund, halfway up a canyon that led to higher reaches in the hills, rich in silver, lead, copper, gold. Silver it was that Casey had found and sold to the men from Tonopah, and it was a freak of luck, he thought whimsically, that had led him and his Ford away over to Starvation Mountains to find their stake when they had probably been driving over millions every day that they made the stage trip from Pinnacle down to Lund.

The trail was rutted in places where the sluicing rains had driven hard across the hills; soft with sand in places where the fierce winds had swept the open. For awhile the thin, wobbly track of a wagon meandered along ahead of him, then turned off up a flat-bottomed draw and was lost in the sagebrush. Some prospector not so lucky as he, thought Casey, with swift, soon forgotten sympathy. A coyote ran up a slope toward him, halted with forefeet planted on a rock, and stared at him, ears perked like an inquisitive dog. Casey stopped, eased his rifle out of the crease in the back of the seat cushion, chanced a shot,—and his luck held. He climbed out, picked up the limp gray animal, threw it into the tonneau and went on. Even with twenty-five thousand dollars in his pocket, Casey told himself that coyote hides are not to be scorned. He had seen the time when the price of a good hide meant flour and bacon and tobacco to him. He would skin it when he stopped to eat.

Eighty miles with never a soul to call good day to Casey. Nor shack nor shelter made for man, and only one place where there was water to wet his lips if they cracked with thirst, —unless, perchance, one of those swift desert downpours came riding on the wind, lashing the clouds with lightning.

Far ahead of Casey such a storm rolled in off the barren hills to the south. "She's a-wettin' up that red lake a-plenty," observed Casey, squinting through the dirty windshield. "No trail around, either, on account of the lava beds. But I guess I can pull acrost, all right." Doubt was in his voice, however, and he was half minded to turn back and take the straight road to Vegas, which had been his first objective. But he discarded the idea.

"No, sir, Casey Ryan never back-trailed yet. Poor time to commence, now when I got the world by the tail and a downhill pull. We'll make out, all right-can't be so terrible boggy with a short rain like that there. I bet," he continued optimistically to the Ford, which was the nearest he had to human companionship, "I bet we make it in a long lope. Git along, there! Shake a wheel —'s the last time you haul Casey around. Casey's goin' to step high, wide and handsome. Sixty miles *an hour*, or he'll ask for his money back. They can't step too fast for Casey! Blue-if I get me a lady friend with yella hair, mebby she'll show up better in a blue car than she will in a white-and-red. This here turnout has got to be tasty and have class. If she was dark —" He shook his head at that. "No, sir, black hair grows too plenty on squaws an' chilli queens. Yella goes with Casey. Clingin' kinda girl with blue eyes-that's the stuff! An' I'll sure show her some drivin'!"

He wondered whether he should try and find the girl first and buy the car to match her beauty, or buy the car first and with that lure the lady of his dreams. It was a nice question and it required thought. It was pleasant to ponder the problem, and Casey became so lost in meditation that he forgot to eat when the sun flirted with the scurrying clouds over his wind-torn automobile top.

So he came bouncing and swaying down the last mesa to the place called Red Lake. Casey had heard it spoken of with opprobrious epithets by men who had crossed it in wet weather. In dry weather it was red clay caked and checked by the sun, and wheels or hoofs stirred clouds of red dust that followed and choked the traveler.

Casey was not thinking at all of the lake when he drove down to it. He was seeing visions, though you would not think it to look at him; a stocky, middle-aged man who needed a shave and a hair-cut, wearing cheap, dirt-stained overalls and a blue shirt and square-toed shoes studded thickly on the soles with hobnails worn shiny; driving a desert-scarred Ford with most of the paint gone and a front fender cocked up and flapping crazily, and tires worn down to the fabric in places. But his eyes were very keen and steady, and there was a humorous twist to his mouth. If he dreamed incongruously of big, luxurious cars gorgeous in paint and nickel trim, and of slim young women with yellow hair and blue eyes, —well, stranger dreams have been hidden away behind exteriors more unsightly than was the shell which holds the soul of Casey Ryan.

Presently the practical, everyday side of his nature nudged him into taking note of his immediate surroundings. Red Lake had received a wetting. The dark, shiny surface betrayed that fact, and it was surprising how real water, when you did see it on a lake subject to mirage, was so unmistakably real. It is like putting flakes of real gold beside flakes of mica; you are ready to swear that the mica is gold-until you see the real gold beside it. So Casey knew at a glance that half of Red Lake was wet, and that the shiny patches here and there were not mirage pictures but shallow pools of water. Moreover, out in the reddest, wettest part of it an automobile stood with its back to him, and pigmy figures were moving slowly upon either side.

Chapter VI

"Stuck," diagnosed Casey in one word, as he caught sight of the group ahead. He tucked his dream into the back of his mind while he pulled down the gas lever a couple of notches and lunged along the muddy ruts that led straight away from the safe line of sagebrush and out upon the platter-like red expanse.

The Ford grunted and lugged down to a steady pull, but Casey drove as he had driven his six horses on a steep grade in the old days, coaxing every ounce of power into action. He juggled with spark and gas and somehow kept her going, and finally stopped with nice judgment on a small island of harder clay within shouting distance of the car ahead. He killed the engine then and stepped down, and went picking his way carefully out to it, his heavy shoes speedily collecting great pancakes of mud that clung like glue.

"Stuck, hey? You oughta kept in the ruts, no matter if they are water-logged. You never want to turn outa the road on one of these lake beds, huntin' dry ground. If it's wet in the road, you can bank on sinkin' in to the hocks the minute you turn out." He carefully removed the mud pancakes from his shoes by scraping them across the hub of the stalled car and edged back to stand with his arms on his hips while he surveyed the full plight of them.

"She sure is bogged down a-plenty," he observed, grinning sympathetically.

"Could you hitch on your car, Mister, and pull us out?" This was a woman's voice, and it thrilled Casey, woman hungry as he was.

Casey put up a hand to his mouth and surreptitiously removed a chew of tobacco almost fresh. With some effort he pulled his feet closer together, and he lifted his old Stetson and reset it at a consciously rakish angle. He glanced at the car, behind it and in front, coming back to the depressed male individual before him. "Yes, ma'am, I'll get you out, all right. Sure, I will."

"We've been stalled here for an hour or more," volunteered the depressed one. "We was right behind the storm. Looked a sorry chance that anybody would come along for the next week or so."

"Mister, you're a godsend, if ever there was one. I'd write your name on the roster of saints in my prayer book, if I ever said prayers and had a prayer book and a pencil and knew what name to write."

"Casey Ryan. Don't you worry, ma'am. We'll get you outa here in no time." Casey grinned and craned his neck. Looking lower this time, he saw a pair of feet which did not seem to belong to that voice, though they were undoubtedly feminine. Still, red mud will work miracles of disfigurement, and Casey was an optimist by nature.

"My wife is trying out a new comedy line," the man observed unemotionally. "Trouble is it never gets over, out front. If she ever did get it across the footlights, I could raise the price of admission and get away with it. How far is it to Rhyolite?"

"Rhyolite? Twenty or twenty-five miles, mebby." Casey gave him an inquiring look.

"Can we get there in time to paper the town and hire a hall to show in, Mister?" Casey saw the mud-caked feet move laboriously toward the rear of the car.

"Yes, ma'am, I guess you can. There ain't any town, though, and it ain't got any hall in it, nor anybody to go to a show."

The woman laughed. "That's like my prayer book. Well, Jack, you certainly have got a powerful eye, but you've been trying to Svengali this out-fit out of the mud for an hour, and I haven't seen it move an inch, so far. Let's just try something else."

"A prayer outa your prayer book, maybe," her husband retorted, not troubling to move or turn his head.

Casey blinked and looked again. The woman who appeared from the farther side of the car might have been the creature of his dream, so far as her face, her hair and her voice went. Her hair was yellow, unmistakably yellow. Her eyes were bluer than Casey's own, and she had nice teeth and showed them in a red-lipped smile. A more sophisticated man would have known that the powder on her nose was freshly applied, and that her reason for remaining so long hidden from his sight while she talked to him was revealed in the moist color on her lips and the fresh bloom on her cheeks. Casey was not sophisticated. He thought she was a beautiful woman and asked no questions of her make-up box.

"Mister, you certainly are a godsend!" she gushed again when she faced him. "I'd call you a direct answer to prayer, only I haven't been praying. I've been trying to tell Jack that the shovel is not packed under the banjos, as he thinks it was, but was left back at our last camp where he was trying to dig water out of a wet spot. Jack, dear, perhaps the gentleman has got a shovel in his car. Ain't it a real gag, Mister, us being stuck out here in a dry lake?"

Casey touched his hat and grinned and tried not to look at her too long. Husbands of beautiful young women are frequently jealous, and Casey knew his place and meant to keep it.

All the way back to his car Casey studied the peculiar features of the meeting. He had been thinking about yellow-haired women-well! But of course, she was married, and therefore not to be thought of save as a coincidence; still, Casey rather regretted the existence of Jack dear, and began to wonder why good-looking women always picked such dried-up little runts for husbands. "Show actors by the talk," he mused. "I wonder now if she don't sing, mebby?"

He started the car and forged out to them, making the last few rods in low gear and knowing how risky it was to stop. They were rather helpless, he had to admit, and did all the standing around while Casey did all the work. But he shoveled the rear wheels out, waded back to the tiny island of solid ground and gathered an armful of brush, which he crowded in front of the wheels, covering himself with mud thereby; then he tied the tow rope he carried for emergencies like this, waded to the Ford, cranked and trusted the rest to luck. The Ford moved slowly ahead until the rope between the two cars tightened, then spun her wheels and proceeded to dig herself in where she stood. The other car, shaking with the tremor of its own engine, ruthlessly ground the sagebrush into the mud and stood upon it roaring and spluttering furiously.

"Nothing like sticking together, Mister," called the lady cheerfully, and he heard her laughter above the churn of their motors.

"Say, ain't your carburetor all off?" Casey leaned out to call back to the husband. "You're smokin' back there like wet wood."

The man immediately stopped the motor and looked behind him.

Casey muttered something under his breath when he climbed out. He looked at his own car standing hub deep in red mud and reached for the solacing plug of chewing tobacco. Then he thought of the lady and withdrew his hand empty.

"We're certainly going to stick together, Mister," she repeated her witticism, and Casey grinned foolishly.

"She'll dry up in a few hours, with this hot sun," he observed hearteningly. "We'll have to pile brush in, I guess." His glance went back to the tiny island and to his double row of tracks. He looked at the man.

"Jack, dear, you might go help the gentleman get some brush," the lady suggested sweetly.

"This ain't my act," Jack dear objected. "I just about broke my spine trying to heave the car outa the mud when we first stuck. Say, I wish there was a beanery of some kind in walking distance. Honest, I'll be dead of starvation in another hour. What's the chance of a bite, Hon?"

Contempt surged through Casey. Deep in his soul he pitied her for being tied to such an insect. Immediately he was glad that she had spirit enough to put the little runt in his place.

"You *would* wait to buy supplies in Rhyolite, remember," she reminded her husband calmly. "I guess you'll have to wait till you get there. I've got one piece of bread saved for Junior. You and I go hungry-and cheer up, old dear; you're used to it!"

"I've got grub," Casey volunteered hospitably. "Didn't stop to eat yet. I'll pack the stuff back there to dry ground and boil some coffee and fry some bacon." He looked at the woman and was rewarded by a smile so brilliant that Casey was dazzled.

"You certainly are a godsend," she called after him, as he turned away to his own car. "It just happens that we're out of everything. It's so hard to keep anything on hand when you're traveling in this country, with towns so far apart. You just run short before you know it."

Casey thought that the very scarcity of towns compelled one to avoid running short of food, but he did not say anything. He waded back to the island with a full load of provisions and cooking utensils, and in three minutes he was squinting against the smoke of a camp-fire while he poured water from a canteen into his blackened coffee pot.

"Coffee! Jack, dear, can you believe your nose!" chirped the woman presently behind Casey. "Junior, darling, just smell the bacon! Isn't he a nice gentleman? Go give him a kiss like a little man."

Casey didn't want any kiss-at least from Junior. Junior was six years old, and his face was dirty and his eyes were old, old eyes, but brown like his father's. He had the pinched, hungry look which Casey had seen only amongst starving Indians, and after he had kissed Casey perfunctorily he snatched the piece of raw bacon which Casey had just sliced off, and tore at it with his teeth like a hungry pup.

Casey affected not to notice, and busied himself with the fire while the woman reproved Junior half-heartedly in an undertone, and laughed stagily and remarked upon the number of hours since they had breakfasted.

Casey tried not to watch them eat, but in spite of himself he thought of a prospector whom he had rescued last summer after a five-day fast. These people ate more than the prospector had eaten, and their eyes followed greedily every mouthful which Casey took, as if they grudged him the food. Wherefore Casey did not take as many mouthfuls as he would have liked.

"This desert air certainly does put an edge on one's appetite," the woman smiled, while she blew across her fourth cup of coffee to cool it, and between breaths bit into a huge bacon sandwich, which Casey could not help knowing was her third. "Jack, dear, isn't this coffee delicious!"

"Mah-mal Do we have to p-pay that there g-godsend? C-can you p-pay for more b-bacon for me, mah-ma?" Junior licked his fingers and twitched a fold of his mother's soiled skirt.

"Sure, give him more bacon! All he wants. I'll fry another skillet full," Casey spoke hurriedly, getting out the piece which he had packed away in the bag.

"He's used to these hold-up joints where they charge you forty cents for a greasy plate," the man explained, speaking with his mouth full. "Eat all yuh want, Junior. This is a barbecue and no collection took up to pay the speaker of the day."

"We certainly appreciate your kindness, Mister," the woman put in graciously, holding out her cup. "What we'd have done, stuck here in the mud with no provisions and no town within miles, heaven only knows. Was you kidding us," she added, with a betrayal of more real anxiety than she intended, "when you said Rhyolite is a dead one? We looked it up on the map, and it was marked like a town. We're making all the little towns that the road shows mostly miss. We give a fine show, Mister. It's been played on all the best time in the country-we took it abroad before the war and made real good money with it. But we just wanted to see the country, you know-after doing the cont'nent and all the like of that. So we thought we'd travel independent and make all the small towns —"

"The movie trust is what put vodeville on the bum," the man interrupted. "We used to play the best time only. We got a first-class act. One that ought to draw down good money anywhere, and would draw down good money, if the movie trust —"

"And then we like to be independent, and go where we like and get off the railroad for a spell. Freedom is the breath of life to he and I. We'd rather have it kinda rough now and then to be free and independent —"

"I've g-got a b-bunny, a-and it f-fell in the g-grease box a-and we c-can't wash it off, a-and h-he's asleep now. C-can I g-give my b-bunny some b-bacon, Mister G-godsend?"

The woman laughed, and Jack dear laughed, and Casey himself grinned sheepishly. Casey did not want to be called a godsend, and he hated the term "Mister" when applied to himself. All his life he had been plain Casey Ryan and proud of it, and his face was very red when he confessed that there was no more bacon. He had not expected to feed a family when he left camp that morning, but had taken rations for himself only.

Junior whined and insisted that he wanted b-bacon for his b-bunny, and the man hushed him querulously and asked Casey what the chances were for getting under way. Casey repacked a lightened bag, emptied the coffee grounds, shouldered his canteen and waded back to the cars and to the problem of red mud with an unbelievable quality of tenacity.

The man followed and asked him if he happened to have any smoking tobacco, afterwards he begged a cigarette paper, and then a match. "The dog-gone helpless, starved bunch!" Casey muttered, while he dug out the wheels of his Ford, and knew that his own haste must wait upon the need of these three human beings whom he had never seen until an hour ago, of whose very existence he had been in ignorance, and who would probably contribute nothing whatever to his own welfare or happiness, however much he might contribute to theirs.

I do not say that Casey soliloquised in this manner while he was sweating there in the mud under hot midday. He did think that now he would no doubt miss the night train to Los Angeles, and that he would not, after all, be purchasing glad raiment and a luxurious car on the morrow. He regretted that, but he did not see how he could help it. He was Casey Ryan, and his heart was soft to suffering even though a little of the spell cast by the woman's blue eyes and her golden hair had dimmed for him.

He still thought her a beautiful woman who was terribly mismated, but he felt vaguely that women with beautiful golden hair should not drink their coffee aloud, or calmly turn up the bottom of their skirts that they might use the underside of the hem for a napkin after eating bacon. I do not like to mention this; Casey did not like to think of it, either. It was with reluctance that he reflected upon the different standard imposed by sex. A man, for instance, might wipe his fingers on his pants and look the world straight in the eye, —but dog-gone it, when a lady's a lady, she ought to *be* a lady.

Later Casey forgot for a time the incident of the luncheon on Red Lake. With infinite labor and much patience he finally extricated himself and the show people, with no assistance from them save encouragement. He towed them to dry land, untied and put away his rope and then discovered that he had not the heart to drive on at his usual hurtling pace and leave them to follow. There was an ominous stutter in their motor, for one thing, and Casey knew of a stiffish hill a few miles this side of Rhyolite, so he forced himself to set a slow pace which they could easily follow.

Chapter VII

It was full sundown when they reached Rhyolite, which was not a town but a camp beside a spring, usually deserted. Three years before, a mine had built the camp for the accommodation of the truck drivers who hauled ore to Lund and were sometimes unable to make the trip in one day. Casey, having adapted his speed to that of the decrepit car of the show people, was thankful that they arrived at all. He still had a little flour and coffee and salt, and he hoped there was enough grease left on the bacon paper to grease the skillet so that bannocks would not stick to the pan. He also hoped that his flour would hold out under the onslaught of their appetites.

But Casey was lucky. A half dozen cowboys were camped there with a pack outfit, meaning to ride the canyons next day for cattle. They were cooking supper, and they had "beefed a critter" that had broken a leg that afternoon running among rocks. Casey shuffled his responsibility and watched, in complete content, while the show people gorged on broiled yearling steaks. (I dislike to use the word gorge where a lady's appetite is involved, but that is the word which Casey thought of first.)

Later, the show people very amiably consented to entertain their hosts. It was then that Casey was once more blinded by the brilliance of the lady and forgot certain little blemishes that had seemed to him quite pronounced. The cowboys obligingly built a bonfire before the tent, into which the couple retired to set their stage and tune their instruments. Casey lay back on a cowboy's rolled bed with his knees crossed, his hands clasped behind his thinning hair, and smoked and watched the first pale stars come out while he listened to the pleasant twang of banjos in the tuning.

It was great. The sale of his silver claim to the men from Tonopah, the check safely pinned in his pocket, the future which he had planned for himself swam hazily through his mind. He was fed to repletion, he was rich, he had been kind to those in need. He was a man to be envied, and he told himself so.

Then the tent flaps were lifted and a dazzling, golden-haired creature in a filmy white evening gown to which the firelight was kind stood there smiling, a banjo in her hands. Casey gave a grunt and sat up, blinking. She sang, looking at him frequently. At the encore, which was livened by a clog danced to hidden music, she surely blew a kiss in the direction of Casey, who gulped and looked around at the others self-consciously, and blushed hotly.

In truth, it was a very good show which the two gave there in the tent; much better than the easiest going optimist would expect. When it was over to the last twang of a banjo string, Casey took off his hat, emptied into it what silver he had in his pockets and set the hat in the fireglow. Without a word the cowboys followed his example, turning pockets inside out to prove they could give no more.

Casey spread his bed apart from the others that night, and lay for a long while smoking and looking up at the stars and dreaming again his dream; only now the golden-haired creature who leaned back upon the deep cushions of his speedy blue car, was not a vague bloodless vision, but a real person with nice teeth and a red-lipped smile, who called him Mister in a tone he thought like music. Now his dream lady sang to him, talked to him, —I consider it rather pathetic that Casey's dream always halted just short of meal time, and that he never pictured her sitting across the table from him in some expensive café, although Casey was rather fond of café lights and music and service and food.

Next morning the glamor remained, although the lady was once more the unkempt woman of yesterday. The three seemed to look upon Casey still as a godsend. They had talked with some of the men and had decided to turn back to Vegas, which was a bigger town than Lund and therefore likely to produce better crowds. They even contemplated a three-night stand, which would make possible some very urgent repairs to their car. Casey demurred, although he could not deny the necessity for repairs. It was a longer trail to Vegas and a rougher trail. Moreover, he himself was on his way to Lund.

"You go to Lund," he urged, "and you can stay there four nights if you want to, and give shows. And I'll take yuh on up to Pinnacle in my car while yours is gettin' fixed, and you can give a show there. You'd draw a big crowd. I'd make it a point to tell folks you give a fine show. And I'll git yuh good rates at the garage where I do business. You don't want nothin' of Vegas. Lund's the place you want to hit fer."

"There's a lot to that," the foreman of the cowboys agreed. "If Casey'swillin' to back you up, you better hit straight for Lund. Everybody there knows Casey Ryan. He drove stage from Pinnacle to Lund for two years and never killed anybody, though he did come close to it now and again. I've saw strong men that rode with Casey and said they never felt right afterwards. Casey, he's a dog-gone good driver, but he used to be kinda hard on passengers. He done more to promote heart failure in them two towns than all the altitude they can pile up. But nobody's going to hold that against a good show that comes there. I heard there ain't been a show stop off in Lund for over a year. You'll have to beat 'em away from the door, I bet." Wherefore the Barrymores-that was the name they called themselves, though I am inclined to doubt their legal right to it-the Barrymores altered their booking and went with Casey to Lund.

They were not fools, by the way. Their car was much more disreputable than you would believe a car could be and turn a wheel, and the Barrymores recognized the handicap of its appearance. They camped well out of sight of town, therefore, and let Casey drive in alone.

Casey found that the westbound train had already gone, which gave him a full twenty-four hours in Lund, even though he discounted his promise to see the Barrymores through. There was a train, to be sure, that passed through Lund in the middle of the night; but that was the De Luxe, standard and drawing-room sleepers, and disdained stopping to pick up plebeian local passengers.

So Casey must spend twenty-four hours in Lund, there to greet men who hailed him joyously at the top of their voices while they were yet afar off, and thumped him painfully upon the shoulders when they came within reach of him. You may not grasp the full significance of this, unless you have known old and popular stage drivers, soft of heart and hard of fist. Then remember that Casey had spent months on end alone in the wilderness, working like a lashed slave from sunrise to dark, trying to wrest a fortune from a certain mountain side. Remember how an enforced isolation, coupled with rough fare and hard work, will breed a craving for lights and laughter and the speech of friends. Remember that, and don't overlook the twenty-five thousand dollar check that Casey had pinned safe within his pocket.

Casey had unthinkingly tossed his last dime into his hat for the show people at Rhyolite. He had not even skinned the coyote, whose hide would have been worth ten or fifteen dollars, as hides go. In the stress of pulling out of the mud at Red Lake, he had forgot all about the dead animal in his tonneau until his nose reminded him next morning that it was there. Then he had hauled it out by the tail and thrown it away. He was broke, except that he had that check in his pocket.

Of course it was easy enough for Casey to get money. He went to the store that sold everything from mining tools to green perfume bottles tied with narrow pink ribbon. The man who owned that store also owned the bank next door, and a little place down the street which was called laconically The Club. One way or another, Dwyer managed to feel the money of every man who came into Lund and stopped there for a space. He was an honest man, too, —or as honest as is practicable for a man in business.

Dwyer was tickled to see Casey again. Casey was a good fellow, and he never needed his memory jogged when he owed a man. He paid before he was asked to pay, and that was enough to make any merchant love him. He watched Casey unpin his vest pocket and remove the check, and he was not too eager to inspect it.

"Good? Surest thing you know. Want it cashed, or applied to your old checking account? It's open yet, with a dollar and sixty-seven cents to your credit, I believe. I'll take care of it, though it's after banking hours."

Casey was foolish. "I'll take a couple of hundred, if it's handy, and a check book. I guess you can fix it so I can get what money I want in Los. I'm goin' to have one hell of a time when I git there. I've earned it."

Dwyer laughed while he inked a pen for Casey's endorsement. "Hop to it, Casey. Glad you made good. But you'd better let me put part of that in a savings account, so you can't check it out. You know, Casey-remember your weak point."

"Aw-that's all right! Don't you worry none about Casey Ryan! Casey'll take care of himself-he's had too many jolts to want another one. Say, gimme a pair of them socks before you go in the bank. I'll pay yuh," he grinned, "when yuh come back with some money. Ain't got a cent on me, Dwyer. Give it all away. Twelve dollars and something. Down to twenty-five thousand dollars and my Ford auty-*mo*-bile-and Bill's goin' to buy that off me as soon as he looks her over to see what's busted and what ain't."

Dwyer laughed again as he unlocked the door behind the overalls and jumpers and disappeared into his bank. Presently he returned with a receipted duplicate deposit slip for twenty-four thousand eight hundred dollars, a little, flat check book and two hundred dollars in worn bank notes. "You ought to be independent for the rest of your life, Casey. This is a fine start for any man," he said.

Casey paid for the socks and slid the change for a ten-dollar bill into his overalls pocket, put the check book and the bank notes away where he had carried the check, and walked out with his hat very much tilted over his right eye and his shoulders swaggering a little. You can't blame him for that, can you?

As he stepped from the store he met an old acquaintance from Pinnacle. There was only one thing to do in a case like that, and Casey did it quite naturally. They came out of The Club wiping their lips, and the swagger in Casey's shoulders was more pronounced.

Face to face Casey met the show lady, which was what he called her in his mind. She had her arms clasped around a large paper sack full of lumpy things, and her eyes had a strained, anxious look.

"Oh, Mister! I've been looking all over for you. They say we can't show in this town. The license for road shows is fifty dollars, to begin with, and I've been all over and can't find a single place where we could show, even if we could pay the license. Ain't that the last word in hard luck? Now what to do beats me, Mister. We've just got to have the old car tinkered up so it'll carry us on to the next place, wherever that is. Jack says he must have a new tire by some means or other, and he was counting on what we'd make here. And up at that other place you've mentioned the mumps have broke out and they wouldn't let us show for love or money. A man in the drug store told me, Mister. We certainly are in a hole now, for sure! If we could give a benefit for something or somebody. Those men back there said you're so popular in this town, I believe I've got an idea. Mister, couldn't you have bad luck, or be sick or something, so we could give a benefit for you? People certainly would turn out good for a man that's liked the way they say you are. I'd just love to put on a show for you. Couldn't we fix it up some way?"

Casey looked up and down the street and found it practically empty. Lund was dining at that hour. And while Casey expected later the loud greetings, and the handshakes and all, as a matter of fact he had thus far talked with Bill, the garage man, with Dwyer, the storekeeper and banker, and with the man from Pinnacle, who was already making ready to crank his car and go home. Lund, as a town, was yet unaware of Casey's presence.

Casey looked at the show lady, found her gazing at his face with eyes that said please in four languages, and hesitated.

"You could git up a benefit for the Methodist church, mebby," he temporized. "There's a church of some kind here —I guess it's a Methodist. They most generally are."

"We'd have to split with them if we did," the show lady objected practically. "Oh, we're stuck worse than when we was back there in the mud! We'd only have to pay five dollars for a six-months' theater license, which would let us give all the shows we wanted to. It's a new law that I guess you didn't know anything about," she added kindly. "You certainly wouldn't have insisted on us coming if you'd knew about the license."

"It's a year, almost, since I was here," Casey admitted; "I been out prospecting."

"Well, we can just work it fine! Can't we go somewhere and talk it over? I've got a swell idea, Mister, if you'll just listen to it a minute, and it'll certainly be a godsend to us to be able to give our show. We've got some crutches amongst our stage props, and some scar patches, Mister, that would certainly make you up fine as a cripple. Wouldn't they believe it, Mister, if it was told that you had been in an accident and got crippled for life?"

In spite of his embarrassment, Casey grinned. "Yeah, I guess they'd believe it, all right," he admitted. "They'd likely be tickled to death to see me goin' around on crutches." He cast a hasty thought back into his past, when he had driven a careening stage between Pinnacle and Lund, strewing the steep trail with wreckage not his own. "Yeah, it'd tickle 'em to death. Them that's rode with me," he concluded.

"Oh, you certainly are a godsend! Duck outa sight somewhere while I go tell Jack dear that we've found a way open for us to show, after all!" While Casey was pulling the sag out of his jaw so that he could protest, could offer her money, do anything save what she wanted, the show lady disappeared. Casey turned and went back into The Club, remained five minutes perhaps and then walked very circumspectly across the street to Bill's garage. It was there that the Barrymores found him when they came seeking with their dilapidated old car, their crutches, their grease paint and scar patches, to make a cripple of Casey whether he would or no.

Bill fell uproariously in with the plan, and Dwyer, stopping at the garage on his way home to dinner, thought it a great joke on Lund and promised to help the benefit along. Casey, with three drinks under his belt and his stomach otherwise empty, wanted to sing,

"Hey, ok Bill! Can-n yuh play the fiddle-o?   Yes, by —"

and stuck there because of the show lady. Casey wouldn't have recognized Trouble if it had walked up and banged him in the eye. He said sure, he'd be a cripple for the lady. He'd be anything once, and some things several times if they asked him in the right way. And then he gave himself into the hands of Jack dear.

Chapter VIII

Casey looked battered and sad when the show people were through with him. He had expected bandages wound picturesquely around his person, but the Barrymores were more artistic than that. Casey's right leg was drawn up at the knee so that he could not put his foot on the ground when he tried, and he did not know how the straps were fastened. His left shoulder was higher than his right shoulder, and his eyes were sunken in his head and a scar ran down along his temple to his left cheek bone. When he looked in the glass which Bill brought him, Casey actually felt ill. They told him that he must not wash his face, and that his week's growth of beard was a blessing from heaven. The show lady begged him, with dew on her lashes, to play the part faithfully, and they departed, very happy over their prospects.

Casey did not know whether he was happy or not. With Bill to encourage him and give him a lift over the gutters, he crossed the street to a restaurant and ordered largely of sirloin steak and French fried potatoes. After supper there was a long evening to spend quietly on crutches, and The Club was just next door. A man can always spend an evening very quickly at The Club-or he could in the wet days-if his money held out. Casey had money enough, and within an hour he didn't care whether he was crippled or not. There were five besides himself at that table, and they had unanimously agreed to remove the lid. Moreover, there was a crowd ten deep around that particular table. For the news had gone out that here was Casey Ryan back again, a hopeless cripple, playing poker like a drunken Rockefeller and losing as if he liked to lose.

At eight o'clock the next morning Bill came in to tell Casey that the show people had brought up their car to be fixed, and was the pay good? Casey replied Without looking up from his hand, which held a pair of queens which interested him. He'd stand good, he said, and Bill gave a grunt and went off.

At noon Casey meant to eat something. But another man had come into the game with a roll of money and a boastful manner. Casey rubbed his cramped leg and hunched down in his chair again and called for a stack of blues. Casey, I may as well confess, had been calling for stacks of blues and reds and whites rather often since midnight.

At four in the afternoon Casey hobbled into the restaurant and ate another steak and drank three cups of black coffee. He meant to go across to the garage and have Bill hunt up the Barrymores and get them to unstrap him for awhile, but just as he was lifting his left crutch around the edge of the restaurant door, two women of Lund came up and began to pity him and ask him how it ever happened. Casey could not remember, just at the moment, what story he had already told of his accident. He stuttered —a strange thing for an Irishman to do, by the way-and retreated into The Club, where they dared not follow.

"H'lo, Casey! Give yuh a chance to win back some of your losin's, if you're game to try it again," called a man from the far end of the room.

Casey swore and hobbled back to him, let himself stiffly down into a chair and dropped his crutches with a rattle of hard wood. Being a cripple was growing painful, besides being very inconvenient. The male half of Lund had practically suspended business that day to hover around him and exchange comments upon his looks. Casey had received a lot of sympathy that day, and only the fact that he had remained sequestered behind the curtained arch that cut across the rear of The Club saved him from receiving a lot more. But of course there were mitigations. Since walking was slow and awkward, Casey sat. And since he was not a man to sit and twiddle thumbs to pass the time, Casey played poker. That is how he explained it afterwards. He had not intended to play poker for twenty-four hours, but tie up a man's leg so he can't walk, and he's got to do *something*.

Wherefore Casey played, —and did not win back what he had lost earlier in the day. Daylight grew dim, and some one came over and lighted a hanging gasoline lamp that threw into tragic relief the painted hollows under Casey's eyes, which were beginning to look very bloodshot around the blue of them.

Once, while the bartender was bringing drinks-you are not to infer that Casey was drunk; he was merely a bit hazy over details-Casey pulled out his dollar watch and looked at it. Eight-thirty —the show must be pretty well started, by now. He thought he might venture to hobble over to Bill's and have those dog-gone straps taken off before he was crippled for sure. But he did not want to do anything to embarrass the show lady. Besides, he had lost a great deal of money, and he wanted to win some of it back. He still had time to make that train, he remembered. It was reported an hour late, some one said.

So Casey rubbed his strapped leg, twisting his face at the cramp in his knee and letting his companions believe that his accident had given him a heritage of pain. He hitched his lifted shoulder into an easier position and picked up another unfortunate assortment of five cards.

At ten o'clock Bill, the garage man, came and whispered something to Casey, who growled an oath and reached almost unconsciously for his crutches before trying to get up; so soon is a habit born in a man.

"What they raisin' thunder about?" he asked apathetically, when Bill had helped him across the gutter and into the street. "Didn't the crowd turn out like they expected?" Casey's tone was dismal. You simply cannot be a cripple for twenty-four hours, and sit up playing unlucky poker all night and all day and well into another night, without losing some of your animation; not even if you are Casey Ryan. "Hell, I missed that train again," he added heavily, when he heard it whistle into the railroad yard.

"Too bad. You oughta be on it, Casey," Bill said ominously.

At the garage the Barrymores were waiting for him in their stage clothes and make-up. The show lady had wept seams down through her rouge, and the beads on her lashes had clotted unbecomingly.

"Mister, you certainly have wished a sorry deal on to us," she exclaimed, when Casey came hobbling through the doorway. "Fifteen years on the stage and *this* never happened to us before. We've took our bad luck with our good luck and lived honest and respectable and self-respecting, and here, at last, ill fortune has tied the can on to us. I know you meant well and all that, Mister, but we certainly have had a raw deal handed out to us in this town. We-certainly-have!"

"We got till noon to-morrow to be outa the county," croaked Jack dear, shifting his Adam's apple rapidly. "And that's real comedy, ain't it, when your damn county runs clean over to the Utah line, and we can't go back the way we come, or-and we can't go anywhere till this big slob here puts our car together. He's got pieces of it strung from here around the block. Say, what kinda town is this you wished on to us, anyway? Holding night court, mind you, so they could can us quicker!"

The show lady must have seen how dazed Casey looked. "Maybe you ain't heard the horrible deal they handed us, Mister. They stopped our show before we'd raised the curtain, —and it was a seventy-five dollar house if it was a cent!" she wailed. "They had a bill as long as my arm for license-we couldn't get by with the five-dollar one-and for lights and hall rent and what-all. There wasn't enough money in the house to pay it! And they was going to send us to jail! The sheriff acted anything but a gentleman, Mister, and if you ever lived in this town and liked it, I must say I question your taste!"

"We wouldn't use a town like this for a garbage dump, back home," cut in Jack with all the contempt he could master.

"And they hauled us over to their dirty old Justice of the Peace, and he told us he'd give us thirty days in jail if we was in the county to-morrow noon, and we don't know how far this county goes, either way!"

"Fifty miles to St. Simon," Bill told them comfortingly. "You can make it, all right —"

"We can make it, hey? How're we going to make it, with our car layin' around all over your garage?" Jack's tone was arrogant past belief.

Casey was fumbling for strap buckles which he could not reach. He was also groping through his colorful, stage-driver's vocabulary for words which might be pronounced in the presence of a lady, and finding mighty few that were of any use to him. The combined effort was turning him a fine purple when the lady was seized with another brilliant idea.

"Jack dear, don't be harsh. The gentleman meant well-and I'll tell you, Mister, what let's do! Let's trade cars till the man has our car repaired. Your car goes just fine, and we can load our stuff in and get away from this horrible town. Why, the preacher was there and made a speech and said the meanest things about you, because you was having a benefit and at the same identical time you was setting in a saloon gambling. He said it was an outrage on civilization, Mister, and an insult to the honest, hard-working people in Lund. Them was his very words."

"Well, hell!" Casey exploded abruptly. "I'm honest and hard-workin' as any damn preacher. You can ask anybody!"

"Well, that's what he said, anyhow. We certainly didn't know you was a gambler when we offered to give you a benefit. We certainly never dreamed you'd queer us like that. But you'll do us the favor to lend us your car, won't you? You wouldn't refuse that, and see me and little Junior languishin' in jail when you know in your heart —"

"Aw, take the darn car!" muttered Casey distractedly, and hobbled into the garage office where he knew Bill kept liniment.

Five minutes, perhaps, after that, Casey opened the office door wide enough to fling out an assortment of straps and two crutches.

The show lady turned and made a motion which Casey mentally called a pounce. "Oh, thank you, Mister! We certainly wouldn't want to go off and forget these props. Jack dear has to use them in a comedy sketch we put on sometimes when we got a good house."

Casey banged the door and said something exceedingly stage-driverish which a lady should by no means overhear.

Sounds from the rear of the garage indicated that Casey's Ford was r'arin' to go, as Casey frequently expressed it. Voices were jumbled in the tones of suggestions, commands, protest. Casey heard the show lady's clear treble berating Jack dear with thin politeness. Then the car came snorting forward, paused in the wide doorway, and the show lady's voice called out clearly, untroubled as the voice of a child after it has received that which it cried for.

"Well, good-by, Mister! You certainly are a godsend to give us the loan of your car!" There was a buzz and a splutter, and they were gone-gone clean out of Casey's life into the unknown whence they had come.

Bill opened the door gently and eased into the office, sniffing liniment. The painted hollows under Casey's eyes gave him a ghastly look in the lamp-light when he lifted his face from examining a chafed and angry knee. Bill opened his mouth for speech, caught a certain look in Casey's eyes and did not say what he had intended to say. Instead:

"You better sleep here in the office, Casey. I've got another bed back of the machine shop. I'll lock up, and if any one comes and rings the night bell-well, never mind. I'll plug her so they can't ring her." The world needs more men like Bill.

Even after an avalanche, human nature cannot resist digging in the melancholy hope of turning up grewsome remains. I know that you are all itching to put shovel into the debris of Casey's dreams, and to see just what was left of them.

There was mighty little, let me tell you. I said in the beginning that twenty-five thousand dollars was like a wildcat in Casey's pocket. You can't give a man that much money all in a lump and suddenly, after he has been content with dollars enough to pay for the food he eats, without seeing him lose his sense of proportion. Twenty-five dollars he understands and can spend more prudently than you, perhaps. Twenty-five thousand he simply cannot gauge. It seems exhaustless. It is as if you plucked from the night all the stars you can see, knowing that the Milky Way is still there and unnumbered other stars invisible, even in the aggregate.

Casey played poker with an appreciative audience and the lid off. Now and then he took a drink stronger than root beer. He kept that up for a night and a day and well into another night. Very well, gather round and look at the remains, and if there's a moral, you are welcome, I am sure.

Casey awoke just before noon, and went out and held his head under Bill's garage hydrant, with the water running full stream. He looked up and found Bill standing there with his hands in his pockets, gazing at Casey sorrowfully. Casey grinned. You can't down the Irish for very long.

"How's she comin', Bill?"

Bill grunted and spat. "She ain't. Not if you mean that car them folks wished on to you. Well, the tail light's pretty fair, too. And in their hurry the lady went off and left a pink silk stockin' in the back seat. The toe's out of it though. Casey, if you wait till you overhaul 'em with that thing they wheeled in here under the name of a car —"

"Oh, that's all right, Bill," Casey grunted gamely. "I was goin' to git me a new car, anyway. Mine wasn't so much. They're welcome."

Bill grunted and spat again, but he did not say anything.

"I'll go see Dwyer and see how much I got left," Casey said presently, and his voice, whether you believe it or not, was cheerful. "I'm going to ketch that evenin' train to Los." And he added kindly, "C'm on and eat with me, Bill. I'm hungry."

Bill shook his head and gave another grunt, and Casey went off without him.

After awhile Casey returned. He was grinning, but the grin was, to a careful observer, a bit sickish. "Say, Bill, talk about poker —I'm off it fer life. Now look what it done to me, Bill! I puts twenty-five thousand dollars into the bank-minus two hundred I took in money-and I takes a check book, and I goes over to The Club and gits into a game. I wears the check book down to the stubs. I goes back and asks Dwyer how much I got in the bank, and he looks me over like I was a sick horse he had doubts about being worth doctorin', and as if he thought he mebby might better take me out an' shoot me an' put me outa my misery.

"'Jest one dollar an' sixty-seven cents, Casey,' he says to me, 'if the checks is all in, which I trust they air!'" Casey got out his plug of chewing tobacco and pried off a blunted corner. "An' hell Bill! I had that much in the bank when I started," he finished plaintively.

"Hell!" repeated Bill in brief, eloquent sympathy.

Casey set his teeth together and extracted comfort from the tobacco. He expectorated ruminatively.

"Well, anyway, I got me some bran' new socks, an' they're paid for, thank God!" He tilted his old Stetson down over his right eye at his favorite, Caseyish angle, stuck his hands in his pockets and strolled out into the sunshine.

Chapter IX

"At that," said Bill, grinning a little, "you'll know as much as the average garage-man. What ain't reformed livery-stable men are second-hand blacksmiths, and a feller like you, that has drove stage for fifteen year —"

"Twenty," Casey Ryan corrected jealously. "Six years at Cripple Creek, and then four in Yellowstone, and I was up in Montana for over five years, driving stage from Dry Lake to Claggett and from there I come to Nevada —"

"Twenty," Bill conceded without waiting to hear more, "knows as much as a man that has kept livery stable. Then again you've had two Fords —"

"Oh, I ain't sayin' I can't *run* a garage," Casey interrupted. "I don't back down from runnin' anything. But if you'd grubstake me for a year, instead of settin' up this here garage at Patmos, I'd feel like I had a better chance of makin' us both a piece uh money. There's a lost gold mine I been wantin' fer years to get out and look for. I believe I know now about where to hit for. It ain't lost, exactly. There's an old Injun been in the habit of packin' in high grade in a lard bucket, and nobody's been able to trail him and git back to tell about it. He's an old she-bear to do anything with, but I got a scheme, Bill —"

"Ferget it," Bill advised. "Now you listen to me, Casey, and lay off that prospectin' bug for awhile. Here's this long strip of desert from Needles to Ludlow, and tourists trailin' through like ants on movin' day. And here's this garage that I can get at Patmos for about half what the buildin's worth. You ain't got any competition, none whatever. You've got a cinch. There'll be cars comin' in from both ways with their tongues hangin' out, outa gas, outa oil, needin' this and needin' that and looking on that garage as a godsend —"

"Say, Bill, if I gotta be a godsend I'll go out somewheres and holler myself to death. Casey's off that godsend stuff for life; you hear me, Bill —"

"Glad to hear it, Casey. If you go down there to Patmos to clean up some money for you 'n' me, you wanta cut out this soft-hearted stuff. Get the money, see? Never mind being kind; you can be kind when you've got a stake to be it with. Charge 'em for everything they git, and see to it that the money's good. Don't you take no checks. Don't trust nobody for anything whatever. That's your weakness, Casey, and you know it. You're too dog-gone trusting. You promise me you'll put a bell on your tire tester and a log chain and drag on your pump and jack-say, you wouldn't believe the number of honest men that go off for a vacation and steal everything, by golly, they can haul away! Pliers, wrenches, oil cans, tire testers-say, you sure wanta watch 'em when they ask yuh for a tester! You can lose more tire testers in the garage business —"

"Well, now, you watch Casey! When it comes to putting things like that over, they wanta try somebody besides Casey Ryan. You ask anybody if Casey's easy fooled. But I'd ruther go hunt the Injun Jim mine, Bill."

"Say, Casey, in this one summer you can make enough money in Patmos to *buy* a gold mine. I've been reading the papers pretty careful. Why, they say tourist travel is the heaviest that ever was known, and this is early May and it's only beginning. And lemme tell yuh something, Casey. I'd ruther have a garage in Patmos than a hotel in Los Angeles, and by all they say that's puttin' it strong. Ever been over the road west uh Needles, Casey?"

Casey never had, and Bill proceeded to describe it so that any tourist who ever blew out a tire there with the sun at a hundred and twenty and running in high, would have confessed the limitations of his own vocabulary.

"And there you are, high and dry, with fifteen miles of the ungodliest, tire-chewinest road on either side of yuh that America can show. About like this stretch down here between Rhyolite and Vegas. And hills and chucks-say, don't talk to me about any Injun packin' gold in a lard bucket. Why, lemme tell yuh, Casey, if you work it right and don't be so dog-gone kind-hearted, you'll want a five-ton truck to haul off your profits next fall. I'd go myself and let you run this place here, only I got a lot of credit trade and you'd never git a cent outa the bunch. And then you're wantin' to leave Lund for awhile, anyway."

"You could git somebody else," Casey suggested half-heartedly. "I kinda hate to be hobbled to a place like a garage, Bill. And if there's anything gits my goat, it's patchin' up old tires. I'll run 'em flat long as they'll stay on, before I'll git out and mend 'em. I'd about as soon go to jail, Bill, as patch tires for tourists; I —"

"You don't have to," said Bill, his grin widening. "You sell 'em new tires, see. There won't be one in a dozen you can't talk into a new tire or two. Whichever way they're goin', tell 'em the road's a heap worse from there on than what it was behind 'em. They'll buy new tires-you take it from me they will. And," he added virtuously, "you'll do 'em no harm whatever. If you got a car, you need tires, and a new one'll always come in handy sometime. You know that yourself, Casey.

"Now, I'll put in an assortment of tires, and I'll trust you to sell 'em. You and the road they got to travel. Why, when I was in Ludlow, a feller blew in there with a big brute of a car —36-6 tires. He'd had a blow-out down the other side of Patmos and he was sore because they didn't have no tires he could use down there. He bought three tires —*three,* mind yuh, and peeled off the bills to pay for 'em! Sa-ay when yuh figure two hundred cars a day rollin' through, and half of 'em comin' to yuh with grief of some kind —"

"It's darn little I know about any car but a Ford," Casey admitted plaintively. "When yuh come to them complicated ones that you can crawl behind the wheel and set your boot on a button and holler giddap and she'll start off in a lope, I don't know about it. A Ford's like a mule or a burro. You take a monkey wrench and work 'em over, and cuss, and that's about all there is to it. But you take them others, and I got to admit I don't know."

"Well," said Bill, and spat reflectively, "you roll up your sleeves and I'll learn yuh. It'll take time for the stuff to be delivered, and you can learn a lot in two or three weeks, Casey, if you fergit that prospectin' idea and put your mind to it."

Casey rolled a cigarette and smoked half of it, his eyes clinging pensively to the barren hills behind Lund. He hunched his shoulders, looked at Bill and grinned reluctantly.

"She's a go with me, Bill, if you can't think of no other way to spend money. I wisht you took to poker more, or minin', or something that's got action. Stakin' Casey Ryan to a garage business looks kinda foolish to me. But if you can stand it, Bill, I can. It's kinda hard on the tourists, don't yuh think?"

Thus are garages born, —too many of them, as suffering drivers will testify. Casey Ryan, known wherever men of the open travel and spin their yarns, famous for his recklessly efficient driving of lurching stagecoaches in the old days, and for his soft heart and his happy-go-lucky ways; famous too as the man who invented ungodly predicaments from which he could extricate himself and be pleased if he kept his shirt on his back; Casey Ryan as the owner of a garage might justly be considered a joke pushed to the very limit of plausibility. Yet Casey Ryan became just that after two weeks of cramming on mechanics and the compiling of a reference book which would have made a fortune for himself and Bill if they had thought to publish it.

"A quort of oil becomes lubrecant and is worth from five to fifteen cents more per quort when you put it into a two-thousand dollar car or over," was one valuable bit of information supplied by Bill. Also: "Never cuss or fight a man getting work done in your place. Shut up and charge him according to the way he acts."

It is safe to assume that Bill would make a fortune in the garage business anywhere, given normal traffic.

Patmos consists of a water tank on the railroad, a siding where trains can pass each other, a ten-by-ten depot, telegraph office and express and freight office, six sweltering families, one sunbaked lodging place with tent bedrooms so hot that even the soap melts, and the Casey Ryan garage. I forgot to mention three trees which stand beside the water tank and try to grow enough at night to make up for the blistering they get during the day. The highway (Coast to Coast and signed at every crossroads in red letters on white metal boards with red arrows pointing to the far skyline) shies away from the railroad at Patmos so that perspiring travelers look wistfully across two hundred yards or so of lava rock and sand and wish that they might lie under those three trees and cool off. They couldn't, you know. It is no cooler under the trees than elsewhere. It merely looks cooler.

Even the water tank is a disappointment to the uninitiated. You cannot drink the water which the pump draws wheezingly up from some deep reservoir of bad flavors. It is very clear water and it has a sparkle that lures the unwary, but it is common knowledge that no man ever drank two swallows of it if he could help himself. So the water supply of Patmos lies twelve miles away in the edge of the hills, where there is a very good spring. One of the six male residents of Patmos hauls water in barrels, at fifty cents a barrel. He makes a living at it, too.

One other male resident keeps the lodging place, —I avoid the term lodging house, because this place is not a house. It is a shack with a sign straddling out over the hot porch to insult the credulity of the passers-by. The sign says that this place is "The Oasis," —and the nearest trees a long rifleshot away, and the coolest water going warm into parched mouths!

The Oasis stands over by the highway, alongside Casey's garage, and the proprietor spends nine tenths of his waking hours sitting on the front porch and following the strip of shade from the west end to the east end, and in watching the trains go by, and counting the cars of tourists and remarking upon the State license plate.

"There's an outfit from Ioway, maw," he will call in to his wife. "Wonder where they're headed fer?" His wife will come to the door and look apathetically at the receding dust cloud, and go back somewhere, —perhaps to put fresh soap in the tents to melt. Toward evening the cars are very likely to slow down and stop reluctantly; sunburned, goggled women and men looking the place over without enthusiasm. It isn't much of a place, to be sure, but any place is better than none in the desert, unless you have your own bed and frying pan with you, roped in dusty canvas to the back of your car.

Alongside the Oasis stands the garage, and in the garage swelters Casey, —during this episode. Just at first Bill came down from Lund and helped him to arrange and mark prices on his stock of tires and "parts" and accessories, and to remember the catalogue names for things so that he would recognize them when a car owner asked for them.

Casey, I must explain, had evolved a system of his own while driving his Ford wickedly here and there to the consternation of his fellow men. Whatever was not a hootin'-annie was a dingbat, and treated accordingly. The hootin'-annie appeared to be the thing that went wrong, while the dingbat was the thing the hootin'-annie was attached to. It was perfectly simple, to Casey and his Ford, but Bill thought it was a trifle limited and was apt to confuse customers. So Bill remained three days mopping his face with his handkerchief and explaining things to Casey. After that Casey hired a heavy-eyed young Mexican to pump tires and fill radiators and the like, and settled down to make his fortune.

Chapter X

Cars came and cars went, in heat and dust and some tribulation. In a month Casey had seen the color of every State license plate in the Union, and some from Canada and Mexico. From Needles way they came, searching their souls for words to tell Casey what they thought of it as far as they had gone. And Casey would squint up at them from under the rim of his greasy old Stetson and grin his Irish grin.

"Cheer up, the worst is yet to come," he would chant, with never a qualm at the staleness of the slogan. "How yuh fixed for water? Better fill up your canteens-yuh don't wanta git caught out between here and Ludlow with a boilin' radiator and not water enough. Got oil enough? Juan, you look and see. Can't afford to run low on oil, stranger. No, ma'am, there ain't any other road-and if there was another road it'd be worse than what this one is. No, ma'am, you ain't liable to git off'n the road. You can't. You'd git stuck in the sand 'fore you'd went the length of your car."

He would walk around them and look at their tires, his hands on his hips perhaps and his mouth damped shut in deep cogitation.

"What kinda shape is your extras in?" he would presently inquire. "She's a tough one, from here on to the next stop. You got a hind tire here that ain't goin' to last yuh five miles up the road." He would kick the tire whose character he was blackening. "Better lay in a supply of blow-out patches, unless you're a mind to invest in a new casing." Very often he would sell a tire or two, complete with new tubes, before the car moved on.

Casey never did things halfway, and Bill had impressed certain things deep on his mind. He was working with Bill's money and he obeyed Bill's commands. He never took a check or a promise for his pay, and he never once let his Irish temper get beyond his teeth or his blackened finger tips. Which is doing remarkably well for Casey Ryan, as you would admit if you knew him.

At the last moment, when the driver was settling himself behind the wheel, Casey would square his conscience for whatever strain the demands of business had put upon it. "Wait and take a good drink uh cold water before yuh start out," he would say, and disappear. He knew that the car wouldwait. The man or woman never lived who refused a drink of cold water on the desert in summer. Casey would return with a pale green glass water pitcher and a pale green glass. He would grin at their exclamations, and pour for them water that was actually cold and came from the coolest water bag inside. Those of you who have never traveled across the desert will not really understand the effect this would have. Those who have will know exactly what was said of Casey as that car moved out once more into the glaring sun and the hot wind and the choking dust.

Casey always kept one cold water bag and one in process of cooling, and he would charge as much as he thought they would pay and be called a fine fellow afterwards. He knew that. He had lived in dry, hot places before, and he was conscientiously trying to please the public and also make money for Bill, who had befriended him. You are not to jump to the conclusion, however, that Casey systematically robbed the public. He did not. He aided the public, helped the public across a rather bad stretch of country, and saw to it that the public paid for the assistance.

Casey saw all sorts and sizes of cars pass to and fro, and most of them stopped at his door, for gas or for water or oil, or perhaps merely to inquire inanely if they were on the right road to Needles or to Los Angeles, as the case might be. Any fool, thought Casey, would know without asking, since there was no other road, and since the one road was signed conscientiously every mile or two. But he always grinned good-naturedly and told them what they wanted him to tell them, and if they shifted money into his palm for any reason whatever he brought out his green glass pitcher and his green glass tumbler and gave them a drink all around and wished them luck.

There were strip-down Fords that tried to look like sixes, and there were six-cylinder cars that labored harder than Fords. There were limousines, sedans, sport cars, —and they all carried suitcases and canvas rolls and bundles draped over the hoods, on the fenders and piled high on the running boards.

Sometimes he would find it necessary to remove a thousand pounds or so of ill-wrapped bedding from the back of a tonneau before he could get at the gas tank to fill it, but Casey never grumbled. He merely retied the luggage with a packer's hitch that would take the greenhorn through his whole vocabulary before he untied it that night, and he would add two bits to the price of the gas because his time belonged to Bill, and Bill expected Casey's time to be paid for by the public.

One day when it was so hot that even Casey was limp and pale from the heat, and the proprietor of the Oasis had forsaken the strip of shade on his porch and had chased his dog out of the dirt hollow it had scratched under the house and had crawled under there himself, a party pulled slowly up to the garage and stopped. Casey was inside sitting on the ground and letting the most recently filled water bag drip down the back of his neck. He shouted to Juan, but Juan had gone somewhere to find himself a cool spot for his siesta, so Casey got slowly to his feet and went out to meet Trouble, sopping his wet hair against the back of his head with the flat of his hand before he put on his hat. He squinted into the sunshine and straightway squared himself for business.

This was a two-ton truck fitted for camping. A tall, lean man whose overalls hung wide from his suspenders and did not seem to touch his person anywhere, climbed out and stood looking at the bare rims of two wheels, as if he had at that moment discovered them.

"Thinkin' about the price uh tires, stranger?" Casey grinned cheerfully. "It's lucky I got your size, at that. Fabrics and cords-and the difference in price is more'n made up in wear. Run yer car inside outa the sun whilst I change yer grief into joy."

"I teen havin' hard luck all along," the man complained listlessly. "Geewhillikens, but it shore does cost to travel!"

Casey should have been warned by that. Bill would have smelled a purse lean as the man himself and would have shied a little. But Casey could meet Trouble every morning after breakfast and yet fail to recognize her until she had him by the collar.

"You ask anybody if it don't!" he agreed sympathetically, mentally going over his rack of tires, not quite sure that he had four in that size, but hoping that he had five and that he could persuade the man to invest. He surely needed rubber, thought Casey, as he scrutinized the two casings on the car. He stood aside while the man backed, turned a wide half-circle and drove into the grateful shade of the garage. It seemed cool in there after the blistering sunlight, unless one glanced at Casey's thermometer which declared a hundred and nineteen with its inexorable red line.

"Whatcha got there? Goats?" Casey's eyes had left the wheels of the trucks and dwelt upon a trailer penned round and filled with uneasy animals.

"Yeah. Twelve, not countin' the little fellers. And m'wife an' six young ones all told. Makes quite a drag on the ole boat. Knocks thunder outa tires, too. You say you got my size? We-ell, I guess I got to have 'em, cost er no cost."

"Sure you got to have 'em. It's worse ahead than what you been over, an' if I was you I'd shoe 'er all round before I hit that lava stretch up ahead here. You could keep them two fer extras in case of accident. Might git some wear outa them when yuh strike good roads again, but they shore won't go far in these rocks. You ask anybody."

"We-ell—I guess mebby I better—I don't see how I'm goin' to git along any other way, but—"

Casey had gone to find where Juan had cached himself and to pluck that apathetic youth from slumber and set him to work. Four casings and tubes for a two-ton truck run into money, as Casey was telling himself complacently. He had not yet sold any tires for a two-ton truck, and he had just two fabrics and two cords, in trade vernacular. He paid no further attention to the man, since there would be no bickering. When a man has only two badly chewed tires, and four wheels, argument is superfluous.

So Casey mildly kicked Juan awake and after the garage jack, and himself wheeled out his four great pneumatic tires, and with his jackknife slit the wound paper covering, and wondered what it was that smelled so unpleasant. A goat bleated plaintively to remind him of their presence. Another goat carried on the theme, and the chorus swelled quaveringly and held to certain minor notes. Within the closed truck a small child whimpered and then began to cry definitely at the top of its voice.

Casey looked up from bending over the fourth tire wrapping. "Better let your folks git out and rest awhile," he invited hospitably. "It's goin' to take a little time to put these tires on. I got some cold water back there-help yourself."

"Well, I'd kinda like to water them goats," the man observed diffidently. "They ain't had a drop sence early yest-day mornin'. You got water here, ain't yuh? An' they might graze around a mite whilst we're here. Travelin' like this, I try to kinda give 'em a chanct when we stop along the road. It's been an awful trip. We come clear from Wyoming. How far is it from here to San Jose, Californy?"

Casey had in the first week learned that it is not wise for a garage man to confess that he does not know distances. People always asked him how far it was to some place of which he had never heard, and he had learned to name figures at random very convincingly. He named now what seemed to him a sufficient number, and the man said "Gosh!" and went back to let down the end gate of the trailer and release the goats. "You said you got water for 'em?" he asked, his tone putting the question in the form of both statement and request.

When you are selling four thirty-six-sixes, two of them cords, to a man, you can't be stingy with a barrel of water, even if it does cost fifty cents. Casey told Juan to go borrow a tub next door and show the man where the water barrel stood. Juan, squatted on his heels while he languidly pumped the jack handle up and down, and seeming pleased than otherwise when the jack slipped and tilted so that he must lower it and begin all over again, got languidly to his bare feet and lounged off obediently. According to Juan's simple philosophy, to obey was better than to dodge hammers, pliers or monkey wrenches, since Casey's aim was direct and there was usually considerable force of hard, prospector's muscle behind it.

Juan was gone a long while, long enough to walk slowly to the station of Patmos and back again, but he returned with the tub, and the incessant bleating of the goats stilled intermittently while they drank. By this time Casey had forgotten the goats, even with the noise of them filling his ears.

Casey was down on his knees hammering dents out of the rim of a front wheel so that the new tire could go on. Four of the six offspring crowded around him, getting in the way of Casey's hammer and asking questions which no man could answer and remain normal. Casey had, while he unwrapped the casings, made a mental reduction in the price. Even Bill would throw off a little, he told himself, on a sale like this. Mentally he had deducted twenty-five dollars from the grand total, but before he had that rim straightened he said to himself that he'd be darned if he discounted more than twenty.

"Humbolt an' Greeley, you git away from there an' git out here an' git these goats a-grazin'," the lean customer called sharply from the rear of the garage. Humbolt and Greeley hastily proceeded to git, which left two unkempt young girls standing there at Casey's elbow so that he could not expectorate where he pleased, or swear at all. Wherefore Casey was appreciably handicapped in his work, and he wished that he were away out in the hills digging into the side of a gulch somewhere, sun-blistered, broke, more than half starving on short rations and with rheumatism in his right shoulder and a bunion giving him a limp in the left foot. He could still be happy —

"*What* yuh doin' that for?" the shrillest voice repeated three times rapidly, with a sniffle now and then by way of punctuation.

"To make little girls ask questions," grunted Casey, glancing around him for the snub-nosed, double-headed, four-pound hammer which he called affectionately by the name Maud. The biggest girl had Maud. She had turned it upright on its handle and was sitting on the head of it. When Casey reached for it and got it, without apology or warning, the girl sprawled backward and howled.

"Porshea, you git up from there! *Shame* on yuh!" A shrill woman voice, very much like the younger voices except that it was worn rough and querulous with age and many hardships, called down from the truck. Casey looked up, startled, and tried to remember just what he had said before the girls appeared to silence him. The woman was very large both in height and in bulk, and she was heaving herself out of the truck in a way that reminded Casey oddly of a disgruntled hippopotamus he had once watched coming out of its tank at a circus. Casey moved modestly away and did not look, after that first glance. A truck, you will please understand, is not a touring car, and ladies who have passed the two-hundred-pound notch on the scales should remain up there and call for a step-ladder.

She descended, and the jack slipped and let the car down with a six-inch lurch. Casey is remarkably quick in his motions. He turned, jumped three feet and caught the lady's full weight in his arms as she was falling toward him. Probably he would have caught it anyway, but then there would have been little left of Casey, and his troubles would have been finished instead of being just begun.

He had just straightened the jack and was beginning to lift the bare wheel off the ground again when the fifth offspring descended. Casey thought again of the hippopotamus in its infancy. The fifth was perhaps fifteen, but she had apparently reached her full growth, which was very nearly that of her mother. She had also reached the age of self-consciousness, and she simpered at Casey when he assisted her to alight.

Casey was not bashful, nor was he over-fastidious; men who have lived long in the wilderness are not, as a rule. Still, he had his little whims, and he failed to react to the young lady's smile. His pale blue eyes were keen to observe details and even Casey did not approve of "high-water marks" on feminine beauty.

Well, that brought the whole family to view save the youngest who had evidently dropped asleep and was left in the truck. Casey went to work on the wheel again, after directing mother and daughter to the desert water bag which swung suspended from ropes in the rear of the garage.

Ten minutes later a dusty limousine stopped for gas and oil, and Casey left his work to wait upon them. There was a very good-looking girl driving, and the man beside her was undoubtedly only her father, and Casey was humanly anxious to be remembered pleasantly when they drove on. He asked them to wait and have a drink of cold water, and was deeply humiliated to find that both water bags were empty,—the overgrown girl having used the last to wash her face. Casey didn't like her any the better for that, or for having accentuated the high-water mark, or for forcing him to apologize to the pretty driver of the limousine.

He refilled the water bags and remarked pointedly that it would take an hour for the water to cool in them and that they must be left alone in the meantime. He did not look at the girl, but from the tail of his eye he saw her pull a contemptuous grimace at him when she thought his back safely turned.

Wherefore Casey finished the putting on of the fourth tire pretty well up toward the boiling point in temper and in blood. I have not mentioned half the disagreeable trifles that nagged at him during the interval,—his audience, for instance, that hovered so close that he could not get up without colliding with one of them, so full of aimless talk that he mislaid tools in his distraction. Juan was a pest and Casey thought malevolently how he would kill him when the job was finished. Juan went around like one in a trance, his heavy-lidded, opaque eyes following every movement of the girl, which kept her younger sisters giggling. But even with interruptions and practically no assistance the truck stood at last with four good tires on its wheels, and Casey wiped a perspiring face and let down the jack, thankful that the job was done; thinking, too, that ten dollars would be a big reduction on the price. He had to count his time, you see.

"Well, how much does it come to, mister?" the lord of the flock asked dolefully, when Casey called him in and told him that he could go at any time now.

Casey told him, and made the price only five dollars lower than the full amount, just because he hated to see men walk around loose in their pants, with their stomachs sagged in as though they never were fed a square meal in their lives.

"It's a pile uh money to pay out for rubber that's goin' to be chewed off on these here danged rocks," sighed the man.

Casey grunted and began collecting his tools, rescuing the best hammer he had from one of the girls. "I wisht it was all profit," he said. "Or even a quarter of it. I'm sellin' 'em close as I can an' git paid fer my time puttin' 'em on."

"Oh, I ain't kickin' about the price. I'm satisfied with that." Men usually are, you notice, when they want credit. "Now I tell yuh. I ain't got that much money with me —"

Casey spat and pointed his thumb toward a sign which he had nailed up just the day before, thinking that it would save both himself and his customers some embarrassment. The sign, except that the letters were not even, was like this:

"CHECKS MUST BE CASHED BY THE ONER OR THEY AIN'T CASHED"

The lean man read and looked at Casey humbly. "Well, I ain't never wrote a check in my life. Now I tell yuh. I ain't got the money to pay for these tires, but I tell yuh what I'll do; I'm goin' on up to my brother-he's got a prune orchard a little ways out from San Jose, an' he's well fixed. Now I'll write out an order on my brother, fer him to send you the money. He's good fer it, an' he'll do it. I'm goin' on up to help him work his place on shares, so I c'n straighten up with him when I get —"

Casey had picked up the jack again and was regretfully but firmly adjusting it under the front axle. "That ain't the first good prospect I ever had pinch out on me," he observed, trying to be cheerful over it. He could even grin while he squinted up at the lean man.

"Well, now, you can't hardly refuse to trust a man in my fix!"

"Think I can't?" Casey was working the jack handle rapidly and the words came in jerks. "You stand there and watch me." He spun the wheel free and reached for his socket wrench. "I wisht you'd spoke your piece before I set these dam nuts so tight," he added.

The lean man turned and looked inquiringly at his wife. "Ain't I honest, maw, and don't I pay my debts? An' ain't my brother Joe honest, an' don't he pay *his* debts? Would you think the man lived, maw, that would set a man with a fambly afoot out on the desert like this?"

"Nev' mind, now, paw. Give him time to think what it means, an' he won't. He's got a heart."

The baby awoke and cried then, and Casey's heart squirmed in his chest. But he thought of Bill and stiffened his business nerve.

"I got a heart; sure I've got a heart. You ask anybody if Casey's got a heart. But I also got a pardner."

"Your pardner's likely gen'l'man enough to trust us, if you ain't," maw said sharply.

"Yes, ma'am, he is. But he's got these tires to pay fer on the first of the month. It ain't a case uh not trustin'; it's a case of git the money or keep the tires. I wisht you had the money-she shore is a good bunch uh rubber I let yuh try on."

They wrangled with him while he removed the tires he had so painstakingly adjusted, but Casey was firm. He had to be. There is no heart in the rubber trust; merely a business office that employs very efficient bookkeepers, who are paid to see that others pay. He removed the new tires; that was his duty to Bill. By then it was five o'clock when all good mechanics throw down their pliers and begin to shed their coveralls.

Casey was his own man after five o'clock. He rolled the tattered tires out into the sunlight, let out the air and yanked them from their rims. "Come on here and help, and I'll patch up your old tires so you c'n go on," he offered good-naturedly, in spite of the things the woman had said to him. "The tire don't live that Casey can't patch if it comes to a showdown."

Before he was through with them he had donated four blow-out patches to the cause, and about five hours of hard labor. The Smith family-yes, they were of the tribe of Smith-were camped outside and quarreling incessantly. The goats, held in spasmodic restraint by Humbolt and Greeley and a little spotted dog which Casey had overlooked in his first inventory, were blatting inconsequently in the sage behind the garage. Casey cooked a belated supper and hoped that the outfit would get an early start, and that their tires would hold until they reached Ludlow, at least. "Though I ain't got nothin' against Ludlow," he added to himself while he poured his coffee.

"Maw wants to know if you got any coffee you kin lend," the shrill voice of Portia sounded unexpectedly at his elbow. Casey jumped,—an indication that his nerves had been unstrung.

"Lend? Hunh! Tell 'er I give her a cupful." Then, because Casey had streaks of wisdom, he closed the doors of the garage and locked them from the inside. Cars might come and honk as long as they liked; Casey was going to have his sleep.

Very early he was awakened by the bleating, the barking, the crying and the wrangling of the Smiths. He pulled his tarp over his ears, hot as it was, to shut out the sound. After a long while he heard the stutter of the truck motor getting warmed up. There was a clamor of voices, a bleating of goats, the barking of the spotted dog, and the truck moved off.

"Thank Gawd!" muttered Casey, and went to sleep again.

Chapter XI

At two o'clock the next afternoon, the Smith outfit came back, limping along on three bare rims. Casey's jaw dropped a little when he saw them coming, but nature had made him an optimist. Now, perhaps, that hungry-looking Smith would dig into his pocket and find the price of new tires. It had been Casey's experience that a man who protested the loudest that he was broke would, if held rigidly to the no-credit rule, find the money to pay for what he must have. In his heart he believed that Smith had money dangling somewhere in close proximity to his lank person.

But if Smith had any money he did not betray the fact. He asked quite humbly for the loan of tools, and tube cement, and more blow-out patches, and set awkwardly to work mending his tattered tires. And once more Casey sent Juan to borrow the Oasis tub, and watered the goats and picked his way amongst the Smith offsprings and pretended to be deaf half of the time, and said he didn't know the other half. His green glass water pitcher was practically useless to travelers, and Juan was worse. A goat got away from Humbolt and Greeley and went exploring in the corner of the garage where Casey lived, and ate three pounds of bacon. You know what bacon costs. Maw Smith became acquainted with Casey and followed him about with a detailed recital of her family history, which she thought would make a real exciting book. What Casey thought I must not tell you.

That night Casey patched tires and tubes. He had to, you see, or go crazy. Next morning he listened to the departure of the Smith family and the Smith goats, and prayed that their tires would hold out even as far as Bagdad, —though I don't see why, since there was no garage in Bagdad, or anything else but a flag station.

That afternoon at three o'clock, they came back again! And Casey neglected to send Juan after the tub to water the goats. Wherefore paw sent Humbolt, and watered the goats himself from Casey's barrel and seemed peevish because he must. Maw Smith came after coffee again, and helped herself with no more formality than a shrill, "I'm borrying some more coffee!" sent to Casey out in front.

That night Casey patched tires and tubes.

At six o'clock Smith pounded on the back door and called in to Casey that he would have to have some gas before he started. So Casey pulled on his pants and gave Smith some gas, and paid the garage out of his own pocket. He didn't swear, either. He was past that.

That afternoon Casey watched apprehensively the road that led west. It was two-thirty when he saw them coming. Casey set his jaw and went in and hid every blow-out patch he had in stock, and all the cement.

Smith went into camp, sent Greeley after the Oasis tub and watered the goats from one of Casey's water barrels. Casey went on with his work, waiting upon customers who paid, and tried not to think of the Smiths, although most of them were underfoot or at his elbow.

"Them tires you mended ain't worth a cuss," Smith came around finally to complain. "I didn't get ten mile out with 'em before I had another blowout. I tell yuh what I'll do. I'll trade yuh goats fer tires. I got two milk goats that's worth a hundred dollars apiece, mebby more, the way goats is selling on the Coast. I hate to part with 'em, but I gotta do somethin'. Er else you'll have to trust me till I c'n get to my brother an' git the money. It ain't," he added grievedly, "as if I wasn't honest enough to pay my debts."

"Nope," said Casey wearily, "I don't want yer goats. I've had more goats a'ready than I want. And tires has gotta roll outa this shop paid for. We talked that all over, the first night."

"What am I goin' to do, then?" Smith inquired in exasperation.

"Hell; I dunno," Casey returned grimly. "I quit guessin' day before yesterday."

Smith went off to confer with maw, and Casey overheard some very harsh statements made concerning himself. Maw Smith was so offended that she refused to borrow coffee from Casey that night, and she called her children out of his garage and told them she would warm their ears for them if they went near him again. Hearing which Casey's features relaxed a little. He could even meet customers with his accustomed grin when Smith in his anger sent the goats over to the water tank next day, refusing to show any friendship for Casey by emptying a water barrel for him. But he had to fire Juan for pouring gasoline into the radiator of a big sedan, and later he had to stalk that lovesick youth into the very camp of the Smiths and lead him back by the collar, and search him for stolen tools. He recovered twice as many as you would believe a Mexican's few garments could conceal.

Casey was harassed for two days by the loud proximity of the Smiths, but not one of them deigned to speak to him or to show any liking for him whatever, beyond helping themselves superciliously to the contents of his water barrel. On the morning of the third day the lean man presented his thin shadow and then himself at the front door of the garage, with a letter in his hand and a hopeful look on his face.

"Well, mebby I c'n talk business to yuh now an' have somethin' to go on," he began abruptly. "I went an' sent off a telegraft to my brother in San Jose about you, and he's wrote a letter to yuh. My brother's a business man. You c'n see that much fer yourself. An' mebby you'll see your way clear t' help me leave this dod-rotten hole. Here's yer letter."

Casey held himself neutral while he read the letter. As it happens that I have a copy, here it is:

(Printed Letterhead)

VISTA GRANDE RANCHO

Smith Bros.
San Jose, Calif.
Garage Owner, Patmos, Calif.

DEAR SIR: I am informed that my brother Eldreth William Smith, having suffered the mishap to lose his tires at your place or thereabouts, and having the misfortune to fall short of immediate funds with which to pay cash for replacement, has been denied credit at your hands.

I regret that because of business requirements in my own business it is impossible for me to place the amount necessary at his immediate disposal. It is therefore my advise that you lend to my brother Eldreth William Smith such money or moneys as will be necessary to purchase railroad tickets for himself and family from Patmos to this place, and

Furthermore that you take as security for said loan such motor truck and equipment etc. as he has now stored at your place of business. I am aware of the fact that a motor truck in any running condition would amply secure such loans as would purchase tickets from Patmos to San Jose, and I hereby enclose note for same, duly made out in blank and signed by me, which signature will be backed by the signature of my brother. Upon receiving from you such money as he may require he will duly deliver note and security duly signed and filled with the amount. I trust this will be perfectly satisfactory to you as amply securing you for the loan of the desired amount.

Thanking you in advance,

Yours very Truly,

J. PAUL SMITH.

In spite of himself, Casey was impressed. The very Spanish name of the prune orchard impressed him, and so did the formal business terms used by J. Paul Smith; and that "thanking you in advance" seemed to place him under a moral obligation too great to shirk. There was the note, too,—heavy green paper with a stag's head printed on it, and looking almost like a check.

"Well, all right, if it don't cost too much and the time don't run too long," surrendered Casey reluctantly. "How much—"

"Fare's a little over twenty-five dollars, an' they'll be four full fares an' three half. I guess mebby I better have a hundred an' seventy-five anyway, so'st we kin eat on the way."

Casey chanced to have almost that much coming to him out of the business, so that he would not be lending Bill's money. He watched the lean Smith fill in the amount and sign the note, identifying the truck by its engine and license numbers, and he went and borrowed fifteen dollars from the proprietor of the Oasis and made up the amount. There was a train at noon, and from his garage door he watched the Smith family start off across the lava rocks to the depot, each one laden with bundles and disreputable grips, the spotted dog trotting optimistically ahead of the party with his pink tongue draped over the right side of his mouth. Smith turned, the baby in his arms, and called back casually to Casey:

"Yuh better tie up them two milk goats when yuh milk 'em. They won't stand if yuh don't."

Casey's jaw sagged. He had not thought of the goats. Indeed, the last two days they had not troubled him except by their bleating at dawn. Humbolt and Greeley had grazed them over by the railroad track so that they could watch the trains go by. Casey looked and saw that the goats were still over there where they had been driven early. He took off his hat and rubbed his palm reflectively over the back of his head, set the hat on his head with a pronounced tilt over one eyebrow, and reached for his plug of tobacco.

"Oh, darn the goats! Me milkin' goats! Well, now, Casey Ryan never milked no goats, an' he ain't goin' to milk no goats! You can ask anybody if they think't he will."

Casey was very busy that day, and he had no dull-eyed Juan to do certain menial tasks about the cars that stopped before his garage. Nevertheless he kept an eye on the station of Patmos until the westbound train had come and had departed, and on the rough road between the railroad and the garage for another half hour, until he was sure that the Smith family were not coming back. Then he went more cheerfully about his work, now and then glancing, perhaps, at the truck which had been driven into the rear of the garage where it was very much in his way, but was safe from pilfering fingers. It was not such a bad truck, give it new tires. Casey had already figured the price at which he could probably sell it, on an easy payment plan, to the man who hauled water for Patmos. It was more than the amount of his loan, naturally. By noon he was rather hoping the "Smith Bros." would fail to take up that note.

Casey, you see, was not counting the goats at all. He had a vague idea that, while they were nominally a part of the security, they were actually of no importance whatever. They would run loose until Smith came after them, he guessed. He did not intend to milk any nanny goats, so that settled the goat question for Casey.

Casey simply did not know anything about goats. He ought to have used a little logic and not so much happy-go-lucky "t'ell with the goats." That is all very well, so far as it goes, and we all know that everybody says it and thinks it. But it does, not settle the problem. It never occurred to Casey, for instance, that the going of Humbolt and Greeley and the little spotted dog would make any difference. It really did make a great deal, you see. And it never occurred to Casey that goats are domesticated animals after they have been hauled around the country for weeks and weeks in a trailer to a truck, or that they will come back to the only home they know.

I don't know how long it takes goats to fill up. I never kept a goat or goats. And I don't know how long they will stand around and blat before they start something. I don't know much more about goats than Casey, or didn't, at least, until he told me. By that time Casey knew a lot more, I suspect, than he could put into words.

Casey says that he heard them blatting around outside, but he was busy trying to straighten a radius rod-Casey *said* he was taking the kinks outa that hootin'-annie that goes behind the front ex and turns the dingbats when you steer-for a man who walked back and forth and slapped his hands together nervously and kept asking how long it was going to take, and how far it was to Barstow, and whether the road from there up across the Mojave was in good condition, and whether the Death Valley road out from Ludlow went clear through the valley and was a cut-off north, or whether it just went into the valley and stopped. Casey says that the only time he ever was in Death Valley it was with a couple of burros and that he like to have stayed there. He got to telling the man about his trip into Death Valley and how he just did get out by a scratch.

So he didn't pay any attention to the goats until he went back after some cold water for the white little woman in the car, that looked all tuckered out and scared. It was then he found the whole corner chewed off one water bag and the other water bag on the ground and a lot more than the corner gone. And the billy was up on his hind feet with his horns caught in the fullest barrel, and was snorting and snuffling in a drowning condition and tilting the barrel perilously. The other goats were acting just like plain damn goats, said Casey, and merely looking for trouble without having found any.

Casey says he had to call the Oasis man to help him get Billy out of the barrel, and that even then he had to borrow a saw and saw off one horn-either that, or cave in the barrel with Maud-and he needed that barrel worse than the billy goat needed two horns; but he told me that if he'd had Maud in his two hands just then he sure would have caved in the goat.

At that, the nervous man got away without paying Casey, which I think rankled worse than a spoiled barrel of water.

Casey told me that he aged ten years in the next two weeks, and lost eighty-nine dollars and a half in damages and wages, not counting the two water bags he had to replace out of his stock, at nearly four dollars wholesale price. When he chased the goats out of his back door they went around and came in at the front, determined, he supposed, to bed down near the truck.

It was late before that occurred to him, and when it did he cranked up and drove the truck a hundred yards down the road that led to the spring. The goats did not follow as he expected, but stood around the trailer and blatted. Casey went back and hooked on the trailer and drove again down the road. The goats would not follow, and he went back to find that Billy had managed to push open the back door and had led his flock into Casey's kitchen. There was no kitchen left but the little camp stove, and that was bent so that it stood skew-gee, Casey said, and developed a habit of toppling over just when his coffee came to a boil.

Casey told me that he had to barricade himself in his garage that night, and he swore that Billy stood on his hind feet and stared at him all night through the window in spite of wrenches and pliers hailing out upon him. However that may be, Billy couldn't have stood there all night, unless Casey got his dates mixed. For at six o'clock the Oasis man came over, stepping high and swinging his fists, and told Casey that them damn goats had et all the bedding out of one tent and the soap, towel and one pillow out of another, and what was Casey going to do about it?

Casey did not know, —and he was famous for his resourcefulness too. I think he paid for the bedding before the thing was settled.

Casey says that after that it was just one thing after another. He told me that he never would have believed twelve goats could cover so much cussedness in a day. He said he couldn't fill a radiator but some goat would be chewing the baggage tied behind the car, or Billy would be rooting suitcases off the running board. One party fell in love with a baby goat and Casey in a moment of desperation told them they could have it. But he was sorry afterward, because the mother stood and blatted at him reproachfully for four days and nights without stopping.

Casey swears that he picked up and threw two tons of rocks every day, and he has no idea how many tons the six families of Patmos heaved at and after the goats. When they weren't going headfirst into barrels of water they were chewing something not meant to be chewed. Casey asserts that it is all a bluff about goats eating tin cans. They don't. He says they never touched a can all the while he had them. He says devastated Patmos wished they would, and leave the two-dollar lace curtains alone, and clotheslines and water barrels and baggage. He says many a party drove off with chewed bedding rolls and didn't know it, and that he didn't tell them, either.

You're thinking about Juan, I know. Well, Casey thought of Juan the first day, and took the trouble to hunt him up and hire him to herd the goats. But Juan developed a bad case of sleeping sickness, Casey says, which unfortunately was not contagious to goats. He swears that he never saw one of those goats lying down, though he had seen pictures of goats lying down and had a vague idea that they chewed their cuds. Casey tried to be funny, then. He looked at me and grinned, and observed, "Hunh! Goats don't chew cuds. That's all wrong. They chew *duds.* You ask anybody in Patmos." So Juan slept under sagebushes and grease-wood, and the goats did not.

Casey declares that he stood it for two weeks, and that it took all he could make in the garage to pay the six families of Patmos for the damage wrought by his security. He lost fifteen pounds of flesh and every friend he had made in the place except the man who hauled water, and he liked it because he was getting rich. Once Casey had a bright idea, and with much labor and language he loaded the goats into the trailer and had the water-hauler take them out to the hills. But that didn't work at all. Part of the flock came back afoot, from sheer homesickness, and the rest were hauled back because they were ruining the spring which was Patmos' sole water supply.

Casey would have shot the goats, but he couldn't bring himself to do anything that would offend J. Paul Smith of the *Vista Grande Rancho.* Whenever he read the letter J. Paul Smith had written him he was ashamed to do anything that would lower him in the estimation of J. Paul Smith, who trusted him and took it for granted that he would do the right thing and do it with enthusiasm.

"If he hadn't wrote so dog-gone polite!" Casey complained to me. "And if he hadn't went an' took it for granted I'd come through. But a man can't turn down a feller that wrote the way he done. Look at that letter! A college perfessor couldn't uh throwed together no better letter than that. And that there 'Thanking you in advance'—a feller *can't* throw a man down when he writes that way. You ask anybody." Casey's tone was one of reminiscent injury, as if J. Paul Smith had indeed taken a mean advantage of him.

One day Casey reached the limit of his endurance,—or perhaps of the endurance of Patmos. There were not enough male residents to form a mob strong enough to lynch Casey, but there was one woman who had lost a sofa pillow and two lace curtains; Casey did not say much about her, but I gathered that he would as soon be lynched as remonstrated with again by that woman. "Sufferin' Sunday! I'd shore hate to be her husband. You ask anybody!" sighed Casey when he was telling me.

Casey moralized a little. "Folks used to look at the goats that I'd maybe just hazed off into the brush fifty yards or so with a thousand pounds mebby of rocks, an' some woman in goggles would say, 'Oh, an' you keep goats! How nice!' like as if it were something peaceful an' homelike to keep goats! Hunh! Lemme tell yuh; never drive past a place that *looks* peaceful, and jump at the idea it *is* peaceful. They may be a woman behind them vines poisinin' 'er husband's father. How could them darn tourists tell 'what was goin' on in Patmos? They seen the goats pertendin' to graze, an' keepin' an eye peeled till my back was turned, an' they thought it was *nice* to keep goats. Hunh!"

At last Casey could bear no more. He gathered together enough hardwood, three-inch crate slats to make twelve crates, and he worked for three nights, making them. And Casey is no carpenter. After that he worked for three days, with all the men in Patmos to help him, getting the goats into the crates and loaded on the truck. Then he drove over to the station and asked for tags, and addressed the crates to J. Paul Smith, *Vista Grande Rancho,* San Jose, Calif. Then he discovered that he could not send them except by express, and that he could not send them by express unless he prepaid the charges. And the charges on goats sent by express, was, as Casey put it, a holy fright.

But he had to do it. Patmos had been led to believe that he would send those goats off on the train, and Casey did not know what would happen if he failed. There were the heads of the six families, and all the children who were of walking age, grouped around the crates and Casey expectantly. Casey went back to the garage safe and got what money he had, borrowed the balance from the male citizens of Patmos and prepaid the express. Patmos helped to load them into the first express car going west, and Casey felt, he said, as if some one had handed him a million dollars in dimes.

Casey seemed to think that ended the story, but I am like the rest of you. I wanted to know what the Smith family did, and J. Paul Smith, and whether Casey kept the truck and sold it to the man who hauled water.

"Who? Me? Say! D'you ever know Casey Ryan to ever come out anywheres but at the little end uh the horn? Ain't I the bag holder pro tem?" I don't know what he meant by that. I think he was mistaken in the meaning of "pro tem."

"You ask anybody. Say, I got a letter sayin' in a gen'ral way that I'm a thief an' a cutthroat an' a profiteer an' so on, an' that I would have to pay fer the goat that was missin' —that there was the one I give away-an' that the damages to the billy goat was worth twenty-five dollars and same would be deducted from the amount of the loan. *Darn* these fancy word slingers!" said Casey. "An' the day before the note come due, here comes that shoestring in pants with the money to pay the note minus the damages, and four new tires fer the truck! Yessir, wouldn't buy tires off me, even! Could yuh beat that fer gall? And he wouldn't hardly speak."

Casey grinned and got his plug of tobacco and inspected the corners absently before he bit into it. "But I got even with 'im," he added. "I laid off till he got his tires on-an' I wouldn't lend him no tools to put 'em on with, neither. And then I looked up an' down the road an' seen there was no dust comin' an' we wouldn't be interrupted, an' I went up to the old skunk an' I says, 'I got a bill to colleck off you. *Thankin' you in advance!*' an' then I shore collected. You ask anybody in Patmos. Say, I bet he drove by-guess-an'-by-gosh to the orange belt, anyway, the way his eyes was swellin' up when he left!"

I mentioned his promise to Bill, that he would not fight a customer. Casey spat disgustedly. "Hell! He wasn't no customer! Didn't he ship his rubber in by express, ruther'n to buy off me?" He grinned retrospectively and looked at his knuckles, one of which showed a patch of new skin, pink and yet tender.

" 'Thankin' you in advance!' that's just what I told 'im. An' I shore got all I thanked 'im for! You ask anybody in Patmos. They seen 'im afterwards."

Chapter XII

"Look there!" Casey rose from the ground where he had been sitting with his hands clasped round his drawn-up knees. He pointed with his pipe to a mountain side twelve miles away but looking five, even in the gloom of early dusk. "Look at that, will yuh! Whadda yuh say that is, just makin' a guess? A fire, mebby?"

"Camp fire. Some prospector boiling coffee in a dirty lard bucket, maybe."

Casey snorted. "It's a darn big fire to boil a pot uh coffee! Recollect, it's twelve miles over to that mountain. A bonfire a mile off wouldn't look any bigger than that. Would it now?" His tone was a challenge to my truthfulness.

"Wel-l, I guess it wouldn't, come to think of it."

"Guess? You know darn well it wouldn't. You watch that there fire. I ain't over there-but if that ain't the devil's lantern, I'll walk on my hands from here over there an' find out for yuh."

"I'd have to go over there myself to discover whether you're right or wrong. But if a fellow can trust his eyes, Casey —"

"Well, you can't," Casey said grimly, still standing, his eyes fixed upon the distant light. "Not here in this country, you can't. You ask anybody. You don't trust your eyes when yuh come to a dry lake an' you see water, an' the bushes around the shore reflected in the water, an' mebby a boat out in the middle. *Do* yuh? You don't trust your eyes when you look at them hills. They look close enough to walk over to 'em in half or three quarters of an hour. *Don't* they? An' didn't I take yuh in my Ford auto-*mo*-bile, an' wasn't it twelve? An' d'yuh trust your eyes when yuh look up, an' it looks like you could knock stars down with a tent pole, like yuh knock apples off'n trees? Sure, you can't trust your eyes! When yuh hit the desert, oletimer, yuh pack two of the biggest liars on earth right under your eyebrows." He chuckled at that. "An' most folks pack another one under their noses, fer luck. Now lookit over there! Prospector nothin'. It's the devil out walkin' an' packin' a lantern. He's mebby found some shin bones an' a rib or two an' mebby a chewed boot, an' he stopped there to have his little laugh. Lemme tell yuh. You mark where that fire is. An' t'-morra, if yuh like, I'll take yuh over there. If you c'n find a track er embers on that slope-Gawsh!"

We both stood staring; while he talked, the light had blinked out like snapping an electric switch. And that was strange because camp fires take a little time in the dying. I stepped inside the tent, fumbled for the field glasses and came out, adjusting the night focus. Casey's squat, powerful form stood perfectly still where I had left him, his face turned toward the mountain. There was no fire on the slope. Beyond, hanging black in the sky, a thunder cloud pillowed up toward the peak of the mountain, pushing out now and then to blot a star from the purple. Now and then a white, ragged gash cut through, but no sound reached up to where we were camped on the high mesa that was the lap of Starvation Mountain. I will explain that Casey had come back to Starvation to see if there were not another good silver claim lying loose and needing a location monument. We faced Tippipah Range twelve miles away, —and to-night the fire on its slope.

"Lightning struck a yucca over there and burned it, probably," I hazarded, seeking the spot through the glasses.

"Yeah-only there ain't no yuccas on that slope. That's a limestone ledge formation an' there ain't enough soil to cover up a t'rantler. And the storm's over back of the Tippipahs anyhow. It ain't on 'em."

"It's burning up again —"

"Hit another yucca, mebby!"

"It looks —" I adjusted the lenses carefully " —like a fire, all right. There's a reddish cast. I can't see any flames, exactly, but —" I suppose I gave a gasp, for Casey laughed outright.

"No, I guess yuh can't. Flames don't travel like that-huh?"

The light had moved suddenly, so that it seemed to jump clean away from the field of vision embraced by the glasses. I had a little trouble in picking it up again. I had to take down the glasses and look; and then I left them down and watched the light with my naked, lying eyes. They did lie; they must have. They said that a camp fire had abruptly picked itself up bodily and was slipping rapidly as a speeding automobile up a bare white slide of rock so steep that a mountain goat would give one glance and hunt up an easier trail. All my life I have had intimate acquaintance with camp fires; I have eaten with them, slept with them, coaxed them in storm, watched them from afar. I thought I knew all their tricks, all their treacheries. I have seen apparently cold ashes blow red quite unexpectedly and fire grass and bushes and go racing away, —I have fought them then with whatever came to hand.

I admit that an odd, prickly sensation at the base of my scalp annoyed me while I watched this fire race up the slope and leave no red trail behind it. Then it disappeared, blinked out again. I opened my mouth to call Casey's attention to it-though I felt that he was watching it with that steady, squinting stare of his that never seems to wink or waver for a second-but there it was again, come to a stop just under the crest of the mountain where the white slide was topped by a black rim capped with bleak, bare rock like a crude skullcap on Tippipah. The fire flared, dimmed, burned bright again, as though some one had piled on dry brush. I caught up the glasses and watched the light for a full minute. They were good glasses, —I ought to have seen the flicker of flames; but I did not. Just the reddish yellow glow and no more.

"Must be fox fire," I said, feeling impatient because that did not satisfy me at all, but having no other explanation that I could think of handy. "I've seen wonderful exhibitions of it in low, swampy ground —"

Casey spat into the dark. "I never heard of nobody boggin' down, up there on Tippipah." He put his cold pipe in his mouth, removed it and gestured with it toward the light. "I've seen jack-o'-lanterns myself. You know darn well that ain't it; not up on them rocks, dry as a bone. A minute ago you said it was lightnin' burnin' a yucca. Why don't yuh come out in the open, an' say you don't *know*? Mebby you'll come closer to believin' what I told yuh about that devil's lantern I follered. He's lit another one-kinda hopin' we'll be fool enough to fall for it. You come inside where yuh can't watch it. That's what does the damage-watchin' and wonderin' and then goin' to see. I bet you wanta strike out right now and see just what it is."

I didn't admit it, but Casey had guessed exactly what was in my mind. I was itching with curiosity and trying to ignore the creepiness of it. Casey went into the tent and lighted the candle and proceeded to unlace his high hiking boots. "You come on in and go to bed. Don't yuh pay no attention to that light-that's what the Old Boy plays for first, every time; workin' your curiosity up. You ask anybody. He played me fer a sucker and I told yuh about it, and yuh thought Casey was stringin' yuh. Well, I can take a joke from the devil himself and never let out a yip-but once is enough for Casey! I'm goin' to bed. Let him set out there and hold his darn lantern and be damned; he ain't going to make nothin' off'n Casey Ryan this time. You can ask anybody if Casey Ryan bites twice on the same hook."

He got into bed and turned his face to the wall with a finality I could not ignore. I let it go at that, but twice I got up and went outside to look. There burned the light, diabolically like a signal fire on the peak, where no fire should be. I began to seek explanations, but the best of them were vague. Electricity playing a prank of some obscure kind, —that was as close as I could get to it, and even that did not satisfy as it should have done, perhaps because the high, barren mesas and the mountains of bare rocks are in themselves weird and sinister, and commonplace explanations of their phenomena seem out of place.

The land is empty of men, emptier still of habitations. There are not many animals, even. A few coyotes, all of them under suspicion of having rabies; venomous things such as tarantulas and centipedes, scorpions, rattlers, hydrophobia skunks. Not so many of them that they are a constant menace, but occasionally to be reckoned with. Great sprawling dry lakes ominous in their very placidity; dust dry, with little whirlwinds scurrying over them and mirages that lie to you most convincingly, painting water where there is only clay dust. Water that is hidden deep in forbidding canyons, water that you must hunt for blindly unless you have been told where it comes stealthily out from some crevice in the rocks. Indians know the water holes, and have told the white men with whom they made friends after a fashion-for Casey tells me he never knew a red man who was essentially noble-and these have told others; and men have named the springs and have indicated their location on maps. Otherwise the land is dry, parched and deadly and beautiful, and men have died terrible, picturesque deaths within its borders.

I was thinking of that, and it seemed not too incongruous that the devil should now and then walk abroad with a lantern of his own devising to make men shrink from his path. But Casey says, and I think he means it, that the light is a lure. He told me a weird adventure of his own to back his argument, but I thought he was inventing most of it as he went along. Until I saw that light on Tippipah I had determined to let his romancing go in at one ear if it must, and stop there without running out at the tips of my fingers. Casey has enough ungodly adventures that are true. I didn't feel called upon to repeat his Irish inventions.

But now I'm going to tell you. If you can't believe it I shall not blame you; but Casey swears that it is all true. It's worth beginning where Casey did, at the beginning. And that goes back to when he was driving stage in the Yellowstone.

Casey was making the trip out, one time, and he had just one passenger because it was at the end of the season and there had been a week of nasty weather that had driven out most of the sightseers and no new ones were coming in. This man was a peevish, egotistical sort, I imagine; at any rate he did a lot of talking about himself and his ill luck, and he told Casey of his misfortunes by the hour.

Casey did not mind that much. He says he didn't listen half the time. But finally the fellow began talking of the wealth that is wasted on folks who can't use it properly or even appreciate the good fortune.

To illustrate that point he told a story that set Casey's mind to seeing visions. The man told about an old Indian who lived in dirt and a government blanket and drank bad whisky when he could get it, and whipped his squaw and behaved exactly like other Indians. Yet that old Indian knew where gold lay so thick that he could pick out pieces of crumbly rock all plastered with free gold. He was too lazy to dig out enough to do him any good. He would come into the nearest town with a rusty old lard bucket full of high grade so rich that the storekeeper once got five hundred dollars from the bucketful. He gave the Indian about twenty dollars' worth of grub and made him a present of two yards of bright blue ribbon, which tickled the old buck so much that in two weeks he was back with more high grade knotted in the bottom of a gunny sack.

Casey asked the man why some one didn't trail the Injun. Casey knew that an Indian is not permitted to file a claim to mineral land. He could not hold it, under the law, if some white man discovered it and located the ground, but Casey thought that some white-hearted fellow might take the claim and pay the buck a certain percentage of the profits.

The man said that couldn't be done. The old buck-Injun Jim, they called him-was an old she-bear. All the Indians were afraid of him and would hide their faces in their blankets when he passed them on his way to the gold, rather than be suspected by Injun Jim of any unwarranted interest in his destination. Casey knew enough about Indians to accept that statement. And white men, it would seem, were either not nervy enough or else they were not cunning enough. A few had attempted to trail Injun Jim, but no one had ever succeeded, because that part of Nevada had not had any gold stampede, which the man declared would have come sure as fate if Injun Jim's mine were ever uncovered.

Casey asked certain questions and learned all that the man could tell him, —or would tell him. He said that Injun Jim lived mostly in the Tippipah district. No free gold had ever been discovered there, nor much gold of any kind; but Injun Jim certainly brought free gold into Round Butte whenever he wanted grub. It must have been ungodly rich, —five hundred dollars' worth in a ten-pound lard bucket!

The tale held Casey's imagination. He dreamed nights of trailing Injun Jim, and if he'd had any money to outfit for the venture he surely would have gone straight to Nevada and to Round Butte. He told himself that it would take an outsider to furnish the energy for the search. Men who live in a country are the last to see the possibilities lying all around them, Casey said. It was true; he had seen it work out even in himself. Hadn't he driven stage in Cripple Creek country and carried out gold by the hundred-thousand,—gold that might have been his had he not been content to drive stage? Hadn't he lived in gold country all his life, almost, and didn't he know mineral formations as well as many a school-trained expert?

But even dreams of gold fluctuate and grow vague before the small interests of everyday living. Casey hadn't the money just then to quit his job of stage driving and go Indian stalking. It would take money,—a few hundred at least. Casey at that time lacked the price of a ticket to Round Butte. So he had to drive and dream, and his first spurt of saving grew half-hearted as the weeks passed; and then he lost all he had saved in a poker game because he wanted to win enough in one night to make the trip.

However, he went among men with his ears wide open for gossip concerning Injun Jim, and he gleaned bits of information that seemed to confirm what his passenger up in the Yellowstone had told him. He even met a man who knew Injun Jim.

Injun Jim, he was told, had one eye and a bad temper. He had lost his right eye in a fight with soldiers, in the days when Indian fighting was part of a soldier's training. Injun Jim nursed a grudge against the whites because of that eye, and while he behaved himself nowadays, being old and not very popular amongst his own people, it was taken for granted that his trigger finger would never be paralyzed, and that a white man need only furnish him a thin excuse and a fair chance to cover all traces of the killing. Injun Jim would attend to the rest with great zeal.

Stranger still, Casey found that the tale of the lard bucket and the gold was true. This man had once been in the store when Jim arrived for grub. He had taken a piece of the ore in his hands. It was free gold, all right, and it must have come from a district where free gold was scarce as women.

"We've got it figured down to a spot about fifty miles square," the man told Casey. "That old Injun don't travel long trails. He's old. And all Injuns are lazy. They won't go hunting mineral like a white man. They know mineral when they see it and they have good memories and can go to the spot afterwards. Injun Jim prob-ly run across a pocket somewheres when he was hunting. Can't be much of it-he'd bring in more at a time if there was, and be Injun-rich. He's just figurin' on making it hold out long as he lives. 'Tain't worth while trying to find it; there's too much mineral laying around loose in these hills."

Casey stored all that gossip away in the back of his head and through all the ups and downs of the years he never quite forgot it.

Chapter XIII

Casey earned a good deal of money, but there are men who are very good at finding original ways of losing money, too. Casey was one. (You should hear Casey unburden himself sometime upon the subject of garages and the tourist trade!) He saved money enough in Patmos to buy two burros and a mule, and what grub and tools the burros could carry. There were no poker games in Patmos, and a discouraged prospector happened along at the right moment, which accounts for it.

In this speed-hungry age Casey had not escaped the warped viewpoint which others assume toward travel. Casey always had craved the sensation of swift moving through space. His old stage horses could tell you tales of that! It was a distinct comedown, buying burros for his venture. That took straight, native optimism and the courage to make the best of things. But he hadn't the price of a Ford, and Casey abhors debt; so he reminded himself cheerfully that many a millionaire would still be poor if he had turned up his nose at burros, sour-dough cans and the business end of pick and shovel, and made the deal.

At that, he was better off than most prospectors, he told himself on the night of his purchase. He had the mule, William, to ride. The prospector had assured Casey over and over that William was saddle broke. Casey is too happy-go-lucky, I think. He took the man's word for it and waited until the night before he intended beginning his journey before he gave William a try-out, down in a sandy swale back of the garage. He returned after dark, leading William. Casey had a pronounced limp and an eyetooth was broken short off, about halfway to the gums, and his lip was cut.

"William's saddle broke, all right," he told his neighbor, the proprietor of the Oasis. "I've saw horses broke like that; cow-punchers have fun in the c'rall with 'em Sundays, seein' which one can stay with the saddle three jumps. William don't mind the saddle at all. All he hates is anybody in it." Then he grinned wryly because of his hurt. "No use arguin' with a mule —I used to be too good a walker."

Casey therefore traded his riding saddle for another packsaddle, and collected six coal-oil cans which he cleaned carefully. William was loaded with cans of water, which he seemed to prefer to Casey, though they probably weighed more. The burros waddled off under their loads of beans, flour, bacon, coffee, lard, and a full set of prospector's tools. Casey set his course by the stars and fared forth across the desert, meaning to pass through the lower end of Death Valley by night, on a trail he knew, and so plod up toward the Tippipah country.

He was happy. He owed no man a nickel, he had grub enough to last him three months if he were careful, he had a body tough as seasoned hickory, and he was headed for that great no-man's-land which is the desert. More, he was actually upon the trail of his dream that he had dreamed years before up in the Yellowstone. An old, secretive Indian was going to find his match when Casey Ryan plodded over his horizon and halted beside his fire.

By the way, don't blame me for showing a fondness for gloom and gore when you read the names Casey carried in his mind the next few weeks. Casey crossed Death Valley and the Funeral Mountains-or a spur of them-and headed up toward Spectre Range, going by way of Deadman's Spring, where he filled his water cans. That does not sound cheerful, but Casey was still fairly happy, —though there were moments when he thought seriously of killing William with a rock.

Every morning, without fail, he and William fought every minute from breakfast to starting time. From his actions you would think that William had never seen a pack before, and expected it to bite him fatally if he came within twenty feet of it. You could tell Casey's camp by the manner in which the sagebrush was trampled and the sand scored with small hoofprints in a wide circle around it. But once the battle was lost to William for that day, and Casey had rested and mopped the perspiration off his face and taken a comforting chew of tobacco and relapsed into silence simply because he could think of nothing more to say, William became a pet dog that hazed the two lazy burros along with little nippings on their rumps, and saw to it that they did not stray too far from camp.

Casey strung into Searchlight one evening at dusk and camped on a little knoll behind the town hall, which was open beyond for grazing, and the village dogs were less likely to bother. Searchlight was not on his way, but miles off to one side. Casey made the detour because he had heard a good deal about the place and knew it as a favorite stamping ground of miners and prospectors who sought free gold. Searchlight is primarily a gold camp, you see. He wanted to hear a little more about Injun Jim.

But there had been a murder in Searchlight a dark night or so before his coming, and three suspects were being discussed and championed by their friends. Searchlight was not in the mood for aimless gossip of Indians. Killings had been monotonously frequent, but they usually had daylight and an audience to rob them of mystery. A murder done on a dark night, in the black shadow of an empty dance hall, and accompanied by a piercing scream and the sound of running feet was vastly different.

Casey lingered half a day, bought a few more pounds of bacon and some matches and ten yards of satin ribbon in assorted colors and went his way.

I mention his stop at Searchlight so that those who demand exact geography will understand why Casey journeyed on to Vegas, tramped its hot sidewalks for half a day and then went on by way of Indian Spring to the Tippipah country and his destination. He was following the beaten trail of miners, now that he was in Jim's country, and he was gleaning a little information from every man he met. Not altogether concerning Injun Jim, understand, —but local tidbits that might make him a welcome companion to the old buck when he met him. Casey says you are not to believe story-writers who assume that an Indian is wrapped always in a blanket and inscrutable dignity. He says an Indian is as great a gossip as any old woman, once you get him thawed to the talking point. So he was filling his bag of tricks as he went along.

From Vegas there is what purports to be an automobile road across the desert to Round Butte, and Casey as he walked cursed his burros and William and sighed for his Ford. He was four days traveling to Furnace Lake, which he had made in a matter of hours with his Ford when he first came to Starvation.

He struck Furnace Lake just before dusk one night and pushed the burros out upon it, thinking he would have cool crossing and would start in the morning with the lake behind him, which would be something of a load off his mind. In his heart Casey hated Furnace Lake, and he had good reason. It was a place of ill fortune for him, especially after the sun had left it. He wanted it behind him where he need think no more about it and the grewsome crevice that cut a deep, wide gash two thirds of the way across it through the middle. Casey is not a coward, and he takes most things as a matter of course, but he admits that he has always hated and distrusted Furnace Lake beyond all the dry lakes in Nevada, —and there are many.

He yelled to William, and William nipped the nearest burro into a shambling half trot, and then went out upon the lake, Casey heading across at the widest part so that he would strike his old trail to Starvation Mountain on the other side. From there to the summit he could make it by noon on the morrow, he planned. Which would be the end of his preliminary journey and the beginning of Casey's last drive toward his goal; for from the top of the divide between Starvation Mountain country and that forbidding waste which lies under the calm scrutiny of Furnace Peak he could see the far-off range of the Tippipahs.

He was a mile out on the Lake when he first glimpsed the light. Casey studied it while he walked ahead, leaving no footprints on the hard-baked clay. He had not known that any road followed just under the crest of the ridge that hid Crazy Woman lake, yet the light was plainly that of an automobile moving with speed across the face of the ridge just under the summit.

Away out in the empty land like that you notice little things and think about them and try to understand just what they mean, unless they are perfectly familiar to you. One print of a foot on the trail may betray the lurking presence of a madman, a murderer, a traveling, friendly, desert dweller or the wandering of some one who is lost and dying of thirst and hunger. You like to know which, and you are not satisfied until you do know.

A light moving swiftly along Crazy Woman ridge meant a car, and a car up there meant a road. If there were a road it would probably lead Casey by a shorter route to the Tippipahs. While he looked there came to his ears a roaring, as of some high-powered car traveling under full pressure of gas. The burros followed him, but William lifted his head and brayed tremulously three times in the dark. Casey had never heard him bray before, and the sudden rasping outcry startled him.

He went back and stood for a minute looking at William, who turned tail and started back toward the shore they had left behind them. Casey ran to head him off, yelling threats, and William, in spite of his six water cans-two of them empty-broke into a lope. Casey glanced over his shoulder as he ran and saw dimly that the burros had turned and were coming after him, their ears flapping loosely on their bobbing heads as they trotted. Beyond him, the light still traveled towards the Tippipahs.

Then, with an abruptness that cannot be pictured, everything was blotted out in a great, blinding swirl of dust as the wind came whooping down upon them. It threw Casey as though some one had tripped him. It spun him round and round on his back like an overturned beetle, and then scooted him across the lake's surface flat as a floor. He thought of the Crevice, but there was nothing he could do save hold his head off the ground and his two palms over his face, shielding his nostrils a little from the smother of dust.

Sometimes he was lifted inches from the surface and borne with incredible swiftness. More than once he was spun round and round until his senses reeled. But all the time he was going somewhere, and I suspect that for once in his life Casey Ryan went fast enough to satisfy him. At last he felt brush sweep past his body, and he knew that he must have been swept to the edge of the lake. He clutched, scratched his hands bloody on the straggly thorns of greasewood, caught in the dark at a more friendly sage and gripped it next the roots. The wind tore at him, howling. Casey flattened his abused body to the hummocky sand and hung on.

Hours later, by the pale stars that peered out breathlessly when the fury of the gale was gone, Casey pulled himself painfully to his feet and looked for the burros and William. Judging by his own experience, they had had a rough time of it and would not go far after the wind permitted them to stop. But as to guessing how far they had been impelled, or in what direction, Casey knew that was impossible. Still, he tried. When the air grew clearer and the surrounding hills bulked like huge shadows against the sky, he saw that he had been blown toward the ridge that guards Crazy Woman lake. His pack animals should be somewhere ahead of him, he thought groggily, and began stumbling along through the brush-covered sand dunes that bordered Furnace Lake for miles.

And then he saw again the light, shining up there just under the crest of the ridge. He was glad the car had escaped, but he reflected that the tricky winds of the desert seldom sweep a large area. Their diabolic fury implies a concentration of force that must of necessity weaken as it flows out away from the center. Up there on the ridge they may not have experienced more than a steady blow.

He walked slowly because of his bruises, and many times he made small detours, thinking that a blotch of shadow off to one side might be his pack train. But always a greasewood mocked him, waving stiff arms at him derisively. In the sage-land distances deceive. A man may walk unseen before your eyes, and a bush afar off may trick you with its semblance to man or beast. Casey finally gave up the hopeless search and headed straight for the light.

It was standing still, —a car facing him with its headlights burning, the distance so great that the two lights glowed as one. "An' it ain't no Ford," Casey decided. "They wouldn't keep the engine runnin' all this time, standin' still. Unless it's one of them old kind with lamps."

I don't suppose you realize, many of you, just what that would mean to a man in the desert country. It is rather hard to define, but the significance would be felt, even by Casey in his present plight. You see, small cars, of the make too famous to be hurt or helped by having its name mentioned in a simple yarn like this, have long been recognized as the proper car for rough trails and no trails. Those who travel the desert most have come to the point of counting "Lizzie" almost as necessary as beans. Wherefore a larger car is nearly always brought in by strangers to the country, who swear solemnly, never to repeat the imprudence. A large car, driven by strangers in the land, means hunters, prospectors from the outside brought in by some special tale of hidden wealth, —or just plain simpletons who only want to see what lies over the mountain. There aren't many of the last-named variety up in the Nevada wastes. Even your nature-loving rovers oddly keep pretty much to the beaten trails of other nature lovers, where gas stations and new tires may be found at regular intervals. The Painted Desert, the Petrified Forest, the National Old Trails they explore, —but not the high, wind-swept mesas of Nevada's barren land.

A fear that was not altogether strange to him crept over Casey. It would be just his grinning enemy Ill-luck on his trail again, if that light should prove to be made by men hunting for Injun Jim and his mine. Casey used to feel a sickness in his middle when that thought nagged him, and he felt a growing anger now when he looked at the twinkling glow. He walked a little faster. Now that the fear had come to him, Casey wanted to come up with the men, talk with them, learn their business if they were truthful, or sense their lying if they tried to hide their purpose from him. He must know. If they were seeking Injun Jim, then he must find some way to head them off, circumvent their plans with strategy of his own. He had dreamed too long and too ardently to submit now to interlopers.

So he walked, limping and cursing a little now and then because of his aches. Up a steep slope made heavy with loose sand that dragged at his feet; over the crest and down the other side among rocks and gravel that made harder walking than the sand. Up another steep slope: it was heartbreaking, unending as the toils of a nightmare, but Casey kept on. He was not worried over his own plight; not yet. He believed that William and his burros were somewhere ahead of him, since they could not cling to a bush as he had done and so resist the impetus of that terrific wind. There was a car standing on the ridge toward which he was laboriously making his way. It did not occur to Casey that morning might show him a rather desperate plight.

Yet the morning did just that. Hours before dawn the light had disappeared abruptly, but Casey had no uneasiness over that. It was foolish for them to run down their battery burning lights when they were standing still, he thought. They had not moved off, and he had well in mind the contour of the ridge where they were standing. He would have bet good money that he could walk straight to the car even though darkness hid it from him until he came within hailing distance.

But daylight found him still below the higher slope of the ridge, and Casey was very tired. He had been walking all day, remember, and he had missed his supper because he wanted to eat it with the lake behind him. He did not walk in a straight line. He was too near exhaustion to forge ahead as was his custom. Now he was picking his way carefully so as to shun the washes out of which he must climb, and the rock patches where he would stumble, and the thick brush that would claw at him. He would have given five dollars for a drink of water, but there would be water at the car, he told himself. People were rather particular about carrying plenty of water when they traveled these wastes.

And then he was on the ridge, and his keen eyes were squinted half-shut while he gazed here and there, no foot of exposed land surface escaping that unwinking stare. He took off his hat and wiped his face, and reached mechanically for a chew of tobacco which he always took when perplexed, as if it stimulated thought.

There was no car. There was no road. There was not even a burro trail along that ridge. Yet there had been the lights of a car, and after the lights had been extinguished Casey had listened rather anxiously for sound of the motor and had heard nothing at all. The most powerful, silent-running car on the market would have made some noise in traveling through that sand and up and down the washes that seamed the mountain side. Casey would have heard it-he had remarkably keen hearing.

"And that's darn funny," he muttered, when he was perfectly sure that there was no car, that there could never have been a car on that trackless ridge. "That's mighty damn funny! You can ask anybody."

Chapter XIV

Other things, however, were not so funny to Casey as he stood staring down over the vast emptiness. There was no sign of his pack train, and without it he would be in sorry case indeed. He thought of the manner in which the tornado had whirled him round and round. Caught in a different set of gyrations and then borne out from the center-flung out would come nearer it-the burros and William might have been carried in any direction save his own. Into that gruesome Crevice, for instance. They had not been more than a mile from the Crevice when the storm struck.

He glanced across to Barren Butte, rising steeply from the farther end of the lake. But he did not think of going to the mine up there, except to tell himself that he'd rot on the desert before he ever asked there for help. He had his reasons, you remember. A man like Casey can face humiliation from men much easier than he can face a woman who had misjudged him and scorned him. Unless, of course, he has a million dollars in his pocket and knows that she knows it.

Having discarded Barren Butte from his plans-rather, having declined to consider it at all-he knew that he must find his supplies, or he must find water somewhere in the Crazy Woman hills. The prospect was not bright, for he had never heard any one mention water there.

He rested where he was for awhile and watched the slope for the pack animals; more particularly for William and the water cans. He could shoot rabbits and live for days, if he had a little water, but he had once tried living on rabbit meat broiled without salt, and he called it dry eating, even with water to wash it down. Without water he would as soon fast and let the rabbits live.

A dark speck moving in the sage far down the slope caught his eyes, and he got up and peered that way eagerly. He started down to meet it hopefully, feeling certain that his present plight would soon merge into a mere incident of the trail. Sure enough, when he had walked for half an hour he saw that it was William, browsing toward him and limping when he moved.

But William was bare as the back of Casey's hand. There was no pack, no coal-oil cans of water; only the halter and lead rope, that dangled and caught on brush and impeded William's limping progress. I suppose even miserable mules like company, for William permitted Casey to walk up and take him by the halter rope. William had a badly skinned knee which gave him the limp, and his right ear was broken close to his head so that the structure which had been his pride dropped over his eye like a wet sunbonnet.

Casey swore a little and started back along William's tracks to find the water cans. He followed a winding, purposeless trail that never showed the track of burros, and after an hour or so he came upon the pack and the cans. Evidently the water supply had suffered in the wind, for only four cans were with the blankets and pack saddle.

William had felt his pack slipping, Casey surmised, and had proceeded to divest himself of the incumbrance in the manner best known to mules. Having kicked himself out of it, he had undoubtedly discovered a leaking can-supposing the cans had escaped thus far-and had battered them with his heels until they were all leaking copiously. William had saved what he could.

Casey read the whole story in the sand. The four cans were bent with gaping seams, and their sides were scored with the prints of William's hoofs. In a corner of one of them Casey found a scant half-cup of water, which he drank greedily. It could no more than ease for a moment his parched throat; it could not satisfy his thirst.

After that he led William back along the trail until the mounting sun warned him that he was making no headway on his journey to the Tippipahs, and that with no tracks in sight he had small hope of tracing the burros.

It was sundown again before he gave up hope, and Casey's thirst was a demon within him. He had wasted a day, he told himself grimly. Now it was going to be a fight.

Through the day he had mechanically studied the geologic formation of those hills before him, and he had decided that the chance for water there was too slight to make a search worth while. He would push on toward the Tippipahs. *Pah*, he knew, meant water in the Indian tongue. He did not know what *Tippi* signified, but since Indians lived in the Tippipah range he was assured that the water was drinkable. So he got stiffly to his feet, studied again the darkling skyline, sent a glance up at the first stars, and turned his face and William's resolutely toward the Tippipahs.

He had applied first aid to William's knee in the form of chewed tobacco, which if it did no more at least discouraged the pestering flies. Now he collected a ride for his pay. He had reasoned that William was probably subdued to the point of permitting the liberty, and that he had other things to think of more important than protecting his mulish dignity. Casey guessed right. William merely switched his tail pettishly, as mules will, and went on picking his way through brush and rocks along the ridge.

It was perhaps nine o'clock when Casey saw the light. William also spied it and stopped still, his long left ear pointed that way, his broken right ear dropping over his eye. William lifted his nose and brayed as if he were tearing loose all his vitals and the operation hurt like the mischief. Casey kicked him in the flanks and urged him on. It must be a camp fire, Casey thought. He did not connect it with that moving light he had seen the night before; that phantom car was a mystery which he would probably never solve, and in Casey's opinion it had nothing to do with a camp fire that twinkled upon a distant hilltop.

From the look of it, Casey judged that it was perhaps eight miles off,—possibly less. But there was a rocky canyon or two between them, and William was lame and Casey was too exhausted to walk more than half a mile before he must lie down and own himself whipped. Casey Ryan had never done that for a man, and he did not propose to do it for Nature. He thought that William ought to have enough stamina to make the trip if he were given time enough. And at the last, if William gave out, then Casey would manage somehow to walk the rest of the way. It all depended upon giving William time enough.

You know, mules are the greatest mind readers in the world. I have always heard that, and now Casey swears that it is so. William immediately began taking his time. Casey told me that a turtle starting nose to nose with William would have had to pull in his feet and wait for him every half mile or so. William must have been very thirsty, too.

The light burned steadily, hearteningly. Whenever they crawled to high ground where a view was possible, Casey saw it there, just under a certain star which he had used for a marker at first. And whenever William saw the light he brayed and tried to swing around and go the other way. But Casey would not permit that, naturally. Nor did he wonder why William acted so queerly. You never wonder why a mule does things; you just fight it out and are satisfied if you win, and let it go at that.

Casey does not remember clearly the details of that night. He knows that during the long hours William balked at a particularly steep climb, and that Casey was finally obliged to get off and lead the Way. It established an unfortunate precedent, for William refused to let Casey on again, and Casey was too weak to mount in spite of William. They compromised at last; that is, they both walked.

The light went out. Moreover, Casey's star that he had used to mark the spot moved over to the west and finally slid out of sight altogether. But Casey felt sure of the direction and he kept going doggedly toward the point where the light had been. He says there wasn't a rod where a snail couldn't have outrun him, and when the sky streaked red and orange and the sun came up, he stood still and looked for a camp, and when he saw nothing at all but bare rock and bushes of the kind that love barrenness, he crawled under the nearest shade, tied William fast to the bush and slept. You don't realize your thirst so much when you are asleep, and you are saving your strength instead of wearing it out in the hot sun. He remained there until the sun was almost out of sight behind a high peak. Then he got up, untied William, mounted him without argument from either, and went on, keeping to the direction in which he had seen the light.

Even the little brown mule was having trouble now. He wavered, he picked his footing with great care when a declivity dipped before him; he stopped every few yards and rested when he was making a climb. As for Casey, he managed to hold himself on the narrow back of William, but that was all. He understood perfectly that the next twenty-four hours would tell the story for him and for William. He had a sturdy body however and a sturdy brain that had never weakened its hold on facts. So he clung to his reason and pushed fear away from him and said doggedly that he would go forward as long as he could crawl or William could carry him, and he would die or he would not die, as Fate decided for him. He wondered, too, about the camp whose fire he had seen.

Then he saw the light. This time it burned suddenly clear and large and very bright, away off to the left of him where he had by daylight noticed a bare shale slide. The light seemed to stand in the very center of the slide, no more than a mile away.

William stopped when Casey pulled on the reins he had fashioned from the lead rope, and turned stiffly so that he faced the light. Casey kicked him gently with his heels to urge him forward, for in spite of what his reason told him about the shale slide his instinct was to go straight to the light. But William began to shiver and tremble, and to swing slowly away. Casey tried to prevent it, but the mule came out in William. He laid his good ear flat along his neck as far as it would go, and took little, nipping steps until he had turned with his tail to the light. Then he thrust his fawn-colored muzzle to the stars and brayed and brayed, his good ear working like a pump handle as he tore the sounds loose from his vitals.

Casey cursed him in a whisper, having no voice left. He kicked William in the flanks, having no other means of coercion at hand. But kicking never yet altered the determination of a mule, and cursing a mule in a whisper is like blowing your breath against the sail of a becalmed sloop. William kept his tail toward the light, and furthermore he momentarily drew his tail farther and farther from that spot. Now and then he would turn his head and glance back, and immediately increase his pace a little. He was long past the point where he had strength to trot, but he could walk, and he did walk and carry Casey on his back, still whispering condemnation.

They did not travel all night. Casey looked at the Big Dipper and judged it was midnight when they stopped on the brink of a deep canyon, halted there in William's sheer despair because the light appeared suddenly on the high point of a hill directly ahead of them. William's voice was gone like Casey's, so that he, too, cursed in a whisper with a spasmodic indrawing of ribs and a wheezing in his throat.

When it was plain that the mule had stopped permanently, Casey slid off William's back and lay down without knowing or caring much whether he would ever get up again. He said he wasn't hungry much; but his mouth was too full of tongue, he added grimly.

He lay and watched through half-closed, staring eyes the light that mocked him so. His dulling senses told him that it was no camp fire, nor any light made by human hands. He did not know what it was. He didn't care any more. William crumpled up and lay down beside him, breathing heavily. It was getting close to the end of things. Casey knew it, and he thinks William knew it too.

The sun found them there and forced Casey to move. He sat up painfully, the fight to live not yet burned out of him, and gazed dully at the forbidding hills that closed around him like great, naked rock demons watching to see him die for want of the things they withheld. Where he remembered the light to have been when last he saw it was bleak, bare rock. It was a devil's light and there was nothing friendly or human about it.

He looked down into the canyon which William had refused to enter. A faint interest revived within him because of a patch of green. Trees, —but they might easily be junipers which will grow in dry canyons as readily, it would seem, as in any other. He kept looking, because green was a great relief from the monotonous gray and black and brown of the hills. It seemed to him after awhile that he saw a small splotch of dead white.

In the barren lands two things will show white in the distance; a white horse and a tent of white canvas. Casey shifted his position and squinted long at the spot, then got up slowly with the help of a bush and took William by the rope. William was on his feet, standing with head dropped, apparently half asleep. Casey knew that William was simply waiting until he could no longer stand.

Together they wabbled down the sloping canyon side and over a grassy bottom to the trees, which were indeed juniper trees, but thriftier looking than their brethren of the dry places. There was water, for William smelled it at last and hurried forward with more briskness than Casey could muster, eager though he was to reach the tent he saw standing there under the biggest juniper.

Beside the tent was a water bucket of bright, new tin. A white granite dipper stood in it. Casey drank sparingly and stopped when he would have given all he ever possessed in the world to have gone on drinking until he could hold no more. But he was not yet crazy with the thirst. So he stopped drinking, filled a white granite basin and soused his head again and again, sighing with sheer ecstasy at the drip of water down his back and chest. After a little he drank two swallows more, put down the dipper and went into the tent.

Chapter XV

We can all remember certain experiences that fill us with incredulity even while we admit that the facts could be proved before a jury of twelve men. So Casey Ryan, having lost his outfit and come so near to death that he could barely keep his feet under him, walked into a tent and stood there thinking it couldn't be true.

A folding camp chair stood near the opening, and Casey sat down from sheer weakness while he looked about him. The tent was a twelve-by-fourteen, which is a bit larger than one usually carries in a pack outfit. It had a canvas floor soiled in strips where the most walking had been done, but white under table and beds, which proved its newness. Casey was not accustomed to seeing tents floored with canvas, and he stared at it for a full half-minute before his eyes went to other things.

There was a folding camp table of the kind shown in the window display of sporting-goods stores, but which seasoned campers find too wobbly for actual comfort. The varnish still shone on legs and braces, which helped to prove its newness. There was a two-burner oil stove with an enamel-rimmed oven that was distinctly out of place in that country and yet harmonized perfectly with the tent and furnishings. The dishes were white enamel of aluminum, and there were boxes piled upon boxes, the labels proclaiming canned things too expensive for ordinary eating. Two spring cots with new blankets and white-cased pillows stood against the tent wall, and beneath each cot sat two yellow pigskin suitcases with straps and brass buckles. They would have been perfectly natural in a Pullman sleeper, but even in his present stress Casey snorted disdainfully at sight of them here.

Things were tumbled about in the disorder of inexperienced campers, but everything was very new and clean except an array of dishes on the table, which told Casey that one man had eaten at least three meals without washing his dishes or putting away his surplus of food. Casey had eaten nothing at all after that one toasted rabbit which he had choked down on the evening when he gave up hope of finding the burros. He got up and staggered stiffly to the table and picked up a piece of burned biscuit, hard as flint.

While he mumbled a fragment of that he looked into various half-filled cans, setting them one by one in a compact group on the table corner; which was habit rather than conscious thought. Poisonous ptomaine lurked in every one of them, which was a shame, since he had to discard half a can of preserved peaches, half a can of roast beef, half a can of asparagus tips, a can of chicken soup scarcely touched and two thirds of a can of sweet potatoes. He salvaged a can of ripe olives which he thought was good, a can of India relish and a can of sweet gherkins (both of the fifty-seven varieties). You will see what I meant when I spoke of expensive camp food.

There was cold coffee in a nickel percolater, and Casey poured himself a cup, knowing well the risk of eating much just at first. It was while he was unscrewing the top of the glass jar that held the sugar that he first noticed the paper. It was folded and thrust into the sugar jar, and Casey pulled it out and held it crumpled in his hand while he sweetened and drank the coffee, forcing himself to take it slowly. When the cup was empty to the last drop he went over and sat down on the edge of a spring cot and unfolded the note. What he read surprised him a great deal and puzzled him more. I leave it to you to judge why.

"I saw it again last night in a different place. The last horse died yesterday down the canyon. You can have the outfit. I'm going to beat it out of here while the going's good. Fred."

"That's mighty damn funny," Casey muttered thickly. "You can-ask —" He lay back luxuriously, with his head on the white pillow and closed his eyes. The reaction from struggling to live had set in with the assurance of his safety. He slept heavily, refreshingly.

He awoke to the craving for food, and immediately started a small fire outside and boiled coffee in a nice new aluminum pail that held two quarts and had an ornamental cover. The oil stove he dismissed from his mind with a snort of contempt. And because nearly everything he saw was catalogued in his mind as a luxury, he opened cans somewhat extravagantly and dined off strange, delectable foods to which his palate was unaccustomed. He still thought it was mighty queer, but that did not impair his appetite.

Afterwards he went out to look after William, remembering that horses were said to have died in this place. William was almost within kicking distance of the spring, as if he meant to keep an eye upon the water supply even though that involved browsing off brush instead of wandering down to good grass below the camp.

Casey knelt stiffly and drank from the spring, laving his face and head afterward as if he never would get enough of the luxury of being wet and cool. He rose and stood looking at William for a few minutes, then took the lead rope and tied him to a juniper that stood near the spring. The note had said that the last horse died down the canyon, the implication of mystery lying heavy behind the words.

Casey went back to the tent and read the note through again twice, studying each word as if he hoped to twist some added information out of it. It sounded as though the writer had expected his partner back from some trip and had left the note for him, since he had not considered it necessary to explain what it was that he had seen again in a different place. Casey wondered if it might not have been that strange light which he himself had followed. Whatever it was, the fellow had not liked it. His going had all the earmarks of flight.

Well, then, why had the last horse died down the canyon? Casey decided that he would go and see, though he was not hankering for exercise that day. He took a long drink of water, somewhat shamefacedly filled a new canteen that lay on a pile of odds and ends near the tent door, and started down the canyon. It couldn't be far, but he might want a drink before he got back, and Casey had had enough of thirst.

He was not long in finding the horse that had died, and in fact all the horses that had died. There had been four, and the manner of their death was not in the least mysterious. They had been staked out to graze in a luxurious patch of loco weed, which is reason enough why any horse should die.

Of course, no man save an unmitigated tenderfoot would picket a horse on loco, which looks very much like wild peavine and is known the West over as the deadliest weed that grows. A little of it mixed with a diet of grass will drive horses and cattle insane, and there is no authentic case of recovery, that I ever heard, once the infection is complete. A lot of it will kill, —and these poor beasts had actually been staked out to graze upon it, I suppose because it looked nice and green, and the horses liked it.

The performance matched very well the enamel-trimmed oil stove and the tinned dainties and the expensive suitcases. Casey went back to camp feeling as though he had stumbled upon a picnic of feeble-minded persons. He wondered what in hell two men of such a type could be doing out there, a hundred miles and more from an ice-cream soda and a barber's chair. He wondered too how "Fred" had expected to get himself across that hundred miles and more of dry desert country. He must certainly be afoot, and the camp itself showed no sign of an emergency outfit having been assembled from its furnishings.

Casey made sure of that, inspecting first the bedding and food and then the cooking utensils. Everything was complete-lavishly so-for two men who loved comfort. Even their sweaters were there; and Casey knew they must have discovered that the nights can be cool even though the days are hot, in that altitude. And there were two canteens of the size usually carried by hikers.

Casey was so worried that he could not properly enjoy his supper of pâté de foi gras and crackers, with pork and beans, plum pudding-eaten as cake-and spiced figs and coffee. That night he turned over on his spring-cot bed as often as if he had been lying on nettles, and when he did sleep he dreamed horribly.

Next morning he set out with William and an emergency camp outfit to trace if he could the missing men. The great outdoors of Nevada is not kind to such as these, and Casey had too lately suffered to think with easy-going optimism that they would manage somehow. They would die if they were left to shift for themselves, and Casey could not pretend that he did not know it.

But there was a difficulty in rescuing them, just as there had been in rescuing the burros. Casey could not find their tracks, and so could not follow them. He and William hunted the canyon from top to bottom and ranged far out on the valley floor without discovering anything that could be called the track of a man. Which was strange, too, in a country where footprints are held for a long, long while by the soil,—as souvenirs of man's passing, perhaps.

So it transpired that Casey at length returned to the new tent just below the spring in the nameless canyon beyond Crazy Woman Lake. Chipmunks had invaded the place and feasted upon an opened package of sweet crackers, but otherwise the tent had been left inviolate. Neither Fred nor his partner had returned. Wherefore Casey opened more cans and "made himself to home," as he naively put it.

He was impatient to continue his journey, but since he had nothing of his own except William, he meant to beg or buy a few things from this camp, if either of the owners showed up. Meantime he could be comfortable, since it is tacitly understood in the open land that a wayfarer may claim hospitality of any man, with or without that man's knowledge. He is expected to keep the camp clean, to leave firewood and to take nothing away with him except what is absolutely necessary to insure his getting safely to the next stopping place. Casey knew well the law, and he busied himself in setting the camp in order while he waited.

But when five days and nights had slipped into history and he and William were still in sole possession, Casey began to take another viewpoint. Fred might possibly have left in a flying machine. The partner might have decamped permanently before Fred lost his nerve. Several things might have happened which would leave this particular camp and contents without a claimant. Casey studied the matter for awhile and then pulled the four suitcases from beneath the cots and proceeded to investigate. The first one that he opened had a note folded and addressed to Fred. Casey read it through without the slightest compunction. The handwriting was different from that of the first note, hurried and scrawly, the words connected with faint lines. Here is what Fred's partner had written:

"Dear Fred: Don't blame me for leaving you. A man that carries the grouch you do don't need company. I'm fed up on solitude, and I don't like the feel of things here. My staying won't help your lung a damn bit and if you want anything you can hunt up the men that carry the light. Maybe they are the ones that are killing off the horses. Any way, you can wash your own dishes from now on. It will do you good. If I had of known you were the crab you are I'll say I would never have come. You are welcome to my share of the outfit. I hope some one shoots me and puts me out of my misery quick if I ever show symptoms of wanting to camp out again. I am going now because if I stayed I'd change your map for you so your own looking glass wouldn't know you. I'll say you are some nut. Art."

Casey had to take a fresh chew of tobacco before his brain would settle down and he could think clearly. Then he observed that it was a damn funny combination and you could ask anybody. After that he began to realize that he was heir to a fine assortment of canned delicacies and an oil stove and four suitcases filled, he hoped, with good clothes. Not omitting possession of two spring cots and several pairs of high-grade blankets, and two sweaters and Lord knows what all.

Those suitcases were enough to make any man sit and bite his nails, wondering if he were crazy. Fred and Art had evidently fitted their wardrobe to their ideas of a summer camp with dancing pavilion and plenty of hammocks in the immediate neighborhood. There were white flannel trousers and white canvas shoes and white silk socks, and fine ties and handkerchiefs and things. There were striped silk shirts which made Casey grin and think how tickled Injun Jim would be with them,—or one or two of them; Casey had no intention of laying them all on the altar of diplomacy. There was an assortment of apparel in those suitcases that would qualify any man as porch hound at Del Monte. And Casey Ryan, if you please, had fallen heir to the lot!

He dressed himself in white flannels with a silk shirt of delf blue and pale green stripes, and wished that there was a looking-glass in camp large enough to reflect all of him at once. Then, because his beard stubble did not harmonize, he shaved with one of the safety razors he found.

After that he sorted and packed a careful wardrobe, and stored strange food into two canvas kyacks. And the next evening he tied the tent flaps carefully and fared forth with William to find the camp of Injun Jim and see if his dream would come true.

You may not believe this next incident. I know I did not, when Casey told me about it, —but now I am not so sure. Casey said that the light appeared again, that night, moving slowly along the lip of the canyon like a man with a large lantern. There was a full moon, which had made him decide to travel at night on account of the heat while the sun was up. But the moon did not reveal the cause of the light, though the canyon crest was plainly visible to him.

William swung away from that light and walked rather briskly in the other direction, and Casey did not argue with him. So they headed almost due west and kept going. It seemed to Casey once or twice that the light followed them; but he could not be sure.

Two full nights he journeyed, and on both nights he had the light behind him. Once it came up swiftly to within a mile or so of him and William, and stopped there for awhile and then disappeared. Casey camped rather early and slept, and took the trail again in the morning. Night travel was getting on his nerves.

All that day he walked and toward evening, with thunder heads piling high above the Tippipahs, he came upon a small herd of Indian ponies feeding out from the mouth of a wide gulch. He knew they were Indian ponies by their size, their variegated colors, and their general unkemptness. They presently spied him and went galloping off up the gulch, and Casey followed until he spied a thin bluish ribbon of smoke wavering up toward the slate-black clouds.

He made camp just out of sight around a point of rocks from the smoke, stretching the canvas tarp which had floored the tent to make shelter between boulders. He changed his clothes, dressing himself carefully in the white flannel trousers, blue-and-green striped silk shirt, tan belt, white shoes and his old Stetson tilted over his right eye at the characteristic Casey angle. He was taking it for granted that an Indian camp lay under that smoke, and he knew Indians. Inquisitiveness would shut them up as effectively as poking a stick at a clam; but there were ways of coaxing their interest, nevertheless, and when an Indian is curious you have the trumps in your own hand and it will be your own fault if you lose.

Casey's manner therefore was extremely preoccupied when he led a suddenly limping William up the gulch and past a stone hut with a patched tepee alongside it. A lean squaw stood erect before the tepee and regarded him fixedly from under the shade of a mahogany-colored hand, and when Casey came closer she stooped and ducked out of sight like a prairie dog diving into its burrow. Casey paid no attention to that. He knew without being told that he was under close scrutiny from eyes unseen; which was what he desired and had prepared for.

The spring, as he had guessed, was above the camp. He threw a rock at two yammering curs that rushed out at him, and drove them back with Caseyish curses. Then he watered William at the trampled spring, made himself a smoke, and went back down the gulch. Opposite the tepee the squaw stood beside the trial. Casey grinned amiably and said hello.

"Yo' ketchum 'bacco? My man, him heap sick. Mebby die. Likeum 'bacco, him." The squaw muttered it as if she would rather not speak, but had been commanded to beg tobacco from the stranger.

"Sure, I got tobacco!" Casey's tone was a bit more friendly than before. He pulled a small red can from his shirt pocket, hesitated and then tied William to a bush. "Too bad your man sick. Mebby I can help him. He in here?"

The squaw gestured dumbly, and Casey stooped and went into the tepee.

Inside it was so dark that he stood still just within the opening to get his bearings. This happened to be very good form in Indian society, and we will assume that Casey lost nothing by the pause. He dimly saw that a few blankets lay untidily against the tepee wall and that an old Indian was stretched upon them, watching Casey with one black eye, the other lid lying in sunken folds across the socket. Casey was for once in his life speechless. He had not expected to walk straight into the camp of Injun Jim. He had thought that of course he would have to go on to Round Butte and glean information there, perhaps; if he were exceptionally lucky he would meet Indians who would tell him what he wanted to know. But here was a one-eyed buck, and he was old, and he lived in the Tippipahs, —Injun Jim by all description.

"Your squaw says you want tobacco." Casey advanced and held out the red can. He knew better than to waste words, especially in the beginning. Indians are peculiar; you must approach them by not seeming to approach at all.

The old fellow grunted and turned the can over and over in clawlike hands, and said he wanted a match and a paper. Casey went farther; he rolled a cigarette and gave it to him and then rolled one for himself. They smoked, there in that unsavoury tepee, saying nothing at all. Casey had achieved the first part of his dream; he was making friends with Injun Jim.

Later he went down to his own camp, leading William. It was hard to wait and watch for the proper moment to broach the subject that filled his mind, and then induce the old Indian to talk. Casey was beginning to understand why no one had wormed the secret from Jim. When you are hundreds of miles and many months distant from a problem, it is easy to decide that you will do so and so, and handle the matter differently from the bungling men you have heard about. To find Injun Jim and get him to tell where his gold mine was had seemed fairly easy to Casey when he was driving stage elsewhere, and could only think about it. But when he sat on his haunches in the tepee, smoking with Injun Jim and conversing intermittently of such vital things as the prospect of rain that night, and the enforced delay in his journey because his pack mule was lame, speaking of gold mines in a properly disinterested and casual manner was not at all easy.

However, Casey ate a very hearty supper and went to bed studying the problem of somehow winning the old fellow's gratitude. Morning did not bring a solution, as it properly should have done, but he ransacked his pack, chose a small glass jar of blackberry jam and a little can of maple syrup, fortified himself with another red can of tobacco and went up to the camp, hoping for a streak of good luck. As for medicine, he hadn't a drop, and if he had he did not know for certain what ailed Injun Jim. He thought it was just old age and general cussedness.

Injun Jim ate the jam, using a deadly looking knife and later his fingers, when the jam got low in the jar. When he had finished that he opened the can and drank the maple syrup just as he would have drunk whisky, —with a relish. He smoked Casey's tobacco in the stone pipe which the squaw brought him and appeared fairly well satisfied with life. But he did not talk much, and what he did say was of no importance whatever. Not once did he mention gold mines.

Casey went back to camp and swore at William as he counted his cans of luxuries. He did not realize that he had established a dangerous precedent, but when he led William up to water, meaning to pass by the camp without stopping, the squaw halted him on his way back and told him briefly that her man wanted him.

Injun Jim did not want Casey; he wanted more jam. Casey went back to camp and got another can, this time of strawberry, and in a spirit of peevishness added a small tin of the liver paste that had caused him a night's discomfort. He took them to the tepee, and Injun Jim ate the complete contents of both cans and seemed disgruntled afterwards; so much so that he would not talk at all but smoked in brooding silence, staring with his one malevolent eye at the stained wall of the tepee.

An hour later he began to move himself restlessly in the blanket and to mutter Piute words, the full meaning of which Casey did not grasp. But he would not answer when he was spoken to, so Casey went back to his camp. And that night Injun Jim was very sick.

Next day however he was sufficiently recovered to want more jam. Casey filled his pockets with small cans and doled them out one by one and gossipped artfully while he watched Injun Jim eat pickles, India relish and jelly with absolute, inscrutable impartiality. Casey felt sympathetic qualms in his own stomach just from watching the performance, but he was talking for a gold mine and he did not stop.

"You know Willow Pete?" he asked garrulously. "Big, tall man. Drinks whisky all the time. Willow Pete found a gold mine two moons ago. He's rich now. Got a big barrel of whisky.

Got silk shirts like this —" he plucked at his own silken sleeve " —got lots of jam all the time. Every day drinks whisky and eats jam."

"Hunh!" Injun Jim ran his forefinger dexterously around the inside of a jelly glass and licked the finger with the nonchalance of a two-year-old. "Hunh. Got heap big gol' mine, me. No can go ketchum two year, mebby. I dunno. Feet no damn good for walk. Back no damn good for ride. No ketchum gol' long time now."

Casey took a chew of tobacco. This was getting to the point he had been aiming for, and he needed his wits working at top speed.

"Well, if you got a gold mine, you can eat jam all the time. Drink whisky, too," he added, hushing his conscience peremptorily. "If you've got a white man that's your friend, he might take your gold to town and buy whisky and jam."

Injun Jim considered, his finger searching for more jelly. "White man no good for Injun, mebby. I dunno. Ketchum gol', mebby no givum. Tell all white mans. Heap mans come. White man horses eat grass. Drink all water. Shootum deer, shootum rabbit, shootum all damn time. Make big house. Heap noise all time. No place for Injuns no more. No good."

"White man not all same, Jim. One white man maybe good friend. Help get gold, give you half. You buy lots of jam, lots of whisky, lots of silk shirts, have good time." Casey looked at him straight. He could do it, because he meant what he said; even the whisky, I regret to say.

Injun Jim accepted a cigarette and smoked it, saying never a word. Casey smoked the mate to it and waited, trying to hide how his fingers trembled. Injun Jim turned himself painfully on the blankets and regarded Casey steadily with his one suspicious eye. Casey met the look squarely.

"You got more shirt?" Jim's finger pointed at the blue and green stripes. "Yo' got more jam? You bringum. Heap sick, me, mebby die. Me no takeum gol' me die. No wantum, me die. Yo' mebby good man. I dunno. Me ketchum heap jam, ketchum heap silk shirt, ketchum heap 'bacco, heap whisky, mebby me tellum you where ketchum gol' mine. Me die, yo' heap rich —"

He turned suddenly, lifted his right arm and sent his knife swishing through the air. It sliced its way through the tepee wall and hung there quivering, Caught by the hilt. Injun Jim called out vicious, Piute words. "Hahnaga!" he commanded fiercely. "Hahnaga!"

The lean old squaw came meekly, stood just within the tepee while her lord spat words at her. She answered apathetically in Piute and backed out. Presently she returned, driving before her a young squaw whom Casey had not before seen. The young squaw was holding a hand upon her other arm, and Casey saw blood between her fingers. The young squaw was not particularly meek. She stood there sullenly while Injun Jim berated her in the Indian tongue, and once she muttered a retort that made the old man's fingers go groping over the blankets for a weapon; whereat the young squaw laughed contemptuously and went out, sending Casey a side glance and a fleeting smile as full of coquetry as ever white woman could employ.

The interruption silenced the old buck upon the subject of gold. Casey sat there and chewed tobacco and waited, schooling his impatience as best he could. Injun Jim muttered in Piute, or lay with his one eye closed. But Casey knew that he did not sleep; his thin lips were drawn too tense for slumber. So he waited.

Injun Jim opened his eye suddenly, looked all around the tepee and then stared fixedly at Casey. "Young squaw no good. Heap much white talk. Stealum gol' mine, mebby. I dunno." He gestured for his knife, and Casey got it for him. Injun Jim fondled it evilly.

"Bimeby killum. Mebby. I dunno. Yo' ketchum jam, ketchum shirt-how many jam yo' ketchum?"

Casey meditated awhile. He had not planned an exclusive jam diet for Injun Jim, therefore his supply was getting low. But at the tenderfoot camp was much more, enough to last Injun Jim to the border of the happy hunting grounds, —if he did not loiter too long upon the way. There was no telling how long Injun Jim would be able to eat jam, but Casey was a good gambler.

"If I go get a lot more, and get silk shirts-six," he counted with his fingers, "you tell me where your gold mine is."

"Yo' bringum heap jam, bringum shirt. Me tellum." His one eye was bright. "Yo' bringum jam. Yo' bringum shirt. Yol giveum me." He patted the bare dirt beside the blankets, signifying that he wanted the jam and shirts there, within reach of his hand. He even twisted his cruel old lips into a smile. "Me tellum. Me shakeum hand."

He held out his left hand and Casey clasped it soberly, though he wanted to jump up and crack his heels together,—as he confided afterwards. Injun Jim laid the blade of his knife across the clasped hands.

"Yo' lie me, yo' die quick. Injun god biteum. Mebby snake. I dunno. How long yo' ketchum heap jam, heap shirt?"

Now that he knew the way, Casey had in mind a certain short-cut that would subtract two days from the round trip. He held up his hand, fingers spread, and got up. Then he thought of the threat and added one of his own.

"I've got a God myself, Jim. You lie about that gold mine and the jam'll choke yuh to death. You can ask anybody."

Casey went out and straightway packed for the journey. Fate, he told himself, was playing partners with him. I don't suppose Casey, even in his most happy-go-lucky mood, had ever been quite so content with life as when he returned to the camp of the tenderfeet for a mule load of jam and silk shirts. Trading an old muzzle-loading shotgun to an Indian chief for the future site of a great city could not have seemed more of a bargain in the days of our forefathers.

He made the trip almost half a day sooner than he had promised and went straight up to Injun Jim's camp with his load. He was whistling all the way up the canyon to the tepee; but then he stopped.

Inside the hut was the sound of wailing. Casey tried not to guess what that meant. He tied William and went to the door of the tepee.

The young squaw came from within and stood just before the opening, regarding Casey with that maddening, Indian immobility so characteristic of the race. She did not speak, though Casey waited for fully two minutes; nor did she move aside to let him go in. Casey grinned disarmingly.

"Me ketchum heap jam for Injun Jim. Heap silk shirts. Me go tellum," he said.

"Are those they?" the young squaw inquired calmly, and pointed to William. Casey jumped. Any man would, hearing that impeccable sentence issue from the lips of a squaw with a blanket over her head.

"Uh-huh," he gulped.

"My father is dead. He died yesterday from eating too much pickles that you gave him. I should like to have what you have brought to give him. I should thank you for the silk shirts. I can fix them so that I can wear them. I will talk to you pretty soon about that gold mine. I know where it is. I have helped my father bring the gold away. My father would not tell you if you gave him all the jam and all the silk in the world. My father was awful mean. I thought he would maybe kill you and that is why I listened beside the tepee. I wished to protect you because I know that you are a good man. Will you give me the silk shirts and the jam?"

She smiled then, and Casey saw that she had a gold tooth in front, which further demonstrated how civilized she was.

"You will excuse the way I am dressed. I have to dress so that I would please my father. He was very mean with me all the time. He did not like me because I have gone to school and got a fine educating. He wanted me to be Indian. But I knew that my father is a chief and that makes me just what you would say a princess, and I wished to learn how to be educate like all white ladies. So I took some gold from my father's mine and I spent the money for going to school. My name," she added impressively, "is Lucy Lily. What is your name?"

"Mr. —Casey Ryan," he stuttered, floundering in the mental backwash left by this flood of amazing eloquence.

"I like that name. I think I will have you for my friend. Do not talk to my mother, Hahnaga. She is crazy. She tells lies all the time about me. She does not like me because I have went to school and got a fine educating. She is mad all the time when she sees that I am not like her. Now you give me the silks. I will put on a pretty dress. My father is dead now and I can do what I wish to do; I am not afraid of my mother. My mother does not know where to find the gold mine. I am the only one who knows."

Casey is a simple soul, too trustful by far. He was embarrassed by the arch smile which Lucy Lily gave him, and he wished vaguely that she was the blanket squaw she looked to be. But it never occurred to Casey that there might be a wily purpose behind her words. He unpacked William and gave her the things he had brought for Injun Jim, and returned with his camp outfit to the spring to think things over while he boiled himself a pot of coffee and fried bacon.

Lucy Lily appeared like an unwarranted vision before him. Indeed, Casey likened her coming to a nightmare. Casey no longer wondered why Injun Jim insisted upon Indian dress for Lucy Lily.

Now she wore a red silk skirt much spotted with camp grease. A three-cornered tear in the side had been sewed with long stitches and coarse white thread, and even Casey was outraged by the un-workmanlike job. She had on one of the silk shirts, which happened to be striped in many shades, none of which harmonized with the basic color of the skirt. She also wore two cheap necklaces whose luster had long since faded, and her hair was coiled on top of her head and adorned with three combs containing many white glass settings. Her face was powdered thickly to the point of her jaws, with very red cheekbones and very red lips. She wore once-white slippers with French heels much run over at the side and dirty white silk stockings with great holes in the heels. I must add that the shirt was too narrow in the bust, so that her arms bulged and there were gaping spaces between the buttons. And for a belt she wore a wide blue ribbon very much creased and soiled, as if she had used it for a long while as a hair bow.

She sat down upon a rock and watched Casey distractedly bungle his cooking. She must have had a great deal of initiative for a squaw, for she plunged straight into the subject which most nearly concerned Casey, and she was frank to the point of appalling him with her bluntness. Casey is a rather case-hardened bachelor, but I suspect that Lucy Lily scared him from the beginning.

"Do you like me when I have pretty dress on?" she inquired, smoothing the red silk complacently over her knees.

Casey swears that he told her it didn't make a darn bit of difference to him what she wore. If that is the truth, Lucy Lily must have been very stupid or very persistent, for she went on blandly stating her plans and her dearest wish.

"That gold mine I am keeping for my husband," she announced. "It is a present for a wedding gift for my man. I shall not marry an Indian man. I am too pretty and I have a gold mine, and I will marry a white man. Indians don't know what money is good for. I want to live in a town and wear silk dresses all the time every day and ride in a red automobile and have lots of rings and go to shows. Have you got lots of money?"

I don't know what Casey told her. He says he swore he hadn't a nickel to his name.

"I think you have got lots of money. I think perhaps you are rich. I don't see white men walk in the desert with silk shirts and have lots of jam and pickles if they are not rich. I think you want that gold mine awful bad. You gave Jim lots of jam so he would tell you. White men want lots of more money when they have got lots of money. It is like that in shows. If a man is poor he don't care. If a man is rich he is hunting all the time for more money and killing people. So I think you are like them rich mans in shows."

Casey told her again that he was poor; but she couldn't have believed him, —not in the face of all the silk and sweets he had displayed.

"I am awful glad Jim is dead. Now you have gave me the things. We will go to Tonopah and you will buy a red automobile and we will ride in it. And you will buy me lots of silk and rings. I shall be a lady like a princess in a show."

"Your mother has got something to say about that gold mine," Casey blurted desperately. "It's hers by rights. She'd have to go fifty-fifty on it. She's got it coming, and I never cheated anybody yet. I ain't going to commence on an old squaw."

"She is a big fool. What you think Hahnaga want of money? The agent he gives her blankets and tea and flour. If you give Hahnaga silk, I will be awful mad. She is old. She will die pretty quick."

"Well," said Casey, "I dunno as any of us has got any cinch on living. And if there's a gold mine in the family, she sure has got to have an even break. What about old Jim? Buried him yet?"

"He is in the tepee. I think Hahnaga will dig a grave. I don't care. I will go with you, and we will find the gold mine. Then you will buy me —"

"I'll buy you nothin'!" Casey's tone was emphatic.

Lucy Lily looked at him steadily. "Before we go for the gold mine we will go to Tonopah and get marriage, and you will give me a gold ring on my finger. Then I will show you where is gold so much you will have money to buy the world full of things." She smiled at him, showing her gold tooth. "I like you for my man," she said. "I am awful pretty. I have lots of fellows. I could marry lots of other white mans, but I will marry you."

"Like hell you will!" snorted Casey, and began to wipe out his frying pan and empty his coffeepot and make other preparations for instant packing. "Like hell you'll marry me! Think I'd marry a squaw —?"

"Then I will not tell you where is the gold! Then I hate you and I will fix you good! You want that gold mine awful bad. You will have to marry me before I tell you."

Casey straightened and looked at her, his frying pan in one hand, his coffeepot in the other. "Say, I never asked you about the darn mine, did I? I done my talkin' to Injun Jim. It's you that butted in here on this deal. Seein' he's dead, I'll talk to his squaw and make a deal with her, mebby." He looked her over measuringly. "Princess-hunh! I'll tell yuh in plain American what you are, if yuh don't git outa here. I may want a gold mine, all right, but I sure don't want it that bad. Git when I tell yuh to git!"

A squaw with no education would have got forthwith. But Lucy Lily had learned to be like white ladies, —or so she said. She screamed at him in English, in Piute, and chose words in each that no princess should employ to express her emotions. Her loud denunciations followed Casey to the tepee, where he stopped and offered his services to Hahnaga as undertaker.

She accepted stolidly and together they buried Injun Jim, using his best blanket and not much ceremony. Casey did not know the Piute customs well enough to follow them, and his version of the white man's funeral service was simple in the extreme. Hahnaga, however, brought two bottles of pickles and one jar of preserves which had outlasted Injun Jim's appetite, and put them in the grave with him, together with his knife and an old rifle and his pipe.

To dig a grave and afterwards heap the dirt symmetrically over a discarded body takes a little time, no matter how cursory is the proceeding. Casey ceased to hear Lucy Lily's raucous voice and so thought that she had settled down. He misjudged the red princess. He discovered that when he went back to where William had stood.

He no longer stood there. He was gone, pack and all, and once more Casey stood equipped for desert journeying with shirt, overalls, shoes and socks, and his old Stetson, and with half a plug of tobacco, a pipe and a few matches in his pocket. On the bush where William had been tied a piece of paper was impaled and fluttered in the wind. Casey jerked it off and read the even, carefully formed script, —and swore.

"Dear Sir: I am going to Tonopah. If you try to come I will tell the sherf to coming and see Jim and put you in jail. I will tell the judge you killed him and the sherf will put you in jail and hung you. Those are fine shirts. I will wear them silk. As ever your friend, Yours truly, LUCY LILY."

Casey sat down on a rock to think it over. The squaw was moving about within the hut, collecting the pitifully few belongings which Lucy Lily had disdained to steal. An Indian does not like to stay where one has died.

Casey could overtake Lucy Lily, if he walked fast and did not stop when dark fell, but he did not want to overtake her. He was not alarmed at her threat of the sheriff, but he did not want to see her again or hear her or think of her.

So Casey tore up the note and went and begged a little food from Hahnaga; then he broached the subject of the gold mine. The squaw listened, looking at him with dull black eyes and a face like a stamped-leather portrait of an Indian. She shook her head and pointed down the gulch.

"No find gol', bad girl. I think killum my mans. I dunno. No fin' gol' —Jim he no tellum. No tellum me, no tellum Lucy, no tellum nobody. I think, all time Jim hide." She made a gesture as of one covering something with dirt. "Lucy all time try for fin' gol'. Jim he no likeum. Lucy my sister girl. Bad. No good. All time heap mean. All time tellum heap big lie so Indian no likeum. One time take monee, go 'way off. School for write. Come back for fin' gol', make Jim tellum. Jim sick long time. Jim no tellum. Jim all time mad for Lucy. Las' night-talk mean-mebby fight-Jim he die quick. Lucy say killum me, I tell.

"Now me go my brother. Walk two day. Give you grub-no got many grub. You takeum gol' you fin'. Me no care. No want. You don' give Lucy. Lucy bad girl all time. No fin' gol' —Jim he no tellum. I dunno."

That left Casey exactly where he had been before he found Injun Jim. There was no getting around it; the squaw repeated her statements twice, which Casey thought was probably more talking that she had done before in the course of six months. She impressed Casey as being truthful. She really did not know any more about Injun Jim's mine than did Casey. Or perhaps a little more, because she knew, poor thing, just how drunk Jim could get on the whisky they gave him for the gold. He used to beat her terribly when he came to camp drunk. Casey learned that much, though it didn't help him any.

Hahnaga did not seem to think that anything need be done about the manner of Jim's death. She said he was heap sick and would die anyway, or words-not many-to that effect. Casey decided to go on and mind his own business. He did not see why, he said, the county of Nye should be let in for a lot of expense on Injun Jim's account, even if Jim had been killed. And as for punishing Lucy Lily, he was perfectly willing that it should be done, only he did not want to do it. I have always believed that Casey was afraid she might possibly marry him in spite of himself if she were in his immediate neighborhood long enough.

They made themselves each a small pack of food and what was more vital, water, and went their different ways. Hahnaga struck off to the west, to her brother at the end of Forty-Mile Canyon. At least, that was where she said her brother mostly camped. Casey retraced his steps for the second time to the camp of the tenderfeet. Loco Canyon, Casey calls the place, claiming it by right of discovery.

Now I don't see, and possibly you won't see, either, what the devil's lantern had to do with Casey's bad luck. Casey maintains rather stubbornly that it had a great deal to do with it. First, he says, it got him all off the trail following it, and was almost the death of him and William. Next, he declares that it drove him to Lucy Lily and had fully intended that he should be tied up to her. Then he suspects that it had something to do with Injun Jim's dying just when he did, and he has another count or two against the lantern and will tell you them, and back them with much argument, if you nag him into it.

It taught him things, he says. And once, after we had talked the matter over and had fallen into silence, he broke out with a sentence I have never forgotten, nor the tone in which he said it, nor the way he glared into the fire, his pipe in his hand where he always had it when he was extremely in earnest.

"The three darndest, orneriest, damndest things on earth," said Casey, as if he were intoning a text, "is a Ford, or a goat, or an Injun. You can ask anybody yuh like if that ain't so."

Chapter XVIII

Casey was restless, and his restlessness manifested itself in a most unusual pessimism. Twice he picked up "float" that showed the clean indigo stain of silver bromyrite in spots the size of a split pea, and cast the piece from him as if it were so much barren limestone, without ever investigating to see where it had come from. Little as I know about mineral, I am sure that one piece at least was rich; high-grade, if ever I saw any. But Casey merely grunted when I spoke to him about it.

"Maybe it is. A coupla hundred ounces, say. What's that, even with silver at a dollar an ounce? It ain't good enough for Casey, and what I'm wastin' my time for, wearing the heels off'n my shoes prospectin' Starvation, is somethin' I can't tell yuh." He looked at me with his pale-blue, unwinking stare for a minute.

"Er —I can-and I guess the quicker it's out the better I'll feel."

He took out his familiar plug of tobacco, always nibbled around the edges, always half the size of his four fingers. I never saw Casey with a fresh plug in his pocket, and I never saw him down to one chew; it is one of the little mysteries in his life that I never quite solved.

"I been thinkin' about that devil's lantern we seen the other night," he said, when he had returned to his pocket the plug with a corner gone. "They's something funny about that-the way it went over there and stood on the Tippipahs again. I ain't sooperstitious. But I can't git things outa my head. I want to go hunt fer that mine of Injun Jim's. This here is just foolin' around-huntin' silver. I want to see where that free gold comes from that he used to peddle. It's mine-by rights. He was goin' to tell me where it was, you recollect, and he woulda if I hadn't overfed him on jam-or if that damn squaw hadn't took a notion for marryin'. I let her stampede me-and that's where I was wrong. I shoulda stayed."

I was foolish enough to argue with him. I had talked with others about the mine of Injun Jim, and one man (who owned cattle and called mines a gamble) told me that he doubted the whole story. A prospectors' bubble, he called it. Free gold, he insisted, did not belong in this particular formation; it ran in porphyry, he said, —and then he ran into mineralogy too technical for me now. I repeated his statement, however, and saw Casey grin tolerantly.

"Gold is where yuh find it," he retorted, and spat after a hurrying lizard. "They said gold couldn't be found in that formation around Goldfield. But they found it, didn't they?"

Casey looked at me steadily for a minute and then came out with what was really in his mind. "You stake me to grub and a couple of burros an' let me go hunt the Injun Jim, and I'll locate yuh in on it when I find it. And if I don't find it, I'll pay yuh back for the outfit. And, anyway, you're makin' money off'n my bad luck right along, ain't yuh? Wasn't it me you was writin' up, these last few days?"

"I was-er-reconsidering that devil's lantern yarn you told me, Casey. But the thing doesn't work out right. It sounds unfinished, as you told it. I don't know that I can do anything with it, after all." I was truthful with him; you all remember that I was dissatisfied with the way Casey ended it. Just walking back across the desert and quitting the search, —it lacked, somehow, the dramatic climax. I could have built one, of course. But I wanted to test out my theory that a man like Casey will live a complete drama if he is left alone. Casey is absolutely natural; he goes out after life without waiting for it to come to him, and he will forget all about his own interests to help a stranger, —and above all, he builds his castles hopefully as a child and seeks always to make them substantial structures afterwards. If any man can prove my theory, that man is Casey Ryan. So I led him along to say what dream held him now.

"Unfinished? Sure it's unfinished! I quit, didn't I tell yuh? It ain't goin' to be finished till I git out and find that mine. I been studyin' things over. I never seen one of them lights till I started out to find Injun Jim's mine. If I'd a-gone along with no bad luck, I wouldn't never a-found that tenderfoot camp, would I? It was keepin' the light at my back done that-and William not likin' the look of it, either. And you gotta admit it was the light mostly that scared them young dudes off and left me the things. And if you'd of saw Injun Jim, you'd of known same as I that it was the jam and the silk shirts that loosened him up. Nothin' in my own pack coulda won him over, —"

"It's all right that far," I cut in. "But then he died, and you were set afoot and all but married by as venomous a creature as I ever heard of, and the thing stops right there, Casey, where it shouldn't."

"And that's what I'm kickin' about! Casey Ryan ain't the man to let it stop there. I been thinkin' it over sence that devil's lantern showed up again, and went and set over there on Tippipah. Mebby I misjudged the dog-gone thing. Mebby it's settin' somewheres around that gold mine. Funny it never showed up no other time and no other place. I been travelin' the desert off'n on all my life, and I never seen anything like it before. And I can tell yuh this much: I been wanting that mine too darn long to give up now. If you don't feel like stakin' me for the trip, I'll go back to Lund and have a talk with Bill. Bill's a good old scout and he'll stake me to an outfit, anyway."

That was merely Casey's inborn optimism speaking. Bill was a good old scout, all right, but if he would grubstake Casey to go hunting the Injun Jim mine, then Bill had changed considerably.

The upshot of it was that we left Starvation the next morning, headed for town. And two days after that I had pulled myself out of bed at daybreak to walk down to his camp under the mesquite grove just outside of town. I drank a cup of coffee with him and wished him luck. Casey did not talk much. His mind was all taken up with the details of his starting, —whether to trust his water cans on the brown burro or the gray, and whether he had taken enough "cold" shoes along for the mule. And he set down his cup of coffee to go rummaging in a kyack just to make sure that he had the hoof rasp and shoeing hammer safe.

He was packed and moving up the little hill out of the grove before the sun had more than painted a cloud or two in the east. A dreamer once more gone to find the end of his particular rainbow, I told myself, as I watched him out of sight. I must admit that I hoped, down deep in the heart of me, that Casey would fall into some other unheard-of experience such as had been his portion in the past. I felt much more certain that he would get into some scrape than I did that he would find the Injun Jim, and I was grinning inside when I went back to town; though there was a bit of envy in the smile, —one must always envy the man who keeps his dreams through all the years and banks on them to the end. For myself, I hadn't chased a rainbow for thirty years, and I could not call myself the better for it, either.

In September the lower desert does not seem to realize that summer is going. The wind blows a little harder, perhaps, and frequently a little hotter; the nights are not quite so sweltering, and the very sheets on one's bed do not feel so freshly baked. But up on the higher mesas there is a heady quality to the wind that blows fresh in your face. There is an Indian-summery haze like a thin veil over the farthest mountain ranges. Summer is with you yet; but somehow you feel that winter is coming.

In a country all gray and dull yellow and brown, you find strange, beautiful tints no artist has yet prisoned with his paints. You dream in spite of yourself, and walk through a world no more than half real, a world peopled with your thoughts.

Casey did, when the burros left him in peace long enough. They were misleading, pot-bellied animals that Casey hazed before him toward the Tippipahs. They never showed more than slits of eyes beneath their drooping lids, yet they never missed seeing whatever there was to see, and taking advantage of every absent-minded moment when Casey was thinking of the Injun Jim, perhaps. They were fast-walking burros when they were following a beaten trail and Casey was hard upon their heels, but when his attention wandered they showed a remarkable amount of energy in finding blind trails and following them into some impracticable wash where Casey wasted a good deal of time in extricating them. He said he never saw burros that hated so to turn around and go back into the road, and he never saw two burros get out of sight as quickly as they could when they thought he wasn't watching. They would choose different directions and hide from him separately,—but once was enough for Casey. He lost them both for an hour in the sand pits twelve miles out of town, and after that he tied them nose to tail and himself held a rope attached to the hindmost, and so made fair time with them, after all.

The mule, Casey said, was just plain damn mule, sloughed off from the army, blasé beyond words,—any words at Casey's command, at least. A lopeared buckskin mule with a hanging lower lip and a chronic tail-switching, that shacked along hour after hour and saved Casey's legs and, more particularly, a bunion that had developed in the past year.

Casey knew the country better than he had known it on his first unprofitable trip into the Tippipahs. He avoided Furnace Lake, keeping well around the Southern rim of it and making straight for Loco Canyon and the spring there while his water cans still had a pleasant slosh. There he rested his longears for a day, and disinterred certain tenderfoot luxuries which he had cached when he was there last time. And when he set out again he went straight on to the old stone hut where Injun Jim had camped. The tepee was gone, burned down according to Indian custom after a death, as he had expected. The herd of Indian ponies were nowhere in sight. Hahnaga's brother, he guessed, had driven them off long ago.

Casey had worked out a theory, bit by bit, and with characteristic optimism he had full faith that it would prove a fact later on. He wanted to start his search from the point where Injun Jim had started, and he had rather a plausible reason for doing so.

Injun Jim was an Indian of the old school, and the old school did a great deal of its talking by signs. Casey had watched Jim with that pale, unwinking stare that misses nothing within range, and he had read the significance of Jim's unconscious gestures while he talked. It had been purely subconscious; Casey had expected the exact location of the mine in words, and perhaps with a crudely accurate map of Jim's making. But now he remembered Jim's words, certain motions made by the skinny hands, and from them he laid his course.

"He was layin' right here-facin' south," Casey told himself, squatting on his heels within the rock circle that marked the walls of the tepee. "He said, 'Got heap big gol' mine, me —' and he turned his hand that way." Casey squinted at the distant blue ridge that was an unnamed spur of the Tippipahs. "It's far enough so an old buck like him couldn't make it very well. Fifteen mile, anyway-mebby twenty or twenty-five. And from the sign talk he made whilst he was talkin', I'd guess it's nearer twenty than fifteen. There's that two-peak butte-looks like that would be about right for distance. And it's dead in line-them old bucks don't waggle their hands permiskus when they talk. Old Jim woulda laid on his hands if he'd knowed what they was tellin' me; but even an ornery old devil like him gits careless when they git old. Casey hits straight fer Two Peak."

That's the way he got his bearings; just remembering the unguarded motion of Injun Jim's grimy hand and adding thereto his superficial knowledge of the country and his own estimate of what an old fellow like Jim could call a long journey. With this and the unquestioning faith in his dream that was a part of him, Casey threw his favorite "packer's hitch" across the packed burros at dawn next morning, boarded his buckskin mule and set off hopefully across the barren valley, heading straight for the distant butte he called Two Peak.

I don't suppose Casey Ryan ever started out to do something for himself-something he considered important to his own personal welfare and happiness-without running straight into some other fellow's business and stopping to lend a hand. He says he can't remember being left alone at any time in his life to follow the beckoning finger of his own particular destiny.

Casey had made camp that night in one of several deep gulches that ridged the butte with two peaks. We had been lucky in our burro buying, and he had two of the fastest walking jacks in the country, so that he was able to give them a good long nooning and still reach the foot of the butte and make camp well before sundown. For the first time since he first heard of the Injun Jim gold mine, Casey felt that he was really "squared away" to the search. As he sat there blowing his unhurried breath upon a blue granite cup of coffee to cool it, his memory slanted back along the years when he had said that some day he would go and hunt for the Injun Jim mine that was so rich a ten-pound lard bucket full of the ore had been known to yield five hundred dollars' worth of gold. Well, it had been a long time since he first said that to himself, but here he was, and to-morrow he would begin his search with daylight, starting with this gulch he was in and working methodically over every foot of Two Peak.

He took two long, satisfying swallows of coffee and poised the cup and listened. After a minute had gone in that way, he finished the coffee in gulps and stood up, dangling the empty cup with a finger crooked in the handle. From somewhere not more than a long rifle-shot away, a Ford was coughing under full pressure of gas and with at least one dirty spark plug to give it a spasmodic stutter. While Casey stood there listening, the stutter slowed and stopped with one wheezy cough. That was all.

"They'll have to clean up her hootin'-annies before they git outa here," Casey observed shrewdly, having intimate and sometimes unpleasant knowledge of Fords and their peculiar ailments. "And I wonder what the sufferin' Chris'mas they're doin' here, anyway. If it's huntin' the Injun Jim they're after, the quicker they scrape the sut off them dingbats and git outa here, the healthier they'll ride. You ask anybody if Casey Ryan's liable to back up now he's on the ground and squared away!"

He stood there uneasily for a minute or two longer, caught a whiff of his bacon scorching and stooped to its rescue. Then he fried a bannock hastily in the bacon grease, folded two slices of bacon within it and ate in a hurry, keeping an ear cocked for any further sounds from the concealed car.

He finished eating without having heard more and piled his dishes without washing them. I don't suppose he had used more than ten minutes at the longest in eating his supper. That was about the limit of Casey's inaction when he smelled a mystery or a scrap. This had the elements of both, and he started out forthwith to trail down the Ford, wiping crumbs from his mouth and getting out his plug of tobacco as he went.

In broken country sounds are deceptive as to direction, but Casey was lucky enough to walk straight toward the spot, which was over a hump in the gulch, a sort of backbone dividing it in two narrow branches there at its mouth. He had noticed when he rode toward it that it was ridged in the middle, and had chosen the left-hand branch for no reason at all except that it happened to be a little smoother traveling for his animals.

He topped the ridge and came full upon a camp below, almost within calling distance from where he first sighted it. There was a stone hut that could not possibly contain more than two small rooms, and there was a tent pitched not far away. There seemed to be a spring just beyond the cabin. Casey saw the silver gleam of water there, and a strip of green grass, and a juniper bush or two.

But these details were not important at the moment. What sent him down the hill in an uneven trot was a group of three that stood beside a car. From their voices, and the gestures that were being made, here was a quarrel building rapidly into a fight. To prove it the smallest person in the group suddenly whipped out a revolver and pointed it at the two. Casey saw the reddening sunlight strike upon the barrel with a brief shine, instantly quenched when the gun was thrust forward toward the other two whom it threatened.

"You get out of my camp and out of my sight just as fast as your legs can take you. This car belongs to me, and you're not going to touch it. You've got your wages-more than your wages, you great hulking shirks! A fine exhibition you're making of yourselves, I must say! You thought you could bluff me-that I'd stand meekly by and let you two bullies have your own way about it, did you? You even waited until you had gorged yourselves on food you've never earned, before you started your highwaymen performance. You made sure of one more good meal, you-you *hogs*. Now go, before I empty this gun into the two of you!"

Casey stopped, puffing a little, I suppose. He is not so young as when they called him the Fightin' Stagedriver, and he had done his long day of travel. The three did not know that he was there, they were so busy with their quarrel. The woman's voice was sharp with contempt, but it was not loud and there was not a tremble in any tone of it. The gun she held was steady in her hand, but one man snarled at her and one man laughed. It was the kind of laugh a woman would hate to hear from a man she was defying.

"Aw, puddown the popgun! Nobody's scared of it-er you. It ain't loaded, and if it was loaded you couldn't hit nothin'. No need to be scared 'long's a woman's pointing a gun at yuh. Crank 'er up, agin, Ole. Don't worry none about *her*. She can't stop nothin', not even her jawin'. Go awn, start the damn Lizzie an' let's go."

Ole bent to the cranking, then complained that the switch must be off. His companion growled that it was nothing of the kind and kept his narrowed gaze fixed upon the woman.

She spied Casey standing there, a few rods beyond the car. The gun dropped in her hand so that its aim was no longer direct. The man who faced her jumped and caught her wrist, and the gun went off, the bullet singing ten feet above Casey's head.

A little girl with flaxen curls and patched overalls on screamed and rushed up to the man, gripping him furiously around the legs just above the knees and trying her little best to shake him. "You leave my mamma alone!" she cried shrilly.

Casey took a hand then, —a hand with a rock in it, I must explain. He managed to kick Ole harshly in the ribs, sending him doubled sidewise and yelping, as he passed him. He laid the other man out senseless with the rock which landed precisely on the back of the head just under his hat.

The woman-Casey had mistaken her for a man at first, because she wore bib overalls and had her hair bobbed and a man's hat on-dropped the gun and held her wrist that showed angry red finger prints. She smiled at Casey exactly as if nothing much had happened.

"Thank you very much indeed. I was beginning to wonder how I was going to manage the situation. It was growing rather awkward, because I should have been compelled to shoot them both, I expect, before I was through. And I dreaded a mess. Wounded, I should have had them on my hands to take care of-their great hulks! —and dead I should have had to bury them, and I detest digging in this rocky soil. You really did me a very great —"

Her eyes ranged to something behind Casey and widened at what they saw. Casey whirled about, ducked a hurtling monkey wrench and rushed Ole, who was getting up awkwardly, his eyes malevolent. He made a very thorough job of thrashing Ole, and finished by knocking him belly down over the un-hooded engine of the Ford.

"I hope Jawn doesn't suffer from that," the little woman commented whimsically. "Babe, run and get that rope over there and take it to the gentleman so he can tie Ole's hands together. Then he can't be naughty any more. Hurry, Baby Girl."

Baby Girl hurried, her curls whipping around her face as she ran. She brought a coil of cotton clothesline to Casey, looking up at him with wide, measuring eyes of a tawny shade like sunlight shining through thin brown silk. "I wish you'd give Joe a beating too," she said with grave earnestness. "He's a badder man than Ole. He hurt my mamma. Will you give Joe a beating and tie his naughty hands jus' like that when he wakes up?" She lifted her plump little body on her scuffed toes, her brown, dimpled fingers clutching the radiator to hold her steady while she watched Casey tie Ole's naughty hands behind his back.

"Now will you tie Joe's naughty hands jus' like that? Don't use up all the rope! My mamma hasn't got any more rope, and you have to tie —"

"Babe! Come over here and don't bother the gentleman. Stand away over there so you can't hear the naughty words Ole is saying." The little woman smiled, but not much. Casey, glancing up from the last efficient knot, felt suddenly sorry that he had not first gagged Ole. Casey had not thought of it before; mere cussing was natural to him as breathing, and he had scarcely been aware of the fact that Ole was speaking. Now he cuffed the Swede soundly and told him to shut up, and yanked him off the car.

"Joe is regaining consciousness. He'll be nasty to handle as a rabid coyote if you wait much longer. Just cut the rope. It's my clothesline, but we must not balk at trifles in a crisis like this." The little woman had recovered her gun and was holding it ready for Joe in case the predicted rabidness became manifest.

Casey tied Joe very thoroughly while consciousness was slowly returning. The situation ceased to be menacing; it became safe and puzzling and even a bit mysterious. Casey reached for his plug, remembered his manners and took away his hand. Robbed of his customary inspiration he stood undecided, scowling at the feebly blinking ruffian called Joe.

"It's very good of you not to ask what it's all about," said the little woman, taking off the man's hat and shaking back her hair like a schoolgirl. "I have some mining claims here-four of them. My husband left them to me, and since that's all he did leave I have been keeping up the assessment work every year. Last year I had enough money to buy Jawn." She nodded toward the Ford. "I outfitted and came out here with an old fellow I'd known for years, kept camp until he'd done the assessment work, and paid him off and that was all there was to it.

"This summer the old man is prospecting the New Jerusalem, I expect. He died in April. I hired these two scoundrels. I was foolish enough to pay half their wages in advance, because they told me a tale of owing money to a widow for board and wanting to pay her. I have," she observed, "a weakness for widows. And they have just pretended to be working the claims. I hurt my ankle so that I haven't been able to walk far for a month, and they took advantage of it and have been prospecting around on their own account, at my expense, while I religiously marked down their time and fed them. They have located four claims adjoining mine, and put up their monuments and done their location work in the past month, if you please, while I supposed they were working for me."

"D'they locate you in on 'em?"

"Locate me-in? You mean, as a partner? They emphatically did not! I went up to the claims to-day, saw that they had not done a thing since the last time I was there; they had even taken away my tools. So we tracked them, Baby and I, and found their location monuments just over the hill, and saw where they had been working. So to-night I asked them about it, and they were very defiant and very cool and decided that they were through out here and would go to town. They were *borrowing* Jawn-so they said. I was objecting, naturally. I was quite against being left alone out here, afoot, with Babe on my hands. It will soon be coming on cold," she said. "I'd have been in a fine predicament, with supplies for only about a month longer. And I must get the assessment work done, too, you know."

"D'you want 'em to stay and finish your work?" Casey reached out with his foot and pushed Joe down upon his back again.

The little woman looked down at Joe and across at Ole by the car. "No, thank you. I should undoubtedly put strychnine in their coffee if they stayed, I should hate the sight of them so. I have some that I brought for the pack rats. No, I don't want them —"

She had sounded very cool and calm, and she had impressed Casey as being quite as fearless as himself. But now he caught a trembling in her voice, and he distinctly saw her lip quiver. He was so disturbed that he went over and slapped Ole again and told him to shut up, though Ole was not saying a word.

"Where's their bed-rolls?" Casey asked, when he turned toward her again. She pointed to the tent, and Casey went and dragged forth the packed belongings of the two. It was perfectly plain that they had deliberately planned their desertion, for everything was ready to load into the car.

Casey went staggering to the Ford, dumped the canvas rolls in and yanked Ole up by the collar, propelling him into the tonneau. Then he came after Joe.

"If you can drive, you'll mebby feel better if yuh go along," he said to the woman. "I'm goin' to haul 'em far enough sos't they won't feel like walkin' back to bother yuh, and seein' you don't know me, mebby you better do the drivin'. Then you'll know I ain't figurin' on stealin' your car and makin' a getaway."

"I can drive, of course," she acquiesced. "Not that I'd be afraid to trust Jawn with you, but they're treacherous devils, those two, and they might manage somehow to make you trouble if you go alone. Jawn is a temperamental car, and he demands all of one's attention at times."

She walked over to the car, reached out in the gathering dusk and fingered the carburetor adjustment. "When they first revealed their plan of making away with Jawn," she drawled, "I came up like this and remonstrated. And while I did so I reached over and turned the screw and shut off the gas feed. Jawn balked with them, of course-but they never guessed why!"

The two in the tonneau muttered something in undertones while the little woman smiled at them contemptuously. Casey thought that was pretty smart-to stall the car so they couldn't get away with it-but he did not tell her so. There was something about the little woman which restrained him from talking freely and speaking his mind bluntly as was his habit.

He cranked the car, waited until she had the adjustment correct, and then went back and stood on the running board, holding with his left hand to a brace of the top and keeping his right free in case he should need it. The little woman helped the little girl into the front seat, slid her own small person behind the wheel and glanced round inquiringly, with a flattering recognition of his masculine right to command.

"Just head towards town and keep a-going till I say when," he told her, and she nodded and sent Jawn careening down over the rough tracks which Casey had missed by a quarter of a mile or less.

She could drive, Casey admitted, almost as recklessly as he could. He had all he wanted to do, hanging on without being snapped off at some of the sharp turns she made. The road wandered down the valley for ten miles, crept over a ridge, then dove headlong into another wide, shallow valley seamed with washes and deep cuts. The little woman never eased her pace except when there was imminent danger of turning Jawn bottomside up in a wash. So in a comparatively short time they were over two summits and facing the distant outline of Crazy Woman Hills. They had come, Casey judged, about twenty miles, and they had been away from camp less than an hour.

Casey leaned forward and spoke to the woman, and she stopped the car obediently. Casey pulled open the door and motioned, and the Swede came stumbling out, sullenly followed by Joe, who muttered thickly that he was sick and that the back of his head was caved in. Casey did not reply, but heaved their bedding out after them. With the little woman holding her gun at full aim, he untied the two and frugally stowed the rope away in the car.

"Now, you git," he ordered them sternly. "There's four of us camped just acrost the ridge from this lady's place, and we'll sure keep plenty of eyes out. If you got any ideas about taking the back trail, you better think agin, both of yuh. You'd never git within shootin' distance of this lady's camp. I'm Casey Ryan that's speakin' to yuh. You ask anybody about me. Git!"

Sourly they shouldered their bed-rolls and went limping down the trail, and when their forms were only blurs beyond the shine of the headlights, the little woman churned Jawn around somehow in the sand and drove back quite as recklessly as she had come. Casey, bouncing alone in the rear seat, did a great deal of thinking, but I don't believe he spoke once.

"Casey Ryan, I have never had much reason for feeling gratitude toward a man, but I am truly grateful to you. You are a man and a gentleman." The little woman had driven close to the stone cabin and had turned and rested her arm along the back of the front seat, half supporting the sleeping child while she looked full at Casey. She had left the engine running, probably for sake of the headlights, and her eyes shone dark and bright in the crisp starlight.

"'Tain't worth mentionin'," Casey protested awkwardly, and got out.

"I've been wondering if I could get a couple of you men to do the work on my claims," she went on. "I'm paying four dollars and board, and it would be a great nuisance to make the long trip to town and find a couple of men I would dare trust. In fact, it's going to be pretty hard for me to trust any one, after this experience. If you men can take the time from your own business —"

"I don't know about the rest," Casey hedged uncomfortably. "They was figurin' on doing something else. But I guess I could finish up the work for yuh, all right. How deep is your shaft?"

"It's a tunnel," she corrected. "My husband started four years ago to drift in to the contact. He'd gone fifty feet when he died. I don't know that I'll strike the body of ore when I do reach the contact, but it's the only hope. I'm working the four claims as a group, and the tunnel is now eighty feet. Those two brigands have wasted a month for me, or it would be a hundred. One man can manage, though of course it's slower and harder. I have powder enough, unless they stole it from me. They did about five feet all told, and tore down part of my wall, I discovered to-day, chasing a stringer of fairly rich ore, thinking, I suppose, that it would lead to a pocket. The old man I had last year found a pocket of high grade that netted me a thousand dollars."

Casey threw up his head. "Gold?" he asked.

"Mostly silver. I sent a truck out from town after the ore, shipped it by express and still made a thousand dollars clear. There wasn't quite a ton and a half of it, though. You'll come, then, and work for me? I wish you could persuade one of your partners to help. It's getting well into September already."

"I wouldn't depend on 'em," Casey demurred uncomfortably. "I can do it alone. And I'll board m'self, if you'd ruther. I've got grub enough. I guess I better be gittin' along back to camp-if you ain't afraid to stay alone. Them two couldn't git back much b'fore daylight, if they run all the way; and by that time I'll be up and on the lookout," and Casey swung off without waiting for an answer.

Casey was out of his blankets long before daylight the next morning and sitting behind a bush on the ridge just back of the cabin, his rifle across his knees. He hoped that his mention of three other men would discourage those two from the attempt to revenge themselves, much as a lone woman would tempt them. But he was not going to take any risk whatever.

At sunrise he went back to his camp-which he had moved closer to the cabin, by the way, just barely keeping it out of sight-and cooked a hasty breakfast. When he returned the little woman was ready to show him her claims, and she seemed to have forgotten those two who had been so ignominiously hauled away and dropped like unwanted cats beside the road. She inquired again about Casey's partners, and Casey lied once more and said that they had gone on over the range, prospecting.

I don't know why he did not tell the little woman that he had lied to Ole and Joe and let it go at that. But he seemed to dread having her discover that he had lied at all, and so he kept on lying about those three imaginary men. Perhaps he had a chivalrous instinct that she would feel safer, more at ease, if she thought that others were somewhere near. At any rate he did not tell her that his only partners were two burros and a mule.

I don't know what the little woman's opinion of Casey was, except that in the first enthusiasm of her gratitude to him she had called him a man and a gentleman. She drove a bargain with him, as she supposed. She would pay him so much more per day if he preferred to board himself, and having named the amount, Casey waited two minutes, as if he were meditating upon the matter, and then replied that it suited him all right.

Casey did not think much of her claims, though he did not tell her so. In his opinion that tunnel should have been driven into the hill at a different point, where the indications of mineral were much stronger and the distance to the contact much less. A light, varying vein had been followed at an incline, and Casey, working alone, was obliged to wheel every pound of dirt up a rather steep grade to the dump outside. The rock was hard to work in, so that it took him a full half a day to put in four shots, and then he would be likely to find that they had "bootlegged." The tunnel also faced the south, from where the wind nearly always blew, so that the gas and smoke from his shots would hang in there sometimes for a full twenty-four hours, making it impossible for him to work.

The little woman seemed slightly surprised when Casey told her, at the end of the first week, to knock off three days on account of gas. She and the little girl came to his camp next day and brought Casey a loaf of light bread and interrupted him in the act of shaving. The little woman looked at the two burros and at the mule, measured the camp outfit with her keen gray eyes, looked at Casey who had nicked his chin, and became thoughtful.

After that she stopped calling him Mr. Ryan and addressed him as Casey Ryan instead, with a little teasing inflection in her voice. Once Casey happened to mention Lund, and when he saw her look of surprise he explained that he drove a stage out of Lund, for awhile.

"Oh! So you *are* that Casey Ryan!" she said. "I might have known it." She laughed to herself, but she did not say why, and Casey was afraid to ask. He could remember so many incidents in his past that he would not want the little woman to know about, and he was afraid that it might be one of them at which she was laughing.

She formed the habit of coming up to the tunnel every day, with Babe chattering along beside her, swinging herself on her mother's hand. At first she said whimsically that she had found it best to keep an eye on her miners, as if that explained her coming. But she always had something good to eat or drink. Once she brought a small bucket of hot chocolate, which Casey gulped down heroically and smacked his lips afterwards. Casey hated chocolate, too, so I think you may take it for granted that by then he was a goner.

He used to smoke his pipe and watch the little woman and Babe go "high-grading" along the tunnel wall. That was what she called it and pretended that she expected to find very rich ore concealed somewhere. It struck him one day, quite suddenly, that the Little Woman (I may as well begin to use capitals, because Casey always called her that in his mind, and the capitals were growing bigger every day) the Little Woman never seemed to notice his smoking, or to realize that it is a filthy habit and immoral and degrading, as that other woman had done.

He began to notice other things, too; that the Little Woman helped him a lot, on afternoons when help was most likely to be appreciated. She sometimes "put down a hole" all by herself, skinning a knuckle now and then with the lightest "single-jack" and saying *"darn!"* quite as a matter of course.

And once, when the rock was particularly hard, she happened along and volunteered to turn the drill while Casey used the "double-jack", which I suppose you know is the big hammer that requires two hands to pound the drill while another turns it slightly after each blow, so that the bitted end will chew its way into hard rock.

You aren't all of you miners, so I will explain further that to drill into rock with a double-jack and steel drill is not sport for greenhorns exactly. The drill-turner needs a lot of faith and a little nerve, because one blow of the double-jack may break a hand clasped just below the head of the drill. And the man with the double-jack needs a steady nerve, too, and some experience in swinging the big hammer true to the head of the drill, —unless he enjoys cracking another man's bones.

Casey Ryan prides himself upon being able to swing a double-jack as well as any man in the country. It is his boast that he never yet broke the skin on the hand of his drill-turner. So I shall have to let you take it for granted that the Little Woman's presence and help was more unnerving than a wildcat on Casey's back. For, while the first, second and third blows fell true on the drill, the fourth went wild. Casey owns that he was in a cold sweat for fear he might hit her. So he did. She was squatted on her heels, steadying one elbow on her knee. The double-jack struck her hand, glanced and landed another blow on her knee; one of those terribly painful blows that take your breath and make you see stars without crippling you permanently.

Casey doesn't like to talk about it, but once he growled that he did about every damn-fool thing he could with a double-jack, except brain her. The Little Woman gave one small scream and went over backward in a faint, and Casey was just about ready to go off and shoot himself.

He took her up in his arms and carried her down to the cabin before she came to. And when she did come to her senses, Babe immediately made matters worse. She was whimpering beside her mother, and when she saw that mamma had waked up, she shrilled consolingly: "It's going to be all well in a minute. Casey Ryan kissed it des like *that!* So now it'll get all well!"

If the Little Woman had wanted to tell Casey what she thought of him, she couldn't just then, for Casey was halfway to his own camp by the time she glanced around the room, looking for him.

Common humanity drove him back, of course. He couldn't let a woman and a child starve to death just because he was a damned idiot and had half-killed the woman. But if there had been another person within calling distance, the Little Woman would probably never have seen Casey Ryan again.

Necessity has a bland way of ignoring such things as conventions and the human emotions. Casey cooked supper for Babe and the Little Woman, and washed the dishes, and wrung out cloths from hot vinegar and salt so that the Little Woman could bathe her knee-she had to do it left-handed, at that-and unbuttoned Babe's clothes and helped her on with her pyjamas and let her kneel on his lap while she said her prayers. Because, as Babe painstakingly explained, she always kneeled on a lap so ants couldn't run over her toes and tickle her and make her laugh, which would make God think she was a bad, naughty girl.

Can you picture Casey Ryan rocking that child to sleep? I can't —yes, I can too, and there's something in the picture that holds back the laugh you think will come.

Before she gave her final wriggle and cheeped her last little cheep, Babe had to be carried over and held down where she could kiss mamma good night. Casey got rather white around the mouth, then. But he didn't say a word. Indeed, he had said mighty little since that fourth blow of the double-jack; just enough to get along intelligently, with what he had to do. He hadn't even told the Little Woman he was sorry.

So Babe was asleep and tucked in her bed, and Casey turned down the light and asked perfunctorily if there was anything else he could do, and had started for the door. And then —

"Casey Ryan," called the Little Woman, with the teasing note in her voice. "Casey Ryan, come back here and listen to me. You are not going off like that to swear at yourself all night. Sit down in that chair and listen to me!"

Casey sat down, swallowing hard. All the Casey Ryan nonchalance was gone, —never had been with him, in fact, while he faced that Little Woman. Somehow she had struck him humble and dumb, from the very beginning. I wish I knew how she did it; I'd like to try it sometime myself.

"Casey Ryan, it's hard for a woman to own herself in the wrong, especially to a man," she said, when he had begun to squirm and wonder what biting words she would say. "I've always thought that I had as good nerve as any one. I have, usually. But that double-jack scared the life out of me after the first blow, and I thought I wouldn't let on. I couldn't admit I was afraid. I was terribly ashamed. I knew you'd never miss, but I was scared, just the same. And like a darn fool I pushed the drill away from me just as you struck. It was coming down-you couldn't change it, man alive. You'd aimed true at the drill, and-the drill wasn't just there at the moment. Serves me right. But it's tough on you, old boy-having to do the cooking for three of us while I'm laid up!"

I'm sure I can't see how Casey Ryan ever got the name of being a devil with the ladies. He certainly behaved like a yap then, if you get my meaning. He gave the Little Woman a quick, unwinking stare, looked away from her shamedly, reached for his plug of tobacco, took away his hand, swallowed twice, shuffled his feet and then grunted —I can use no other word for it:

"Aw, I guess I c'n stand it if you can!"

He made a motion then to rise up and go to his own camp where he would undoubtedly think of many tender, witty things that he would like to have spoken to the Little Woman. But she was watching him. She saw him move and stopped him with a question.

"Casey Ryan, tell me the truth about that tunnel. Do you think it's ever going to strike the ore body at all?"

Start Casey off on the subject of mining and you have him anchored and interested for an hour, at least. The Little Woman had brains, you must see that.

"Well, I don't want to discourage you, ma'am," Casey said reluctantly, the truth crowding against his teeth. "But I'd 'a' gone in under that iron capping, if I'd been doing it. The outcropping you followed in from the surface never has been in place, ma'am. It's what I'd call a wild stringer. It pinched out forty foot back of where we're diggin' now. That's just an iron stain we're following, and the pocket of high grade don't mean nothin'. You went in on the strength of indications —" He stopped there and chuckled to himself, in a way that I'd come to know as the "indications" of a story, —which usually followed.

The Little Woman probably guessed. I suppose she was lonely, too, and the pain of her hurts made her want entertainment. "What are you laughing at, Casey Ryan?" she demanded. "If it's funny, tell *me*."

Casey blushed, though she couldn't have seen him in the dusky light of the cabin. "Aw, it ain't anything much," he protested bashfully. "I just happened to think about a little ol' Frenchman I knowed once, over in Cripple Creek, ma'am." He stopped.

"Well? Tell me about the little ol' Frenchman. It made you laugh, Casey Ryan, and it's about the first time I've seen you do that. Tell me."

"Well, it ain't nothin' very funny to tell about," Casey hedged like a bashful boy; which was mighty queer for Casey Ryan, I assure you. For if there was anything Casey liked better than a funny story, it was some one to listen while he told it. "You won't git the kick, mebby. It's knowin' the Frenchman makes it seem kinda funny when I think about it. He was a good little man and he kept a little hotel and was an awful good cook. And he wanted a gold mine worse than anybody I ever seen. He didn't know a da-nothin' at all about minin' ma'am, but every ol' soak of a prospector could git a meal off him by tellin' him about some wildcat bonanza or other. He'd forgit to charge 'em, he'd be so busy listenin'.

"Well, there was two ol' soaks that got around him to grubstake 'em. They worked it all one year. They'd git a burro load of grub and go out somewheres and peck around till it was all et up, and then they'd come back an' tell Frenchy some wild tale about runnin' acrost what looked like the richest prospect in the country. They'd go on about havin' all the indications of a big body uh rich ore. He'd soak it in, an' they'd hang around town-one had a sore foot one time, I remember, that lasted 'em a month of good board at Frenchy's hotel before he drove 'em out agin to his mine, as he called it.

"They worked that scheme on him for a long time-and it was the only da-scheme they wasn't too lazy to work. They'd git money to buy powder an' fuse an' caps, ma'am, an' blow it on booze, y'see. An' they'd hang in town, boardin' off Frenchy, jest as long as they c'ld think of an excuse fer stayin'.

"So somebody tipped Frenchy off that he was bein' worked for grub an' booze money, an' Frenchy done a lot uh thinkin'. Next time them two come in, he was mighty nice to 'em. An' when he finally got 'em pried loose an' headed out, he appeared suddenly and says he's goin along to take a look at his mine. They couldn't do nothin' but take him, uh course. So they led him out to an old location hole somebody else had dug, an' they showed him iron cappin' an' granite contact an' so on-just talkin' wild, an' every few minutes comin' in with the 'strong indications of a rich ore body.' That was their trump suit, y'see, ma'am.

"Frenchy listened, an' his eyes commenced to snap, but he never said nothin' for awhile. Then all at once he pulled one uh these ol'-style revolvers an' points it at 'em, an' yells: *'Indicaziones! Indicaziones!* T'ell weez your *indicaziones!* Now you show me zee me-*tall!*'" Casey stopped, reached for his plug and remembered that he mustn't. The Little Woman laughed. She didn't seem to need the tapering off of the story, as most women demand.

"And so you think I have plenty of *indicaziones*, but mighty little chance of getting the me-*tall*," she pointed the moral. "Well, then tell me what to do."

It was in the telling, I think, that Casey for the first time forgot to be shy and became his real, Casey Ryan best. The Little Woman saw at once, when he pointed it out to her, that she ought to drift and cut under the iron capping instead of tunnelling away from it as they had been doing.

But she was not altogether engrossed in that tunnel. I think her prospecting into the soul of Casey Ryan interested her much more; and being a woman she followed the small outcropping of his Irish humor and opened up a distinct vein of it before the evening was over. Just to convince you, she led him on until Casey told her all about feeding his Ford syrup instead of oil, and all about how it ran over him a few times on the dry lake, —Casey was secretly made happy because she saw at once how easily that could happen, and never once doubted that he was sober! He told her about the goats in Patmos and made her laugh so hard that Babe woke and whimpered a little, and insisted that Casey take her up and rock her again in the old homemade chair with crooked juniper branches hewn for rockers.

With Babe in his arms he told her, too, about his coming out to hunt the Injun Jim mine. He must have felt pretty well acquainted, by then, because he regaled her with a painstaking, Caseyish description of Lucy Lily and her educated wardrobe, and-because she was a murderous kind of squaw and entitled to no particular chivalry-even repeated her manner of proposing to a white man, and her avowed reason and all. That was going pretty far, I think, for one evening, but we must keep in mind the fact that Casey and the Little Woman had met almost a month before this, and that Casey had merely thrown wide open the little door to his real self.

At any rate it was after ten o'clock by Casey's Ingersoll when he tucked Babe into her little bed, brought a jelly glass of cold water for the Little Woman to drink in the night, and started for the door.

There he stopped for a minute, debated with his shyness and turned back.

"You mebby moved that steel at the wrong time," he said abruptly, "I guess you musta, the way it happened. But I was so scared I'd hit yuh, my teeth was playin' the dance to *La Paloma*. I was in a cold sweat. I never did hit a man with a double-jack in my life, and I guess I've put down ten miles uh holes, ma'am, if you placed 'em end to end. I always made it my brag I never scraped a knuckle at that game. But-them little hands of yours on the drill —I was shakin' all over for fear I might-hurt yuh. I —I never hated anything so bad in my life —I'd ruther kill a dozen men than hurt you —"

"Man alive," the Little Woman exclaimed softly from her dusky corner, "you'd never have hurt me in the world, if I'd had the nerve to trust you." And she added softly, "I'll trust you, from now on, Casey Ryan. Always."

I think Casey was an awful fool to walk out and never let her know that he heard that "Always."

"Casey Ryan," the Little Woman began with her usual abruptness one evening, when she was able to walk as far as the mine and back without feeling; the effect of the exercise, but was still nursing a bandaged right hand; "Casey Ryan, tell me again just what old Injun Jim looked like."

Casey laughed and shifted Babe to a more secure perch on his shoulder, and drew his head to one side in an effort to slacken Babe's terrific pull on his hair. "Him? Mean an' ornery as the meanest thing you can think of. Sour as a dough can you've went off an' left for a coupla weeks in July."

"Oh, yes; very explicit, I admit. But just what did he look like? Height, weight, age and chief characteristics. I have," she explained, "a very-good reason for wanting a description of him."

"What yuh want a description of him for? He's good an' dead now." You see, Casey had reached the point of intimacy where he could argue with the Little Woman quite in his everyday Irish spirit of contention.

The Little Woman had spirit of her own, but she was surprisingly meek with Casey at times. "It struck me quite suddenly, to-day, that I may know where that gold mine is; or about where it is," she said, with a hidden excitement in her voice. "I've been thinking all day about it, and putting two and two together. I merely need a fair description now of Injun Jim, to feel tolerably certain that I do or do not know something about the location of that mine."

"How'd *you* come to know anything about it?" Casey stopped to move Babe to his other shoulder. He had put in a long hard day in the tunnel, and Babe was a husky youngster for four-and-a-half. Also she had developed a burr-like quality toward Casey, and she liked so well to be carried home from the mine that she would sit flat on the ground and rock her small body and weep until she was picked, up and placed on Casey's shoulder. "Set still, now, Babe, or Casey'll have to put yuh down an' make yuh walk home. Le'go my ear! Yuh want Casey to go around lop-sided, with only one ear?"

"Yes!" assented Babe eagerly, kicking Casey in the stomach. "Give me your knife, Casey Wyan, so I can cut off one ear an' *make* you lop-sided!"

"An' you'd do it, too!" Casey exclaimed admiringly.

"Baby Girl, you interrupted mother when mother was speaking of something important. You make mother very sad."

Babe's mouth puckered, her eyelids puckered, and she give a small wail. "Now Baby's sad! You hurt-my —*feelin's* when you speak to me cross!" She shook her yellow curls into her eyes and wept against them.

There was no hope of grown-ups talking about anything so foolish as a gold mine when Babe was in that mood. So Casey cooked supper, washed the dishes and helped Babe into her pyjamas; then he let her kneel restively in his lap while she said her prayers, and told her a story while he rocked her to sleep-it was a funny, Caseyish story about a bear, but we haven't time for it now-before he attempted to ask the Little Woman again what she meant by her mysterious curiosity concerning Injun Jim. Then, when he had his pipe going and the stove filled with piñon wood, he turned to her with the question in his eyes.

The Little Woman laughed. "Now, if that terrible child will kindly consent to sleep for fifteen minutes, *I'll* tell you what I meant," she said. "It had slipped my mind altogether, and it was only to-day, when Babe was scratching out a snake's track-so the snake couldn't find the way back home, she said-that I chanced to remember. Just a small thing, you know, that may or may not mean *something* very large and *important* —like a gold mine, for instance."

"I don't have to go to work 'til sunup," Casey hinted broadly, "and I've set up many a night when I wasn't havin' half as much fun as I git listenin' to you talk."

Again the Little Woman laughed. I think she had been rambling along just to bait Casey into something like that."

"Very well, then, I'll come to the point. Though it is such a luxury to talk, sometimes! For a woman, that is.

"Three years ago we had two burros to pack water from your gulch, where there were too many snakes, to this gulch where there never seemed to be so many. We hadn't developed this spring then. One night something or other frightened the burros and they disappeared, and I started out to find them, leaving Babe of course with her father at the tunnel.

"I trailed those burros along the mountain for about four miles, I should think. And by that time I was wishing I had taken a canteen with me, though when I started out from camp I hated the thought of being burdened with the weight of it. I thought I could find water in some of the gulches, however, so I climbed a certain ridge and sat down to rest and examine the canyon beneath with that old telescope Babe plays with. It has been dropped so many times it's worthless now, but three years ago you could see a lizard run across a rock a mile away. Don't you believe that?" she stopped to demand sternly.

"Say! You couldn't tell me nothin' I wouldn't believe!" Casey retorted, fussing with his pipe to hide the grin on his face.

"This is the truth, as it happens. I merely speak of the lizard to convince you that a man's features would show very distinctly in the telescope. And please observe, Casey Ryan, that I am very serious at the moment. This may be important to you, remember.

"I was sitting among a heap of boulders that capped the ridge, and it happened that I was pretty well concealed from view because I was keeping in the shade of a huge rock and had crouched down so that I could steady the telescope across a flat rock in front of me. So I was not discovered by a man down in the canyon whom I picked up with the telescope while I was searching the canyon side for a spring.

"The man was suddenly revealed to me as he parted the branches of a large greasewood and peered out. I think it was the stealthiness of his manner that impressed me most. He looked up and down and across, but he did not see me. After a short wait, while he seemed to be listening, he crept out from behind the bush, turned and lifted forward a bag which hadn't much in it, yet appeared quite heavy. He went down into the canyon, picking his way carefully and stepping on rocks, mostly. But in one place where he must cross a wash of deep sand, he went backward and with a dead branch he had picked up among the rocks he scratched out each track as he made it. Babe reminded me of that to-day when she scratched out the snake's track in the sand up by the mine."

Casey was leaning toward her, listening avidly, his pipe going cold in his hand. "Was he —?"

"He was an Indian, and very old, and he walked with that bent, tottery walk of old age. He had one eye and —"

"Injun Jim, that was-couldn't be anybody else!" Casey knocked his pipe against the front of the little cookstove, emptying the half-burned tobacco into the hearth. The Little Woman probably wondered why he seemed so unexcited, but she did not know all of Casey's traits. He put away his pipe and almost immediately reached for his plug of tobacco, taking a chew without remembering where he was. "If you feel able to ride," he said, "I'll ketch up the mule in the morning, and we'll go over there."

"So your heart is really set on finding it, after all. I've been wondering about that. You haven't seemed to be thinking much about it, lately."

"A feller can prospect," Casey declared, "when he can't do nothin' else." And he added rather convincingly, "Good jobs is scarce, out this way. I'd be a fool to pass up this one, when I'd have the hull winter left fer prospectin'."

"And what about those partners of yours?"

"Oh, them?" Casey hesitated, tempted perhaps to tell the truth. "Oh, they've quit on me. They quit right away after I went to work. We-we had a kinda fuss, and they've went back to town." He stopped and added with a sigh of relief, "We can just as well count them out, fr'm now on-an' fergit about 'em."

"Oh," said the Little Woman, and smiled to herself. "Well, if you are anxious about that patch of brush in the canyon, we'll go and see what's behind it. To-morrow is Sunday, anyway."

"I'd a made up the time, if it wasn't," Casey assured her with dignity. "I've been waitin' a good many years for a look at that Injun Jim gold."

"And it's just possible that I have been almost within reach of it for the past four years and didn't know it! Well, I always have believed that Fate weaves our destinies for us; and a curious pattern is the weaving, sometimes! I'll go with you, Casey Ryan, and I hope, for your sake, that Indian Jim's mine is behind that clump of bushes. And I hope," she added, with a little laugh whose meaning was not clear to Casey, "I hope you get a million dollars out of it! I should like to point to Casey Ryan, the mining millionaire and say, 'That plutocratic gentleman over there once knocked me down with a hammer, and washed my dishes for two weeks, and really, my dears, you should taste his sour-dough biscuits!'"

Casey went away to his camp and lay awake a long time, not thinking about the Injun Jim mine, if you please, but wondering what he had done to make the Little Woman give him hell about his biscuits. Good Lord! Did she still blame him for hitting her with that double-jack? —when he knew and she knew that she had made him do it! —and if she didn't like his sour-dough biscuits, why in thunder had she kept telling him she did?

He tucked the incident away in the back of his mind, meaning to watch her and find out just what she did mean, anyway. Her opinion of him had become vital to Casey; more vital than the Injun Jim mine, even.

He saddled the buckskin mule next morning and after breakfast the three set out, with a lunch and two canteens of water. The Little Woman was in a very good humor and kept Casey "jumpin' sideways," as he afterwards confessed to me, wondering just what she meant or whether she meant nothing at all by her remarks concerning his future wealth and dignity and how he would forget old friends.

She even pretended she had forgotten the place, and was not at all sure that this was the right canyon, when they came to it. She studied landmarks and then said they were all wrong and that the place was marked in her mind by something entirely different and not what she first named. She deviled Casey all she could, and led him straight to the spot and suggested that they eat their lunch there, within twenty feet of the bushes from which she had seen the Indian creep with the sack on his back.

She underrated Casey's knowledge of minerals; or perhaps she wanted to test it, —you never can tell what a woman really has in the back of her mind. Casey sat there eating a sour-dough biscuit of his own making, and staring at the steep wall of the canyon because he was afraid to stare at the Little Woman, and so his uncannily keen eye saw a bit of rock no larger than Babe's fist. It lay just under that particular clump of bushes, in the shade. And in the shade he saw a yellow gleam on the rock.

He looked at the Little Woman then and grinned, but he didn't say anything until he had taken the coffeepot off the fire, and had filled her cup.

"This ain't a bad canyon to prospect in. You can brush up your memory whilst I take a look around. Mebby I can find Jim's mine myself," he said impudently. Then he got up and went poking here and there with his prospector's pick, and finally worked up to the brush and disappeared behind it. In five minutes or less he came back to her with a little nugget the size of Babe's thumb.

"If yuh want to see something pretty, come on up where I got this here," he told her. "I'll show yuh what drives prospectors crazy. This ain't no free gold country, but there's a pile uh gold in a dirt bank I can show yuh. Mebby you forgot the place, and mebby yuh didn't. I've quit guessin' at what yuh really do mean an' what yuh don't mean. Anyway, this is where we headed for."

"Well, you really are a prospector, after all. I just wondered." The Little Woman did not seem in the least embarrassed. She just laughed and took Babe by the hand, and they went up beyond the clump of bushes to what lay hidden so cunningly behind it.

Cunning-that was the mood Nature must have been in when she planted free gold in that little wrinkle on the side of Two Peak, and set the bushes in the mouth of the draw, and piled an iron ledge across the top and spread barren mountainside all around it. In the hiding Injun Jim had done his share, too. He had pulled rubble down over the face of the bank of richness, and eyes less keen than Casey's would have passed it by without a second glance.

The Little Woman knelt and picked out half a dozen small nuggets and stood up, holding them out to Casey, her eyes shining. "Casey Ryan, here's the end of your rainbow! And you're luckier than most of us; you've got your pot o' gold."

Casey looked down at her oddly. "It's mebby the end of one," he said. "But they's another one, now, 't I can see plainer than this one. I dunno's I'll ever git to where that one points."

"A man's never satisfied," scoffed the Little Woman, turning the precious little yellow fragments over thoughtfully in her palm. "I should think this ought to be enough for you, man alive."

"Mebby it had. But it ain't." He looked at her, hesitating,—and I think the Little Woman waited and held her breath for what he might say next. But Casey was scarcely himself in her presence. He turned away without another glance at the nuggets.

"You'n the kid can gopher around there whilst I go step off the lines of a claim an' put up the location notice," he said, and left her standing there with the gold in her palm.

That night it was the Little Woman who planned great things for Casey, and it was Casey who smoked and said little about it. But once he shook his head when she described the gilded future she saw for him.

"Money in great gobs like that ain't much use to me," he demurred. "Once I blew into Lund, over here, with twenty-five thousand dollars in my pocket that I got outa silver claims. All I ever saved outa that chunk was two pairs of socks. No need of you makin' plans on my being a millionaire. It ain't in me. I guess I'm nothin' but a rough-neck stagedriver an' prospector, clear into the middle of my bones. If I had the sense of a rabbit I never'd gone hellin' through life the way I've done. I'd amount to somethin' by now. As it is I ain't nothin' and I ain't nobody—"

"You're Casey Wyan! You make me sad when you say that!" Babe protested sleepily, lifting her head from his shoulder and spatting him reprovingly on the cheek. "You're my bes' friend and you've got a lots more sense than a wabbit!"

"And your rainbow, Casey Ryan?" the Little Woman asked softly. "What about this other, new rainbow?"

"It's there," said Casey gloomily. "It'll always be there-jest over the ridge ahead uh me. I c'n see it, plain enough, but I got more sense 'n to think I'll ever git m'hands on it."

"I'll go catch your wainbow, Casey Wyan. I'll run fas' as I can, an' I'll catch it for you!"

"Will yuh, Babe?" Casey bent his head until his lips touched her curls. And neither Casey nor the Little Woman spoke of it again.

Oddly enough, it was Lucy Lily who unconsciously brought Casey to his rainbow. Lucy Lily did not mean to do Casey any favor, I can assure you, but Fate just took her and used her for the moment, and Lucy Lily had nothing to say about it.

Don't think that a squaw who wants to live like a white princess will forget to go hunting a gold mine whose richness she had seen, —in a lard bucket, perhaps. Lucy Lily did not abandon her bait. She used it again, and a renegade white man snapped at it, worse luck. So they went hunting through the Tippipahs for the mine of Injun Jim. What excuses the squaw made for not being able to lead the man directly to the spot, I can't say, of course; but I suppose she invented plenty.

She did one clever thing, at least. In their wanderings she led the way into the old camp of Injun Jim. There had been no storm to dim the tracks Casey had made, and Lucy Lily, Indian that she was, knew that these were the tracks of Casey Ryan and guessed what was his errand there. So she and her white man trailed him across the valley to Two Peak.

They came first to the camp, and there the Little Woman met them, and by some canny intuition knew who they were and what they wanted, —thanks to Casey's garrulous mood when he told her of Lucy Lily. They said that they were hunting horses, and presently went on over the ridge; not following Casey's plain trail to the tunnel, but riding off at an angle so that they could come into the trail once they were hidden from the house.

Casey, as it happened, was not at the tunnel at all, but over at the gold mine, doing the location work. Doing it in the side hill a good two hundred feet away from the gold streak, too, I will add.

The Little Woman watched until the squaw and her man were out of sight, and then she took a small canteen and filled it, got her rifle, pocketed her automatic revolver, and tied Babe's sunbonnet firmly under Babe's double chin. She could not take the mule, because Casey had ridden him, so she walked, and carried Babe most of the way on her back. She kept to the gulches until she was too far away to be seen in the sage, even when a squaw was squinting sharp-eyed after her.

She came, in the course of two hours or so, to the lip of the canyon, and who-whooed to Casey, mucking out after a shot he had put down in the location hole. Casey looked up, waved his hand and then came running. No whim would send the Little Woman on a four-mile walk with a heavy child like Babe to carry, and Casey was as white as he'll ever get when he met her halfway to the bottom of the canyon.

"Take Babe and let's get back to the claim," she panted. "I came to tell you that squaw is on your trail with a white man in tow, and it'll be a case of claim-jumping if they can see their way tolerably clear. He's a mate for the two you helped me haul out of camp, and I think, Casey Ryan, the squaw would kill you in a minute if she gets the chance."

Casey did rather a funny thing, considering how scared he was usually of the Little Woman. "You pack that kid all the way over here?" he grunted, and picked up the Little Woman and carried her, and left Babe to walk. Of course he helped Babe, holding her hand over the roughest spots, but it was the Little Woman whom he carried the rest of the way. And Babe, if you please, was quite calm about it and never once became "sad" so that she must sit down and cry.

"All the claim-jumpin' they'll do won't hurt nobody," Casey observed unexcitedly, when he had set the Little Woman down on a rock beside his location "cut" in the canyon's side. "She likely picked on a white man so's he could locate under the law, but this claim's located a'ready." He waved a hand toward the monument, a few rods up the canyon. "And Casey Ryan ain't spreadin' no rich gold vein wide open for every prowlin' desert rat to pack off all he kin stagger under. I'm callin' it the Devil's Lantern. You c'n call a mine any name yuh darn want to. And if it wasn't fer the Devil's Lantern, I wouldn't be here. That name won't mean nothin' to 'em. Let 'em come." His eyes turned toward the hidden richness and dwelt there, studying the tracks, big and little, that led up to it, and deciding that tracks do not necessarily mean a gold mine, and that it would be better to leave them as they were and not attempt to cover them.

"You just say it's your claim, if they come snoopin' around here. I'm supposed to be workin' for yuh," he said abruptly, giving her one of his quick, steady glances.

"They can go and read the location notice," the Little Woman pointed out. Casey did not make any reply to that, but picked up his shovel and went to work again, mucking out the dirt and broken rocks which the dynamite had loosened in the cut.

"She's a bird, ain't she?" he grinned over his shoulder, his mind reverting to Lucy Lily. "Did she have on her war paint?"

"She will have, when she sees you," the Little Woman retorted, watching the farther rim of the canyon. Then she remembered Babe and called to her. That youngster was always prospecting around on her own initiative, and she answered shrilly now from up the canyon. The Little Woman stood up, looking that way, never dreaming how wishfully Casey was watching her, —and how reverently.

"Baby Girl, you must not run off like that! Mother will be compelled to tie a rope on you."

"I was jes' getting-Casey Wyan's —'bacco. Poor Casey Wyan forgot-his 'bacco! He's my frien'. I have to give him his 'bacco," Babe defended herself, coming down from the location monument in small jumps and scrambles. Close to her importantly heaving chest she clutched a small, red tobacco can of the kind which smokers carelessly call "P.A." "Casey Wyan lost it up in the wocks," Babe explained, when her mother met her disapprovingly and caught her by the hand.

"Why, Babe! You've been naughty. This must be Casey Ryan's location notice. It must be left in the rocks, Baby Girl, so people will know that Casey Ryan owns this claim."

"It's his 'bacco!" Babe insisted stubbornly. "Casey Wyan needs his 'bacco."

The Little Woman knew that streak of stubbornness of old. There was just one way to deal with it, and that was to prove to Babe that she was mistaken. So she opened the red can and pulled out a folded paper, unfolded the paper and began to read it aloud. Not that Babe would understand it all, but to make it seem very convincing and important, —and I think partly to enjoy for herself the sense of Casey's potential wealth.

"'Notice of Location-Quartz,'" she read, and glanced over the paper at her listening small daughter. "'To Whom it May Concern: Please take notice that: The name of this claim is the Devil's Lantern Quartz Mining Claim. Said Claim is situated in the-Unsurveyed-Mining District, County of Nye, State of Nevada. Located this twenty-fifth day of September, 19 — .This discovery is made and this notice is posted this twenty-fifth day of September,19 —.

"'2. That the undersigned locators are citizens of he United States or have declared their intention to become such, and have discovered mineral-bearing rock —!'"

"What's mineral-bearing wock, mother?"

"That's the gold, Baby Girl. ' —in place thereon and do locate and claim same for mining purposes.

"'3. That the number of linear feet in length along the course of the vein each way from the point of discovery whereon we have erected a monument —'That's the monument, up there, and Babe must not touch it — ' —is Easterly 950 feet; Westerly 550 feet; that the total length does not exceed 1500 feet. That the width on the Southerly side is 300 feet; that the width on the Northerly side is 300 feet; that the end lines are parallel; that the general course of the vein or lode as near as may be is in an Easterly and Westerly direction; that the boundaries of this claim may be readily traced and are defined as follows, to-wit: —!'"

She skipped a lot of easterly and westerly technique in Casey's clear, uncompromising hand-writing-done in an indelible pencil-and came down to the last paragraph:

"'That all the dips, variations, spurs, angles and all veins, ledges, or deposits within the lines of said claim, together with all water and timber and any other rights appurtenant, allowed by the law of this State or of the United States are hereby claimed.

"'Locators
Jack I. Gleason,
Margaret Sutten.'

"Why-why-y—Good Lord!"
"Here they come," Casey called at that moment. "Put 'er back in the monument and don't let on like we think they're after this claim at all. It's a darn sight harder to start a fuss when the other fellow don't act like he knows there's any fuss comin'. You ask anybody that ever had a fight."

The Trail of the White Mule

Chapter I

Casey Ryan, hunched behind the wheel of a large, dark blue touring car with a kinked front fender and the glass gone from the left headlight, slid out from the halted traffic, shied sharply away from a hysterically clanging street car, crossed the path of a huge red truck coming in from his right, missed it with two inches to spare and was halfway down the block before the traffic officer overtook him.

The traffic officer was Irish too, and bigger than Casey, and madder. For all that, Casey offered to lick the livin' tar outa him before accepting a pale, expensive ticket which he crumbled and put into his pocket without looking at it.

"What I know about these here fancy city rules ain't sufficient to give a horn-toad a headache-but it's a darn sight more'n I care," Casey declaimed hotly. "I never was asked what I thought of them tin signs you stick up on the end of a telegraft pole, to tell folks when to go an' when to quit goin'. Mebby it's all right fer these here city drivers —"

"This'll mean thirty days for you," spluttered the officer. "I ought to call the patrol right now —"

"Get the undertaker on the line first!" Casey advised him ominously.

Traffic was piling up behind them, and horns were honking a blatant chorus that extended two blocks up the street. The traffic officer glanced into the troubled gray eyes of the Little Woman beside Casey and took his foot off the running board.

"Better go put up your bail and then forfeit it," he advised in a milder tone. "The judge will probably remember you; I do, and my memory ain't the best in the world. Twice you've been hooked for speeding through traffic; and parking by fire-plugs and in front of the No Park signs and after four, seems to be your big outdoor sport. Forfeit your bail, old boy-or it's thirty days for you, sure."

Casey Ryan made bitter retort, but the traffic cop had gone to untangle two furious Fords from a horse-drawn mail wagon, so he did not hear. Which was good luck for Casey.

"Why do you persist in making trouble for yourself?" the Little Woman beside him exclaimed. "It can't be so hard to obey the rules; other drivers do. I know that I have driven this car all over town without any trouble whatever."

Casey hogged the next safety-zone line to the deep disgust of a young movie star in a cream-and-silver racer, and pulled in to the curb just where he could not be passed.

"All right, ma'am. You can drive, then." He slid out of the driver's seat to the pavement, his face a deeper shade of red than usual.

"For pity's sake, Casey! Don't be silly," his wife cried sharply, a bit of panic in her voice.

"You was in a hurry to git home," Casey pointed out to her with that mildness of manner which is not mild. "I was hurryin', wasn't I?"

"You aren't hurrying now-you're delaying the traffic again. Do be reasonable! You know it costs money to argue with the police."

"Police be damned! I'm tryin' to please a woman, an' I'm up agin a hard proposition. You can ask anybody if I'm the unreasonable one. You hustled me out of the show soon as the huggin' commenced. You wouldn't even let me stay to see the first of Mutt and Jeff. You said you was in a hurry. I leaves the show without seein' the best part, gits the car an' drills through the traffic tryin' to git yuh home quick. Now you're kickin' because I did hurry."

"Hey! Whadda yuh mean, blockin' the traffic?" a domineering voice behind him bellowed. "This ain't any reception hall, and it ain't no free auto park neither."

Another traffic officer with another pencil and another pad of tickets such as drivers dread to see began to write down the number of Casey's car. This man did not argue. He finished his work briskly, presented another notice which advised Casey Ryan to report immediately to police headquarters, waved Casey peremptorily to proceed, and returned to his little square platform to the chorus of blatting automobile horns.

"The cops in this town hands out tickets like they was Free Excursion peddlers!" snorted Casey, his eyes a pale glitter behind his half-closed lids. "They can go around me, or they can honk and be darned to 'em. Git behind the wheel, ma'am-Casey Ryan's drove the last inch he'll ever drive in this darned town. If they pinch me again, it'll have to be fer walkin'."

The Little Woman looked at him, pressed her lips together and moved behind the wheel. She did not say a word all the way out to the white apartment house on Vermont which held the four rooms they called home. She parked the car dexterously in front and led the way to their apartment (ground floor, front) before she looked at me.

"It's coming to a show-down, Jack," she said then with a faint smile. "He's on probation already for disobeying traffic rules of one sort and other, and his fines cost more than the entire upkeep of the car. I think he really will have to go to jail this time. It just isn't in Casey Ryan to take orders from any one, especially when his own personal habits of driving a car are concerned."

"Town life is getting on his nerves," I tried to defend Casey, and at the same time to comfort the Little Woman. "I didn't think it would work, his coming here to live, with nothing to do but spend money. This is the inevitable result of too much money and too much leisure."

"It sounds much better, putting it that way," murmured Mrs. Casey. "I think you're right-though he did behave back there as if it were too much matrimony. Jack, he's been looking forward to your visit. I'm sorry this has happened to spoil it."

"It isn't spoiled," I grinned. "Casey Ryan is, always and ever shall be Casey Ryan. He's running true to form, though tamer than one would expect. When do you think he'll show up?"

Mrs. Casey did not know. She ventured a guess or two, but there was no conviction in her tone. With two nominal arrests in five minutes chalked against him, and with his first rebellion against the Little Woman to rankle in his conscience and memory, she owned herself at a loss.

With a cheerfulness that was only conversation deep, we waited for Casey and finally ate supper without him. The evening was enlivened somewhat by Babe's chatter of kindergarten doings; and was punctuated by certain pauses while steps on the sidewalk passed on or ended with the closing of another door than the Ryans'. I fought the impulse to call up the police station, and I caught the eyes of the Little Woman straying unconsciously to the telephone in the hall while she talked of things remote from our inner thoughts. Margaret Ryan is game, I'll say that. We played cribbage for an hour or two, and the Little Woman beat me until finally I threw up my hands and quit.

"I can't stand it any longer, Mrs. Casey. Do you think he's in jail, or just sulking at a movie somewhere?" I blurted. "Forgive my butting in, but I wish you'd talk about it. You know you can, to me. Casey Ryan is a friend and more than a friend: he's a pet theory of mine —a fad, if you prefer to call him that.

"I consider him a perfect example of human nature in its unhampered, unbiased state, going straight through life without deviating a hair's breadth from the viewpoint of youth. A fighter and a castle builder; a sort of rough-edged Peter Pan. Till he gums soft food and hobbles with a stick because the years have warped his back and his legs, Casey Ryan will keep that indefinable, bubbling optimism of spiritual youth. So tell me all about him. I want to know who has licked, so far; luxury or Casey Ryan."

The Little Woman laughed and picked up the cards, evening their edges with sensitive fingers that had not been manicured so beautifully when first I saw them.

"Well-sir," she drawled, making one word of the two and failing to keep a little twitching from her lips, "I think it's been about a tie, so far. As a husband-Casey's a darned good bachelor." Her chuckle robbed that statement of anything approaching criticism. "Aside from his insisting on cooking breakfast every morning and feeding me in bed, forcing me to eat fried eggs and sour-dough hotcakes swimming in butter and honey-when I crave grapefruit and thin toast and one French lamb chop with a white paper frill on the handle and garnished with fresh parsley-he's the soul of consideration. He wants four kinds of jam on the table every meal, when fresh fruit is going to waste. He's bullied the laundryman until the poor fellow's reached the point where he won't stop if the car's parked in front and Casey's liable to be home; but aside from that, Casey's all right.

"After serving time in the desert and rustling my own wood and living on bacon and beans and sour-dough bread, I'm perfectly willing to spend the rest of my life doing painless house-keeping with all the modern built-in features ever invented; and buying my bread and cakes and salads from the delicatessen around the corner. I never want to see a sagebush again as long as I live, or feel the crunch of gravel under my feet. I expect to die in French-heeled pumps and embroidered silk stockings and the finest, silliest silk things ever put in a show window to tempt the soul of a woman. But it took just two weeks and three days to drive Casey back to his sour-dough can."

"He craved luxury more than you seemed to do," I remembered aloud.

"He did, yes. But his idea of luxury is sitting down in the kitchen to a real meal of beans and biscuits and all the known varieties of jam and those horrible whitewashed store cookies and having the noise of the phonograph drowned every five minutes by a passing street car. Casey wants four movies a day, and he wants them all funny. He brings home silk shirts with the stripes fairly shrieking when he unwraps them-and he has to be thrown and tied to get a collar on him.

"He will get up at any hour of the night to chase after a fire engine, and every whipstitch he gets pinched for doing something which is perfectly lawful and right in the desert and perfectly awful in the city. You saw him," said the Little Woman, "to-day." And she added wistfully, "It's the first time since we were married that he has ever talked back-to me.

"And you know," she went on, shuffling the cards and stopping to regard the joker attentively (though I am sure she didn't know what card she was looking at), "just chasing around town and doing nothing but square yourself for not playing according to the rules costs money without getting you anywhere. Fifty-five thousand dollars isn't so much just to play with, in this town. Casey's highest ambition now seems to be nickel disk wheels on a new racing car that can make the speed cops go some to catch him. His idea of economy is to put six or seven thousand dollars into a car that will enable him to outrun a twenty-dollar fine!

"We have some money invested," she went on. "We own this apartment house-and fortunately it's in my name. So long as the housing problem continues critical, I think I can keep Casey going without spending our last cent."

"He did one good stroke of business," I ventured, "when he bought this place. Apartment houses are good as gold mines these days."

The Little Woman laughed. "Well-sir, it wasn't so much a stroke as it was a wallop. Casey bought it just to show who was boss, he or the landlord. The first thing he did when we moved in was to take down the nicely framed rules that said we must not cook cabbage nor onions nor fish, nor play music after ten o'clock at night, nor do any loud talking in the halls.

"Every day for a week Casey cooked cabbage, onions and fish. He sat up nights to play the graphophone. He stayed home to talk loudly and play bucking bronk with Babe all up and down the stairs and in the halls. Our rent was paid for a month in advance, and the landlord was too little and old to fight. So he sold out cheap-and it really was a good stroke of business for us, though not deliberate.

"Well-sir, at first we lost tenants who didn't enjoy the freedom of their neighbors' homes. But really, Jack, you'd be surprised to know how many people in this city just LOVE cabbage and onions and fish, and to have children they needn't disown whenever they go house-hunting. I had ventilator hoods put over every gas range in the house, and turned the back yard into a playground with plenty of sand piles and swings. I raised the price, too, and made the place look very select, with a roof garden for the grown-ups. We have the house filled now with really nice families-avoiding the garlic brand-and as an investment I wouldn't ask for anything better.

"Casey enjoyed himself hugely while he was whipping things into shape, but the last month he's been going stale. The tenants are all so thankful to do as they please that they're excru-ciatingly polite to him, no matter what he does or says. He's tired of the beaches and he has begun to cuss the long, smooth roads that are signed so that he couldn't get lost if he tried. It does seem as if there's no interest left in anything, unless he can get a kick out of going to jail. And, Jack, I do believe he's gone there."

The telephone rang and the Little Woman excused herself and went into the hall, closing the door softly behind her.

I'm not greatly given to reminiscence, but while I sat and watched the flames of civilization licking tamely at the impregnable iron bark of the gas logs, the eyes of my memory looked upon a picture:

Desert, empty and with the mountains standing back against the sky, the great dipper up-tilted over a peak and the stars bending close for very friendliness. The licking flames of dry greasewood burning, with a pungent odor in my nostrils when the wind blew the smoke my way. The far-off hooting of an owl, perched somewhere on a juniper branch watching for mice; and Casey Ryan sitting cross-legged in the sand, squinting humorously at me across the fire while he talked.

I saw him, too, bolting a hurried breakfast under a mesquite tree in the chill before sunrise, his mind intent upon the trail; facing the desert and its hardships as a matter of course, with never a thought that other men would shrink from the ordeal.

I saw him kneeling before a solid face of rock in a shallow cut in the hillside, swinging his "single-jack" with tireless rhythm; a tap and a turn of the steel, a tap and a turn-chewing tobacco industriously and stopping now and then to pry off a fresh bit from the plug in his hip pocket before he reached for the "spoon" to muck out the hole he was drilling.

I saw him larruping in his Ford along a sandy, winding trail it would break a snake's back to follow, hot on the heels of his next adventure, dreaming of the fortune that finally came. . . .

The Little Woman came in looking as if she had been talking with Destiny and was still dazed and unsteady from the meeting.

"Well-sir, he's gone!" she announced, and stopped and tried to smile. But her eyes looked hurt and sorry. "He has bought a Ford and a tent and outfit since he left us down on Seventh and Broadway, and he just called me up on long-distance from San Bernardino. He's going out on a prospecting trip, he says. I'll say he's been going some! A speed cop overhauled him just the other side of Claremont, he told me, and he was delayed for a few minutes while he licked the cop and kicked him and his motorcycle into a ditch. He says he's sorry he sassed me, and if I can drive a car in this darned town and not spend all my loose change paying fines, I'm a better man than he is. He doesn't know when he'll be back-and there you are."

She sat down wearily on the arm of an over-stuffed armchair and looked up at the gilt-and-onyx clock which I suspected Casey of having bought. "If he isn't lynched before morning," she sighed whimsically, "he'll probably make it to the Nevada line all right."

I rose, also glancing at the clock. But the Little Woman put up a hand to forbid the plan she read in my mind.

"Let him alone, Jack," she advised. "Let him go and be just as wild and devilish as he wants to be. I'm only thankful he can take it out on a Ford and a pick and shovel. There really isn't any trouble between us two. Casey knows I can look out for myself for awhile. He's got to have a vacation from loafing and matrimony. I'm so thankful he isn't taking it in jail!"

I told her somewhat bluntly that she was a brick, and that if I could get in touch with Casey I'd try to keep an eye on him. It would probably be a good thing, I told her, if he did stay away long enough to let this collection of complaints against him be forgotten at the police station.

I went away, hoping fervently that Casey would break even his own records that night. I really intended to find him and keep an eye on him. But keeping an eye on Casey Ryan is a more complicated affair than it sounds.

Wherefore, much of this story must be built upon my knowledge of Casey and a more or less complete report of events in which I took no part, welded together with a bit of healthy imagination.

Chapter II

Casey Ryan knew his desert. Also, from long and not so happy experience, he knew Fords, or thought he did. He made the mistake, however, of buying a nearly new one and asking it to accomplish the work of a twin six from the moment he got behind the wheel.

He was fortunate in buying a demonstrator's car with a hundred miles or so to its credit. He arrived in Barstow before the proprietor of a supply store had gone to bed-for which he was grateful to the Ford. He loaded up there with such necessities for desert prospecting as he had not waited to buy in Los Angeles, turned short off the main highway where traffic officers might be summoned by telephone to lie in wait for him, and took the steeper and less used trail north. He was still mad and talking bitterly to himself in an undertone while he drove-telling the new Ford what he thought of city rules and city ways, and driving it as no Ford was ever meant by its maker to be driven.

The country north of Barstow is not to be taken casually in the middle of a dark night, even by Casey Ryan and a Ford. The roads, once you are well away from help, are all pretty much alike, and all bad. And although the white, diamond-shaped signs of a beneficent automobile club are posted here and there, where wrong turnings are most likely to prove disastrous to travelers, Casey Ryan was in the mood to lick any man who pointed out a sign to him. He did see one or two in spite of himself and gave a grunt of contempt. So, where he should have turned to the east (his intention being to reach Nevada by way of Silver Lake) he continued traveling north and didn't know it.

Driving across the desert on a dark night is confusing to the most observant wayfarer. On either side, beyond the light of the car, illusory forest stands for mile upon mile. Up hill or down or across the level it is the same —a narrow, winding trail through dimly seen woods. The most familiar road grows strange; the miles are longer; you drive through mystery and silence and the world around you is a formless void.

Dawn and a gorgeous sunrise painted out the woods and revealed barren hilltops which Casey did not know. Because he did not know them, he guessed shrewdly that he was on his way to the wilderness of mountains and sand which lies west of Death Valley. Small chance he had of hearing the shop whistles blow in Las Vegas at noon, as he had expected.

He was telling himself that he didn't care where he went, when the car, laboring more and more reluctantly up a long, sandy hill, suddenly stopped. In Casey's heart was a thrill at the sheer luxury of stopping in the middle of the road without having some thick-necked cop stride toward him bawling insults. That he was obliged to stop, and that a hill uptilted before him, and the sand was a foot deep outside the ruts failed to impress him with foreboding. He gloried in his freedom and thought not at all of the Ford.

He climbed stiffly out, squinted at the sky line, which was jagged, and at his immediate surroundings, which were barren and lonely and soothing to his soul that hungered for these things. Great, gaunt "Joshua" trees stood in grotesque groups all up and down the narrow valley, hiding the way he had come from the way he would go. It was as if the desert had purposely dropped a curtain before his past and would show him none of his future. Whereat Casey Ryan grinned, took a chew of tobacco and was himself again.

"If they wanta come pinch me here, I'll meet 'em man to man. Back in town no man's got a show. They pile in four deep and gang a feller. Out here it's lick er git licked. They can all go t' thunder. Tahell with town!"

The odor of coffee boiling in a new pot which the sagebrush fire was fast blackening; the salty, smoky smell of bacon frying in a new frying pan that turned bluish with the heat; the sizzle of bannock batter poured into hot grease-these things made the smiling mouth of Casey Ryan water with desire.

"Hell!" said Casey, breathing deep when, stomach full and resentment toward the past blurred by satisfaction with his present, he filled his pipe and fingered his vest pocket for a match. "Gas stoves can't cook nothin' so there's any taste to it. That there's the first real meal

I've et in six months. Light a match and turn on the gas and call that a fire! Hunh! Good old sage er greasewood fer Casey Ryan, from here on!"

He laid back against the sandy sidehill, tilted his hat over his eyes and crossed his legs luxuriously. He was in no hurry to continue his journey. Now that he and the desert were alone together, haste and Casey Ryan held nothing in common. For awhile he watched a Joshua palm that looked oddly like a giant man with one arm hanging loose at its side and another pointing fixedly at a distant, black-capped butte standing aloof from its fellows. Casey was tired after his night on the trail. Easy living in town had softened his muscles and slowed a little that untiring energy which had balked at no hardship. He was drowsy, and his brain stopped thinking logically and slipped into half-waking fancy.

The Joshua seemed to move, to lift its arm and point more imperatively toward the peak. Its ungainly head seemed to turn and nod at Casey. What did the darned thing want? Casey would go when he, got good and ready. Perhaps he would go that way, and perhaps he would not. Right here was good enough for Casey Ryan at present; and you could ask anybody if he were the man to follow another man's pointing, much less a Joshua tree.

Battering rain woke Casey some hours later and drove him to the shelter of the Ford. Thunder and lightning came with the rain, and a bellowing wind that rocked the car and threatened once or twice to overturn it. With some trouble Casey managed to button down the curtains and sat huddled on the front seat, watching through a streaming windshield the buffeted wilderness. He was glad he had not unloaded his outfit; gladder still that the storm had not struck which he was traveling. Down the trail toward him a small river galloped, washing deep gullies where the wheels of his car offered obstruction to its boisterousness.

"She's a tough one," grinned Casey, in spite of the chattering of his teeth. "Looks like all the water in the world is bein' poured down this pass. Keeps on, I'll have to gouge out a couple of Joshuays an' turn the old Ford into a boat-but Casey'll keep agoin'!"

Until inky dark it rained like the deluge. Casey remained perched in his one-man ark and tried hard to enjoy himself and his hard-won freedom. He stabbed open a can of condensed milk, poured it into a cup, and drank it and ate what was left of his breakfast bannock, which he had fortunately put away in the car out of the reach of a hill of industrious red ants.

He thought vaguely of cranking the car and going on, but gave up the notion. One sidehill, he decided, was as good as another sidehill for the present.

That night Casey slept fitfully in the car and discovered that even a wall bed in a despised apartment house may be more comfortable than the front seat of a Ford. His bones ached by morning, and he was hungry enough to eat raw bacon and relish it. But the sun was fighting through the piled clouds and shone cheerfully upon the draggled pass, and Casey boiled coffee and fried bacon and bannock beside the trail, and for a little while was happy again.

From breakfast until noon he was busy as a beaver repairing the washout beneath the car and on to the top of the hill. She was going to have to get down and dig in her toes to make it, he told the Ford, when at last he heaved pick and shovel into the tonneau, packed in his cooking outfit and made ready to crank up.

From then until supper time he wore a trail around the car, looking to see what was wrong and why he could not crank. He removed hootin'-annies and dingbats (using Casey's mechanical terms) looked them over dissatisfiedly, and put them back without having done them ny good whatever. Sometimes they were returned to a different place, I imagine, since I know too well how impartial Casey is with the mechanical parts of a Ford.

He made camp there that night, pitching his little tent in the trail for pure cussedness, and defying aloud a traveling world to make him move until he got good and ready. He might have saved his vocabulary, for the road was impassable before him and behind; and had Casey managed to start the car, he could not have driven a mile in either direction.

Since he did not know that, the next day he painstakingly cleaned the spark plugs and tried again to crank the Ford; couldn't, and removed more hootin'-annies and dingbats than he had touched the day before. That night he once more pitched his tent in the trail, hoping in his heart that some one would drive along and dispute his right to camp there; when he would lick the doggone cuss.

On the fourth day, after a long, fatiguing session with the vitals of a Ford that refused to be cranked, Casey was busy gathering brush, for his supper fire when Fate came walking up' the trail. Fate appears in many forms. In this instance it assumed the shape of a packed burro that poked its nose around a group of Joshuas, stopped abruptly and backed precipitately into another burro which swung out of the trail and went careening awkwardly down the slope. The stampeding burro had not seen the Ford at all, but accepted the testimony of its leader that something was radically wrong with the trail ahead. His pack bumped against the yuccas as he went; after him lurched a large man, heavy to the point of fatness, yelling hoarse threats and incoherent objurgations.

Casey threw down his armful of dead brush and went after the lead burro which was blazing itself a trail in an entirely different direction. The lead burro had four large canteens strapped outside its pack, and Casey was growing so short of water that he had begun to debate seriously the question of draining the radiator on the morrow.

I don't suppose many of you would believe the innate cussedness of a burro when it wants to be that way. Casey hazed this one to the hills and back down the trail for half a mile before he rushed it into a clump of greasewood and sneaked up on it when it thought itself hidden from all mortal eyes. After that he dug heels into the sand and hung on. Memory resurrected for his need certain choice phrases coined in times of stress for the ears of burros alone. Luxury and civilization and fifty-five thousand dollars and a wife were as if they had never been. He was Casey Ryan, the prospector, fighting a stubborn donkey all over a desert slope. He led it conquered back to the Ford, tied it to a wheel and lifted off the four canteens, gratified with their weight and hoping there were more on the other burro. He had quite forgotten that he had meant to lick the first man he saw, and grinned when the fat man came toiling back with the other animal.

By the time their coffee was boiled and their bacon fried, each one knew the other's past history and tentative plans for the future, censored and glossed somewhat by the teller but received without question or criticism.

The fat man's name was Barney Oakes, and he had heard of Casey Ryan and was glad to meet him. Though Casey had never heard of Barney Oakes, he discovered that they both knew Bill Masters, the garage man at Lund; and further gossip revealed the amazing fact that Barney Oakes had once been the husband of the woman whom Casey had very nearly married, the widow who cooked for the Lucky Lode.

"Boy, you're sure lucky she turned loose on yuh before yuh went an' married her!" Barney congratulated Casey, slapping his great thigh and laughing loudly. "She shore is handy with her tongue-that old girl. Ever hear a sawmill workin' overtime? That's her-rippin' through knots an' never blowin' the whistle fer quittin' time. I never knowed a man could have as many faults as what she used t' name over fer me." He drained his cup and sighed with great content. "At that, I stayed with her seven months and fourteen days," he boasted. "I admit, two of them months I was laid up with a busted ankle an' shoulder blade. Tunnel caved in on me."

They talked late that night and were comrades, brothers, partners share and share alike before they slept. Next morning Casey tried again to start the Ford; couldn't; and yielded to Barney's argument that burros were better than a car for prospectin' in that rough country. They over-hauled Casey's outfit, took all the grub and as much else as the burros could carry and debated seriously what point in the Panamints they should aim for.

"Where's that there Joshuay tree pointin' to?" Casey asked finally. "She's the biggest and oldest in the bunch, and ever since I've been here she's looked like she's got somethin' on 'er mind. Whadda yuh think, Barney?"

Barney walked around the yucca, stood behind the extended arm, squinted at the sharp-peaked butte with the black capping, toward which the gaunt tree seemed to point. He spat out a stale quid of tobacco and took a fresh one, squinted again toward the butte and looked at Casey.

"She's country I never prospected in, back in there. I've follered poorer advice than a Joshuay. Le's try it a whirl."

Thus it came to pass that Casey Ryan forsook his Ford for a strange partner with two burros and a clouded past, and fared forth across the barren foothills with no better guidance than the rigid, outstretched limb of a great, gaunt Joshua tree.

Chapter III

In a still sunny gulch which shadows would presently fill to the brim, Casey Ryan was reaching, soiled bandanna in his hand, to pull a pot of bubbling coffee from the coals, —a pot now blackened with the smoke of many campfires to prove how thoroughly a part of the open land it had become. Something nipped at his right shoulder, and at the same instant ticked the coffeepot and overturned it into a splutter of steam and hot ashes. The spiteful crack of a rifle shot followed close. Casey ducked behind a nose of rock, and big Barney Oakes scuttled for cover, spilling bacon out of the frying pan as he went.

For a week the two had been camped in this particular gulch, which drew in to a mere wrinkle on the southwestern slope of the black-topped butte, toward which the Joshua tree in the pass had directed them. Nearly a week they had spent toiling across the hilly, waterless waste, with two harrowing days when their canteens flopped empty on the burros and big Barney stumbled oftener than Casey liked to see. Casey himself had gone doggedly ahead, his body bent forward, his square shoulders sagging a bit, but with never a thought of doing anything but go on.

A red splotch high up on the side of this gulch promised "water formation" as prospectors have a way of putting it. They had found the water, else adventure would have turned to tragedy. Near the water they had also found a promising outcropping of silver-bearing quartz. Barney's blowpipe had this very day shown them silver in castle-building quantities.

Just at this moment, however, they were not thinking of mines. They were eyeing a round hole in the coffeepot from which a brown rivulet ran spitting into the blackening coals.

Casey was the more venturesome. He raised himself to see if he could discover where the bullet had come from, and very nearly met the fate of the coffeepot. He felt the wind of a second bullet that spatted against a boulder near Barney. Barney burrowed deeper into his covert.

Casey went down on all fours and crawled laboriously toward a concealing bank covered thick with brush. A third bullet clipped a twig of sage just about three inches above the middle of his back, and Casey flattened on his stomach and swore. Some one on the peak of the hill had good eyesight, he decided. Neither spoke, other than to swear in undertones; for voices carried far in that clear atmosphere, and nothing could be gained by conversation.

Darkness never had poured so slowly into that gulch since the world was young. The campfire had died to black embers before Casey ventured from his covert, and Barney Oakes seemed to have holed up for the season. Unless you have lived for a long while in a land altogether empty of any human life save your own, you cannot realize the effect of having mysterious bullets zip past your ears and ruin your supper for you.

"Somebody's gunnin' fer us, looks like t' me," Barney observed belatedly in a hoarse whisper, from his covert.

"Found that out, did yuh? Well, it ain't the first time Casey's been shot at and missed," Casey retorted peevishly in the lee of the bank. "Say! I knowed the sing of bullets before I was old enough to carry a tune."

"So'd I," boasted Barney, "but that ain't sayin' I learned t' like the song."

"What I'm figurin' out now," said Casey, "is how to get up there an' AT 'am. An' how we kin do it without him seein' us. Goin' t' be kinda ticklish-but it ain't the first ticklish job Casey Ryan ever tackled."

"It can't be did," Barney stated flatly. "An' if it could be did, I wouldn't do it. I ain't as easy t' miss as what you be. I got bulk."

"A hole bored through your tallow might mebbe do you good," Casey suggested harshly. "Might let in a little sand. You can't never tell —"

"My vitals," said Barney with dignity, "is just as close to the surface as what your vitals be. I ain't so fat —I'm big. An' I got all the sand I need. I also have got sense, which some men lacks."

"What yuh figurin' on doin'?" Casey wanted to know. "Set here under a bush an' let 'em pick yuh up same as they would a cottontail, mebbe? We got a hull night to work in, an' Casey's eyes is as good as anybody's in the dark. More'n that, Casey's six-gun kin shoot just as hard an' fast as a rifle—let 'im git close enough."

Barney did not want to be left alone and said so frankly. Neither did he want to climb the butte. He could see no possible gain in climbing to meet an enemy or enemies who could hear the noise of approach. It was plain suicide, he declared, and Barney Oakes was not ready to die.

But Casey could never listen to argument when a fight was in prospect. He filled a canteen, emptied a box of cartridges into his pocket, stuck his old, Colt six-shooter inside his trousers belt, and gave Barney some parting instruction under his breath.

Barney was to move camp down under the bank by the spring, and dig himself in there, so that the only approach would be up the narrow gulch. He would then wait until Casey returned.

"Somebody's after our outfit, most likely," Casey reasoned. "It ain't the first time I've knowed it to happen. So you put the hull outfit outa sight down there an' stand guard over it. If we'd 'a' run when they opened up, they'd uh cleaned us out and left us flat. They's two of us, an' we'll git 'em from two sides."

He stuffed cold bannock into the pocket that did not hold the cartridges and disappeared, climbing the side of the gulch opposite the point which held their ambitious marksman.

To Barney's panicky expostulations he had given little heed. "If yore vitals is as close to your hide as what you claim," Casey had said impatiently, "an' you don't want any punctures in 'em, git to work an' git that hide of yourn outa sight. It'll take some diggin'; they's a lot of yuh to cover."

Barney, therefore, dug like a badger with a dog snuffing at its tail. Casey, on the other hand, climbed laboriously in the darkness a bluff he had not attempted to climb by daylight. It was hard work and slow, for he felt the need of going quietly. What lay over the rim-rock he did not know, though he meant to find out.

Daylight found him leaning against a smooth ledge which formed a part of the black capping he had seen from the road. He had spent the night toiling over boulders and into small gulches and out again, trying to find some crevice through which he might climb to the top. Now he was just about where he had been several hours before, and even Casey Ryan could not help realizing what a fine target he would make if he attempted to climb back down the bluff to camp before darkness again hid his movements.

Standing there puffing and wondering what to do next, he saw the two burros come picking their way toward the spring for their morning drink and a handful apiece of rolled oats which Barney kept to bait them into camp. The lead burro was within easy flinging distance of a rock, from camp, when the thin, unmistakable crack of a rifle-shot came from the right, high up on the rim somewhere beyond Casey. The lead burro pitched forward, struggled to get up, fell again and rolled over, lodging against a rock with its four feet sticking up at awkward angles in the air.

The second burro, always quick to take alarm, wheeled and went galloping away down the draw. But he couldn't outgallop the bullet that sent him in a complete somersault down the slope. Barney might keep the rest of his rolled oats, for the burros were through wanting them.

Casey squinted along the rim of black rock that crested the peak irregularly like a stiff, ragged frill of mourning stuff the gods had thrown away. He could not see the man who had shot the burros. By the intervals between shots, Casey guessed that one man was doing the shooting, though it was probable there were others in the gang. And now that the burros were dead, it became more than ever necessary to locate the gang and have it out with them. That necessity did not worry Casey in the least. The only thing that troubled him now was getting up on the rim without being seen.

It was characteristic of Casey Ryan that, though he moved with caution, he nevertheless moved toward their unseen enemy. Not for a long, long while had Casey been cautious in his behavior, and the necessity galled him. If the hidden marksman had missed that last burro, Casey would probably have taken a longer chance. But to date, every bullet had gone straight to its destination; which was enough to make any man think twice.

Once during the forenoon, while Casey was standing against the rim-rock staring glumly down upon the camp, Barney's hat, perched on a pick handle, lifted its crown above the edge of his hiding place; an old, old trick Barney was playing to see if the rifle were still there and working. The rifle worked very well indeed, for Barney was presently flattened into his retreat, swearing and poking his finger through a round hole in his hat.

Casey seized the opportunity created by the diversion and scurried like a lizard across a bare, gravelly slide that had been bothering him for half an hour. By mid-afternoon he reached a crevice that looked promising enough when he craned up it, but which nearly broke his neck when he had climbed halfway up. Never before had he been compelled to measure so exactly his breadth and thickness. It was drawing matters down rather fine when he was compelled to back down to where he had elbow room, and remove his coat before he could squeeze his body through that crack. But he did it, with his six-shooter inside his shirt and the extra ammunition weighting his trousers pockets.

In spite of his long experience with desert scenery, Casey was somewhat astonished to find himself in a new land, fairly level and with thick groves of pinon cedar and juniper trees scattered here and there. Far away stood other barren hills with deep canyons between. He knew now that the black-capped butte was less a butte than the uptilted nose of a high plateau not half so barren as the lower country. From the pointing Joshua tree it had seemed a peak, but contours are never so deceptive as in the high, broken barrens of Nevada.

He looked down into the gulch where Barney was holed up with their outfit. He could scarcely distinguish the place, it had dwindled so with the distance. He had small hope of seeing Barney. After that last leaden bee had buzzed through his hat crown, you would have to dig faster than Barney if you wanted a look at him. Casey grinned when he thought of it.

When he had gotten his breath and had scraped some loose dirt out of his shirt collar, Casey crouched down behind a juniper and examined his surroundings carefully, his pale, straight-lidded eyes moving slowly as the white, pointing finger of a searchlight while he took in every small detail within view. Midway in the arc of his vision was a ledge, ending in a flat-topped boulder.

The ledge blocked his view, except that he could see trees and a higher peak of rocks beyond it. He made his way cautiously toward the ledge, his eyes fixed upon the boulder. A huge, sloping slab of the granite outcropping it seemed, scaly with gray-green fungus in the cracks where moisture longest remained; granite ledge banked with low junipers warped and stunted and tangled with sage. The longer Casey looked at the boulder, the less he saw that seemed unnatural in a country filled with boulders and outcroppings and stunted vegetation.

But the longer he looked at it, the stronger grew his animal instinct that something was wrong. He waited for a time —a long time indeed for Casey Ryan to wait. There was no stir anywhere save the sweep of the wind blowing steadily from the west.

He crept forward, halting often, eyeing the boulder and its neighboring ledge, distrust growing within him, though he saw nothing, heard nothing but the wind sweeping through branches and bush. Casey Ryan was never frightened in his life. But he was Irish born-and there's something in Irish blood that will not out; something that goes beyond reason into the world of unknown wisdom.

It's a tricksy world, that realm of intuitions. For this is what befell Casey Ryan, and you may account for it as best pleases you.

He circled the rock as a wolf will circle a coiled rattler which it does not see. Beyond the rock, built close against it so that the rear wall must have been the face of the ledge, a little rock cabin squatted secretively. One small window, with two panes of glass was set high under the eaves on the side toward Casey. Cleverly concealed it was, built to resemble the ledge. Visible from one side only, and that was the side where Casey stood. At the back the sloping boulder, untouched, impregnable; at the north and west, a twist of the ledge that hid the cabin completely in a niche. It was the window on the south side that betrayed it.

So here was what the boulder concealed, —and yet, Casey was not satisfied with the discovery. Unconsciously he reached for his gun. This, he told himself, must be the secret habitation of the fiend who shot from rim-rocks with terrible precision at harmless prospectors and their burros.

Casey squinted up at the sun and turned his level gaze again upon the cabin. Reason told him that the man with the rifle was still watching for a pot shot at him and Barney, and that there was nothing whatever to indicate the presence of only one man in the camp below. Had he been glimpsed once during the climb, he would have been fired upon; he would never have been given the chance to gain the top and find this cabin.

The place looked deserted. His practical, everyday mind told him it was empty for the time being. But he felt queer and uncomfortable, nevertheless. He sneaked along the ledge to the cabin, flattened himself against the corner next the gray boulder and waited there for a minute. He felt the flesh stiffening on his jaws as he crept up to the window to look in. By standing on his toes, Casey's eyes came on a level with the lowest inch of glass, —the window was so high.

Just at first Casey could not see much. Then, when his eyes had adjusted themselves to the half twilight within, his mind at first failed to grasp what he saw. Gradually a dimly sensed dread took hold of him, and grew while he stood there peering in at commonplace things which should have given him no feeling save perhaps a faint surprise.

A fairly clean, tiny room he saw, with a rough, narrow bed in one corner and a box table at its head. From the ceiling hung a lantern with the chimney smoked on one side and the warped, pole rafter above it slightly blackened to show how long the lantern had hung there lighted. A door opposite the tiny window was closed, and there was no latch or fastening on the inner side. An Indian blanket covered half the floor space, and in the corner opposite the bed was a queer, drumlike thing of sheet iron with a pipe running through the wall; some heating arrangement, Casey guessed.

In the center of the room, facing the window, a woman sat in a wooden rocking chair and rocked. A pale old woman with dark hollows under her eyes that were fixed upon the pattern of the Indian rug. Her hair was white. Her thin, white hands rested limply on the arms of the chair, and she was rocking back and forth, back and forth, steadily, quietly, —just rocking and staring at the Indian rug.

Casey has since told me that she was the creepiest thing he ever saw in his life. Yet he could not explain why it was so. The woman's face was not so old, though it was lined and without color. There was a terrible quiet in her features, but he felt, somehow, that her thoughts were not quiet. It was as if her thoughts were reaching out to him, telling him things too awful for her thin, hushed lips to let pass.

But after all, Casey's main object was to locate the man with the rifle, and to do it before he himself was seen on the butte. He watched a little longer the woman who rocked and rocked. Never once did her eyes move from that fixed point on the rug. Never once did her fingers move on the arm of the chair. Her mouth remained immobile as the lips of a dead woman. He had to force himself to leave the window; and when he did, he felt guilty, as if he had somehow deserted some one helpless and needing him. He sneaked back, lifted himself and took another long look. The old woman was rocking back and forth, her face quiet with that terrible, pent placidity which Casey could not understand.

Away from the cabin a pebble's throw, he shook his shoulders and pulled his mind away from her, back to the man with the rifle-and to Barney. Rocking in a chair never hurt anybody that he ever heard of. And shooting from rim-rocks did. And Barney was down there, holed up and helpless, though he had grub and water. Casey was up here in a mighty dangerous place without much grub or water but-he hoped-not quite helpless. His immediate, pressing job was not to peek through a high-up window at an old woman rocking back and forth in a chair, but to round up the man who was interfering with Casey's peaceful quest for-well, he called it wealth; but I think that adventure meant more to him.

He picked his way carefully along the edge of the rim-rock, keeping under cover when he could and watching always the country ahead. And without any artful description of his progress, I will simply say that Casey Ryan combed the edge of that rampart for two miles before dark, and found himself at last on the side farthest from Barney without having discovered the faintest trace of any living soul save the woman who rocked back and forth in the little, secret cabin.

Casey sat down on a rock, took a restrained drink from his canteen, and said everything he knew or could invent that was profane and condemnatory of his luck, of the unseen assassin, of the country and his present predicament. He got up, looked all around him, sniffed unavailingly for some tang of smoke in the thin, crisp air, reseated himself and said everything all over again.

Presently he rose and made his way straight across the butte, going slowly to lessen his chance of making a noise for unfriendly ears to hear, and with the stars for guidance.

Chapter IV

The night was growing cold, and Casey had no coat. At least he could go down and tell Barney what he had discovered and had failed to discover, and get something to eat. Barney would probably be worrying about him, though there was a chance that a bullet had found Barney before dark. Casey was uneasy, and once he was down the fissure again, he hurried as much as possible.

He managed to reach the camp by the little spring without being shot at and without breaking a leg. But Barney was not there. Just at first Casey believed he was dead; but a brief search told Casey that two of the largest canteens were gone, together with a side of bacon, some flour and all of the tobacco. White assassins would have made a more thorough job of robbing the camp. Barney, it was evident, had fled the fate of the burros.

Casey told the stars what he thought of a partner like Barney. Afterward he ate what was easiest to swallow without cooking, overhauled what was left of their outfit, cached the remainder in a clump of bushes, and wearily climbed the bluff again under a capacity load. He concealed himself in the bottom of the fissure to sleep, since he could search no farther.

If he thought wistfully of the palled comfort of his apartment in Los Angeles, and of the Little Woman there, he still did not think strongly enough to send him back to them. For with a canteen or two of water, some food and his two capable legs to carry him, Casey Ryan could have made it to Barstow easily enough. But because he was Casey Ryan, and Irish, and because he was always on the hunt for trouble without recognizing it when he met it in the trail, it never occurred to him to follow Barney down to safer country.

"That there Joshuay tree meant a lot more'n what it let on, pointin' up this way!" Casey muttered, staring down upon a somnolent wilderness blanketed with hushed midnight. "If it thinks it's got Casey whipped, it better think agin and think quick. I'll give it somethin' to point at, 'fore I leave this here butte.

"Funny, the way it kept pointin' up this way. I've saw Joshuays before-miles of 'em. But I never seen one that looked so kinda human and so kinda like it was tryin' to talk. Seems kinda funny; an' that old lady rockin' an' lookin' —seems like her an' the Joshuay has kinda throwed in together, hopin' somebody might come along with savvy enough to kinda-aw, hell!" So did Casey and his Irish belief in the supernatural fall plump against the limitations of his vocabulary.

Against the limitations proscribed by his material predicament, however, Casey Ryan set his face with a grin. Somebody was going to get the big jolt of his life before long, he told himself over a careful breakfast fire built cunningly far back in the crevice where a current of air sucked into the rock capping of the butte. Something was going on up here that shouldn't go on. He did not know what it was, but he meant to stop it. He did not know who was making Indian war on peaceful prospectors, but Casey felt that they were already as good as licked, since he was here with breakfast under his belt and his six-shooter tucked handily inside his waistband.

He squinted up the crack in the ledge, made certain mental alterations in its narrow, jagged walls, and reached for the tough-handled, efficient prospector's pick he had thoughtfully included in his meagre equipment. Slowly and methodically he worked up the crevice, knocking off certain sharp points of rock, and knowing all the while what would probably happen to him if he were overheard.

He was not discovered, however. When he laid elbows on the upper level of the rim and pulled himself up, his coat was on his back where it belonged, and even Barney could have followed him. Yet the top showed no evidence of a widening of the fissure. The bushy junipers hid him completely while he reconnoitred and considered what he should do.

Because the place was close and the invisible call was strong, Casey went first to the rock hut, circled it carefully and found that it was exactly what it had seemed at first sight; a hidden place with no evident opening save that high, small window under the eaves. There was no sign of pathway leading to it, no trace of life outside its wall. But when he crept close and peeked in again, there sat the old woman rocking back and forth. But to-day she stared at the wall before her.

Casey felt a distinct sensation of relief just in knowing that she was, after all, capable of moving. Now her head was not bent, but rested against the back of her chair. She was rocking steadily, quietly, with never a halt.

Casey rapped on the window and waited, fighting a nameless dread of the mystery of her. But she continued to rock and to stare at the wall; if she heard the tapping she gave no sign whatever. So presently he turned away and set himself to the work of finding the man with the rifle.

To that end he first of all climbed the tallest pinon tree in sight; a tree that stood on a rise of ground apart from its brothers. From the concealment of its branches, he surveyed his surroundings carefully, noting especially the notched unevenness of the butte's rim and how just behind him it narrowed unexpectedly to a thin ridge not more than a couple of hundred yards in breadth. A jagged outcropping cut straight across and Casey saw how yesterday he had mistaken that ledge for the rim of the butte. His man must have been out on the point beyond him all the while. He was out there now, very likely; there, or down in the camp he had watched yesterday like a vulture.

His search having narrowed to an area easily covered in an hour or two, Casey turned his head and examined as well as he could the deep canyon that had bitten into the butte and caused that narrow peak. Trees blocked his view there, and he was feeling about for a lower foothold so that he could make the descent when a voice from the ground startled him considerably.

"Come down outa there, before I shoot yuh down!"

Casey looked down and saw what he afterwards declared was the meanest looking man on earth, pointing straight at him the widest muzzled shotgun he had ever seen in his life.

Casey came down. The last ten feet of the distance he made in a clean jump, planting his feet full in the old man's stomach. The meanest looking man on earth gave a grunt and crumpled, with Casey's fingers digging into his throat.

Whether Casey would have killed him or not will never be known. For just as the man was falling limp in his hands, another heavy body landed upon Casey's back. Casey felt a hard, chill circle pressed against his perspiring temple. His hands relaxed and fall away from the throat, leaving finger marks there in the flesh.

"Git up off'n him!" a new voice commanded harshly, and Casey obeyed. His captor shifted the gun muzzle to the back of Casey's neck and poked the gasping, bearded old man with his toe.

"Git up, Paw, you old fool, you! What'd you let 'im light on yuh fer? Why couldn't you a stood back a piece, outa reach? You like to got croaked."

Casey found it prudent to hold his head rather still, as a man does when he carries a boil on his neck. The muzzle of a six-shooter has a quieting effect, when applied to the person by an unfriendly hand. Casey did not at once see the intruder. But presently "Paw" recovered himself and his shotgun, and swung it menacingly toward Casey. Whereupon the cold circle left Casey's medulla oblongata and a long-faced, long-legged youth stepped somewhat hastily to one side.

"Paw, you ol' fool, you, get your finger off'n that trigger whilst you're aimin' at me!" he exclaimed pettishly.

"I wa'n't aimin' at you. I was aimin' at this 'ere —" Casey heard himself called many names, any one of which was good for a fight when Casey was free.

"Aw, you shut up, Paw. You ain't gittin' nobody nowhere," the son interrupted. "You can't cuss 'im t' death-he looks like he could cut loose a few of them pet names hisself if he got a chancet. Yuh might tell us what you was doin' up that there tree, mister. An' what you're doin' on this here butte, anyhow."

Casey looked at him. Knowing Casey, I should say that his eyes were not pleasant. "Talk to Paw," he advised contemptuously. "The two of yuh may possibly be able to stand each other without gittin' sick; but me, I never did git used to skunks!"

That remark very nearly got him a through ticket to Land Beyond. But, being very nearly what Casey had called them, they contented themselves with mouthing vile epithets.

"Better take 'im down to the mine an' keep 'im till Mart gets back, Paw," the long-jawed youth suggested, when he ran short of objurgations. "Mart'll fix 'im when he comes."

"I'd fix 'im, here an', now," threatened Paw, "but Mart, he's so damned techy lately-what we oughta do is bust 'is head with a rock an' pitch 'im over the rim. That'd fix 'im."

They wrangled over the suggestion, and finally decided to take him down and turn him over to one whom they called Joe. Casey went along peaceably, hopeful that he would later have a chance to fight back. He told himself that they both had heads like peanuts, and whenever they moved, he swore, he could hear their brains rattle in their skulls. It doesn't take brains to shoot straight, and he decided that the lanky young man was the one who had shot from the rim-rock. They drove him down into the narrow, deep gulch, following a steep trail that Casey had not seen the day before. The trail led them to the mouth of a tunnel; and by the size of the dump Casey judged that the workings were of a considerable extent. They were getting out silver ore, he guessed, after a glance or two at stray pieces of rock.

Joe was a big, glum-looking individual with his left hand bandaged. He chewed tobacco industriously and maintained a complete silence while Hank, frequently telling Paw to shut up, told how and where they had found Casey spying up on the butte.

"We don't fancy stray desert rats prowlin' around without no reason," said Joe. "Our boss that we're workin' for ain't at home. We're lookin' for 'im back any day now, an' we'll just hold yuh till he comes. He can do as he likes about yuh. You'll have to work fer your board —c'm on an' I'll show yuh how."

Hank followed Casey and Joe into the tunnel. Casey made no objections whatever to going. The tunnel was a fairly long one, he noticed, with drifts opening out of it to left and right. At the end of the main tunnel, Joe turned, took Casey's candle from him and stuck it into a seam in the wall, as he had done with his own.

"Ever drill in rock?" he asked shortly.

"Mebbe I have an' mebbe I ain't," Casey returned defiantly.

"Here's a drill, an' here's your single-jack. Now git t' work. There ain't any loafin' around this camp, and spies never meant good to nobody. Yuh needn't expect to be popular with us-but you'll git your grub if yuh earn it."

Casey looked at the drill, took the double-headed, four-pound hammer and hesitated. He has said that it was pretty hard to resist braining the two of them at once. But there would still be the old man with the shotgun, and he admitted that he was curious about the old woman who rocked and rocked. He decided to wait awhile and see, why these miners found it necessary to shoot harmless prospectors who came near the butte. So he spat into the dust of the tunnel floor, squinted at Joe for a minute and went to work.

That day Casey was kept underground except during the short interval of "shooting" and waiting for the dynamite smoke to clear out of the tunnel; which process Casey assisted by operating a hand blower much against his will. Joe remained always on guard, eyeing Casey suspiciously. When at last he was permitted to pick up his coat and leave the tunnel, night had fallen so that the gulch was dim and shadowy. Casey was conducted to a dugout cabin where bacon was frying too fast and smoking suffocatingly. Paw was there, in a vile temper which seemed to be directed toward the three impartially and to have been caused chiefly by his temporary occupation as camp cook.

Casey watched the old man place food for one person in little dishes which he set in a bake pan for want of a tray. He added a small tin teapot of tea and disappeared from the dugout.

"Two of us waitin' to see your boss, huh?" Casey inquired boldly of Joe. "Can't we eat together?"

"You can call yourself lucky if you eat at all," Joe retorted glumly. "The old man's pretty sore at the way you handled him. He's runnin' this camp; I ain't."

Casey let it go at that, chiefly because he was hungry and tired and did not want to risk losing his supper altogether. Hounds like these, he told himself bitterly, were capable of any crime-from smashing a man's skull and throwing him off the rim-rock to starving him to death.

He was Casey Ryan, ready always to fight whether his chance of winning was even or merely microscopical; but even so, Casey was not inclined toward suicide.

When the old man presently returned and the three sat down to the table, Casey obeyed a gesture and sat down with them. In spite of Joe's six-shooter laid handily upon the table beside his plate, Casey ate heartily, though the food was neither well cooked nor over plentiful.

After supper he rose and filled his pipe which they had permitted him to keep. A stranger coming into the cabin might not have guessed that Casey was a prisoner. When the table was cleared and Hank set about washing the dishes, Casey picked up a grimy dish towel branded black in places where it had rubbed sooty kettles, and grinned cheerfully at Paw while he dried a tin plate. Paw eyed him dubiously over a stinking pipe, spat reflectively into the woodbox and crossed his legs the other way, loosely swinging an ill-shod foot.

"Y'ain't told us yet what brung yuh up on the butte," Paw observed suddenly. "Yuh wa'n't lost-yuh ain't got the mark uh no tenderfoot. What was yuh doin' up in that tree?"

"Mebbe I mighta been huntin' mountain sheep," Casey retorted calmly.

"Huntin' mountain sheep up a tree is a new one," tittered Hank. "Wish you'd give me a swaller uh that brand. Must have a kick like a brindle mule."

"More likely 'White Mule.' " Casey cocked a knowing eye at Hank. "You're too late, young feller. I chewed the cork day before yesterday," he declared.

While he fished another plate out of the pan, Casey observed that Paw looked at Joe inquiringly, and that Joe moved his head sidewise a careful inch, and back again.

"Moonshine, huh?" Paw hazarded hopefully. "Yuh peddlin' it, er makin' it?"

Casey grinned secretively. "A man can't be pinched without the goods," he observed shrewdly. "I was raised in a country where they took fools out an' brained 'em with an axe. You fellers ain't been none too friendly, recollect. When's your boss expected home, did yuh say? I'd kinda like to meet 'im."

"He'll kinda like to meet you," Joe returned darkly. "Your actions has been plumb suspicious.

"Nothin' suspicious about MY actions," Casey stated truculently, throwing discretion behind him. "The suspiciousness lays up here somewheres on this butte. If yuh want to know what brung me up here, Casey Ryan's the man that can tell yuh to your faces. I come up here to find out who's been gittin' busy with a high-power on my camp down below. Ain't it natural a man'd want to know who'd shot his two burros-an' 'is pardner?" Casey had impulsively decided to throw in Barney for good measure. "Casey Ryan ain't the man to set under a bush an' be shot at like a rabbit. You can ask anybody if Casey ever backed up fer man er beast. I come up here huntin'. Shore I did. It wasn't sheep I was after-that there's my mistake. It was goats."

"Guess I got yourn," Hank leered "when stuck my gun in your back hair."

"If any one's 'been usin' a high-power it wasn't on this butte," Joe growled. "None uh this bunch done any shootin'. Pap an' Hank, they was up here huntin' burros an I caught yuh up a tree spyin'. We got a little band uh antelope up here we're pertectin'. Our boss got himself made a deppity fer just such cases as yourn appears t' be-pervidin' your case ain't worse.

"Now you say your pardner was shot down below in your camp. That shore looks bad fer you, old-timer. The boss'll shore have t' look into it when he gits here. Lucky we made up our minds t' hold yuh —a murderer, like as not." He filled his pipe with deliberation, while Casey, his jaw sagging, stared from one to the other.

Casey had meant to accuse them to their faces of shooting Barney and the burros from the rim-rock. It had occurred to him that if they believed Barney dead, they might reveal something of their purpose in the attack. Concealment, he felt vaguely, would serve merely to sharpen their suspicion of him. It had seemed very important to Casey that these three should not know that Barney was probably well on his way to Barstow by now.

Barney in Barstow would mean Barney bearing news that Casey Ryan was undoubtedly murdered by outlaws in the Panamints; which would mean a few officers on the trail, with Barney to guide them to the spot. Paw and Hank and Joe-outlaws all, he would have sworn would get what Casey called their needin's. His jaw muscles tightened when he thought of that, and the prospect held him quiet under Joe's injustice.

"I can prove anything I'm asked to prove when the time comes," he said sourly, and began to roll himself a cigarette, since his pipe had gone out. "But I ain't in any courtroom yet, an' you fellers ain't any judge an' jury."

"We got to hold ye," Paw spoke up unctiously, as if the decision had been his. "Ef a crime's been committed, like you say it has, we got to do our duty an' hold ye. The boss'll know what to do with ye-like I said all along; when I hauled ye down outa that tree, for instance.

"Aw, shut up, Paw, you ol' fool, you," Hank commanded again with filial gentleness. "He had yore tongue hangin' out a foot when I come along an' captured 'im. Don't go takin' no credit to yourself-you ain't got none comin'. Mart'll know what to do with 'im, all right. But yuh needn't go an' try to let on to Mart that you was the one that caught 'im. He had you caught. An' he'd a killed yuh if I hadn't showed up an' pulled 'im off'n yuh."

"Well now, when it comes to KILLIN'," Casey interjected spitefully, "I guess I coulda put the two of yuh away if I'd a wanted to right bad. Casey Ryan ain't no killer, because he don't have to be. G'wan an' hold me if yuh feel that way. Grub ain't none too good, but I can stand it till your boss comes. I want a man-to-man talk with him, anyway."

Chapter V

That night Casey slept soundly in a bunk built above Joe's bed in the dugout, with Hank and Paw on the opposite side of the room with their guns handy. In the morning he thought well enough of his stomach to get up and start breakfast when Hank had built the fire. He was aware of Joe's suspicious gaze from the lower bunk, and of the close presence of Joe's six-shooter eyeing him balefully from underneath the top blanket. Hank, too, was watchful as a coyote, which he much resembled, in Casey's opinion. But Casey did not mind trifles of that kind, once his mind was at ease about the breakfast and he was free to slice bacon the right thickness, and mix the hot-cake batter himself. For the first time in many weeks he sang-if you could call it singing-over his work.

When Casey Ryan sings over a breakfast fire, you may expect the bacon fried exactly right. You may be sure the hot-cakes will be browned correctly with no uncooked dough inside, and that the coffee will give you heart for whatever hardship the day may hold.

Even Paw's surliness lightened a bit by the time he had speared his tenth cake and walloped it in the bacon grease before sprinkling it thick with sugar and settling the eleventh cake on top. Casey was eyeing the fourteenth cake on Hank's plate when Joe looked up at him over a loaded fork.

"Save out enough dough for three good uns," Joe ordered, "an' fill that little coffee pot an' set it to keep hot, before Hank hogs the hull thing. Dad, seems like you're, too busy t' think uh some things Mart wouldn't want forgot." Paw looked quickly at Casey; but Casey Ryan had played poker all his life, and his weathered face showed no expression beyond a momentary interest, which was natural.

"Other feller hurt bad?" he inquired carelessly, looking at Joe's bandaged hand. He almost grinned when he saw the relieved glances exchanged between Joe and Paw.

"Leg broke," Joe mumbled over a mouthful. "Dad, he set it an' it's doin' all right. He's up in another cabin." Through Hank's brainless titter, Joe added carefully, "Bad ground in the first right-hand drift. We had to abandon it. Rocks big as your head comin' in on yuh onexpected. None uh them right-hand drifts is safe fer a man t' walk in, much less work."

Thereupon Casey related a thrilling story of a cave-in, and assured Joe that he and his partner were lucky to get off with mere broken bones. Casey, you will observe, was running contrary to his nature and leaning to diplomacy.

For himself, I am sure he would never have troubled to placate them. He would have taken the first slim chance that offered-or made one-and fought the three to a finish.

But there was the old woman in the rock hut above them, rocking back and forth and staring at a wall that had no visible opening save one small window to let in the light of outdoors. Prisoner she must be-though why, Casey could only guess.

Perhaps she was some desert woman, the widow of some miner who had been shot as these three had tried to shoot him and Barney Oakes. Mean, malevolent as they were, they would still lack the brutishness necessary to shoot an old woman. So they had shut her up there in the rock hut, not daring to take her back to civilization where she would tell of the crime. It was all plain enough to Casey. The story of the crippled miner made him curl his lip contemptuously when his back was safely turned from Joe.

That day Casey thought much of the old woman in the hut, and of Paw's worse than inferior cooking. Though he did not realize the change in himself, six months of close companionship with the Little Woman had changed Casey Ryan considerably. Time was when even his soft-heartedness would not have impelled him to patient scheming that he might help an old woman whose sole claim upon his sympathy consisted of four rock walls and a look of calm despair in her eyes. Now, Casey was thinking and planning for the old woman more than for himself.

Wherefore, Casey chose the time when he was "putting in an upper" (which is miner's parlance for drilling a hole in the upper face of the tunnel). He gritted his teeth when he swung back the single-jack and landed a glancing blow on the knuckles of his left hand instead of the drill end. No man save Casey Ryan or a surgeon could have told positively whether the metacarpal bones were broken or whether the hand was merely skinned and bruised.

Joe came up, regarded the bleeding hand sourly, led Casey out to the dugout and bandaged the hand for him. There would be no more tunnel work for Casey until the hand had healed; that was accepted without comment.

That night Casey proved to Paw that, with one hand in a sling much resembling Joe's, he could nevertheless cook a meal that made eating a pleasure to look forward to. After that the old woman in the little stone hut had pudding, sometimes, and cake made without eggs, and pie; and the potatoes were mashed or baked instead of plain boiled. Casey had the satisfaction of seeing the dishes return empty to the dugout, and know that he was permitted to add something to her comfort and well-being. The Little Woman would be glad of that, Casey thought with a glow. She might never hear of it, but Casey liked to feel that he was doing something that would please the Little Woman.

For the first few days after Casey was installed as cook, one of the three remained always with him, making it plain that he was under guard. Two were always busy elsewhere. Casey saw that he was expected to believe that they were at work in the tunnel, driving it in to a certain contact of which they spoke frequently and at length.

At supper they would mention their footage for that day's work, and Casey would hide a grin of derision. Casey knew rock as he knew bacon and beans and his sour-dough can. To make the footage they claimed to be making in that tunnel, they would need to shoot twice a day, with a round of, say, five holes to a shot.

As a matter of fact, two holes a day, one shot at noon and one at night, were the most Casey ever heard fired in the tunnel or elsewhere about the mine. But he did not tell them any of the things he thought; not even Joe, who had intelligence far above Paw and Hank, ever guessed that Casey listened every day for their shots and could tell, almost to an inch what progress they were actually making in the tunnel. Nor did he guess that Casey Ryan with his mouth shut was more unsafe than "giant powder" laid out in the sun until it sweated destruction.

Persistent effort, directed by an idea based solely upon an abstract theory, must be driven by a trained intelligence. In this case the abstract theory that every prisoner must be watched must support itself unaided by Casey's behavior. Not even Joe's intelligence was trained to a degree where the theory in itself was sufficient to hold him to the continuous effort of watching Casey.

Wherefore Paw, Hank and Joe presently slipped into the habit of leaving Casey alone for an hour or so; being careful to keep the guns out of his reach, and returning to the dugout at unexpected intervals to make sure that all was well.

Casey Ryan knew his pots and pans, and how to make them fill his days if need be. With savory suppers and his care-free, Casey Ryan grin, he presently lulled them into accepting him as a handy man around camp, and into forgetting that he was at least a potential enemy. Afoot and alone in that unfriendly land, with his left hand smashed and carried in a sling, and on his tongue an Irish joke that implied content with his captivity, Casey Ryan would not have looked dangerous to more intelligent men than these three.

They should have looked one night under the bedding in Casey's bunk. More important still would have been the safeguarding of their "giant powder" and caps and fuse. They should not have left it in a gouged, open hollow under a boulder near the dugout. They were not burdened by the weight of their brains, I imagine.

Just here I should like to say a few words to those who are wholly ignorant of the devastating power contained in "giant powder"—which is dynamite. If you have never had any experience with the stuff, you are likely to go out with a bang and a puff of bluish-brown smoke when you go. On the other hand, you may believe the weird tales one reads now and then, of how whole mountainsides have been thrown down by the discharge of a few sticks of dynamite. Or of one man striking terror to the very souls of a group of mutinous miners by threatening to throw a piece at them. Very well, now this is the truth without any frills of exaggeration or any belittlement:

Dynamite MAY go off by being thrown so that it lands with a jar, but it is not likely to be so hasty as all that. Whole boxes of it have been dropped off wagons traveling over rough trails, with no worse effect than a nervous chill down the spine of the driver of the wagon. It is true that old stuff, after lying around for months and months through varying degrees of temperature, may perform erratically, exploding when it shouldn't and refusing to explode when it should. The average miner refuses to take a chance with stale "giant" if he can get hold of fresh.

One stick the size of an ordinary candle, and from that to a maximum amount of four sticks, may be used to "load" a hole eighteen to twenty-four inches long, drilled into living rock. The amount of dynamite used depends upon the quality of rock to be broken and the skill and good judgment of the miner. In average hard-rock mining, from three to five of these holes are drilled in a space four-by-six feet in area.

A stick of dynamite is exploded by inserting in one end of the stick a high-power detonating cap which will deliver a twenty-pound blow per X —whatever that means. From three- to six-X caps are used in ordinary mining. Three-X caps sometimes fail to explode a stick of dynamite. A six-X cap, delivering a one-hundred-and-twenty-pound blow, may be counted upon to do the work without fail.

The cap itself is exploded by a spark running through a length of fuse, the length depending altogether upon the time required to reach a point of safety after the fuse is lighted. The cap is really more dangerous to handle than is the dynamite itself. The cap is a tricky thing that may go off at any jar or scratch or at a spark from pipe or cigarette. You can, if you are sufficiently careless of possible results, light the twisted paper end of a stick of dynamite and watch the dynamite burn like wax in your fingers; it MAY go off and set your friends to work retrieving portions of your body. More likely, it will do nothing but burn harmlessly.

Well, then, a piece of fuse is inserted in the open end of the cap, and the metal pressed tight against the fuse to hold it in place. Pressed down by the miner's teeth, sometimes, if he has been long in the business and has grown careless about his head; otherwise he crimps the cap on with a small pair of pliers or the back of his knife blade-and feels a bit easier when it is done without losing a hand.

You would think, unless you are accustomed to the stuff, that when five holes are loaded with, probably, ten or twelve sticks of dynamite to the lot, each hole containing a six-X exploding cap as well, that the first shot would likewise be the last shot and that the whole tunnel would cave in and the mountain behind it would shake. Nothing like that occurs. If there are five loaded holes in the tunnel face, and you do not hear, one after the other, five muffled BOOMS, you will know that one hole failed to go off-and that the miner is worried. It happens sometimes that four holes loaded with eight sticks of dynamite explode within a foot or so of the fifth hole and yet the fifth hole remains "dead" and a menace to the miner until it is discharged.

So please don't swallow those wild tales of a stick of dynamite that threw down a mountainside. I once read a story-it was not so long ago-of a Chinaman who wiped out a mine with a little piece of dynamite which he carried in his pocket. I laughed.

Casey Ryan, on the first day when he was left alone with his crippled hand and his pots and pans for company, did nothing whatever that he would not have done had one of the three been present. He was suspicious of their going and thought it was a trap set to catch him in an attempted escape.

On the second day when the three went off together and left him alone, Casey went out gathering wood and discovered just where the "powder," fuse and caps were kept under a huge, black boulder between the tunnel portal and the dugout. On the third day he also gathered wood and helped himself to two sticks of dynamite, three caps and eighteen inches of fuse. Not enough to be missed unless they checked their supply more carefully than Casey believed they did; but enough for Casey's purpose nevertheless.

That night, while the moon shone in through the dingy window at the head of his bunk and gave him a little light to work by, Casey sat up in bed and snored softly and with a soothing rhythm while he cut a stick of dynamite in two, capped five inches of fuse for each piece working awkwardly with his one good hand and pinching the caps tight with his teeth, which might have sent him with a bang into Kingdom Come-and very carefully worked the caps into the powder until no more than three inches of fuse protruded from the end of the half stick. It would have been less dangerous to land with a yell in the middle of the floor and fight the three men with one bare hand, but Casey's courage never turned a hair.

Still snoring mildly, he held up to the moonlight two deadly weapons and surveyed them with much satisfaction. They would not be so quick, as fiction would have them, but if his aim was accurate in throwing, they would be deadly enough. Moreover, he could count with a good deal of certainty upon a certain degree of terror which the sight of them in his hand would produce.

When Casey Ryan cooked breakfast next morning, he carried two half-sticks of loaded dynamite under his hand in the sling. Can you wonder that even he shied at standing over the stove cooking hot cakes and complained that his broken hand pained him a lot and that the heat made it worse? But a shrewd observer would have noticed on his face the expression of a cat that has been shut in the pantry over night.

Joe volunteered to take another look at the hand and see if blood poison was "setting in"; but Casey said it didn't feel like blood poison. He had knocked it against the bunk edge in his sleep, he declared. He'd dose 'er with iodine after a while, and she'd be all right.

Joe let it go at that, being preoccupied with other matters at which Casey could only guess. He conferred with Paw outside the dugout after breakfast, called Hank away from the dish-washing and the three set off toward the tunnel with a brisker air than usually accompanied them to work. Casey watched them go and felt reasonably sure of at least two hours to himself.

The first thing Casey did after he had made sure that he was actually alone was to remove the deadly stuff from the sling and lay it on a shadowed shelf where it would be safe but convenient to his hand. Then, going to his bunk, he reached under the blankets and found the other stick of dynamite which he had not yet loaded. This he laid on the kitchen table and cut it in two as he had done last night with the other stick. With his remaining cap he loaded a half and carried it back to his bunk. He was debating in his mind whether it was worth while purloining another cap from a box under the boulder when another fancy took him and set him grinning.

Four separate charges of dynamite, he reasoned, would not be necessary. It was an even chance that the sight of a piece with the fuse in his hand would be sufficient to tame Paw or Hank or Joe-or the three together, for that matter-without going further than to give them a sight of it.

With that idea uppermost, Casey split the paper carefully down the side of the remaining half-stick, took out the contents in a tin plate and carried it outside where he buried it in the sand beneath a bush. Returning to the dugout he made a thick dough of leftover pancake batter and molded it into the dynamite wrapping with a fragment of harmless fuse protruding from the opened end. When the thing was dry, Casey thought it would look very deadly and might be useful. After several days of helplessness for want of a weapon, Casey was in a mood to supply himself generously.

He finished the dish-washing, working awkwardly with one hand. After that he put a kettle of beans on to boil, filled the stove with pinon sticks and closed the drafts. He armed himself with the two loaded pieces of dynamite from the cupboard, filled his pockets with such other things as he thought he might need, and went prospecting on his own account.

At the portal of the tunnel he stopped and listened for the ping-g, ping-g of a single-jack striking steadily upon steel. But the tunnel was silent, the ore car uptilted at the end of its track on the dump. Yet the three men were supposedly at work in the mine, had talked at breakfast about wanting to show a certain footage when the boss returned, and of needing to hurry.

Casey went into the tunnel, listening and going silently; sounds travel far in underground workings. At the mouth of the first right-hand drift he stopped again and listened. This, if he would believe Joe, was the drift where the bad ground had caused the accident to Joe and his partner whose leg had been broken. Casey found the drift as silent as the main tunnel. He went in ten feet or so and lighted the candle he had pulled from inside his shirt. With the candle held in the swollen fingers of his injured hand, and a prospector's pick taken from the portal in his other, Casey went on cautiously, keeping an eye upon the roof which, to his wise, squinting eyes, looked perfectly solid and safe.

If a track had ever been laid in this drift it had long since been removed. But a well-defined path led along its center with boot tracks going and coming, blurring one another with much passing. Casey grinned and went on, his ears cocked for any sound before or behind, his shoes slung over his arm by their tied laces.

So he came, in the course of a hundred feet or so, to a crude door of split cedar slabs, the fastening padlocked on his side. Casey had vaguely expected some such bar to his path, and he merely gave a grunt of satisfaction that the lock was old and on his side of the door.

With his jackknife Casey speedily took off one side of the lock and opened it. Making the door appear locked behind him when he had passed through was a different matter, and Casey did not attempt it. Instead, he merely closed the door behind him, carrying the padlock in with him.

As Casey reviewed his situation, being on the butte at all was a risk in itself. One detail more or less could not matter so much. Besides, he was a bold Casey Ryan with two loaded half-sticks of dynamite in his sling.

A crude ladder against the wall of a roomy stope beyond the door did not in the least surprise him. He had expected something of this sort. When he had topped the ladder and found himself in a chamber that stretched away into blackness, he grunted again his mental confirmation of a theory working out beautifully in fact. His candle held close to the wall, he moved forward along the well-trodden path, looking for a door. Mechanically he noticed also the formation of the wall and the vein of ore-probably high-grade in pockets, at least-that had caused this chamber to be dug. The ore, he judged, had long since been taken out and down through the stope into the tunnel and so out through the main portal. These workings were old and for mining purposes abandoned. But just now Casey was absorbed in solving the one angle of the mystery which he had stumbled upon at first, and he gave no more than a glance and a thought to the silent testimony of the rock walls.

He found the door, fastened also on the outside just as he had expected it would be. Beside it stood a rather clever heating apparatus which Casey did not examine in detail. His Irish heart was beating rather fast while he unfastened the door. Beyond that door his thoughts went questing eagerly but he hesitated nevertheless before he lifted his knuckles and rapped.

There was no reply. Casey waited a minute, knocked again, then pulled the door open a crack and looked in. The old woman sat there rocking back and forth, steadily, quietly. But her thin fingers were rolling a corner of her apron hem painstakingly, as if she meant to hem it again. Her eyes were fixed absently upon the futile task. Casey watched her as long as he dared and cleared his throat twice in the hope that she would notice him. But the old woman rocked back and forth and rolled her apron hem; unrolled it and carefully rolled it again.

"Good morning, ma'am," said Casey, clearing his throat for the third time and coming a step into the room with his candle dripping wax on the floor.

For just an instant the uneasy fingers paused in their rolling of the apron hem. For just so long the rockers hesitated in their motion. But the old woman did not reply nor turn her face toward him; and Casey pushed the door shut behind him and took two more steps toward her.

"I come to see if yuh needed anything, ma'am; a friend, mebbe." Casey grinned amiably, wanting to reassure her if it were possible to make her aware of his presence. "They had yuh locked in, ma'am. That don't look good to Casey Ryan. If yuh wanta get out-if they got yuh held a prisoner here, or anything like 'that, you can trust Casey Ryan any old time. Is-can I do anything for yuh, ma'am?" The old woman dropped her hands to her lap and held them there, closely clasped. Her head swung slowly round until she was looking at Casey with that awful, fixed stare she had heretofore directed at the wall or the floor.

"Tell those hell-hounds they have a thousand years to burn-every one of them!" she said in a deep, low voice that had in it a singing resonance like a chant. "Every cat, every rat, every mouse, every louse, has a thousand year's to burn. Tell Mart the hounds of hell must burn!" Her voice carried a terrible condemnation far beyond the meaning of the words themselves. It was as if she were pronouncing the doom of the whole world. "Every cat, every rat, every mouse, every louse —"

Casey Ryan's jaw dropped an inch. He backed until he was against the door. He had to swallow twice before he could find his voice, and those of you who know Casey Ryan will appreciate that. He waited until she had finished her declaration.

"No, ma'am, you're wrong. I come up here to see if I could help yuh."

"Hounds of hell-black as the bottomless pit that spewed you forth to prey upon mankind! The world will have to burn. Tell those hounds of hell that bay at the gibbous moon the world will have to burn. Every cat, every rat, every mouse, every louse has a thousand years to burn!"

Casey Ryan, with his mouth half open and his eyes rather wild, furtively opened the door behind him. Still meeting fixedly the dull glare of the old woman's eyes, Casey slid out through the door and fastened it hastily behind him. With an uneasy glance now and then over his shoulder as if he feared the old woman might be in pursuit of him, he hurried back down the ladder to the closed door in the drift, pulled the door shut behind him and put the padlock in place before he breathed naturally.

He stopped then to put on his shoes, made his way to the drift opening and listened again for voices or footsteps. When he found the way clear he hurried out and back to the dugout. The first thing he did was to fill his pipe and light it. Even then the sonorous voice of the old woman intoning her dreadful proclamation against the world rang in his ears and sent occasional ripples of horror down his spine. Seen through the window, she had looked a sad, lonely old lady who needed sympathy and help. At closer range she was terrible. Casey was trying to forget her by busying himself about the stove when Joe walked in unexpectedly.

Joe stood just inside the door, staring at Casey with a glassy look in his eyes. Something in Joe's face warned Casey of impending events; but with that terrible old woman still fresh in his mind, Casey was in the mood to welcome distraction of any sort. He shifted his hand in the sling so that his concealed weapons lay more comfortably therein, secure from detection, and waited.

Joe leaned forward, lifted an arm slowly and aimed a finger at Casey accusingly.

"Pap says that you're a Federal officer!" he began, waggling his finger at Casey. "Pap thinks you come here spyin' around t' see what we're up to on this here butte. Now, you can't pull nothin' like that! You can't get away with it.

"Hank, he wants t' bump yuh off an' say nothin' to anybody. Now, I come t' have it out with yuh. If you're a Federal officer we're goin' t' settle with yuh an' take no chances. Mart, he's more easy-goin' in some ways, on account of havin' his crazy ol' mother on 'is hands t' take care of. Mart don't want no killin' —on account of his mother goin' loony when 'is dad got killed. But Mart ain't here. Pap an' Hank, they been at me all mornin' t' let 'em bump yuh off.

"But Pap an' Hank, they're drunk, see? I'm the only sober man left on the job. So I come up here t' settle with yuh myself. Takes a sober man with a level head t' settle these things. Now, if you come up here spyin' an' snoopin', you git bumped off an' no argument about it. Mart's got his mother t' take care of-an' we aim t' pertect Mart. If you're a Federal officer, I want t' know it here an' now. If yuh ain't, I want yuh t' sample some uh the out-kickin'est 'White Mule' yuh ever swallered. Now which are yuh, and what yuh goin' t' do? I want my answer here an' now, an' no argument an' no foolin'!"

Casey blinked but his mouth widened in a grin. "Me, I never went lookin' fer nothin, I wouldn't put under my vest, Joe," he declared convincingly. So that was it! He was thinking against time. Moonshiners as well as would-be murderers they were-and Joe drunk and giving them away like a fool. Casey wished that he knew where Hank and Paw were at this moment. He hoped, too, that Joe was right-that Hank and Paw were drunk. He'd have the three of them tied in a row before dark, in any case. The thing to do now was to humor Joe along-leave it to Casey Ryan!

Joe was uncorking a small, flat bottle of pale liquor. Now he held it out to Casey. Casey took it, thinking he would pretend to drink, would urge Joe to take a drink; it would be simple, once he got Joe started. But Joe had a few ideas of his own concerning the celebration. He pulled a gun unexpectedly, leaned against the closed door to steady himself and aimed it full at Casey.

"In just two minutes I'm goin' t' shoot if that there bottle ain't empty," he stated gravely, nodding his head with intense pride in his ability to handle the situation. "If you're a Federal officer, yuh won't dast t' drink. If yuh ain't, you'll be almighty glad to. Anyway, it'll be settled one way or t'other. Drink 'er down!"

Casey blinked again, but this time he did not grin. He debated swiftly his chance of scaring Joe with the dynamite before Joe would shoot. But Joe had his finger crooked with drunken solemnity upon the trigger. The time for dynamite was not now.

"Pap an' Hank, they lap up anything an' call it good. I claim that's got a back-action kick to it. Drink 'er down!"

Casey drank 'er down. It was like swallowing flames. It was a half-pint flask, and it was full when Casey, with Joe's eyes fixed upon him, tilted it and began to drink. Under Joe's baleful glare Casey emptied the flask before he stopped.

Joe settled his shoulders comfortably against the doorway and watched Casey make for the water bucket.

"I claim that's the out-kickin'est stuff that ever was made on Black Butte. How'd yuh like it?"

"All right," Casey bore witness, keeping his eyes fixed on Joe and the gun and trying his best to maintain a nonchalant manner. "I'd call it purty fair hootch."

"It's GOOD hootch!" Joe declared impressively, apparently quite convinced that Casey was not a Federal officer. "Can yuh feel the kick to it?"

Casey backed until he sat on the edge of the table his good right hand supporting his left elbow outside the sling. He grinned at Joe and while he still keenly realized that he was playing a part for the sole purpose of gaining somehow an advantage over Joe, he was conscious of a slight giddiness. An unprejudiced observer would have noticed that his grin was not quite the old, Casey Ryan grin. It was a shade foolish.

"Bet your life I can feel the kick!" he agreed, nodding his head. "You can ask anybody." Then Casey discovered something strange in Joe's appearance. He lifted his head, held it very still and regarded Joe attentively.

"Say, Joe, what yuh tryin' to do with that six-gun? Tryin' to write your name in the air with it?"

Joe looked inquiringly down at the gun, eyeing it as if it were a new and absolutely unknown object. He satisfied himself apparently beyond all doubt that the gun was doing nothing it should not do, and finally turned his attention to Casey sitting on the table and grinning at him meaninglessly.

"Ain't writin' nothin'," Joe stated solemnly. "It's yore eyes. Gun's all right-yo'r seein' crooked. It's the hootch. Back-action kick to it. Ain't that right?"

"That's right," nodded Casey and he added, grinning more foolishly, "Darn right, that's right! Back-action kick-bet your life."

Joe pushed the gun inside his waistband and crooked his finger at Casey, beckoning myste-riously. "C'mon an' I'll show yuh how it's made," he invited with heavy enthusiasm. "Yore a judge uh hootch all right—I can see that. I'll show yuh how we do it. Best White Mule in Nevada. Ain't that right? Ain't that the real hootch?"

"'S right, all right," Casey agreed earnestly. "Puttin' the hoot in hootch-you fellers. You can ask anybody if that ain't right."

Joe laughed hoarsely. "Puttin' the hoot in hootch-that's right. I knowed you was all right. Didn't I say you was? I told Hank an' Pap you wasn't no Federal officer. They know it, too. I was foolin' back there. I knowed you didn't need no gun pulled on yuh t' make yuh put away the hootch. Lapped it up like a thirsty hound. I knowed yuh would —I was kiddin' yuh, runnin' that razoo with the gun. Ain't that right?"

"Darn right, that's right! I knew you was foolin' all along. You knew Casey Ryan's all right-sure, you knowed it!" Casey laid his good hand investigatively against his stomach. "Pretty hot hootch-you can ask anybody if it ain't! Workin' like an air drill a'ready."

He blinked inquisitively at Joe, who stared back inquiringly. "Who's your friend?" Casey demanded pugnaciously. "He sneaked in on yuh. I never seen 'im come in."

Joe turned slowly and looked behind him at the blank boards of the unpainted door. Just as slowly he turned back to Casey. A slow grin split his leathery face.

"Ain't nobody. It's the hootch. Told yuh, didn't I? Gittin' the best of yuh, ain't it? C'mon — I'll show yuh how it's made."

"Take a barr'l t' git the besta-Casey Ry'n," Casey boasted, his words blurring noticeably. "Where's y'r White Mule? Let 'er kick-Casey Ry'n can lead 'er an' tame 'er-an' make'r eat outa 's hand!" Following Joe, Casey stepped high over a rock no bigger than his fist.

With a lurch he straightened and tried to pull his muddled wits out of the fog that was fast enveloping them. Dimly he sensed the importance of this discovery which Joe had forced upon him. In flashes of normalcy he knew that he must see all he could of their moonshine operations. He must let them think he was drunk until he knew all their secrets. He assured himself vaguely that he must, above all things, keep his head.

But it was all pretty hazy and rapidly growing hazier. Casey Ryan, you must know, was not what is informally termed a drinking man. In his youth he might have been able to handle a sudden half-pint of moonshine whisky and keep as level a head as he now strove valiantly to retain. But Casey's later years had been more temperate than most desert men would believe. Unfortunately virtue is not always it own reward; at least Casey now found himself the worse for past abstinences.

Joe led him into the tunnel, laughing sardonically because Casey found it scarcely wide enough for his oscillating progress. They turned into a drift. Casey did not know which drift it was, though he tried foggily to remember. He was still, you must know, trying to keep a level head and gain valuable information for the sheriff who he hoped would return to the butte with Barney.

Paw and Hank were wrangling somewhere ahead. Casey could hear their raised voices mingled in a confused rumbling in the pent walls of the drift. Casey thought they passed through a doorway, and that Joe closed a heavy door behind them, but he was not sure.

Memory of the old woman intoning her horrible anathema surged back upon Casey with the closing of the door. The voices of Hank and Paw he now mistook for the ravings of the woman in the stone hut. Casey balked there, and would not go on. He did not want to face the old woman again, and he said so repeatedly-or believed that he did.

Joe caught him by the arm and pulled him forward by main strength. The voices of Paw and Hank came closer and clarified into words; or did Casey and Joe walk farther and come into their presence?

They were all standing together somewhere, in a large, underground chamber with a hole letting in the sunlight high up on one side. Casey was positive there was a hole up there, because the sun shone in his eyes and to avoid it he moved aside and fell over a bucket or a keg or something. Hank laughed loudly at the spectacle, and Paw swore because the fall startled him; but it was Joe who helped Casey up.

Casey knew that he was sitting on a barrel-or something-and telling a funny story. He thought it must be very funny indeed, because every one was laughing and bending double and slapping legs while he talked. Casey realized that here at last were men who appreciated Casey Ryan as he deserved to be appreciated. Tears ran down his own weathered cheeks-tears of mirth. He had never laughed so much before in all his life, he thought. Every one, even Paw, who was normally a mean, cantankerous old cuss, was having the time of his life.

They attempted to show Casey certain intricacies of their still, which made it better than other stills and put a greater kick in the White Mule it bred. Somewhere back in the dim recesses of Casey's mind, he felt that he ought to listen and remember what they told him.

Vaguely he knew that he must not take another drink, no matter how insistent they were. In the brief glow of that resolution Casey protested that he could hoot without any more hootch. But he hated to hurt Paw's feelings, or Hank's or Joe's. They had made the hootch with a new and different twist, and they were honestly anxious for his judgment and approval. He decided that perhaps he really ought to take a little more just to please them; not much —a couple of drinks maybe. Wherefore, he graciously consented to taste the "run" of the day before. Thereafter Casey Ryan hooted to the satisfaction of everybody, himself most of all.

After an indeterminate interval the four left the still, taking a bottle with them so that it might be had without delay, should they meet a snake or a hydrophobia skunk or some other venomous reptile. It was Casey who made the suggestion, and he became involved in difficulties when he attempted the word venomous. Once started Casey was determined to pronounce the word and pronounce it correctly, because Casey Ryan never backed up when he once started. The result was a peculiar humming which accompanied his reeling progress down the drift (now so narrow that Casey scraped both shoulders frequently) to the portal.

They stopped on the flat of the dump and argued over the advisability of taking a drink apiece before going farther, as a sort of preventive. Joe told them solemnly that they couldn't afford to get drunk on the darn' stuff. It had too hard a back-action kick, he explained, and they might forget themselves if they took too much. It was important, Joe explained at great length, that they should not forget themselves. The boss had always impressed upon them the grim necessity of remaining sober whatever happened.

"We never HAVE got drunk," Joe reiterated, "and we can't afford t' git drunk now. We've got t' keep level heads, snakes or no snakes."

Casey Ryan's head was level. He wabbled up to Joe and told him so to his face, repeating the statement many times and in many forms. He declaimed it all the way up the path to the dugout, and when they were standing outside. Beyond all else, Casey was anxious that Joe should feel perfectly certain that he, Casey Ryan, knew what he was doing, knew what he was saying, and that his head was and always had been perr-rf'c'ly level-l-l.

"Jus' t' prove-it —I c'n kill that jack-over-there —without-no-gun!" Casey bragged bubblingly, running his words together as if they were being poured in muddy liquid from his mouth. "B'lieve it? Think-I-can't?"

The three turned circumspectly and stared solemnly at a gray burro with a crippled front leg that had limped to the dump heap within easy throwing distance from the cabin door. Hobbling on three legs it went nosing painfully amongst a litter of tin cans and bent paper cartons, hunting garbage. As if conscious that it was being talked about, the burro lifted its head and eyed the four mournfully, its ears loosely flopping.

"How?" questioned Paw, waggling his beard disparagingly. "Spit 'n 'is eye?"

"Talk 'm t' death," Hank guessed with imbecile shrewdness.

"Think-I-can't? What'll —y'bet?"

They disputed the point with drunken insistence and mild imprecations, Hank and Paw and Joe at various times siding impartially for and against Casey. Casey gathered the impression that none of them believed him. They seemed to think he didn't know what he was talking about. They even questioned the fact that his head was level. He felt that his honor was at stake and that his reputation as a truthful man and a level-headed man was threatened.

While they wrangled, the fingers of Casey's right hand fumbled unobserved in the sling on his left, twisting together the two short lengths of fuse so that he might light both as one piece. Even in his drunkenness Casey knew dynamite and how best to handle it. Judgment might be dethroned, but the mechanical details of his profession were grooved deep into habit and were observed automatically and without the aid of conscious thought.

He braced himself against the dugout wall and raised his hand to the cigarette he had with some trouble rolled and lighted. A spitting splutter arose, that would have claimed the attention of the three, had they not been unanimously engaged in trying to out-talk one another upon the subject of Casey's ability to kill a burro seventy-five feet away without a gun.

Casey glanced at them cunningly, drew back his right hand and pitched something at the burro.

"Y' watch 'im!" he barked, and the three turned around to look, with no clear conception of what it was they were expected to watch.

The burro jerked its head up, then bent to sniff at the thin curl of powder smoke rising from amongst the cans. Paw and Hank and Joe were lifted some inches from the ground with the explosion. They came down in a hail of gravel, tin cans and fragments of burro. Casey, flattened against the wall in preparation for the blast, laughed exultantly.

Paw and Hank and Joe picked themselves up and clung together for mutual support and comfort. They craned necks forward, goggling incredulously at what little was left of the burro and the pile of tin cans.

"'Z that a bumb?" Paw cackled nervously at last, clawing gravel out of his uncombed beard. "'Z got me all shuck up. Whar's that 'r bottle?"

"'Z goin' t' eat a bumb—ol' fool burro!" Hank chortled weakly, feeling tenderly certain nicks on his cheeks where gravel had landed. "Paw, you ol' fool, you, don't hawg the hull thing—gimme a drink!"

"Casey's sure all right," came Joe's official O.K. of the performance. "Casey said 'e c'd do it —'n' Casey done it!" He turned and slapped Casey somewhat uncertainly on the back, which toppled him against the wall again. "Good'n on us, Casey! Darn' good joke on us —'n' on the burro!"

Whereupon they drank to Casey solemnly, and one and all, they proclaimed that it was a VERY good joke on the burro. A merciful joke, certainly; as you would agree had you seen the poor brute hungry and hobbling painfully, hunting scraps of food amongst the litter of tin cans.

After that, Casey wanted to sleep. He forced admissions from the three that he, Casey Ryan, was all right and that he knew exactly what he was doing and kept a level head. He crawled laboriously into his bunk, shoes, hat and all; and, convinced that he had defended his honor and preserved the Casey Ryan reputation untarnished, he blissfully skipped the next eighteen hours.

Chapter VI

Casey awoke under the vivid impression that some one was driving a gadget into his skull with a "double-jack." The smell of bacon scorching filled his very soul with the loathing of food. The sight of Joe calmly filling his pipe roused Casey to the fighting mood-with no power to fight. He was a sick man; and to remain alive was agony.

The squalid disorder and the stale aroma of a drunken orgy still pervaded the dugout and made it a nightmare hole to Casey. Hank came tittering to the bunk and offered him a cup of coffee, muddy from too long boiling, and Joe grinned over his pipe at the colorful language with which Casey refused the offering.

"Better take a brace uh hootch," Joe suggested with no more than his normal ill nature. "I got some over at the still we made awhile back that, ain't quite so kicky. Been agin' it in wood an' charcoal. That tones 'er down. I'll go git yuh some after we eat. Kinda want a brace, myself. That new hootch shore is a kickin' fool."

Paw accepted this remark, as high praise, and let three hot cakes burn until their edges curled while he bragged of his skill as a maker of moonshine. Paw himself was red-eyed and loose-lipped from yesterday's debauch. Hank's whole face, especially in the region of his eyes, was puffed unbecomingly. Casey, squinting an angry eye at Hank and the cup of coffee, spared a thought from his own misery to acknowledge surprise that anything on earth could make Hank more unpleasant to look upon. Joe had a sickly pallor to prove the potency of the brew.

For such is the way of moonshine when fusel oil abounds, as it does invariably in new whisky distilled by furtive amateurs working in secret and with neither the facilities nor the knowledge for its scientific manufacture. There is grim significance in the sardonic humor of the man who first named it White Mule. The kick is certain and terrific; frequently it is fatal as well. The worst of it is, you never know what the effect will be until you have drunk the stuff; and after you have drunk it, you are in no condition to resist the effect or to refrain from courting further disaster.

That is what happened to Casey. The poison in the first half-pint, swallowed under the eye of Joe's six-shooter, upset his judgment. The poison in his further potations made a wholly different man of Casey Ryan; and the after effect was so terrific that he would have swallowed cyanide if it promised relief.

He gritted his teeth and suffered tortures until Joe returned and gave him a drink of whisky in a chipped granite cup. Almost immediately he felt better. The pounding agony in his head eased perceptibly and his nerves ceased to quiver. After a while he sat up, gazed longingly at the water bucket and crawled down from the bunk. He drank largely in great gulps. His bloodshot eyes strayed meditatively to the coffee pot. After an undecided moment he walked uncertainly to the stove and poured himself a cup of coffee.

Casey lifted the cup to drink, but the smell of it under his nose sickened him. He weaved uncertainly to the door, opened it and threw out the coffee-cup and all. Which was nature flying a storm flag, had any one with a clear head been there to observe the action and the look on Casey's face.

"Gimme another shot uh that damn' hootch," he growled. Joe pushed the bottle toward Casey, eyeing him curiously.

"That stuff they run yesterday shore is kicky," Joe ruminated sympathetically. "Pap's proud as pups over it. He thinks it's the real article-but I dunno. Shore laid yuh out, Casey, an' yuh never got much, neither. Not enough t' lay yuh out the way it did. Y' look sick."

"I AM sick!" Casey snarled, and poured himself a drink more generous than was wise. "When Casey Ryan says he's sick, you can put it down he's SICK! He don't want nobody tellin' 'im whether 'e's sick 'r not. —he KNOWS 'e's sick!" He drank, and swore that it was rotten stuff not fit for a hawg (which was absolute truth). Then he staggered to the stove, picked up the coffee pot, carried it to the door and flung it savagely outside because the odor offended him.

"Mart got back last night," Joe announced casually. "You was dead t' the world. But we told 'im you was all right, an' I guess he aims t' give yuh steady work an' a cut-in on the deal. We been cleanin' up purty good money-but Mart says the market ain't what it was; too many gone into the business. You're a good cook an' a good miner an' a purty good feller all around-only the boss says you'll have t' cut out the booze."

"'J you tell 'im you MADE me drink it?" Casey halted in the middle of the floor, facing Joe indignantly.

"I told 'im I put it up t' yuh straight-what your business is, an' all. You got no call t' kick-didn't I go swipe this bottle uh booze for yuh t' sober up on, soon as the boss's back was turned? I knowed yuh needed it; that's why. We all needed it. I'm just tellin' yuh the boss don't approve of no celebrations like we had yest'day. I got up early an' hauled that burro outa sight 'fore he seen it. That's how much a friend I be, an' it wouldn't hurt yuh none to show a little gratitude!"

"Gratitude, hell! A lot I got in life t' be grateful for!" Casey slumped down on the nearest bench, laid his injured hand carefully on the table and leaned his aching head on the other while he discoursed bitterly on the subject of his wrongs.

His muddled memory fumbled back to his grievance against traffic cops, distorting and magnifying the injustice he had received at their hands. He had once had a home, a wife and a fortune, he declared, and what had happened? Laws and cops had driven him out, had robbed him of his home and his family and sent him out in the hills like a damned kiotey, hopin' he'd starve to death. And where, he asked defiantly, was the gratitude in that?

He told Joe ramblingly but more or less truthfully how he had been betrayed and deserted by a man he had befriended; one Barney Oakes, upon whom Casey would like to lay his hands for a minute.

"What I done to the burro ain't nothin' t' what I'd do t' that hound uh hell!" he declared, pounding the table with his good fist.

Homeless, friendless; but Joe was his friend, and Paw and Hank were his friends-and besides them there was in all the world not one friend of Casey Ryan's. They were good friends and good fellows, even if they did put too much hoot in their hootch. Casey Ryan liked his hootch with a hoot in it.

He was still hooting (somewhat incoherently it is true, with recourse now and then to the bottle because he was sick and he didn't give a darn who knew it) when the door opened and he whom they called Mart walked in. Joe introduced him to Casey, who sat still upon the bench and looked him over with drunken disparagement. Casey had a hazy recollection of wanting to see the boss and have it out with him, but he could not recall what it was that he had been so anxious to quarrel about.

Mart was a slender man of middle height, with thin, intelligent face and a look across the eyes like the old woman who rocked in the stone hut. He glanced from the bottle to Casey, eyeing him sharply. Drunk or sober, Casey was not the man to be stared down; nevertheless his fingers strayed involuntarily to his shirt collar and pulled fussily at the wrinkles.

"So you're the man they've been holding here for my inspection," Mart said coolly, with a faint smile at Casey's evident discomfort. "You're still hitting it up, I see. Joe, take that bottle away from him. When he's sober enough to talk straight, I'll give him the third degree and see what he really is, anyway. Guess he's all right-but he sure can lap up the booze. That's a point against him."

Casey's hand went to the bottle, beating Joe's by three inches. He did not particularly want the whisky, but it angered him to hear Mart order it taken from him. Away back in his mind where reason had gone into hiding, Casey knew that some great injustice was being done him; that he, Casey Ryan, was not the man they were calmly taking it for granted that he was.

With the bottle in his hand he rose and walked unsteadily to his bunk. He did not like this man they called the boss. He remembered that in his bunk, under the bedding, he had concealed something that would make him the equal of them all. He fumbled under the blankets, found what he sought and with his back turned to the others he slipped the thing into his sling out of sight.

Mart and Joe were talking together by the table, paying no attention to Casey, who was groggily making up his mind to crawl into his bunk and take another sleep. He still meant to have it out with Mart, but he did not feel like tackling the job just now.

Mart turned to the door and Joe got up to follow him, with a careless glance over his shoulder at Casey, who was lifting a foot as if it weighed a great deal, and was groping with it in the air trying to locate the edge of the lower bunk. Joe laughed, but the laugh died in his throat, choked off suddenly by what he saw when Mart pulled open the door.

Casey turned suspiciously at the laugh and the sound of the door opening. He swung round and steadied himself with his back against the bunk when he saw Mart and Joe lift their hands and hold them there, palms outward, a bit higher than their heads. Something in the sight enraged Casey unreasoningly. A flick of the memory may have carried him back to the old days in the mining camps when Casey drove stage and hold-ups were frequent.

"What 'r yuh tryin' to pull on me now?" he bawled, and rushed headlong toward them, pushing them forcibly out into the open with a collision of his body against Joe. Outside, a voice harshly commanded him to throw up his hands-and it was then that Casey Ryan's Irish fighting blood boiled and bubbled over. Unconsciously he pushed his hat forward over one eye, drew back his lips in a fighting grin, stepped down off the low doorsill with a lurch that nearly sent him sprawling and went weaving belligerently toward a group of five men whose attitude was anything but conciliatory.

"Casey Ryan! I'm dogged if it ain't Casey!" exclaimed a familiar voice in the group, whereat the others looked astonished. Through his slits of swollen lids Casey glared toward the voice and recognized Barney Oakes, grinning at him with what Casey considered a Judas treachery. He saw two men step away from Joe and the boss, leaving them in handcuffs.

"Take them irons off'n my friends!" bellowed Casey as he charged. "Whadda yuh think you're doin', anyway? Take 'em off! It's Casey Ryan that's tellin' yuh, an' yuh better heed what he says, before you're tore from limb to limb!"

"B-but, Casey! This 'ere's a shurf's possy!" The voice of Barney rose in a protesting 'squawk. "I brung 'em all the way over here to your rescue! They brung a cor'ner to view your remains! Don't you know your pardner, BARNEY OAKES?

"Ah-h —I know yuh think I don't? I know yuh to a fare-yuh-well! Brung a cor'ner, did yuh? Tha's all right-goin' t' need a cor'ner-but he won't set on Casey Ryan's remains-you c'n ask anybody if any cor'ners ever set on Casey Ryan yit! Naw." Casey snarled as contemptuously as was possible to a man in his condition. "No cor'ner ever set on Casey Ryan, an' he ain't goin' to!"

The men glanced questioningly at one another. One laughed. He was a large, smooth-jowled man inclined to portliness, and his laugh vibrated his entire front contagiously so that the others grinned and took it for granted that Casey Ryan was a comedy element introduced unexpectedly where they had thought to find him a tragedy.

"No, you're a pretty lively man for me to sit on; I admit it," the portly man remarked. "I'm the coroner, and it looks as if I wouldn't sit, this trip."

Casey eyed him blearily, not in the least mollified but instead swinging to a certain degree of lucidity that was nevertheless governed largely by the hoot he had swallowed in the hootch.

"There's part of a burro 'round here some'er's you c'n set on," Casey informed him grimly, and fumbled in his coat pocket for his pipe. He drew it out empty, looked at it and returned it to his pocket. One who knew Casey intimately would have detected a hidden purpose in his manner. The warning was faint, indefinable at best, and difficult to picture in words. One might say that an intimate acquaintance would have detected a false note in Casey's defiance. His manner was restrained just when violence would have been more natural.

"Damn a pipe," Casey grumbled with drunken petulance. "Anybody got a cigarette? I'm single-handed an' I ain't able t' roll 'em."

It was the coroner himself who handed Casey a "tailor-made." Casey nodded glumly, accepted a match and lighted the cigarette almost as if he were sober. He looked the group over noncommittally, eyed again the handcuffs on Mart and Joe, sent a veiled glance toward Barney Oakes and turned away. He still held the center of the stage. Fully expecting to find him dead, the sheriff and his men were slow to adjust themselves to the fact that he was very much alive and very drunk and apparently not greatly interested in his rescue.

Casey halted in his unsteady progress toward the dugout. The sheriff was already questioning his two prisoners about other members of the gang; but he looked up when Casey lifted up his voice and spoke his mind of the moment.

"Brung a cor'ner, did yuh, lookin' for some one to set on! Barney Oakes is the man that'll need a cor'ner in a minute. You're all goin' to need 'im. Casey Ryan never stood around yit whilst his friends was hobbled up by a shurf—turn 'em loose an' turn 'em loose quick! An' git back away from Barney Oakes so he won't drop on yuh in chunks —I'll fix 'im for yuh to set on!"

His hand had gone up to his cigarette, but only Joe knew what was likely to follow. Joe gave a yell of warning, ducked and ran straight away from the group. The sheriff yelled also and gave chase. The group was broken-luckily-just as Casey heaved something in that direction.

"I blowed up a jackass yesterday when they thought I couldn't —I'll blow up a bunch of 'em to-day! Yuh c'n set on what's left uh Barney Oakes!"

The explosion scattered dirt and small stones-and the sheriff's posse. Casey sent one malevolent glance over his shoulder as he stumbled into the dugout.

"Missed 'im!" he grumbled disgustedly to himself when he saw no fragments of Barney falling. His ferociousness, like the dynamite, annihilated itself with the explosion. "Missed 'im! Casey Ryan's gittin' old; old an' sick an' a damn' fool. Missed 'im with the last shot-drunk-drunk an' don't give a darn!"

He slammed the door shut behind him, pushed his hat forward so violently that it rested on the bridge of his nose, and wabbled over to his bunk. This time his foot found the edge of the lower bunk, and he scratched and clawed his way up and rolled in upon the blankets.

He was asleep and snoring when the sheriff, edging his way in as if he were an animal trainer's apprentice entering the lion's cage, sneaked on his toes to the bunk and slipped the handcuffs on Casey.

Casey awoke almost sober and considerably surprised when he discovered the handcuffs. His injured hand was throbbing from the poison in his system and the steel band on his swollen wrist. His head still ached frightfully and his tongue felt thick and dry as flannel in his mouth.

He rolled over and sat up, staring uncomprehendingly at the cabin full of men. The sight of Barney Oakes recalled in a measure his performance with the dynamite; at least, he felt a keen disappointment that Barney was alive and whole and grinning. Casey could not see what there was to grin about, and he took it as a direct insult to himself.

Mart and Joe sat sullenly on a bench against the wall, and Paw reclined in his bunk at the farther end of the room. A blood-stained bandage wrapped Paw's head turbanwise, and his little, deep-set eyes gleamed wickedly in his pallid face. Casey looked for Hank, but he was not there.

A strange man was cooking supper, and Casey wanted to tell him that he was slicing the bacon twice as thick as it should be. The corpulent man, whom he dimly remembered as a coroner, was talking with a big, burly individual whom Casey guessed was the sheriff. A man came in and announced to the big man that the car was fixed and they could go any time. Mart, who had been staring morosely down at his shackled wrists, lifted his head and spoke to the sheriff.

"You'll have to do something about my mother," he said, and bit his lip at the manner in which every head swung his way.

"What about your mother?" the sheriff asked moving toward him. "Is she here?" His eyes sent a quick glance around the room which obviously had four outside walls.

Mart swallowed. "She has a cabin to herself," he explained constrainedly. "She-she isn't quite right. Strangers excite her. She-hasn't been well since my father was killed in the mine; she's quiet enough with us-she knows us. I don't know how she'll be now. I'm afraid-but she can't be left here alone; all I ask is, be as gentle as you can."

The sheriff looked from him to Joe. Joe nodded confirmation. "Plumb harmless," he said gruffly. "It IS kinda-pitiful. Thinks everybody in the world is damned and going to hell on a long lope." He gave a snort that resembled neither mirth nor disgust. "Mebbe she's right at that," he added grimly.

The sheriff asked more questions, and Mart stood up. "I'll show you where she is, sure. But can't you leave her be till we're ready to start? She-it ain't right to bring her here."

"She'll want her supper," the sheriff reminded Mart. "We'll be driving all night. Is she sick abed?"

Casey lay down again and turned his face to the wall. He remembered the old woman now, and he hoped sincerely they would not bring her into the cabin. But whatever they did, Casey wanted no part in it whatever. He wanted to be left alone, and he wanted to think. More than all else he wanted not to see again the old woman who chanted horrible things while she rocked and rocked.

He was roused from uneasy slumber by two officious souls, one of whom was Barney Oakes. Their intentions were kindly enough, they only wanted to give him his supper. But Casey wanted neither supper nor kindly intentions, and he was still unregenerately regretful that Barney Oakes was not lying out on the garbage heap in a more or less fragmentary condition. They raised him to a sitting posture, and Casey swung his legs over the edge of the bunk and delivered a ferocious kick at Barney Oakes.

He caught Barney under the chin, and Barney went down for several counts. After that Casey wore hobbles on his feet, and was secretly rather proud of the fact that they considered him so dangerous as all that. Had his mood not been a sulky one which refused to have speech with any one there, they would probably have found it wise to gag him as well.

That is one night in Casey's turbulent life which he never recalled if he could help it. Two cars had brought the sheriff's party, and one was a seven-passenger. In the roomy rear seat of this car, Casey, shackled and savage, was made to ride with Mart and his mother. Two deputies occupied the folding seats and never relaxed their watchfulness.

Casey's head still ached splittingly, and the jolting of the car did not serve to ease the pain. The old woman sat in the middle, with a blanket wound round and round her to hold her quiet; which it failed to do. Into Casey's ear rolled the full volume of her rich contralto voice as she monotonously intoned the doom of all mankind-together with every cat, every rat, etc. Mart's fear had proved well-founded. Strangers had excited the woman and it was not until sheer exhaustion silenced her that she ceased for one moment her horrible chant.

I read the story in the morning paper, and made a flying trip to San Bernardino. Casey was in jail, naturally; but he didn't care much about that so long as he owned a head with an air-drill going inside. At least, that is what he told me when I was let in to see him. I was working to get him out of there on bail if possible before I sent word to the Little Woman, hoping she had not read the papers. I had some trouble piecing the facts together and trying to get the straight of things before I sent word to the Little Woman. I went out and got him some medicine guaranteed, by the doctor who wrote the prescription, to take the hoot out of the hootch Casey had swallowed. That afternoon Casey left off glaring at me, sat up, accepted a cigarette and consented to talk.

"—an' all I got to say is, Barney Oakes is a liar an' the father uh liars. I never was in cahoots with him at no time. When he says I got 'im to foller a Joshuay palm jest to git 'im out in the hills an' kill 'im off, he lies. Let 'im come an' tell me that there story!"

Casey was still slightly abnormal, I noticed, so I calmed him as best I could and left him alone for a time. There was some hesitancy about the bail, too, which I wished to overcome. Throwing that half-stick of dynamite might be construed as an attempt at wholesale murder. I did not want the county officials to think too long and harshly about the matter.

I explained later to Casey that Barney Oakes had reported his disappearance to the officials in Barstow. The sheriff's office had long suspected a nest of moonshiners somewhere near Black Butte, and it was rumored that one Mart Hanson, who owned a mine up there, was banking more money than was reasonable, these hard times, for a miner, who ships no ore. Casey's disappearance had crystallized the suspicions into an immediate investigation. And Barney's assertion that Casey had been murdered took the coroner along with the posse.

It had all been straight and fairly simple until they reached the mine and discovered Casey uproariously one of the gang. Throwing loaded dynamite at sheriffs is frowned upon nowadays in the best official circles, I told Casey; he would have to explain that in court, I was afraid.

Then Barney, after Casey had kicked him in the chin, had reversed his first report of the trouble and was now declaiming to all who would listen that he had been decoyed to Black Butte by Casey Ryan and there ambushed and nearly killed. Casey, as Barney now interpreted the incident, had joined his confederates under the very thin pretense of climbing the butte to come at them from behind. Barney now remembered that he had been shot at from three different angles, and that the burros had been killed by pistol shots fired at close range-presumably by Casey Ryan.

It was like taming tigers to make Casey sit still and listen to all this, but I had to do it so that he would know what to disprove. Afterwards I had a talk with Joe and Paw, separately, and so got at the whole truth. They bore no malice toward Casey and were perfectly willing to see him out of the scrape. They were a sobered pair; Hank, like a fool, had fired at the posse and was killed.

The next day came the Little Woman to the rescue. I told her the whole story, not even omitting the burro, before she went to the jail to see Casey. It was a pretty mess-take it all around-and I was secretly somewhat doubtful of the outcome.

The Little Woman is game as women are made. She went with me to the jail, and she met Casey with a whimsical smile. We found him sitting on the side of his bunk with his legs stretched out and his feet crossed, his good hand thrust in his trousers pocket and a cigarette in one corner of his mouth, which turned sourly downward. He cocked an eye up at us and rose, as the Little Woman had maybe taught him was proper. But he did not say a word until the Little Woman walked up and kissed him on both cheeks, turning his face this way and that with her hand under his chin.

Casey grinned sheepishly then and hugged her with his good arm. I wish you could have seen the look in his eyes when they dwelt on the Little Woman!

"Casey Ryan, you need a shave. And your shirt collar is a disgrace to a Piute," she drawled reprovingly.

Casey looked at me over her shoulder and grinned. He hadn't a word to say for himself, which was unusual in Casey Ryan.

"It's lucky for you, Casey Ryan, that I remembered to go down to the police station and get the proof that you were pinched twice on Broadway just five days before Barney Oakes says he found you stalled in the trail north of Barstow; and that you had been pinched pretty regularly every whip-stitch for the last six months, and were a familiar and unwelcome figure in downtown traffic and elsewhere.

"The sheriff who raided Black Butte admitted to me that it is utterly impossible for the world to hold more than one Casey Ryan at a time; and that he, for one, is willing to accept the word of the city police that you were there raising the record for traffic trouble and not moonshining at Black Butte. He doesn't approve of throwing dynamite at people, but-well, I talked with the prosecuting attorney, too, and they both seem to be mighty nice men and reasonable. I'm afraid Barney Oakes will see his beautiful story all spoiled."

"He'll forget it when he feels the ruin to his face I'm goin' t' create for him if I ever meet up with 'im again," Casey commented grimly.

"Babe sent you a pincushion she made in school. I think she made beautiful, neat stitches in that C," went on the Little Woman in a placid, gossipy tone invented especially for domestic conversation. "And-oh, yes! There's a new laundryman on our route, and he PERSISTS in running across the lawn and dumping the laundry in the front hall, though I've told him and TOLD him to deliver it at the back. And there's a new tenant in Number Six, and they hadn't been in more than three days before he came home drunk and kept everybody in the house awake, bellowing up and down the hall and abusing his wife and all. I told him held have to go when his month is up, but he says he'll be damned if he will. He says he won't and I can't make him."

"He won't, hey?" A familiar, pale glitter came into Casey's eyes. "You watch and see whether he goes or not! He better tell Casey Ryan he won't go! Who'd, they think's runnin' the place? Lemme ketch that laundry driver oncet, runnin' across our lawn; I'll run 'im across it-on his nose! They take advantage of you quick as my back's turned. I'll learn 'em they got Casey Ryan to reckon with!"

The Little Woman gave me a smiling glance over Casey's shoulder, and lowered a cautious eyelid. I left them then and went away to have a satisfying talk with the sheriff and the prosecuting attorney.

Chapter VIII

In the desert, where roads are fewer and worse than they should be, a man may travel wherever he can negotiate the rocks and sand, and none may say him nay. If any man objects, the traveler is by custom privileged to whip the objector if he is big enough, and afterwards go on his way with the full approval of public opinion. He may blaze a trail of his own, return that way a year later and find his trail an established thoroughfare.

In the desert Casey gave trail to none nor asked reprisals if he suffered most in a sudden meeting. In Los Angeles Casey was halted and rebuked on every corner, so he complained; hampered and annoyed by rules and regulations which desert dwellers never dreamed of.

Since he kept the optimistic viewpoint of a child, experience seemed to teach him little. Like the boy he was at heart, he was perfectly willing to make good resolutions-all of which were more or less theoretical and left to a kindly Providence to keep intact for him.

So here he was, after we had pried him loose from his last predicament, perfectly optimistic under his fresh haircut, and thinking the traffic cops would not remember him. Thinking, too-as he confided to the Little Woman-that Los Angeles looked pretty good, after all. He was resolved to lead henceforth a blameless life. It was time he settled down, Casey declared virtuously. His last trip into the desert was all wrong, and he wanted you to ask anybody if Casey Ryan wasn't ready at any and all times to admit his mistakes, if he ever happened to make any. He was starting in fresh now, with a new deal all around from a new deck. He had got up and walked around his chair, he told us, and had thrown the ash of a left-handed cigarette over his right shoulder; he'd show the world that Casey Ryan could and would keep out of gunshot of trouble.

He was rehearsing all this and feeling very self-righteous while he drove down West Washington Street. True, he was doing twenty-five where he shouldn't, but so far no officer had yelled at him and he hadn't so much as barked a fender. Down across Grand Avenue he larruped, never noticing the terrific bounce when he crossed the water drains there (being still fresh from desert roads). He was still doing twenty-five when he turned into Hill Street.

Busy with his good resolutions and the blameless life he was about to lead, Casey forgot to signal the left-hand turn. In the desert you don't signal, because the nearest car is probably forty or fifty miles behind you and collisions are not imminent. West-Washington-and-Hill-Street crossing is not desert, however. A car was coming behind Casey much closer than fifty miles; one of those scuttling Ford delivery trucks. It locked fenders with Casey when he swung to the left. The two cars skidded as one toward the right-hand curb; caught amidships a bright yellow, torpedo-tailed runabout coming up from Main Street, and turned it neatly on its back, its four wheels spinning helplessly in the quiet, sunny morning. Casey himself was catapulted over the runabout, landing abruptly in a sitting position on the corner of the vacant lot beyond, his self-righteousness considerably jarred.

A new traffic officer had been detailed to watch that intersection and teach a driving world that it must not cut corners. A bright, new traffic button had been placed in the geographical center of the crossing; and woe be unto the right-hand pocket of any man who failed to drive circumspectly around it. New traffic officers are apt to be keenly conscientious in their work. At twenty-five dollars per cut, sixteen unhappy drivers had been taught where the new button was located and had been informed that twelve miles per hour at that crossing would be tolerated, and that more would be expensive.

Not all drivers take their teaching meekly, and the new traffic officer near the end of his shift had pessimistically decided that the driving world is composed mostly of blamed idiots and hardened criminals.

He gritted his teeth ominously when Casey Ryan came down upon the crossing at double the legal speed. He held his breath for an instant during the crash that resounded for blocks. When the dust had settled, he ran over and yanked off the dented sand of the vacant lot a dazed and hardened malefactor who had committed three traffic crimes in three seconds: he had exceeded the speed limit outrageously, cut fifteen feet inside the red button, and failed to signal the turn.

"You damned, drunken boob!" shouted the new traffic cop and shook Casey Ryan (not knowing him).

Shaking Casey will never be safe until he is in his coffin with a lily in his hand. He was considerably jolted, but he managed a fourth crime in the next five minutes. He licked the traffic cop rather thoroughly —I suppose because his onslaught was wholly unexpected-kicked an expostulating minister in the pit of the stomach, and was profanely volunteering to lick the whole darned town when he was finally overwhelmed by numbers and captured alive; which speaks well for the L. A. P.

Wherefore Casey Ryan continued his ride down town in a dark car that wears a clamoring bell the size of a breakfast plate under the driver's foot, and a dark red L. A. Police Patrol sign painted on the sides. Two uniformed, stern-lipped cops rode with him and didn't seem to care if Casey's nose WAS bleeding all over his vest. A uniformed cop stood on the steps behind, and another rode beside the driver and kept his eye peeled over his shoulder, thinking he would be justified in shooting if anything started inside. Boys on bicycles pedaled furiously to keep up, and many an automobile barely escaped the curb because the driver was goggling at the mussed-up prisoner in the "Black Maria."

The Little Woman telegraphed me at San Francisco that night. The wire was brief but disquieting. It merely said, "CASEY IN JAIL SERIOUS NEED HELP." But I caught the Lark an hour later and thanked God it was running on time.

The Little Woman and I spent two frantic days getting Casey out of jail. The traffic cop's defeat had been rather public; and just as soon as he could stand up straight in the pulpit, the minister meant to preach a series of sermons against the laxity of a police force that permits such outrages to occur in broad daylight. More than that, the thing was in the papers, and people were reading and giggling on the street cars and in restaurants. Wherefore, the L. A. P. was on its tin ear.

Even so, much may be accomplished for a man so wholesomely human as Casey Ryan. On the third day the charge against him was changed from something worse to "Reckless driving and disturbing the peace." Casey was persuaded to plead guilty to that charge, which was harder to accomplish than mollifying the L. A. P.

He paid two fifty-dollar fines and was forbidden to drive a car "in the County of Los Angeles, State of California, during the next succeeding period of two years." He was further advised (unofficially but nevertheless with complete sincerity) to pay all damages to the two cars he had wrecked and to ask the minister's doctor what was his fee; a new uniform for the traffic cop was also suggested, since Casey had thrust his foot violently into the cop's pocket which was not tailored to resist the strain. The judge also observed, in the course of the conversation, that desert air was peculiarly invigorating and that Casey should not jeopardize his health and well-being by filling his lungs with city smoke.

I couldn't blame Casey much for the mood he was in after a setback like that to his good resolutions. I was inclined to believe with Casey that Providence had lain down on the job.

Chapter IX

At the corner of the Plaza where traffic is heaviest, a dingy Ford loaded with camp outfit stalled on the street-car track just as the traffic officer spread-eagled his arms and turned with majestic deliberation to let the East-and-West traffic through. The motorman slid open his window and shouted insults at the driver, and the traffic cop left his little platform and strode heavily toward the Ford, pulling his book out of his pocket with the mechanical motion born of the grief of many drivers.

Casey Ryan, clinging to the front step of the street car on his way to the apartment house he once more called home, swung off and beat the traffic officer to the Ford. He stooped and gave a heave on the crank, obeyed a motion of the driver's head when the car started, and stepped upon the running board. The traffic officer paused, waved his book warningly and said something. The motorman drew in his head, clanged the bell, and the afternoon traffic proceeded to untangle.

"Get in, old-timer," invited the driver whom Casey had assisted. Casey did not ask whether the driver was going in his direction, but got in chuckling at the small triumph over his enemies, the police.

"Fords are mean cusses," he observed sympathetically. "They like nothing better than to get a feller in bad. But they can't pull nothin' on me. I know 'em to a fare-you-well. Notice how this one changed 'er mind about gettin' you tagged, soon as Casey Ryan took 'er by the nose?"

"Are you Casey Ryan?" The driver took his eyes off the traffic long enough to give Casey an appraising look that measured him mentally and physically. "Say, I've heard quite a lot about you. Bill Masters, up at Lund, has spoke of you often. He knows you, don't he?"

"Bill Masters sure had ought t' know me," Casey grinned. In a big, roaring, unfriendly city, here sounded a friendly, familiar tone; a voice straight from the desert, as it were. Casey forgot what had happened when Barney Oakes crossed his path claiming acquaintance with Bill Masters, of Lund. He bit off a chew of tobacco, hunched down lower in the seat, and prepared himself for a real conflab with the man who spoke the language of his tribe.

He forgot that he had just bought tickets to that evening's performance at the Orpheum, as a sort of farewell offering to his domestic goddess before once more going into voluntary exile as advised by the judge. Pasadena Avenue heard conversational fragments such as, "Say! Do you know —? Was you in Lund when —?"

Casey's new friend drove as fast as the law permitted. He talked of many places and men familiar to Casey, who was in a mood that hungered for those places and men in a spiritual revulsion against the city and all its ways.

Pasadena, Lamanda Park, Monrovia-it was not until the car slowed for the Glendora speed-limit sign that Casey lifted himself off his shoulder blades, and awoke to the fact that he was some distance from home and that the shadows were growing rather long.

"Say! I better get out here and 'phone to the missus," he exclaimed suddenly. "Pull up at a drug store or some place, will yuh? I got to talkin' an' forgot I was on my way home when I throwed in with yuh."

"Aw, you can 'phone any time. There is street cars running back to town all the time I or you can catch a bus anywhere's along here. I got pinched once for drivin' through here without a tail-light; and twice I've had blowouts right along here. This town's a jinx for me and I want to slip it behind me."

Casey nodded appreciatively. "Every darn' town's a jinx for me," he confided resentfully. "Towns an' Casey Ryan don't agree. Towns is harder on me than sour beans."

"Yeah —I guess L. A.'s a jinx for you all right. I heard about your latest run-in with the cops. I wish t' heck you'd of cleaned up a few for me. I love them saps the way I like rat poison. I've got no use for the clowns nor for towns that actually hands 'em good jack for dealin' misery to us guys. The bird never lived that got a square deal from 'em. They grab yuh and dust yuh off —"

"They won't grab Casey Ryan no more. Why, lemme tell yuh what they done!"

Glendora slipped behind and was forgotten while Casey told the story of his wrongs. In no particular, according to his version, had he been other than law-abiding. Nobody, he declaimed heatedly, had ever taken HIM by the scruff of the neck and shaken him like a pup, and got away with it, and nobody ever would. Casey was Irish and his father had been Irish, and the Ryan never lived that took sass and said thank-yuh.

His new friend listened with just that degree of sympathy which encourages the unburdening of the soul. When Casey next awoke to the fact that he was getting farther and farther away from home, they were away past Claremont and still going to the full extent of the speed limit. His friend had switched on the lights.

"I GOT to telephone my wife!" Casey exclaimed uneasily. "I'll gamble she's down to the police station right now, lookin' for me. An' I want the cops t' kinda forgit about me. I got to talkin' along an' plumb forgot I wasn't headed home."

"Aw, you can 'phone from Fontana. I'll have to stop there anyway for gas. Say, why don't yuh stall 'er off till morning? You couldn't get home for supper now if yuh went by wireless. I guess yuh wouldn't hate a mouthful of desert air after swallowing smoke and insults, like yuh done in L. A. Tell her you're takin' a ride to Barstow. You can catch a train out of there and be home to breakfast, easy. If you ain't got the change in your clothes for carfare," he added generously, "Why, I'll stake yuh just for your company on the trip. Whadda yuh say?"

Casey looked at the orange and the grapefruit and lemon orchards that walled the Foothill Boulevard. All trees looked alike to Casey, and these reminded him disagreeably of the fruit stalls in Los Angeles.

"Well, mebby I might go on to Barstow. Too late now to take the missus to the show, anyway. I guess I can dig up the price uh carfare from Barstow back." He chuckled with a sinful pride in his prosperity, which was still new enough to be novel. "Yuh don't catch Casey Ryan goin' around no more without a dime in his hind pocket. I've felt the lack of 'em too many times when they was needed. Casey Ryan's going to carry a jingle louder'n a lead burro from now on. You can ask anybody."

"You bet it's wise for a feller to go heeled," the friend of Bill Masters responded easily. "You never know when yuh might need it. Well, there's a Bell sign over there. You can be askin' your wife's consent while I gas up."

Innocent pleasure; the blameless joy of riding in a Ford toward the desert, with a prince of a fellow for company, was not so easily made to sound logical and a perfectly commonplace incident over a long-distance telephone. The Little Woman seemed struck with a sense of the unusual; her voice betrayed trepidation and she asked questions which Casey found it difficult to answer. That he was merely riding as far as Barstow with a desert acquaintance and would catch the first train back, she apparently failed to find convincing.

"Casey Ryan, tell me the truth. If you're in a scrape again, you know perfectly well that Jack and I will have to come and get you out of it. San Bernardino sounds bad to me, Casey, and you're pretty close to the place. Do you really want me to believe that you're coming back on the next train?"

"Sure as I'm standin' here! What makes yuh think I'm in a scrape? Didn't I tell yuh I'm goin' to walk around trouble from now on? When Casey tells you a thing like that, yuh got a right to put it down for the truth. I'm going to Barstow for a breath uh fresh air. This is a feller that knows Bill Masters. I'll be home to breakfast. I ain't in no trouble an' I ain't goin' to be. You can believe that or you can set there callin' Casey Ryan a liar till I git back. G'by."

Whatever the Little Woman thought of it, Casey really meant to do exactly what he said he would do. And he really did not believe that trouble was within a hundred miles of him.

Chapter X

"Wanta drive?" Casey's friend was rolling a smoke before he cranked up. "They tell me up in Lund that no man livin' ever got the chance to look back and see Casey Ryan swallowing dust. I've heard of some that's tried. But I reckon," he added pensively, while he rubbed the damp edge of the paper down carefully with a yellowed thumb, "Fords is out of your line, now. Maybe you don't toy with nothin' cheaper than a twin-six."

"Well, you can ask anybody if Casey Ryan's the man to git big-headed! Money don't spoil ME none. There ain't anybody c'n say it does. Casey Ryan is Casey Ryan wherever an' whenever yuh meet up with him. Yuh might mebby see me next, hazin' a burro over a ridge. Or yuh might see me with ten pounds uh flour, a quart uh beans an' a sour-dough bucket on my back. Whichever way the game breaks-you'll be seein' Casey Ryan; an' you'll see 'im settin' in the game an' ready t' push his last white chip to the center."

"I believe it, Casey. Darned if I don't. Well, you drive 'er awhile; till yuh get tired, anyway." He bent to the crank, gave a heave and climbed in, with Casey behind the wheel, looking pleased to be there and quite ready to show the world he could drive.

"Say, if I drive till I'm TIRED," he retorted, "I'm liable to soak 'er hubs in the Atlantic Ocean before I quit. And then, mebby I'll back 'er out an' drive 'er to the end of Venice Pier just for pastime."

"Up in Lund they're talkin' yet about your drivin'," his new friend flattered him. "They say there's no stops when you get the wheel cuddled up to your chest. No quittin' an' no passin' yuh by with a merry laugh an' a cloud of alkali dust. I guess it's right. I've been wantin' to meet yuh."

"That there last remark sounds like a traffic cop I had a run-in with once!" Casey snorted-merely to hide his gratification. "You sound good, just to listen to, but you ain't altogether believable. There's men in Lund that'd give an ear to meet me in a narrow trail with a hairpin turn an' me on the outside an' drunk.

"They'd like it to be about a four-thousand-foot drop, straight down. Lund as a town ain't so crazy about me that they'd close up whilst I was bein' planted, an' stop all traffic for five minutes. A show benefit was sprung on Lund once, to help Casey Ryan that was supposed to be crippled. An' I had to give a good Ford —a DARN' good Ford! —to the benefitters, so is they could git outa town ahead uh the howlin' mob. That's how I know the way Lund loves Casey Ryan. Yuh can't kid ME, young feller."

Meanwhile, Casey swung north into Cajon Pass; up that long, straight, cement-paved high-way to the hills he showed his new friend how a Ford could travel when Casey Ryan juggled the wheel. The full moon was pushing up into a cloud bank over a high peak beyond the Pass. The few cars they met were gone with a whistle of wind as Casey shot by.

He raced a passenger train from the mile whistling-post to the crossing, made the turn and crossed the track with the white finger of the headlight bathing the Ford blindingly. He completed that S turn and beat the train to the next crossing half a mile farther on; where he "spiked 'er tail", as he called it, stopping dead still and waiting jeeringly for the train to pass. The engineer leaned far out of the cab window to bellow his opinion of such driving; which was unfavorable to the full extent of his vocabulary.

"Nothin' the matter with a Ford, as I can see," Casey observed carelessly, when he was under way again.

"You sure are some driver," his new friend praised him, letting go the edge of the car and easing down again into the seat. "Give yuh a Ford and all the gas yuh can burn and I can't see that you'd need to worry none about any of them saps that makes it their business to interfere with travelin'. I'm glad that moon's quit the job. Gives the headlights a show. Hit 'er up now, fast as yuh like. After that crossin' back there I ain't expectin' to tremble on no curves. I see you're qualified to spin 'er on a plate if need be. And for a Ford, she sure can travel."

Casey therefore "let 'er out", and the Ford went like a scared lizard up the winding highway through the Pass. At Cajon Camp he slowed, thinking they would need to fill the radiator before attempting to climb the steep grade to the summit. But the young man shook his head and gave the "highball." (Which, if you don't already know it, is the signal for full speed ahead.)

Full speed ahead Casey gave him, and they roared on up the steep, twisting grade to the summit of the Pass. Casey began to feel a distinct admiration for this particular Ford. The car was heavily loaded-he could gauge the weight by the "feel" of the car as he drove yet it made the grade at twenty-five miles an hour and reached the top without boiling the radiator; which is better than many a more pretentious car could do.

"Too bad you've made your pile already," the young man broke a long silence. "I'd like to have a guy like you for my pardner. The desert ain't talkative none when you're out in the middle of it, and you know there ain't another human in a day's drive. I've been going it alone. Nine-tenths of these birds that are eager to throw in with yuh thinks that fifty-fifty means you do the work and they take the jack. I'm plumb fed upon them pardnerships. But if you didn't have your jack stored away —a hull mountain of it, I reckon —I'd invite yuh to set into the game with me; I sure would."

Casey spat into the dark beside the car. "They's never a pile so big a feller ain't willin' to make it bigger," he replied sententiously. "Fer, as I'm concerned, Casey's never backed up from a dollar yet. But I ain't no wild colt no more, runnin' loose an' never a halter mark on me. I'm bein' broke to harness, and it's stable an' corral from now on, an' no more open range fer Casey. The missus hopes to high-school me in time. She's a good hand-gentle but firm, as the preacher says. And I guess it's time fer Casey Ryan to quit hellin' around the country an' settle down an' behave himself."

"I could put you in the way of adding some easy money to your bank roll," the other suggested tentatively.

But Casey shook his head. "Twenty years ago yuh needn't have asked me twice, young feller. I'd 'a' drawed my chair right up and stacked my chips a mile high. Any game that come along, I played 'er down to the last chip. Twenty years ago-yes, er ten! —Casey Ryan woulda tore that L. A. jail down rock by rock an' give the roof t' the kids to make a playhouse. Them L. A. cops never woulda hauled me t' jail in no wagon. I mighta loaded 'em in behind, and dropped 'em off at the first morgue an' drove on a-whistlin'. That there woulda been Casey Ryan's gait a few years back. Take me now, married to a good woman an' gettin' gray —" Casey sighed, gazing wishfully back at the Casey Ryan he had been and might never be again.

"No, sir, I ain't so darned rich I ain't willin' to add a few more iron men to the bunch. But on account of the missus I've got to kinda pick my chances. I ain't had money so long but what it feels good to remind myself I got it. I carry a thousand dollars or so in my inside pocket, just to count over now an' then to convince myself I needn't worry about a grubstake. I've got to soak it into my bones gradual that I can afford to settle down and live tame, like the missus wants. Stand-up collars every day, an' step into a chiny bathtub every night an' scrub-when you ain't doin' nothin' to git dirt under your finger nails even! Funny, the way city folks act. The less they do to git dirty, the more soap they wear out. You can ask anybody if that ain't right.

"Can't chew tobacco in the house, even, 'cause there's no place yuh dast to spit. I stuck m' head out of the bedroom window oncet, an I let fly an' it landed on a lady; an' the missus went an' bought her a new hat an took my plug away from me. I had to keep my chewin' tobacco in the tool-box of my car, after that, an' sneak out to the beach now an' then an' chew where I could spit in the ocean. That's city life for yuh!"

"When I git to thinkin' about hittin' out into the hills prospectin, or somethin', that roll uh dough I pack stands right on its hind legs an' says I got no excuse. I've got enough to keep me in bacon an' beans, anyway. An' the missus gits down in the mouth when I so much as mention minin'."

"A guy grows old fast when he quits the game and sets down to do the grandpa-by-the-fire. First you know, a clown that thinks it's time he took it easy is gummin' 'is grub, and shiverin' when yuh open the door, an' takin' naps in the daytime same as babies. Let a guy once preach he's gettin' old —"

Casey jerked the gas lever and jumped the car ahead viciously. "Well, now, any time yuh see CASEY RYAN gummin' 'is grub an' needin' a nap after dinner—"

"A clown GITS that way once he pulls out of the game. I've saw it happen time an' again." The young man laughed rather irritatingly. "Say, when I tell it to Bill Masters that Casey Ryan has plumb played out his string an' laid down an' QUIT, by hock, and can be seen hereafter SETTIN' WITH A SHAWL OVER HIS SHOULDERS—"

Casey nearly turned the Ford over at that insult. He jerked it back into the road and sent it ahead again at a faster pace.

"Well, now, any time yuh see CASEY RYAN settin' with a shawl over his shoulders—"

"Well, maybe not YOU; but the bird sure comes to it that thinks he's too old to play the game. Why, you'll never be ready to settle down! Take yuh twenty years from now—I'd rather bank on a pardner like you'd be than some young clown that ain't had the experience. From the yarns I've heard about yuh, yuh don't back down from nothing. And you're willing to give a pardner a chance to get away with his hide on him. I'd rather be held up by the law than by some clown that's workin' with me."

He paused; and when he, spoke again his tone had changed to meet a prosaic detail of the drive.

"Stop here in Victorville, will yuh, Casey? I'll take a look at the radiator and maybe take on some more gas and oil. I've been stuck on the desert a few times with an empty tank-and that learns a guy to keep the top of his gas tank full and never mind the bottom."

"Good idea," said Casey shortly, his own tone relaxing its tension of a few minutes before. "I run a garage over at Patmos once, an' the boobs I seen creepin' in on their last spoonful uh gas-walkin' sometimes for miles to carry gas back to where they was stalled-learnt Casey Ryan to fill 'er up every chancet he gits."

But although the subject of age had been dropped half a mile back in the sand, certain phrases flung at him had been barbed and had bitten deep into Casey Ryan's self-esteem. They stung and rankled there. He had squirmed at the picture his new friend had so ruthlessly drawn with crude words, but bold, of doddering old age. Casey resented the implication that he might one day fill that picture.

He began vaguely to resent the Little Woman's air of needing to protect him from himself. Casey Ryan, he told himself boastfully, had never needed protection from anybody. He had managed for a good many years to get along on his own hook. The Little Woman was all right, but she was making a mistake—a big mistake-if she thought she had to close-herd him to keep him out of trouble.

He rolled a smoke and wished that the Little Woman would settle down with him somewhere in the desert, where he could keep a couple of burros and go prospecting in the hills. Where sagebrush could grow to their very door if it wanted to, and the moon could show them long stretches of mesa land shadowed with mystery, and then drop out of sight behind high peaks.

He felt that he might indeed grow old fast, shut up in a city. It occurred to him that the Little Woman was unreasonable to expect it of him. Her idea of getting him out of town for a time, as the judge had advised, was to send him up to San Francisco to be close-herded there. Casey had promised to go, but now the prospect jarred. He wasn't feeble-minded, that he knew of; it seemed natural to want to do his own deciding now and then. When he got back home in the morning, Casey meant to have a serious talk with the Little Woman, and get right down to cases, and tell her that he was built for the desert, and that you can't teach an old dog new tricks.

"They been tryin' to make Casey Ryan over into something he ain't," he muttered under his breath, while his new friend was in the garage office paying for the gas. "Jack an' the Little Woman's all right, but they can't drive Casey Ryan in no town herd. Cops is cops; and they got 'em in San Francisco same as they got 'em in L. A. If they got 'em, I'll run agin' 'em. I'll tell 'em so, too."

The young man came out, sliding silver coins into his trousers pocket. He glanced up and down the narrow, little street already deserted, cranked the Ford and climbed in.

"All set," he observed cheerfully, "Let's go!"

Casey slipped his cigarette to the upper, left-hand corner of his whimsical, Irish mouth, forced a roar out of the little engine and whipped around the corner and across the track into the faintly lighted road that led past shady groves and over a hill or two, and so into the desert again.

His new friend had fallen into a meditative mood, staring out through the windshield and whistling under his breath a pleasant little melody of which he was probably wholly unaware. Perhaps he felt that he had said enough to Casey just at present concerning a possible partnership. Perhaps he even regretted having said anything at all.

Casey himself drove mechanically, his rebellious mood slipping gradually into optimism. You can't keep Casey Ryan down for long; in spite of his past unpleasant experiences he was presently weaving optimistic plans of his own. The young fellow beside him seemed to return Casey's impulsive friendship. Casey thought pleasureably of the possibility of their driving over the desert together, sharing alike the fortunes of the game and the adventures of the trail. Casey himself had learned to be shy of partnerships-witness Barney Oakes! —but any man with a drop of Irish in his blood and a bit of Irish twinkle in his eye would turn his back on defeat and try again for a winning.

They had just passed over a hilly stretch with many turns and windings, the moon blotted out completely now by the cloud bank. For half an hour they had not seen any evidence that other human beings were alive in the world. But when they went rattling across a small mesa where the sand was deep, a car with one brilliant spotlight suddenly showed itself around a turn just ahead of them.

Casey slowed down automatically and gave a twist to the steering wheel. But the sand just here was deep and loose, and the front wheels of the Ford gouged unavailingly at the sides of the ruts. Casey honked the horn warningly and stopped full, swearing a good, Caseyish oath. The other car, having made no apparent effort to turn out, also stopped within a few feet of Casey, the spotlight fairly blinding him.

The young man beside Casey slid up straight in the seat and stopped whistling. He leaned out of the car and stared ahead without the dusty interference of the windshield.

"You can back up a few lengths and make the turn-out all right," he suggested.

"If I can back up, so can he. He's got as much road behind him as what I'VE got," Casey retorted stubbornly. "He never made a try at turnin' out. I was watchin'. Any time I can't lick a road hawg, he's got a license to lick me. Make yourself comf'table, young feller-we're liable to set here a spell." Casey grinned. "I spent four hours on a hill once, out-settin, a road hawg that wanted me to back up."

The man in the other car climbed out and came toward them, walking outside the beams cast by his own glaring spotlight. He bulked rather large in the shadows; but Casey Ryan, blinking at him through the windshield, was still ready and willing to fight if necessary. Or, if stubbornness were to be the test, Casey could grin and feel secure. A little man, he reflected, can sit just as long as a big man.

The big man walked leisurely up to the car and smiled as he lifted a foot to the running board. He leaned forward, his eyes going past Casey to the other man.

"I kinda thought it was you, Kenner," he drawled. "How much liquor you got aboard to-night?"

Casey, slanting a glance downward, glimpsed the barrel of a big automatic looking toward them.

"What if I ain't got any?" the young man parried glumly. "You're taking a lot for granted."

The big man chuckled. "If you ain't loaded with hootch, it's because one of the boys met up with yuh before I did. Open 'er up. Lemme see what you got."

The young fellow scowled, swore under his breath and climbed out, turning toward the loaded tonneau with reluctant obedience.

"I can't argue with the law," he said, as he began to pull out a roll of bedding wedged in tightly. "But, for cripes sake, go as easy as you can. I'm plumb lame from my last fall!"

The big man chuckled again. "The law's merciful as, it can afford to be, and I've got a heart like an ox. Got any jack on yuh?"

"I'm just about cleaned, and that's the Gawd's truth. Have a heart, can't yuh? A man's got t' live."

"Slip me five hundred, anyway. How much is your load?"

"Sixty gallons-bottled, most of it. Two kegs in bulk." Young Kenner was proceeding stoically with the unloading. Casey, his mouth clamped tight shut, was glaring stupifiedly straight out through the windshield.

"Pile out thirty gallons of the bottled goods by that bush. You can keep the kegs." The big man's eyes shifted to Casey Ryan's expressionless profile and dwelt there curiously.

"Seems like I know you," he said abruptly. "Ain't you the guy that was brought in with that Black Butte bunch of moonshiners and got off on account of a nice wife and an L. A. alibi? Sure you are! Casey Ryan. I got yuh placed now." He threw back his head and laughed.

Casey might have been an Indian making a society call for all the sign of life he gave. Young Kenner, having deposited his camp outfit in a heap on the ground, began lifting out tall, round bottles, four at a time and ricking them neatly beside the large sagebush indicated by the officer.

Standing upon the running board at Casey's shoulder where he had a clear view, the big man watched the unloading and at the same time kept an eye on Casey. It was perfectly evident that for all his easy good nature, he was not a man who could be talked out of his purpose.

"All right, pile in your blankets," the big man ordered at last, and young Kenner unemotionally began to reload the camp outfit. The big man's attention shifted to Casey again. He looked at him curiously and grinned.

"Say, that's a good one you pulled! You had all the county officials bluffed into thinking you were the victim of that Black Butte bunch, instead of being in cahoots. That alibi of yours was a bird. Does Kenner, here, know you hit the hootch pretty strong at times? Bootlegging's bad business for a man that laps it up the way you do. Where's that piece of change, Kenner?"

"Aw, can't yuh find some way to leave me jack enough to buy gas and grub?" Young Kenner asked sullenly, reaching into his pocket. The big man shook his head.

"I'm doing a lot for you boys, when I let yuh get past me with the Lizzie, to say nothing of half your load. I'd ought to trundle yuh back to San Berdoo; you both know that as well as I do. I'm too soft-hearted for this job, anyway. Hand over the roll."

Young Kenner swore and extended his arm behind Casey. "That leaves me six bits," he growled, as the big man dropped something into his coat pocket. "You might give me back ten, anyway."

"Couldn't possibly. I have to have something to square myself with if this leaks out. Just back up, till you can get around my car. Turn to the left where the sand ain't so deep and you ain't likely to run over the booze."

With the big man still standing at his shoulder on the running board, Casey Ryan did what he had rashly declared he never would do; he backed the Ford, turned it to the left as he had been commanded to do, and drove around the other car. It was bitter work for Casey; but even he recognized the fact that the "settin'" was not good that evening. Back in the road again, he stopped when he was told to stop, and waited, with a surface calm altogether strange to Casey, while the officer stepped off and gave a bit of parting advice.

"Better keep right on going, boys. I'd hate to see yuh get in trouble, so you'd better take this old road up ahead here. That'll bring yuh out at Dagget and you'll miss Barstow altogether. I just came from there; there's a hard gang hanging around on the lookout for anything they can pick up. Don't get caught again. On your way!"

Casey drove for half a mile still staring straight before him. Then young Kenner laughed shortly.

"That's Smilin' Lou," he said. "He's a mean boy to monkey with. Talk about road hawgs-he's one yuh can't outset!"

Chapter XI

"So that's the kind uh game yuh asked me to set in on!" Casey broke another long silence. He had felt in his bones that young Kenner was watching him secretly, waiting for him to take his stand for or against the proposition.

"I'd like to know who passed the word around amongst outlaws that Casey Ryan is the only original easy mark left runnin' wild, an' that he can be caught an' made a goat of any time it's handy! Look at the crowd of folks bunched on that crossing this afternoon! Why didn't yuh pick some one else for the goat? Outa all them hundreds uh people, why'n hell did yuh have to go an' pick on Casey Ryan? Ain't he had trouble enough tryin' to keep outa trouble?

"Naw! Casey Ryan's went an' blowed hisself to show tickets, an' he's headed home, peaceful an' on time, so's he can shave an' put on a clean collar an' slick up to please his wife an' take 'er to the show! Nothin' agin the law in that! Not a damn' thing yuh can haul 'im to jail fer! So YOU had to come along, loaded to the guards with hootch-stall your Ford on the car track right under m' nose, an' tell Casey Ryan to git in! Couldn't leave 'im to go home peaceful to 'is wife-naw! You had t' haul 'im away out here an' git 'im in wrong with a cop agin! That's a fine game you're playin'! That's a DARNED fine game!"

"Sure, it is! It's better than the game you've been playing," young Kenner stated calmly. "Take your own story, for instance. You've been dubbin' along, tryin' t' play the way the law tells you to. An' the saps has been flockin' to yuh like a bunch uh hornets-every bird tryin' t' sink his stinger in first. Ain't that right?

"Keepin' the law has laid yuh in jail twice in the last month, by your own tell. Why, a clown like you, that's aimin' t' keep the law an' live honest, is the easiest mark in the world. Them's the guys that do the most harm-they make graftin' so darned easy! Them's the guys the saps lay for and dust off regular in the shape of fines an' taxes an' the like uh that. Oncet in awhile they'll snatch yuh fer somethin' yuh never done at all an' lay yuh away fer a day or two, just t' keep yuh scared and easy t' handle next time.

"Now, yuh take me, fer instance. I play agin' the law-an' I'm cleanin' up right along, and have yet to take my morning sunlight in streaks. I know as much about the inside of a jail as I know about the White House-an' no more. I've hauled hootch all over the country, an' I never yet was dusted off so hard by the law that I didn't come through with a roll uh jack they'd overlooked.

"Take this highjackin' to-night, for instance. Look what Smilin' Lou took off'n me! And yet," Kenner turned and grinned impudently at Casey, "don't never think I didn't come out a long jump ahead! I carry nothin' cheap; nothin' but good whisky an' brandy that the liquor houses failed to declare when the world went dry. Then there's real, honest-to-gosh European stuff run in from Mexico; now you're in, Casey, I'll tell yuh the snap. When I said easy money, I was in my right mind.

"You can count on highjackers leavin' yuh half your load; mebby a little more, if yuh set purty. They don't aim t' force yuh out uh the business. They grab what the traffic'll bear, an' let yuh go on an make a profit so you'll stay.

"Now there's a card you can slip up your sleeve for this game. Yuh load in the best stuff first-see? Anything real special you wanta put in kegs with double sides an' ends which you fill with moonshine. Yuh never can tell-they might wanta sample it. Smilin' Lou did once-an' you notice to-night he left the kegs be. So they get a good grade of whisky from the liquor houses. And they pass up the best, imported stuff that can be got to-day. We'll have regular customers for that; and you can gamble they'll pay the price!" He laughed at some secret joke which he straightway shared with Casey.

"You noticed I got my gas-tank behind —a twenty-gallon tank at that. Well, what if I tell yuh that right under this front seat there's a false bottom to the tool-box and under that-well, suppose you're settin' on forty pints uh French champagne? More'n all that, this cushion we're settin' on has got a concealed pocket down both sides-for hop. So yuh see, Casey, a man can make an honest livin' at this game, even if he's highjacked every trip. Now you're in, I can show yuh all kinds uh tricks."

The muscles, along Casey's jaw had hardened until they looked bunched. His eyes, fixed upon the winding trail in front of him, were a pale, unwinking glitter.

"Who says I'm in? Yuh ain't heard Casey Ryan say it yet, have yuh? Yuh better wait till Casey says he's in b'fore yuh bank on 'im too strong. Casey may be an easy mark-he may be the officious goat pro tem of every darn' bootlegger an' moonshiner an' every darn' cop that crosses his trail; but you can ask anybody if Casey Ryan don't do 'is own decidin'!

"Before you go any further, young feller, I'll tell yuh just how fur Casey's in your game-an' that's as fur as Barstow. When Casey says he'll do a thing he comes purty near doin' it. I ain't playin' no bootleg game, young feller; White Mule an' me ain't an' never was trail pardners. Make me choose between bootleggers an' cops, an' I'd have to flip a dollar on it. Only fer Bill Masters bein' your friend, I dunno but what I'd take yuh right back with me t' L. A. an' let yuh sleep in a jail oncet-seein' you've never had the pleasure!"

The young man laughed imperturbably. "Flip that dollar for me, Casey, to see whether I shoot yuh now an' dump yuh out in the brush somewheres, or make yuh play the hootch game an' like it. Why, you didn't think for one minute, did yuh, that I was takin' any chance with you? Not a chance in the world! Go squeal to the law-an' what would it get yuh?

"You was drivin' this car yourself when Smilin' Lou stopped us, recollect. He had yuh placed as one of that Black Butte gang quick as he lamped yuh. Yuh think Smilin' Lou is goin' to take a chance? You was caught with the goods t'night, old-timer, an' it's the second time inside a month. It'd be the third time you an' the law has tangled. Why, you set there yourself an' told me how you was practically run outa L. A., right this week. You set still a minute and figure out about how many years they'd give yuh!

"How come Smilin' Lou overlooked cleanin' yuh of your roll when he took mine, do yuh think? He was treatin' yuh white, an' givin' yuh a chance to come back strong next time-that's why. They got so much on yuh now after to-night, that he knows you got just one chance to sidestep a stretch in the pen. That's to play the game with pertection. Smilin' Lou never to my knowledge throwed down a guy that come through on demand.

"Smilin' Lou stood there an' sized yuh up about the same as I did, somethin' like this: 'Here Is Casey Ryan —a clown that's safe anywhere in the desert States. He got honest prospector wrote all over 'im. Why, if you boarded a street car the conductor would be guessin', wild-eyed, how much gold dust it takes to make a nickel, expectin' you to haul out your poke an' look around fer the gold scales. Why, you could git by where a town guy couldn't. You've got a rep a mile long as a fightin', squareshootin' Irishman that's a drivin' fool an' knows the desert like he knows ham-an'-eggs. Tie on some picks an' shovels an' put you behind the wheel, and only the guys that are in the know would ever get wise in a thousand years.

"Why, look what he said about you havin' 'em all bluffed in San Berdoo! Grabbed you with a bunch uh moonshiners, and you fightin' the saps harder'n any of 'em-and then, by heck, you slips the noose an' leaves 'em thinkin' you're honest but unlucky.

"So you 'n' me is pardners till I say when. We'll clean up some real jack together. Minin' ain't in it, no more, with hootch runnin' —if yuh play it right. The good old White Mule goes under the wire, old-timer, an' takes the money. Burros is extinct."

"Burros ain't any extincter than what you'll be when I git through with yuh," gritted Casey savagely, shutting off the gas. "Bill Masters can like it or not —I'm goin' to lick the livin' tar outa you here an' now. When I'm through with yuh, if you're able to wiggle the wheel, yuh can take your load uh hootch an' go tahell! I'll hoof it down here to the next station on the railroad an' ketch a ride back to L. A."

Kenner laughed. "An' what would I be doin', you poor nut? Set here meek till yuh tell me to git out an' take a lickin'? Yuh feel that gun proddin' yuh in the ribs, don't yuh? I can't help wonderin' how your wife would feel towards you if you was found with a hole drilled through your middle, an' a carload uh booze. That'd jar the faith of the most believin' woman on earth.

You take this cut-off road up here an' drive till I tell yuh t' stop. As you may know, a man can't be chickenhearted and peddle hootch-an' I'm called an expert. So you think that over, Casey-an' drive purty, see?"

Casey drove as "purty" as was possible with a six-shooter pressed irritatingly against his lowest floating rib; but he did not dwell upon the spectacle of himself found dead with a carload of booze. He wished to heaven he hadn't let the Little Woman talk him out of packing a gun, and waited for his chance.

Young Kenner was thoughtful, brooding through the hours of darkness with his head slightly bent and his eyes, so far as Casey could determine, fixed steadily on the uneven trail where the headlights revealed every rut, every stone, every chuck-hole. But Casey was not deceived by that quiescence. The revolver barrel never once ceased its pressure against his side, and he knew that young Kenner never for an instant forgot that he was riding with Casey Ryan at the wheel, waiting for a chance to kill him.

By daylight, such was Casey's driving, they were well down the highway which leads to Needles and on through Arizona. Casey was just thinking that they would soon run out of gas, and that he would then have a fighting chance, when he was startled almost into believing that he had spoken his plan.

"I told you there's a twenty-gallon tank on this car; well, it holds twenty-five. I've got a special carburetor that gives an actual mileage of twenty-two miles to the gallon on ordinary desert roads. I filled 'er till she run over at Victorville-and I notice you're easy on the gas with your drivin'. Figure it yourself, Casey, and don't be countin' on a stop till I'm ready t' stop."

Casey grunted, more crestfallen than he would ever admit. But he hadn't given up; the give-up quality had been completely forgotten when Casey's personality was being put together. He drove on, around the rubbly base of a blackened volcano long since cold and bleak, and bored his way through the sandy stretch that leads through Patmos.

Patmos was a place of unhappy memories, but he drove through the little hamlet so fast that he scarcely thought of his unpleasant sojourn there the summer before. Young Kenner had fallen silent again and they drove the sixty miles or so to Goffs with not a word spoken between them.

Casey spent most of that time in mentally cursing the Ford for its efficiency. He had prayed for blowouts, a fouled timer, for something or anything or everything to happen that could possibly befall a Ford. He couldn't even make the radiator boil. Worst and most persistent of his discomforts was the hard pressure of that six-shooter against his side. Casey was positive that the imprint of it would be worn as a permanent brand upon his person for the rest of his life. Young Kenner's voice speaking to him came so abruptly that Casey jumped.

"I've been thinking over your case," Kenner said cheerfully. "Stop right here while we talk it over."

Casey stopped right there.

"I've changed my mind about havin' you for a pardner," young Kenner went on. "You'd be a valuable man all right; but when a harp like you gets stubborn-bitter, my hunch tells me to break away clean. You're a mick-an' micks is all alike when they git a grudge. I can't be bothered keepin' yuh under my eye all the time, and the way I've felt yuh oozin' venom all this while shows me I'd have to. An' bumpin' yuh off would be neither pleasant ner safe.

"Now, the way I've doped this out, I'm goin' to sell yuh the outfit fer just what jack yuh got in your clothes. Fork it over, an' I'll give yuh the layout just as she stands."

"Yuh better wait till Casey says he wants t' buy!" Swallowing resentment all night had made his voice husky; and it was bitter indeed to sit still and hear himself called a harp and a mick.

"Why wait? Hand over the roll, and that closes the deal. I didn't ask yuh would yuh buy — I'm givin' yuh somethin' fer your money, is all. I could take it off yuh after yuh quit kickin' and drive your remains in to this little burg, with a tale of how I'd caught a bootlegger that resisted arrest. So fork over the jack, old-timer. I want to catch that train over there that's about ready to pull out." He prodded sharply with the gun, and Casey heard a click which needed no explanation.

Casey fumbled for a minute inside his vest and glumly "forked over." Young Kenner inspected the folded bank notes, smiled and slipped the flat bundle inside his shirt.

"You're stronger on the bank roll than what yuh let on," he remarked contentedly. "I don't stand to lose so much, after all. Sixteen hundred, I make it. What's in your pants pockets?"

Casey, still balefully silent, emptied first one pocket and then the other into Kenner's cupped palm. With heavy sarcasm he felt in his watch pocket and produced a nickel slipped there after paying street-car fare. He held it out to young Kenner between his finger and thumb, still gazing straight before him.

Young Kenner took it and grinned. "Oh, well-you're rich! Drive on now, and when you get about even with that caboose, slow to twelve miles whilst I hop off; and then hit 'er up again an' keep 'er goin'. If yuh don't, I'll grab yuh fer a bootlegger, sure. And I'd have the hull train crew to help me wrassle yuh down. They'd be willin' to sample the evidence, I guess, an' be witnesses against yuh. An' bear in mind, Casey, that yuh got a darned good Ford and all its valuable contents for sixteen hundred and some odd bucks. If you meet up with the law, you can treat 'em white an' still break even on the deal yuh just consummated with me."

"Like hell I consummated the deal!" Casey was goaded into muttering.

He drove abreast of the caboose, and at a final prod in the ribs Casey slowed down. Young Kenner dropped off the running board, alighted running with his body slanted backwards and his lips smiling friendly-wise.

"Don't take any bad money-an' don't let 'em catch yuh!" he cried mockingly, as he headed for the caboose.

At a crossing, two miles farther on, Casey came larruping out of the sand hills and was forced to wait while the freight train went rattling past, headed east on a downhill grade.

Young Kenner, up in the cupola, leaned far out and waved his hat as the caboose flicked by.

The highway north from the Santa Fe Railroad just west of Needles climbs an imperceptible grade across barren land to where the mesa changes and becomes potentially fertile. Up this road, going north, a cloud of yellow dust rolled swiftly. See at close range, the nose of a dingy Ford protruded slightly in front of the enveloping cloud-and behind it Casey Ryan, hard-eyed and with his jaw set to the fighting mood, gripped the wheel and drove as if he had a grudge against the road.

At the first signpost Casey canted a malevolent eye upward and went lurching by at top speed. The car bulked black for a moment, dimmed, and merged into the fleeing cloud that presently seemed no more than a dust-devil whirling across the mesa. At the second signpost Casey slowed, his eyes dwelling speculatively upon the legend:

The arrow pointed to the right where a narrow, little-used trail angled crookedly away through the greasewood. Casey gave a deciding twist to the steering wheel and turned into the trail.

Juniper Wells is not nearly so nice a place as it sounds. But it is the first water north of the Santa Fe, and now and then a wayfarer of the desert leaves the main highway and turns that way, driven by necessity. It is a secluded spot, too unattractive to tempt people to linger; because of its very seclusion it therefore tempted Casey Ryan.

When a man has driven a Ford fifteen hours without once leaving the wheel or taking a drink of water or a mouthful of food, however great his trouble or his haste, his first thought will be of water, food and rest. Even Casey's deadly rage at the diabolical trick played upon him could not hold his thoughts from dwelling upon bacon and coffee and a good sleep afterwards.

Wind and rain and more wind, buffeting that trail since the last car had passed, made "heavy going." The Ford labored up small hills and across gullies, dipping downward at last to Juniper Wells; there Casey stopped close beside the blackened embers left by some forgotten traveler of the wild. He slid stiffly from behind the wheel to the vacant seat beside him, and climbed out like the old man he had last night determined never to become. He walked away a few paces, turned and stood glaring back at the car as if familiarizing himself with an object little known and hated much.

Fate, he felt, had played a shabby trick upon an honest man. Here he stood, a criminal in the eyes of the law, a liar in the eyes of the missus. An honest man and a truthful, here he was-he, Casey Ryan-actually afraid to face his fellow men.

"HE wasn't no friend of Bill Masters; the divil himself wouldn'ta owned him fer a friend!" snarled Casey, thinking of Kenner. "Me-CASEY RYAN! —with a load uh booze wished onto me-and a car that may have been stolen fer all I know-an' not a darn' nickel to my name! They can make a goat uh Casey Ryan once, but watch clost when they try it the second time! Casey MAY be gittin' old; he might possibly have softenin' of the brain; but he'll git the skunk that done this, or you'll find his carcass layin' alongside the trail bleachin' like a blowed-out tire! I'll trail 'im till my tongue hangs down to my knees! I'll git 'im an' I'll drown 'im face down in a bucket of his own booze!" Whipped by emotion, his voice rose stridently until it cracked just under a shout.

"That sounds pretty businesslike, old man," a strange voice spoke whimsically behind Casey. "Who's all this you're going to trail till your tongue hangs down to your knees? Going to need any help?"

Casey whirled belligerently upon the man who had walked quietly up behind him.

"Where the hell did YOU come from?" he countered roughly.

"Does it matter? I'm here," the other parried blandly. "But by the way! If you've got the makings of a meal in your car-and you look too old a hand in the desert to be without grub —I won't refuse to have a snack with you. I hate to invite myself to breakfast, but it's that or go hungry-and an empty belly won't stand on ceremony."

The hard-bitten features of Casey Ryan, tanned as they were by wind and sun to a fair imitation of leather, were never meant to portray mixed emotions. His face, therefore, remained impassive except for a queer, cornered look in his eyes. With a sick feeling at the pit of his stomach he wondered just how much of his impassioned soliloquy the man had overheard; who and what this man was, and how he had managed to approach within six feet of Casey without being overheard. With a sicker feeling, he wondered if there were any grub in the car; and if so, how he could get at it without revealing his contraband load to this stranger.

But Casey Ryan was nothing if not game. He reached for his trusty plug of tobacco and pried off a corner with his teeth. He lifted his left hand mechanically to the back of his head and pushed his black felt hat forward so that it rested over his right eyebrow at a devil-may-care angle. These preparations made involuntarily and unconsciously, Casey Ryan was himself again.

"All right-if you're willin' to rustle the wood an' start a fire, I'll see if I can dig up somethin'."
He cocked an eye up at the sun. "I et my breakfast long enough ago so I guess it's settled. I
reckon mebby I c'd take on some bacon an' coffee myself. Feller I had along with me I ditched,
back here at the railroad. He done the packin' up-an' I'd hate to swear to what he put in an' what
he left out. Onery cuss —I wouldn't put nothin' past him. But mebby we can make out a meal."

The stranger seemed perfectly satisfied with this arrangement and studied preamble. He
started off to gather dead branches of greasewood; and Casey, having prepared the way for
possible disappointment, turned toward the car.

Fear and Casey Ryan have ever been strangers; yet he was conscious of a distinct, prickly chill
down his spine. The glance he cast over his shoulder at the stranger betrayed uneasiness, best
he could do. He turned over the roll of bedding and cautiously began a superficial search which
he hoped would reveal grub in plenty-without revealing anything else. He wished now that he
had taken a look over his shoulder when young Kenner was unloading the car at Smiling Lou's
command. He would be better prepared now for possible emergencies. He remembered, with
a bit of comfort, that the bootlegger had piled a good deal of stuff upon the ground before
Casey first heard the clink of bottles.

A grunt of relief signaled his location of a box containing grub. A moment later he lifted out
a gunny sack bulging unevenly with cooking utensils. He fished a little deeper, turned back a
folded tarp and laid naked to his eyes the top of a whisky keg. With a grunt of consternation
he hastily replaced the tarp, his heart flopping in his chest like a fresh-landed fish.

The stranger was kneeling beside a faintly crackling little pile of twigs, his face turned inquiringly toward Casey. Casey, glancing guiltily over his shoulder, felt the chill hand of discovery
reaching for his very soul. It was as if a dead man were hidden away beneath that tarp. It
seemed to him that the eyes of the stranger were sharp, suspicious eyes, and that they dwelt
upon him altogether too attentively for a perfectly justifiable interest even in the box of grub.

Black coffee, drunk hot and strong, gave the world a brighter aspect. Casey decided that the
situation was not so desperate, after all. Easy enough to bluff it out-easiest thing in the world!
He would just go along as if there wasn't a thing on his mind heavier than his thinning, sandy
hair. No man living had any right or business snooping around in his car, unless he carried a
badge of an officer of the law. Even with the badge, Casey told himself sternly, a man would
have to show a warrant before he could touch a finger to his outfit.

Over his third cup of coffee Casey eyed the stranger guardedly. He did not look like an
officer. He was not big and burly, with arrogant eyes and the hint of leashed authority in his
tone. Instead, he was of medium height, owned a pair of shrewd gray eyes and an easy drawl,
and was dressed in the half military style so popular with mining men, surveyors and others
who can afford to choose what garb they will adopt for outdoor living.

He had shown a perfect familiarity with cooking over a campfire, and had fried the bacon
in a manner which even Casey could not criticize. Before the coffee was boiled he had told
Casey that his name was Mack Nolan. Immediately afterward he had grinned and added the
superfluous information that he was Irish and didn't care who knew it.

"Well, I'm Irish, meself," Casey returned approvingly and with more than his usual brogue.
"You can ask anybody if Casey Ryan has ever showed shame fer the blood that's in' 'im. 'Tis the
Irish that never backs up from a rough trail or a fight." He poured a fourth cup of coffee into
a chipped enamel cup and took his courage in his two hands. Mack Nolan, he assured himself
optimistically, couldn't possibly know what lay hidden under the camp outfit in the Ford. Until
he did know, he was harmless as anybody, so long as Casey kept an eye on him.

During the companionable smoke that followed breakfast, Casey learned that Mack Nolan had spent some time in Nevada, ambling through the hills, examining the geologic formation of the country with a view to possible future prospecting in districts yet undeveloped.

"The mineral possibilities of Nevada haven't been more than scratched," Mack Nolan observed, lying back with one arm thrown up under his head as a makeshift pillow and the other hand negligently attending to the cigarette he was smoking. His gray army hat was tilted over his eyes, shielding them from the sun while they dwelt rather studiously upon the face of Casey Ryan.

"Every spring I like to get out and poke around through these hills where folks as a rule don't go. Never did much prospecting-as such. Don't take kindly enough to a pick and shovel for that. What I like best is general field work. If I run across something rich, time enough then to locate a claim or two and hire a couple of strong backs to do the digging.

"I've been out now for about three weeks; and night before last, just as I stopped to make camp and before I'd started to unpack, my two mules got scared at a rattler and quit the country. Left me flat, without a thing but my clothes and six-shooter, and what I had in my pockets." He lifted the cigarette from between his lips-thin, they were, and curved and rather pitiless, one could guess, if the man were sufficiently roused.

"I wasted all yesterday trying to trail 'em. But you can't do much tracking in these rocks back here toward the river. I was hitting for the highway to catch a ride if I could, when I saw you topping this last ridge over here. Don't blame me much for bumming a breakfast, do you?" And he added, with a sigh of deep physical content, "It sure-lee was some feed!"

His lids drooped lower as if sleep were overtaking him in spite of himself. "I'd ask yuh if you'd seen anything of those mules-only I don't give a damn now. I wish this was night instead of noon; I could sleep the clock around after that bacon and bannock of yours. Haven't a care in the world," he murmured drowsily. "Happy as a toad in the sun, first warm day of spring. How soon you going to crank up?"

Casey stared at him unwinkingly through narrowed lids. He pushed his hat forward with a sharp tilt over his eyebrow-which meant always that Casey Ryan had just O. K.'d an idea-and reached for his chewing tobacco.

"Go ahead an' take a nap if yuh want to," he urged. "I got some tinkerin' to do on the Ford, an' I was aimin' to lay over here an' do it. I'm kinda lookin' around, myself, for a likely prospect; I got all the time there is. I guess I'll back the car down the draw a piece where she'll set level, an' clean up 'er dingbats whilst you take a sleep."

Casey left the breakfast things where they were, as a silent reassurance to Mack Nolan that the car would not go off without him. It was a fine, psychological detail of which Casey was secretly rather proud. A box of grub, a smoked coffee pot and dirty breakfast dishes left beside a dead campfire establishes evidence, admissible before any jury, that the owner means to return.

Casey went over and cranked the Ford, grimly determined to make the coffee pot lie for him if necessary. He backed the car down the draw a good seventy-five yards, to where a wrinkle in the bank hid him from the breakfast camp. He stopped there and left the engine running while he straddled out over the side and went forward to the dip of the front fender to see if the Ford were still visible to Mack Nolan. He was glad to find that by crouching and sighting across the fender he could just see the campfire and the top of Nolan's hat beyond it. The man need only lift his head off his arm to see that the Ford was standing just around the turn of the draw.

"The corner was never yet so tight that Casey Ryan couldn't find a crack somewhere to crawl through," he told himself vaingloriously. "An' I hope to thunder the feller sleeps long an' sleeps solid!"

For fifteen minutes the mind of Casey Ryan was at ease. He had found a shovel in the car, placed conveniently at the side where it could be used for just such an emergency as this. For fifteen minutes he had been using that shovel in a shelving bank of loose gravel just under an outcropping of rhyolite a rod or so behind the car and well out of sight of Nolan.

He was beginning to consider his excavation almost deep enough to bury two ten-gallon kegs and forty bottles of whisky, when the shadow of a head and shoulders fell across the hole. Casey did not lift the dirt and rocks he had on his shovel. He froze to a tense quiet, goggling at the shadow.

"What are yuh doing, Casey? Trying to outdig a badger?" Mack Nolan's chuckle was friendliness itself.

Casey's head snapped around so that he could cock an eye up at Nolan. He grinned mechanically. "Naw. Picked up a rich-lookin' piece uh float. Thought I'd just see if it didn't mebby come from this ledge."

Mack Nolan stepped forward interestedly and looked at the ledge.

"Where's the piece you found?" he very naturally inquired. "The formation just here wouldn't lead me to expect gold-bearing rock; but of course, anything is possible with gold. Let's have a look at the specimen."

Casey had once tried to bluff a stranger with two deuces and a pair of fives, and two full stacks of blue chips pushed to the center to back the bluff. The stranger had called him, with three queens and a pair of jacks. Casey felt like that now.

He had laughed over his loss then, and he grinned now and reached carelessly to the bank beside him as if he fully expected to lay his hand on the specimen of gold-bearing rock. He went so far as to utter a surprised oath when he failed to find it. He felt in his pockets. He went forward and scanned the top of the ledge almost convincingly. He turned and stood a-straddle, his hands on his hips, and gazed on the pile of dirt he had thrown out of the hole. Last, he pushed his hat back so that with the next movement he could push it forward again over his eyebrow.

"Now if that there lump uh high-grade ain't went an' slid down the bank an' got covered up with the muck!" he exclaimed disgustedly. "I'm a son of a gun if Fate ain't playin' agin' Casey Ryan with a flock uh aces under its vest!"

Mack Nolan laughed, and Casey slanted a look his way. "Thought I left you takin, a nap," he said brazenly. "What's the matter? Didn't your breakfast set good?"

Mack Nolan laughed again. It was evident that he found Casey Ryan very amusing.

"The breakfast was fine," he replied easily. "A couple of lizards got to playing tag over me. That woke me up, and the sun was so hot I just thought I'd come down and crawl into the car and go to sleep there. Go ahead with your prospecting, Casey—I won't bother you."

Casey went on with his digging, but his heart was not in it. With every laggard shovelful of dirt, he glanced over his shoulder apprehensively, watching Mack Nolan crawl into the back of the car and settle himself, with an audible sigh of satisfaction, on top of the load. He had one wild, wicked impulse to lengthen the hole and make it serve as a grave for more than bootleg whisky; but it was an impulse born of desperation, and it died almost before it had lived.

Chapter XIV

Casey left his digging and returned to the Ford, still determined to carry on the bluff and pretend that much tinkering was necessary before he could travel further. With a great show of industry he rummaged for pliers and wrenches, removed the hood from the motor and squinted down at the little engine.

By that time Mack Nolan was snoring softly in deep slumber. Casey listened suspiciously, knowing too well how misleading a snore could be. But his own eyelids were growing exceeding heavy, and the soporific sound acted hypnotically upon his sleep-hungry brain. He caught himself yawning, and suddenly threw down the wrench.

"Aw, hell!" he muttered disgustedly, and went and crawled under the back of the car where it was shady.

The sun was nearly down when Casey awoke and crawled out. Mack Nolan was still curled comfortably in the car, his back against the bed roll. He opened his eyes and yawned when Casey leaned and looked in upon him.

"By Jove, that was a fine sleep I had," he announced cheerfully, lifting himself up and dangling his legs outside the car. "Strike anything yet?"

"Naw." Casey's grunt was eloquent of the mood he was in.

"Get the car fixed all right?" Mack Nolan's cheerfulness seemed nothing less than diabolical to Casey.

"Naw." Then Casey added grimly, "I'm stuck. I dunno what ails the damned thing. Have to send to Vegas fer new parts, I guess. It's only three miles out here to the road. Mebby you better hike over to the highway an' ketch a ride with somebody. I might send in for a timer an' some things, too. No use waitin' fer me, Nolan-can't tell how long I'll be held up here."

Mack Nolan climbed out of the car. Casey's spirits rose instantly. Nolan came forward and looked down at the engine as casually as he would glance at a nickel alarm clock.

"She was hitting all right when you backed down here," Nolan remarked easily. "I'll just take a look at her myself. Fords are cranky sometimes. But I've assembled too many of them in the factory to let one get the best of me in the desert."

Casey could almost hear his heart when it slumped down into his boots. But he wasn't licked yet.

"Aw, let the darned thing alone till we eat," he said, pushing his hat forward to hurry his wits.

"Well—I can throw a Ford together in the dark, if necessary," smiled Mack Nolan. "Eat, it is, if you want it that way. That breakfast I put away seems to have sharpened my appetite for supper. Tell you what, Ryan. I'll do a little trouble-shooting here while you cook supper. How'll that be?"

That wouldn't be, if Casey could prevent it. His pale, narrow-lidded eyes dwelt upon Nolan unwinkingly.

"Well, mebby I'm kind of a crank about my car," he hedged, with a praiseworthy calmness. "Fords is like horses, to me. I drove stage all m' life till I took to prospectin'—an' I never could stand around and let anybody else monkey with my teams. I ain't a doubt in the world, Mr. Nolan, but what you know as much about Fords as I do. More, mebby. But Casey Ryan's got 'is little ways, an' he can't seem to ditch 'em. We'll eat; an' then mebby we'll look 'er over together."

"At the same time," he went on with rising courage, "I'm liable to stick around here for awhile an' prospect a little. If you wanta find them mules an' outfit, don't bank too strong on Casey Ryan. He's liable to change 'is mind any old time. Day or night, you can't tell what Casey might take a notion to do. That there's a fact. You can ask anybody if it ain't."

Mack Nolan laughed and slapped Casey unexpectedly on the shoulder. "You're a man after my own heart, Casey Ryan," he declared enigmatically. "I'll stick to you and take a chance. Darn the mules! Somebody will find them and look after them until I show up."

Casey's spirits, as he admitted to himself, were rising and falling like the hammer of a pile driver; and like the pile driver, the hammer was driving him deeper and deeper into hopelessness.

He would have given an ear to know for certain whether Mack Nolan were as innocent and friendly as he seemed. Until he did know, Casey could see nothing before him but to wait his chance to give Nolan the slip.

Sitting cross-legged in the glow of the campfire after supper, with a huge pattern of stars drawn over the purple night sky, Casey pulled out the old pipe with which he had solaced many an evening and stuffed it thoughtfully with tobacco. Across the campfire, Mack Nolan sat with his hat tilted down over his eyes, smoking a cigarette and seeming at peace with all the world.

Casey hoped that Nolan would forget about fixing the Ford. He hoped that Nolan would sleep well to-night. Casey was perfectly willing to sacrifice a good roll of bedding and the cooking outfit for the privilege of traveling alone. No man, he told himself savagely, could ask a better deal than he was prepared to give Nolan. He bent to reach a burning twig for his pipe, and found Nolan watching him steadily from under his hat brim.

"What sort of looking fellows were those, Ryan, that left a load of booze on your hands?" Nolan asked casually when he saw that he was observed.

Casey burned his fingers with the blazing twig. "Who said anything about any fellers leavin' me booze?" he evaded sharply. "If it's a drink you're hintin' for, you won't get it. Casey Ryan ain't no booze peddler, an' now's as good a time as any to let that soak into your system."

Mack Nolan's gray eyes were still watching Casey with a steadfastness that was disconcerting to a man in Casey's dilemma.

"It might help us both considerably," he said quietly, "if you told me all about it. You can't cache that booze you've got in the car —I won't let you, for one thing; for another, that would be merely dodging the issue, and if you'll forgive my frankness, dodging doesn't seem to be quite in your line."

Casey puffed hard on his pipe. "The world's gittin' so darned full uh crooks, a man can't turn around now'days without bumpin' into a few!" he exploded bitterly. "What kind uh hold-up game YOU playin', Mr. Nolan? If that's your name," he added fiercely.

Mack Nolan laughed to himself and rubbed the ash from his cigarette against the sole of his shoe. "Why," he answered genially, "my game is holding up bootleggers-and crooked cops. Speaking off-hand (which I don't often do) I should say you have a fine chance to sit in with me. I'm just guessing, now," he added dryly, "but I'm tolerably good at guessing; a man's got to be, these days."

"A man's got to do better than guess-with Casey Ryan," Casey remarked ominously. "The last man that guessed Casey Ryan, guessed 'im plumb wrong."

"Meaning that you'd refuse to help me round up bootleggers and the officers that protect them?" A steel edge crept into Mack Nolan's voice. He leaned forward, his elbows on his knees, his eyes boring into Casey's mind.

"Man, don't stall with me! You've got brains enough to know that if I were a crook I'd have held you up long before now. You gave me three splendid opportunities to stick a gun in your back-and I could have made others. And," he added with a smile, "if I had thought that you were a bootlegger or a crook of any other kind, I'd have had you in Las Vegas jail by this time. You're no more a crook than I am. You've got neither the looks nor the actions of a slicker. I may say I know you pretty well —"

Casey thrust out a pugnacious chin. "Say! D' you know Bill Masters, too? That's all I wanta know!"

"Bill Masters? Why, is he the fellow who stepped out from under this load of hootch? If he is, he must have picked himself a new name; I never heard it."

Casey glared suspiciously for twenty seconds before he settled back glumly into his mental corner.

"Ryan, I've been all day sizing you up. I'm going to be perfectly honest with you and tell you why I think you're straight-although you must admit the evidence is rather against you.

"I happened to be right close when you drove down in here and stopped. As a matter of fact, I was behind that little clump of junipers. Had you driven around them instead of stopping this side, you couldn't have failed to see me.

"You came down here mad at the trick that had been played you. You were so mad, you started talking to yourself as a safety valve-blowing off mental steam. You've spent a lot of time in the desert-alone. Men like that frequently talk aloud their thoughts, just to hear a human voice. You made matters pretty plain to me before you knew there was any one within miles of you. For instance, you're not at all sure this car you've got wasn't stolen. You're inclined to think it was. You're broke-robbed, I take it, by the men who somehow managed to leave you with the car and a load of booze on your hands. The trick must have been turned this morning; down at the railroad, I imagine-because you hadn't taken time to stop and size up the predicament you were in until you got here.

"Your main idea was to get off somewhere out of sight. You were scared. You didn't hear me behind you until I spoke-which proves you're a green hand at dodging. And that, Ryan, is a very good recommendation to a man in my line of work. But you're shrewd, and you're game-dead game. You're a peach at thinking up schemes to get yourself out of a hole. Of course, being new at it, you don't think quite far enough. For instance, because you found me afoot it never occurred to you that I might know something about a car; but the rest of your plan was a dandy.

"Your idea of backing down there around the turn and burying the booze was all right. With almost any other man it would have worked. Once you got that hootch off your mind, I rather think you'd have been glad to have me along with you, instead of giving me broad hints to leave. But you haven't got the booze buried yet, and you've been figuring all the evening. You don't see how the devil you're going to manage it with me around.

"I'll do a little more guessing, now: I guess you've doped it out that you'll pack the bedroll up here, tuck me in and pray to the Lord I'll sleep sound. You're hoping you can cache the booze and make your getaway while I've gone bye-low. Or possibly, if you got the booze put away safe from my prying eyes, you might come back to bed and I'd find you here in the morning just as if nothing had happened. How Is that for guesswork?"

"You go tahell!" growled Casey, swallowing a sickly grin. He pressed down the tobacco in his pipe, eyeing Nolan queerly. "If them damn' lizards had uh let yuh alone, I wouldn't have nothin' on m' mind now but my hat." He looked across the fire and grinned again.

"Keep on; you'll be tellin' me what the missus an' I was arguin' about last night over long-distance. I've heard tell uh this four-bit mind reading an' forecastin' your horrorscope fer a dime; but I never met up with it before. If you're aimin' to take up a collection after the show, you'll fare slim. I've been what a feller called 'dusted off'." He added, after a pause that was eloquent, "They done it thorough!"

Mack Nolan laughed. "They usually are thorough, when they're 'dusting off a chump', as I believe they call it."

Casey grunted. "'Chump' is right, mebby. But anyways, you're too late, Mr. Nolan. I'm cleaned."

Mack Nolan rolled another cigarette, lighted it and flipped the match into the campfire. He smoked it down to the last inch, staring into the fire and saying nothing the while. When the cigarette stub followed the match, he leaned back upon one elbow and began tracing a geometrical figure in the sand with a stick.

"Ryan," he said abruptly, "you're square and I know it. The very nature of my business makes me cautious about trusting men-but I'm going to trust you." He stopped again, taking great pains with the point of a triangle he was drawing.

Casey knocked the ashes out of his pipe against a rock. "Puttin' it that way, Mr. Nolan, the man's yet to live that Casey Ryan ever double-crossed. Cops I got no use for; nor yet bootleggers. Whether I got any use for you, Mr. Nolan, I can say better when I've heard yuh out. A goat I've been for the last time. But I'm willin' to HEAR yuh out-and that there's more'n what I'd uh said this morning."

"And that's fair enough, Ryan. If you jumped into things with your eyes shut, I don't think I'd want you with me."

Casey squirmed, remembering certain times when he had gone too headlong into things.

"I'm going to ask you, Ryan, to tell me the whole story of this car and its load of whisky. Before you do that, I'll tell you this much to show good faith and prove to you how much I trust you: I'm an officer, and my special work right now is to clean up a gang of bootleggers and the crooked officers who are protecting them. What I know about your case leads me to believe that you've run afoul of them and that you're the man I've been looking for that can help me set a trap for them. Would you like to do that?"

"If it's that bunch you're after, Mr. Nolan, I'd ruther land 'em in jail than to find a ledge of solid gold ten feet thick an' a mile long. One thing I'd like to know first. Are yuh or ain't yuh huntin' mules?"

Mack Nolan laughed. "I am, yes. But the mule I'm hunting is white!"

Casey studied that until he had the fresh pipeful of tobacco going well. Then he looked up and grinned understandingly.

"So it's White Mule you're trailin'." He kicked a stub of greasewood branch back into the flames and laughed. "Well, the tracks is deep an' plenty, and if that's the trail you're takin', I'm with yuh. You ain't a cop-leastways you don't spread your arms every time you turn around. Gosh, I hate them wing-floppin' kind! They's one thing an' one only that I hate worse-an' that's bootleggers an' moonshiners. If you got a scheme to give them cusses their needin's, you can ask anybody if Casey Ryan ain't the feller you can bank on."

"Yes. That's what I've been thinking. Now, I wish you'd tell me exactly what you've been up against. Don't leave out anything, however trivial it might seem to you."

Wherefore, Casey sat with the firelight flickering across his seamed, Irish face and told the story of his wrongs. Trivial details Nolan had asked for-and he got them with the full Casey Ryan flavor. Even the old woman who rocked, Casey pictured-from his particular angle. Mack Nolan sat up and listened, his eyes steady and his mouth, that had curved to laughter many times during the recital, once more firm and somewhat pitiless when Casey finished.

"This Smiling Lou; you'd know him again, of course?"

"Know him! Say, I'd know him after he'd fried a week in hell!" Casey's tone left no doubt of his meaning.

"And I suppose you could tell this man Kenner a mile off and around a corner. Now, I'll tell you what I want you to do, Casey. This may jar you a little-until I explain. I want you —" Mack Nolan paused, his lips twitching in a faint smile —"to do a little bootlegging yourself."

"Yuh-WHAT?" In the firelight Casey's eyes were seen to bulge.

"I want you to bootleg this whisky you've got in the car." Nolan's eyes twinkled. "I want you to go back and peddle this booze, and I want you to do it so that Smiling Lou or one of his bunch will hold you up and highjack you. Do you see what I mean? You don't —so I'll tell you. We'll put it in marked bottles. I have the bottles and the seals and labels for every brand of liquor to be had in the country to-day. With marked money and marked bottles, we ought to be able to get the goods on that gang."

Casey thought of something quite suddenly and held out an imperative, pointing finger.

"There's something else that feller told me was in the car!" he cried agitatedly. "He said he had forty pints of French champagne cached in a false bottom under the front seat. And he said the front cushion had a blind pocket around the edges that was full uh dope. Hop, he called it."

Mack Nolan whistled under his breath.

"And he turned the whole outfit over to you for sixteen hundred dollars or so?" He stared thoughtfully into the fire. Abruptly he looked at Casey.

"What the deuce had you done to him, Ryan?" he asked, with a quizzical intentness. "He must have been scared stiff, to let go of all that stuff for sixteen hundred. Why, man, the 'junk' —that's dope-alone must be worth more than that. And the champagne-forty pints, you say? He ought to get twenty dollars a pint for that. Figure it yourself. I hope," he added seriously, "the fellow wasn't too scared to show up again."

"Well," Casey said grimly, "I dunno how scart he is-but he knows darn' well I'll kill 'im. I told im I would."

Again Mack Nolan laughed. "Catching's much better than killing, Ryan. It hurts a man worse, and it lasts a heap longer. What do you say to turning in? To-morrow we'll have a full day at my private bottling works."

They moved their cooking outfit down near the Ford for safety's sake. While it was wholly improbable that the car would be robbed in the night, Mack Nolan was a man who took as few chances as possible. It happened that the excavation Casey had so hopefully made that morning formed a convenient level for their bed; wherefore they spread it there, talking in low tones of their plans until they went to sleep.

Dawn was just thinning the curtain of darkness when Nolan woke Casey with a shake of the shoulder.

"I think we'd better be moving from here before the world's astir. You can back on down this draw, Ryan, and strike an old trail that cuts over the ridge and up the next gulch to an old, deserted mine where I've made headquarters. It isn't far, and we can have breakfast at my camp."

Casey swallowed his astonishment, and for once in his life he did as he was told without argument.

Mack Nolan's camp was fairly accessible by roundabout trail with a few tire tracks to point the way for Casey. Straight across the ridges, it would not have been more than two miles to Juniper Wells. Nevertheless not one man in a year would be tempted to come this way, unless it were definitely known that some one lived here.

As the camp of a man who was prospecting for pastime rather than for a grubstake, the place was perfect. Mack Nolan had taken possession of a cabin dug into the hill at the head of a long draw. A brush-covered shed of makeshift construction sheltered a car of the ubiquitous Ford make. Fifty yards away and in full sight of the cabin, the mouth of a tunnel yawned blackly under a rhyolite ledge.

Casey swept the camp with an observant glance and nodded approval as and stopped before the cabin.

"As a prospector, Mr. Nolan, I'll say 'tis a fine layout you got here. An' tain't the first time an honest-lookin' mine has been made to cover things far off from minin'. Like the Black Butte bunch, f'r instance. But if any one was to ride up on yuh unexpected here, I'll say yuh could meet 'em with a grin an' feel easy about your secrets."

"That's praise indeed, coming from an old hand like you," Nolan declared. "Now I'll tell you something else. With Casey Ryan in the camp the whole thing's twice as convincing. Come in. I want to show you what I call an artistic interior."

Grinning, Casey followed him inside and exclaimed profanely in admiration of Mack Nolan's genius. The cabin showed every mark of the owner's interest in the geologic formation of that immediate district.

On the floor along the wall lay specimens of mineralized rock, a couple of prospector's picks, a single-jack and a set of drills; a sample sack, grimed and with a hole in the corner mended by the simple process of gathering the cloth together around it and tying it tightly with a string, hung from a nail above the tools. On the window sill were specimens of ore; two or three of the pieces showed a richness that lighted Casey's eyes with the enthusiasm of an old prospector. Mining journals and a prospector's manual lay upon a box table at the foot of the bunk. For the rest, the cabin looked exactly what it was-the orderly home of a man quite accustomed to primitive living far off from his fellows.

They had a very satisfactory breakfast cooked by Mack Nolan from his own supplies and eaten in a leisurely manner while Nolan talked of primary formations and secondary, and of mineral intrusions and breaks. Casey listened and learned a few things he had not known, for all his years of prospecting. Mack Nolan, he decided, could pass anywhere as a mining expert.

"And now," said Nolan briskly, when he had hung up the dishpan and draped the dishcloth over it to dry, "I'll show you the bottling works. We'll have to do the work by lantern-light. There's not one chance in fifty that any one would show up here-but you never can tell. We could get the stuff out of sight easily enough while the car was coming up the gulch. But the smell is a different matter. We'll take no chances."

At the head of the bunk, a curtained space beneath a high shelf very obviously did duty as a wardrobe. A leather motor coat hung there, one sleeve protruding beyond the curtain of flowered calico. Other garments bulged the cloth here and there. Nolan, smiling over his shoulder at Casey, nodded and pushed the clothing aside. A door behind opened inward, admitting the two into a small recess from which another door opened into a cellar dug deep into the hill.

Undoubtedly this had once been used as a frost-proof storeroom. A small ventilator pipe opened-so Nolan told Casey-in the middle of a greasewood clump. Nolan lighted a gasoline lantern that shed a white brilliance upon the room. On the long table which extended down one side of the room, Casey saw boxes of bottles and other supplies which he did not at the moment recognize.

"We'll have to rebottle all the whisky," said Nolan.

"You'll see a certain mark blown into the bottom of each one of these. The champagne, I'm afraid, I must either confiscate and destroy or run the risk of marking the labels. The hop we'll lay aside for further consideration."

Casey grinned, thinking of the speedy downfall of his enemies, Smiling Lou and Kenner-and, as a secondary consideration other crooks of their type.

"So now we'll unload the stuff, Ryan, and get to work here." Nolan adjusted the white flame in the mantle of the gasoline lantern and led the way outside. "Take in the seat-cushion, Casey. I don't fancy opening it outside, even in this howling wilderness."

"I think I'll just pack in the kegs first, Mr. Nolan." For the first time since the shock of Mr. Nolan's "mind-reading" the night before, Casey ventured a suggestion. "Anybody comes along, it's the kegs they'd look at cross-eyed. Cushions is expected in Fords-if I ain't buttin' in," he added meekly.

"Which you're not. You're acting as my agent now, Ryan, and it will take two heads to put this over without a hitch. Sure, put the kegs out of sight first. The bottles next-and then we'll make short work of the dope in the cushion."

Casey carried in the kegs while Nolan kept watch for inopportune visitors. It was thought inadvisable to unload the camp outfit from the car until the whisky was all removed. The outfit effectually hid what was below-and they were taking no chances. They both breathed freer when the two kegs were in the cellar. Nolan was pleased; too, when Casey came out with the sample bag and announced that he would carry the bottles in the bag. Then Nolan fancied he heard a car, and walked away to where he would have a longer view down the gulch. He would whistle, he said, and warn Casey if someone was coming.

He had not proceeded fifty yards when Casey yelled and brought him back at a run. Casey was rummaging in the car, throwing things about with a recklessness which ill-became an agent of the self-possessed Mack Nolan.

"There ain't a damn' bottle here!" he bellowed indignantly. "Them crooks gypped me outa ten gallons uh good, bottle whisky! Now what do you know about that, Mr. Nolan? That feller said it was high-grade stuff he had packed away at the bottom. He lied. There ain't nothin' here but a set uh skid chains an' a jack. An' the champagne, mebby, under the front seat!"

Mack Nolan's eyes narrowed. "I think Ryan, I'll have a look under that front seat."

He had a look-several looks, in fact. There was the false bottom under the seat, but there was nothing in it. He took his pocket knife, opened a blade and split the edge of the seat-cushion at the bottom. He inserted a finger and thumb and drew out a bit of hair stuffing. He stood up and eyed Casey sharply, and Casey stared back defensively.

"He was a darned liar from start t' finish. He said there was champagne an' he said there was hop," Casey stated flatly.

"I wondered at his letting go of stuff as valuable as that," said Nolan. "I think we'd better take a look at those kegs."

They went into the cellar and took a look at the kegs. Both kegs. Afterward they stood and looked at each other. Casey's hands went to his hips, and the muscles along his jaw hardened into lumps. He spat into the dirt of the cellar floor.

"Water!" He snorted disgustedly. "Casey Ryan with the devil an' all scart outa him, thinkin' he had ownership of a load uh booze an' hop sufficient t' hang 'im!" His hand slid into his trousers pocket, reaching for the comforting plug of tobacco. "Stuck up an' robbed is what happens t' Casey. You can ask anybody if it ain't highway robbery!"

Nolan stopped whistling under his breath. "There's the Ford," he reminded Casey comfortingly.

"Which I wisht it wasn't!" snarled Casey. "You know yourself, Mr. Nolan, it's likely stole, an' the first man I meet in the trail'll likely take it off me, claimin' it's his'n!"

Mack Nolan started whistling again, but checked himself abruptly. "Well, our trap's wanting bait, I see. This leaves me still hunting the White Mule."

"Aw, tahell with your White Mule! Tahell with everything!" Casey kicked the nearest keg viciously and went out into the sunshine, swearing to himself.

Chapter XVI

In the shade of a juniper that grew on the highest point of the gulch's rim, Mack Nolan lay sprawled on the flat of his back, one arm for a pillow, and stared up into the serene blue of the sky with cottony flakes of cloud swimming steadily to the northeast. Three feet away, Casey Ryan rested on left hip and elbow and stared glumly down upon the cabin directly beneath them. Whenever his pale, straight-lidded eyes focussed upon the dusty top of the Ford car standing in front of the cabin, Casey said something under his breath. Miles away to the south, pale violet, dreamlike in the distance, the jagged outline of a small mountain range stood as if painted upon the horizon. A wavy ribbon of smudgy brown was drawn uncertainly across the base of the mountains. This, Casey knew, when his eyes lifted to look that way, marked the line of the Sante Fe and a train moving heavily upgrade to the west.

Toward it dipped the smooth stretch of barren mesa cut straight down the middle with a yellow line that was the highway up which Casey had driven the morning before. The inimitable magic of distance and high desert air veiled greasewood, sage and sand with the glamour of unreality. The mountains beyond, unspeakably desolate and forbidding at close range, and the little black buttes standing afar, off-small spewings of age-old volcanos dead before man was born-seemed fascinating, unknown islets anchored in a sea of enchantment. Across the valley to the west nearer mountains, all amethyst and opal tinted, stood bold and inscrutable, with jagged peaks thrust into the blue to pierce and hold the little clouds that came floating by. Even the gulch at hand had been touched by the enchanter's wand and smiled mysteriously in the vivid sunlight, the very air a-quiver with that indescribable beauty of the high mesa land which holds desert dwellers in thrall.

When first Casey saw the smoke smudge against the mountains to the south, he remembered his misadventure of the lower desert and swore. When he looked again, the majestic sweep of distance gave him a satisfied feeling of freedom from the crowded pettinesses of the city. For the first time since trouble met him in the trail between Victorville and Barstow, Casey heaved a sigh of content because he was once more out in the big land he loved. Those distant, painted mountains, looking as impossible as the back drop of a stage, held gulches and deep canyons he knew. The closer hills he had prospected. The mesa, spread all around him, seemed more familiar than the white apartment house in Los Angeles which Casey had lately called home. And if the thought of the Little Woman brought with it the vague discomfort of a schoolboy playing hookey, Casey could not have regretted being here with Mack Nolan if he had tried.

They were lying up here in the shade-following the instinct of other creatures of the wild to guard against surprises-while they worked out a nice problem in moonshine. And since the desert had never meant a monotonously placid life to Casey-who carried his problems philosophically as a dog bears patiently with fleas-he had every reason now for feeling very much at home. When he reached mechanically into his pocket for his Bull Durham and papers, any man who knew him well would have recognized the motion as a sign that Casey was himself again, once more on his mental feet and ready to go boring optimistically into his next bunch of trouble.

Mack Nolan raised his head off his arm and glanced at Casey quizzically.

"Well-we can't catch fish if we won't cut bait," he volunteered sententiously. "I've a nice little job staked out for you, Casey."

Casey gave a grunt that might mean one of several things, and which probably meant them all. He waited until he had his cigarette going. "If it ain't a goat's job I'm fer it," he said. "Casey Ryan ain't the man t' set in the shade whilst there's men runnin' loose he's darned anxious t' meet."

"I've been thinking over the deal those fellows pulled on you. If the man Kenner had left you the booze and dope he told you was in the car, I'd say it was a straight case of a sticky-fingered officer letting a bootlegger by with part of his load, and a later attack of cold feet on the part of the bootlegger. But they didn't leave you any booze. So I have doped it this way, Ryan.

"The thing's deeper than it looked, yesterday. Those two were working together, part of a gang, I should say, with a fairly well-organized system. By accident-and probably for a greater degree of safety in getting out of the city, Kenner invited you to ride with him. He wanted no argument with that traffic cop-no record made of his name and license number. So he took you in. When he found out who you were, he knew you were at outs with the law. He knew you as an experienced desert man. He had you placed as a valuable member of their gang, if you could be won over and persuaded to join them.

"As soon as possible he got you behind the wheel-further protection to himself if he should meet an officer who was straight. He felt you out on the subject of a partnership. And when you met Smiling Lou-well, this Kenner had decided to take no chance with you. He still had hopes of pulling you in with them, but he was far from feeling sure of you. He undoubtedly gave Smiling Lou the cue to make the thing appear an ordinary case of highjacking while he ditched his whole load so that there would be no evidence against him if he lost out and you turned nasty.

"I'm absolutely certain, Casey, that if you had not been along, Smiling Lou would not have touched that load. They'd probably have stopped there for a talk, exchanged news and perhaps perfected future plans, and parted like two old cronies. It's possible, of course, that Smiling Lou might have taken some whisky back with him-if he had needed it. Otherwise, I think they split more cash than booze, as a rule."

Casey sat up. "Well, they coulda played me for a sucker easy enough," he admitted reluctantly. "An' if it'll be any help to yuh, Mr. Nolan, I'll say that I never seen the money passed from Kenner to Smilin' Lou, an' I never seen a bottle unloaded from the car. I heard 'em yes. An' I'll say there was a bunch of 'em all right. But what I SEEN was the road ahead of me and that car of Smilin' Lou's standin' in the middle of it. He had a gun pulled on me, mind yuh-and you can ask anybody if a feller feels like rubberin' much when there's only the click of a trigger between him an' a six-foot hole in the ground."

"All the more reason," said Nolan, also sitting up with his hands clasped around his knees, "why it's important to catch them with the goods. You'll have to peddle hootch, Casey, until we get Smiling Lou and his outfit."

"And where, Mr. Nolan, do I git the booze to peddle?" asked Casey practically.

Nolan laughed to himself. "It can be bought," he said, "but I'd rather not. Since you've never monkeyed with the stuff, it might make you conspicuous if you went around buying up a load of hootch. And of course I can't appear in this thing at all. But I have what I think is a very good plan."

Casey looked at him inquiringly, and again Nolan laughed.

"Nothing for it, Casey, —we'll have to locate a still and rob it. That, or make some of our own, which takes time. And it's an unpleasant, messy job anyway."

Casey stared dubiously down into the gulch. "That'd be fine, Mr. Nolan, if we knew where was the still. Or mebby yuh do know."

Mack Nolan shook his head. "No, I don't, worse luck. I haven't been long enough in the district to know as much about it as I hope to know later on. Prospecting for this headquarters took a little time; and getting my stuff moved in here secretly took more time. A week ago, Casey, I shouldn't have been quite ready to use you. But you came when you were needed, and so —I feel sure the White Mule will presently show up."

Casey lifted his head and stared meditatively out across the immensity of the empty land around them.

"She's a damn' big country, Mr. Nolan. I dunno," he remarked doubtfully. "But Casey Ryan has yet t' go after a thing an' fail t' git it. I guess if it's hootch we want, it ought t' be easy enough t' find; it shore has been hard t' dodge it lately! If yuh want White Mule, Mr. Nolan, you send Casey out travelin' peaceful an' meanin' harm t' nobody. Foller Casey and you'll find 'im tangled up with a mess uh hootch b'fore he gits ten miles from camp."

"You could go out and highjack some one." Nolan agreed, taking him seriously-which Casey had not intended. "I think we'll go down and load the camp outfit into my car, Ryan, and I'll start you out. Go up into your old stamping ground where people know you. If you're careful in picking your men, you could locate some hootch, couldn't you, without attracting attention?"

Casey studied the matter. "Bill Masters could mebby help me out," he said finally. "Only I don't like the friends Bill's been wishin' onto me lately. This man Kenner, that held me up, knowed Bill Masters intimate. I'm kinda losin' my taste fer Bill lately."

Mack Nolan seized upon the clue avidly. Before Casey quite realized what he had done, he found himself hustled away from camp in Mack Nolan's car, headed for Lund in the service of his government. Since young Kenner had been able to talk so intimately of Bill Masters, Mack Nolan argued that Bill Masters should likewise be able to give some useful information concerning young Kenner. Moreover, a man in Bill Masters' position would probably know at least a few of the hidden trails of the White Mule near Lund.

"If you can bring back a load of moonshine Ryan, by all means do so," Nolan instructed Casey at the last moment. "Here's money to buy it with. We should have enough to make a good haul for Smiling Lou. Twenty gallons at least-forty, if you can get them. Keep your weather eye open, and whatever happens, don't mention my name or say that you are working with the law. In five days, if you are not here, I shall drive to Las Vegas. Get word to me there if anything goes wrong. Just write or wire to General Delivery. But I look for you back, Ryan, not later than Friday midnight. Take no unnecessary risk; this is more important than you know."

Nolan's crisp tone of authority remained with Casey mile upon mile. And such was the Casey Ryan driving that midnight found him coasting into Bill Masters' garage in Lund with the motor shut off and a grin on the Casey Ryan face.

Mack Nolan had just crawled into his bunk on Wednesday night when he thought he heard a car laboring up the gulch. He sat up in bed to listen and then got hurriedly into his clothes. He was standing just around the corner of the dugout where the headlights could not reach him, when Casey killed the engine and stopped before the door. Steam was rising in a small cloud from the radiator cap, and the sound of boiling water was distinctly audible some distance away.

Mack Nolan waited until Casey had climbed out from behind the wheel and headed for the door. Then he stepped out and hailed him. Casey started perceptibly, whirling as if to face an enemy. When he saw that it was Nolan he apparently lost his desire to enter the cabin. Instead he came close to Nolan and spoke in a hoarse whisper.

"We better run 'er under the shed, Mr. Nolan, and drain the darned radiator. I dunno am I follered or not, but I was awhile back. But the man that catches Casey Ryan when he's on the trail an' travelin, has yet t' be born. An' you can ask anybody if that ain't so."

Mack Nolan's eyes narrowed. "And who followed you then?" he asked quietly. "Did you bring any hootch?"

"Did yuh send Casey Ryan after hootch, or was it mebby spuds er somethin'?" Casey retorted with heavy dignity. "Will yuh pack it in, Mr. Nolan, whilst I back the car in the shed, or shall I bring it when I come? It ain't so much," he added drily, "but it cost the trouble of a trainload."

"I'll take it in," said Nolan. "If any one does come we want no evidence in reach."

Casey turned to the car, clawed at his camp outfit and lifted out a demijohn which he grimly handed to Nolan. "Fer many a mile it rode on the seat with me so I could drink 'er down if they got me cornered," he grinned. "One good swaller is about the size of it, Mr. Nolan."

Nolan grinned in sympathy and turned into the cabin, bearing the three-gallon, wicker-covered glass bottle in his arms. Presently he returned to the doorway and stood there listening down the gulch until Casey came up, walking from the shed.

"'Tis a good thing yuh left this other car standin' here cold an' peaceful, Mr. Nolan," Casey, observed, after he also had stood for a minute listening. "If they're follerin' they'll be here darn' soon. If they ain't I've ditched 'em. Let's git t' bed an' I'll tell yuh my tale uh woe."

Without a word Nolan led the way into the cabin. In the dark they undressed and got into the bed which was luckily wide enough for two.

"Had your supper?" Nolan asked belatedly when they were settled.

"I did not," Casey grunted. "I will say, Mr. Nolan, there's few times in my life when you'd see Casey Ryan missin' 'is supper whilst layin' tracks away from a fight. But if it was light enough you could gaze upon 'im now. And I must hand it t' the Gallopin' Gussie yuh give me the loan of fer the trip. She brung me home ahead of the sheriff-and you can ask anybody if Casey Ryan himself can't be proud uh that!"

"The sheriff?" Nolan's voice was puzzled. He seemed to be considering something for a minute, before he spoke again. "You could have explained to the sheriff, couldn't you, your reason for having booze in the car?"

Casey raised to one elbow. "When yuh told Casey Ryan 'twas not many men you'd trust, and that you trusted me an' the business was t' be secret-Mr. Nolan, you 'was talkin' t' CASEY RYAN!" He lay down again as if that precluded further argument.

"Good! I thought I hadn't made a mistake in my man," Nolan approved, in a tone that gave Casey an inner glow of pride in himself. "Let's have the story, old man. Did you see Bill Masters?"

"Bill Masters," said Casey grimly, "was not in Lund. His garage is sold an' Bill's in Denver-which is a long drive for a Ford t' git there an' back before Friday midnight. Yuh put a time limit me, Mr. Nolan, an' nobody had Bill's address. I didn't foller Bill t' Denver. I asked some others in Lund if they knowed a man named Kenner, and they did not. So then I went huntin' booze that I could git without the hull of Nevada knowin' it in fifteen minutes. An' Casey's got this t' say: When yuh WANT hootch, it's hard t' find as free gold in granite. When yuh

DON'T want it, it's forced on yuh at the point of a gun. This jug I stole-seein' your business is private, Mr. Nolan.

"I grabbed it off some fellers I knowed in Lund an' never had no use for, anyway. They're mean enough when they're sober, an' when they're jagged they're not t' be mentioned on a Sunday. I mighta paid 'em for it, but money's no good t' them fellers an' there's no call t' waste it. So they made a holler and I sets the jug down an' licks them both, an' comes along home mindin' my own business.

"So I guess they 'phoned the sheriff in Vegas that here comes a bootlegger and land 'im quick. Anyway, I was goin' t' stop there an' take on a beefsteak an' a few cups uh coffee, but I never done it. I was slowin' down in front uh Sam's Place when a friend uh mine gives me the high sign t' put 'er in high an' keep 'er goin'. Which I done.

"Down by Ladd's, Casey looks back an' here comes the sheriff's car hell bent fer 'lection (anyway it looked like the sheriff's car). An' I wanta say right here, Mr. Nolan, that's a darn' good Ford yuh got! I was follered, and 'I was follered hard. But I'm here an' they' ain't —an' you can ask anybody if that didn't take some going'!"

In the darkness of the cabin Casey turned over and heaved a great sigh. On the heels of that came a chuckle.

"I got t' hand it t' the L. A. traffic cops, Mr. Nolan. They shore learned me a lot about dodgin'. So now yuh got the hull story. If it was the sheriff behind me an' if he trails me here, they got no evidence an' you can mebby square it with 'im. You'd know what t' tell 'im-which is more'n what Casey Ryan can say."

Casey fell asleep immediately afterward, but Mack Nolan lay for a long while with his eyes wide open and his ears alert for strange sounds in the gulch. He was a new man in this district, working independently of sheriff's offices. Casey Ryan was the first man he had confided in; all others were fair game for Nolan to prove honest or dishonest with the government. The very nature of his business made it so. For when whisky runners drove openly in broad daylight through the country with their unlawful loads, somewhere along the line officers of the law were sharing the profits. Nolan knew none of them, —by sight. If he carried the records of some safely memorized and pigeonholed for future use, that was his own business. Mack Nolan's thoughts were his own and he guarded them jealously and slept with his lips tightly closed. He wanted no sheriff coming to him for explanation of his movements. Wherefore he listened long, and when he slept his slumber was light.

At daylight he was up and abroad. Two hours after sunrise Casey awoke with the smell of breakfast in his nostrils. He rolled over and blinked at Mack Nolan standing with his hat on the back of his head and a cigarette between his lips, calmly turning three hot-cakes with a kitchen knife. Casey grinned condescendingly. He himself turned his cakes by the simple process of tossing them in the air a certain kind of flip, and catching them dexterously as they came down. Right there he decided that Mack Nolan was not after all a real outdoors man.

"Well, the sheriff didn't arrive last night," Nolan observed cheerfully, when he saw that Casey was awake. "I don't much look for him, either. Your driving on past the turn to Juniper Wells and coming up that other old road very likely threw him off the track. You must have been close to the State line then and he gave you up as a bad job."

"It was a GOOD job!" Casey maintained reaching for his clothes. "I made 'em think I was headed clean outa the country. If they knowed who it was at all, they'd know I belong in L. A., and I figured they'd guess I was headed there. They stopped for something this side of Searchlight an' so I pulls away from 'em a couple of miles. They never seen where I went to."

While he washed for breakfast, Casey began to take stock of certain minor injuries.

"That darned Pete Gibson has got tushes in his mouth like a wild hawg; the kind that sticks out," he grumbled, touching certain skinned places on his knuckles. "Every time I landed on 'im yesterday I run against them tushes uh his'n." But he added with a grin, "They ain't so solid as they was when I met up with 'im. I felt one of 'em give 'fore I got through."

"Brings the price of moonshine up a bit, doesn't it?" Nolan suggested drily. "I rather think you might better have paid the men their price. A fight is well enough in its way —I'm Irish myself. But as my agent, Ryan, the main idea is to let the law fight for you. Our work is merely to give the law a chance. I like your not wanting to explain to the sheriff. Prohibition officers do not explain, as a rule. The law behind them does that.

"And since the price seems to be rather hard on the knuckles —" He glanced down at Casey's hands and grinned. " —I think it may come cheaper to make the stuff ourselves. Licking two men for three gallons, and getting the officers at your tail light into the bargain, is all right as an experiment; but I don't believe, Ryan, we ought to adopt that as a habit."

Casey cocked an eye up at him. "Did yuh ever make White Mule, Mr. Nolan?" he asked grimly.

Nolan laughed his easy little chuckle. "Why, no, Ryan, I never did. Did you?"

"Naw. I seen some made once, but I had too much of it inside me at the time to learn the receipt for it. I'd rather steal it, if it's all the same to you, Mr. Nolan." His hand went up to the back of his head and moved forward, although there was no hat to push. "I've lived honest all these years-an', dammit, it's kinda tough to break out with stealin I what yuh don't want! Couldn't we fill them bottles with somethin' that LOOKS like hootch? Cold tea should get by, Mr. Nolan. It'd be a fine joke on Smilin' Lou."

"A good joke, maybe-but no evidence. It isn't against the law, Ryan, to have cold tea in your possession. No, it's got to be whisky, and there's got to be a load of it. Enough to look like business and tempt him or any other member of the gang you happen to meet. If they caught you with three gallons, Casey, they'd probably run you in and feel very virtuous about it. Nothing for it, I'm afraid. We'll have to become real moonshiners ourselves for awhile."

Casey ate with less appetite after that. Making moonshine did not appeal to him at all. Given his choice, I think he would even prefer drinking it, unhappy as the effect had been on him.

"We'll need a still, and we'll need the stuff. I'm going to leave you in charge of the camp, Ryan, while I make a trip to Needles. I'll deputize you to assist me in cleaning up this district. And this district, Ryan, touches salt water. So if revenge looks good to you, you'll have a fine chance to get even with the bootleggers. And in the meantime, just kill time around camp here while I'm gone. If any one shows up, you're prospecting."

That day, doubt-devils took hold of Casey Ryan and plucked at his belief. How did he know that Mack Nolan wasn't another bootlegger, wanting to rope Casey in on a job for some fell purpose of his own? He had Mack Nolan's word and nothing more. For that matter, he had also had young Kenner's word. Kenner had fooled him completely. Mack Nolan could also fool him-perhaps.

"Well, anyhow, he never claimed to know Bill Masters, and that's a point in 'is favor. And if it's some dirty work he's up to, he coulda made it shorter than what he's doin'. An' if he's double-crossin' Casey Ryan-well, anyway, Casey Ryan 'll be present at the time an' place when he does it!"

Upon that comforting thought, Casey decided to trust Mack Nolan until he caught him playing crooked; and proceeded to kill time as best he could.

It was noon the next day when Nolan returned, and he did not explain why he was eighteen hours overdue. Casey eyed him expectantly, but Nolan's manner was brisk and preoccupied.

"Help me unload this stuff, Ryan," he said, "and put it out of sight in the cellar. We won't have to go through the process of making moonshine, after all."

Casey looked into the car, pulling aside the tarp. Four kegs he counted, and lifted out one.

"An' how many did YOU lick, Mr. Nolan?" he grinned over his shoulder as he started for the door.

Nolan laughed noncommittally.

"Perhaps I'm luckier at picking my bootleggers," he retorted. "If you carry the right brand of bluff, you can keep the skin on your knuckles, Ryan. This beats making it, at any rate."

That afternoon and the next day, Casey Ryan did what he never dreamed was possible. With Mack Nolan to show him how, Casey performed miracles. While he did not, literally change water into wine, he did give forty-three gallons of White Mule a most imposing pedigree.

He turned kegs of crude, moonshine whisky into Canadian Club, Garnkirk, Tom Pepper, Three Star Hennessey and Cognac-if you were to believe the bottles, labels and government seals. Under Mack Nolan's instruction and with his expert assistance, the forgery was perfect. While the cellar reeked with the odor of White Mule when they had finished, the bottled array on the table whispered of sybaritic revelings to glisten the eyes of the most dissipated man about town.

"When it's as easy done as that, Mr. Nolan, the feller's a fool that drinks it. You've learnt Casey Ryan somethin' that mighta done 'im some good a few years back." He picked up a flat, pint bottle and caressed its label with reminiscent finger tips.

"Many's the time me an' old Tommy Pepper drove stage together," he mused. "Throwed 'im at a bear once that I met in the trail over in Colorado when I hadn't no gun on me. Busted a pint on his nose-man! Then I never waited to see what happened. I was a wild divil them days when me an' Tommy Pepper was side pardners. But a yaller snake with a green head crawled out of a bottle of 'im once-and that there was where Casey Ryan says good-by to booze. If I hadn't quit 'im then, I'd sure as hell quit 'im now. After this performance, Mr. Nolan, Casey Ryan's goin' to look twice into his coffee pot. I wouldn't believe in cow's milk, if I done the milkin' myself!"

"Most of the stuff that's peddled nowadays is doctored," Nolan replied, with the air of one who knows. "When it isn't White Mule, it's likely to be something worse. That's one of the chief reasons why I'm fighting it. If they only peddled decent whisky it wouldn't be so bad, Ryan. But it's rank poison. I've seen so many go stone blind-or die-that it makes me pretty savage sometimes. So now I'll coach you in the part you're to play as hootch runner; and to-morrow you can start for Los Angeles."

Casey did not answer. He felt absently for his pipe, filled and lighted it and went out to sit on the doorstep in gloomy meditation while he smoked.

Returning to Los Angeles, even without a bootlegger's load, was not a matter which Casey liked to contemplate. He would have to face the Little Woman if he went back; either as a deliberate liar, who lied to his wife to gain the freedom he might have had without resorting to deceit, or as the victim once more of crooks. Casey thought he would prefer the accusation of lying deliberately to the Little Woman, though it made him squirm to think of it. He wished she had not openly taunted him with getting into trouble and needing her always to get him out.

He would like to tell her that he was now working for the government. The secrecy of his mission, the danger it involved, would impress even her amused cynicism. But the very secrecy of his mission in itself made it impossible for him to tell her anything about it. Casey would not admit it, but it was a real disappointment to him that he could not wear a star on his coat.

All that day and evening he was glum, a strange mood for Casey Ryan. But if Mack Nolan noticed his silence, he gave no sign. Nolan himself was wholly absorbed by the business in hand. The success of this plan meant a good deal to him, and he told Casey so very frankly; which lightened Casey's gloom perceptibly.

Casey was to drive to Los Angeles-even to San Diego if necessary-and return within a week, unless Nolan's hopes were fulfilled and Casey was held up and highjacked. If he were apprehended by officers who were honestly discharging their duty, Casey was to do thus-and-so, and presently be free to drive on with his load. If he were highjacked (Casey gritted his teeth and said he hoped the highjacker would be Smiling Lou), he was to permit himself to be robbed, worm himself as far as possible into their confidence and return for further orders.

If Mack Nolan should chance to be absent from the cabin, then Casey was to wait until he returned. And Nolan intimated that hereafter the making of moonshine might be a part of Casey's duties. Then, without warning, Mack Nolan struck at the heart of Casey's worry.

"I don't want to dictate to any man in family affairs, Ryan. But I've got to speak of one other matter," he said diffidently. "I suppose naturally you'll want to go home and let your wife know you're still alive, anyway. But if you can manage to keep your present business a secret for the time being, I think you'd better do it. You said you were planning to be away on a trip for some time, I remember. If you can just let it go that way, or say that you are prospecting over here, I wish you would. Think you can manage that all right?"

"I'd rather manage a six-horse team of bronk mules," Casey admitted. "But after the way the missus thinks I lied to 'er about takin' the next train home from Barstow, anything I say 'll be used agin' me. My wife's got brains. She ain't put it down that the trains have quit runnin'. Accordin' to her figures, Casey's lied and he's in a hole again, an' it'll be up to her an' Jack to run windlass an' pull 'im out. Don't matter what I say she won't believe me anyhow-so Casey won't say nothin'. Can't lie with your mouth shut, can yuh?"

"Oh, yes, it's been done," Mack Nolan chuckled. "Now we'll set down the serial numbers and the bank name of this 'jack', —and here's your expense money separate. And if there's anything that isn't clear to you, Ryan, speak up. You won't hear from me again, probably, until you're back from this fishing trip."

Casey thought that everything was perfectly clear, and rashly he said so, as he started off.

From Barstow to Victorville, from Victorville to Camp Cajon Casey drove expectantly, hoping to meet Smiling Lou. He scanned each car that approached and slowed for every meeting like a searching party or a man who is lost and wishes to inquire the way. His pace would have been law-abiding in Los Angeles at five o'clock on Broadway between Fourth and Eighth streets. Goggled women tourists eyed him curiously, and one car stopped full to see what he wanted. But his "Tom Pepper" rode safe under the tarp behind him, and the "Three Star Hennessey" beaded daintily with the joggling it got, and Casey was neither halted nor questioned as he passed.

At Camp Cajon Casey stopped and cooked an early supper, because the summer crowd was there and a real bootlegger would have considered stopping rather unsafe. Casey boiled coffee over one of the camp fireplaces and watched furtively the sunburned holiday group nearest. He placed his supper on one of the round, cement tables near the car, and every man who passed that way Casey watched unblinkingly while he ate.

He succeeded in making three different parties swallow their supper in a hurry and pack up and leave, glancing back uneasily at Casey as they drove away. But Casey himself was unmolested, and no one asked about his load.

From Camp Cajon to San Bernardino Casey drove furiously, remembering young Kenner's desire for speed. He stopped there for the night, and nearly had a fight with the garage man where he put up, because he showed undue caution concerning the safety of his car from prowlers during the night.

He left the car there that day and returned furtively after dark, asking the night man if he had seen any saps around his car. The night man looked at him uncomprehendingly.

"I dunno-nothin's been picked up since I come on at six. We ain't responsible for lost articles, anyway. See that sign?"

Casey grunted, cranked up and drove away, wondering whether the night man was as innocent as he tried to act.

From San Bernardino to Los Angeles Casey drove placidly as a load of oranges in February. He put up at a cheap place on San Pedro Street, with his car in the garage next door and a five-dollar tip in the palm of a rat-faced mechanic with Casey's injunction to clean 'er dingbats and keep other people away.

He did not go out to see the Little Woman, after all. He had sent her a wire from Goffs the day before, saying that he was prospecting with a fellow and he hoped she was well. This, after long pondering, had seemed to him the easiest way out of an argument with the Little Woman. The wire had given no address whereby she might reach him, but the omission was not the oversight Casey hoped she would consider it. He wanted to be reassuring without starting anything.

Los Angeles with no Little Woman at his elbow was a dismal hole, and Casey got out of it as soon as possible. As per instructions, he drove down to San Diego, ventured perilously close to the Mexico line, fooled around there for a day looking for trouble, failed to find so much as a frown and drove back.

He headed straight for San Bernardino, which was Smiling Lou's headquarters. He killed time there and met the sheriff on the street the day he arrived. The sheriff had a memory trained to hold faces indefinitely. He smiled a little, made a polite gesture in the general direction of his hat and passed on. Casey swore to himself and resolved to duck guiltily around the nearest corner if he saw the sheriff coming his way again.

On the day when his time limit expired Casey drove up the gulch to Nolan's camp. In the car behind him rode undisturbed his Canadian Club, Garnkirk, Three-Star Hennessey, Cognac and Tom Pepper; bottles, labels, government seals and all. Nolan was walking over from the tunnel when Casey arrived. He smiled inquiringly as he shook hands, —a ceremony to which Casey was plainly unaccustomed.

"What luck, Ryan? I beat you back by about two hours. Getting things ready to begin making it. Did they catch you all right?"

"Naw!" Casey spat disgustedly. "Never seen a booze peddler, never seen a cop look my way. I went around actin' like I just killed a man an' stole a lady's diamonds, and the sheriff at San Berdoo TIPS 'IS HAT TO ME, by golly! Drove through L. A. hella-whoopin' an' not a darned traffic cop knowed it was Casey Ryan. You can ask anybody if I didn't do every thing possible to git in bad or give bootleggers a tip I was one of 'em.

"You can't git Casey Ryan up agin' the gang you're after, Mr. Nolan. Only way Casey Ryan can git up agin' the law is to go along peaceable tryin' to please the missus an' mindin' his own business. I coulda peddled that damn' hootch on a hangin' tray like circus lemonade. I coulda stood on the corner in any uh them damned towns with the hull works piled out on a table in front of me, an' I coulda hollered my damn' head off; an' Smilin' Lou woulda passed me by like I was sellin' chewin' gum and shoe strings."

Mack Nolan looked at Casey, turned and went into the cabin, sat down on the edge of the bed and laughed until the tears dripped over his lashes. Casey Ryan followed him, and sat on the edge of the table with his arms folded. Whenever Mack Nolan lifted his face from his palms and looked at Casey, Casey swore. Whereat Mack Nolan would give another whoop.

You can't wonder if relations were somewhat strained, between them for the rest of that day.

Nature had made Casey Ryan an optimist. The blood of Ireland had made him pugnacious. And Mack Nolan had a way with him. Wherefore, Casey Ryan once more came larruping down the grade to Camp Cajon and turned in there with a dogged purpose in his eyes and with his jaw set stubbornly. History has it that whenever Casey Ryan gets that look in his face, the man underneath might just as well holler and crawl out; because holler he must, before Casey would ever let him up.

Behind him, stowed under the bedding, grub and camp dishes, rode his eight cases of bootlegger's bait, packed convincingly in the sawdust, straw and cardboard of the wet old days when Uncle Sam himself O. K.'d the job. A chain of tiny beads at the top of each bottle lied and said it was good liquor. The boxes themselves said, "This side up" —when any side up would thrill the soul of the man who owned a wet appetite and a dry throat.

It was a good job Mack Nolan had made of the bottling. Uncle Sam himself must needs polish his spectacles and take another look to detect the fraud. It was a marvelous job of bottling, —and the proof lay only in the drinking. "Tommy" Pepper rode in pint flasks designed to slip safely into a man's coat pocket. Beside him two cases of Canadian Club (if you were satisfied with the evidence of your eyes) sat serene in round-shouldered bottles-conventional, secure in its reputation. Cognac and Garnkirk, a case for each, rode in tall, slim bottles with no shoulders at all. Plumper than they, Three Star Hennessey sat smugly waiting until the joke was turned upon its victim. A tempting load it was, to men of certain minds and morals. Casey grinned sardonically when he thought of it.

Casey drove deep into the grove of sycamores and made camp there, away from the chattering picnic parties at the cement tables. By Mack Nolan's advice he was adopting a slightly different policy. He no longer shunned his fellow men or glared suspiciously when strangers approached. Instead he was very nearly the old Casey Ryan, except that he failed to state his name and business to all and sundry with the old Casey Ryan candor, but instead avoided the subject altogether or evaded questions with vague generalities.

But as an understudy for Ananias, Casey Ryan would have been a failure. In two hours or less he had made easy trail acquaintance with six different men, and he had unconsciously managed to vary his vague account of himself six different times. Wherefore he was presently asked cautiously concerning his thirst.

"They's times," said Casey, hopefully lowering an eyelid, "when a feller dassent take a nip, no matter how thirsty he gits."

The questioner stared at him for a minute and slowly nodded. "You're darn' right," he assented. "I scursely ever touch anything, myself." And he added vaguely, "Quite a lot of it peddled out here in this camp, I guess. Tourists comin' through are scared to pack it themselves-but they sure don't overlook any chances to take a snort."

"Yeah?" Casey cocked a knowing eye at the speaker. "They must pay a pretty fair price fer it, too. Don't the cops bother folks none?"

"Some —I guess."

Casey filled his pipe and offered his tobacco sack to the man. The fellow took it, nodding listless thanks, and filled his own pipe. The two sat down together on the knee of a deformed sycamore and smoked in circumspect silence.

"Arizona, I see." The man nodded toward the license plates on Casey's car.

"Uh-huh." Casey glanced that way. "Know a man name of Kenner?" He asked abruptly.

The fellow looked at Casey sidelong, without turning his head.

"Some. Do you?"

"Some." Casey felt that he was making headway, though it was a good deal like playing checkers with the king row wide open and only two crowned heads to defend his men.

"Friend uh yours?" The fellow turned his head and looked straight at Casey.

Casey returned him a pale, straight-lidded stare. The man's glance flickered and swung away.

"Who wants to know?" Casey asked calmly.

"Oh, you can call me Jim Cassidy. I just asked." He removed his pipe from his mouth and inspected it apathetically. "He's a friend of Bill Masters, garage man up at Lund. Know Bill?"

"Any man says I don't, you can call 'im a liar." Casey also inspected his pipe. "Bought that car off'n Kenner," Casey added boldly. Getting into trouble, he discovered, carried almost the thrill of trying to keep out of it.

"Yeah?" The self-styled Jim Cassidy looked at the Ford more attentively. "And contents?"

Casey snorted. "What do you know about goats, if anything?" he asked mysteriously.

Jim Cassidy eyed Casey sidelong through a silence. Then he brought his palm down flat on his thigh and laughed.

"You pass," he stated, with a relieved sigh. "He's a dinger, ain't he?"

"You know 'im, all right." Casey also laughed and put out his hand. "If you're a friend of Kenner's, shake hands with Casey Ryan! He's damned glad to meet yuh-an' you can ask anybody if that ain't the truth."

After that the acquaintance progressed more smoothly. By the time Casey spread his bed close alongside the car-he knew just how much booze Jim Cassidy carried, just what Cassidy expected to make off the load, and a good many other bits of information of no particular use to Casey.

A strange, inner excitement held Casey awake long after Jim Cassidy was asleep snoring. He lay looking up into the leafy branches of the sycamore beside him and watched a star slip slowly across an open space between the branches. Farther up the grove a hilarious group of young hikers sang snatches of songs to the uncertain accompaniment of a ukelele. A hundred feet away on his right, occasional cars went coasting past on the down grade, coming in off the desert, or climbed more slowly with motors working, on their way up from the valley below. The shifting brilliance from their headlights flicked the grove capriciously as they went by. Now and then a car stopped. One, a big, high-powered car with one dazzling spotlight swung into the narrow driveway and entered the grove.

Casey lifted his head like a desert turtle and blinked curiously at the car as it eased past him a few feet and stopped. A gloved hand went out to the spotlight and turned it slowly, lighting the grove foot by foot and pausing to dwell upon each silent, parked car. Casey sat up in the blankets and waited.

Luck, he told himself, was grinning at him from ear to ear. For this was Smiling Lou himself, and none other. He was alone, —a big, hungry, official fish searching the grove greedily. Casey swallowed a grin and tried to look scared. The light was slowly working around in his direction.

I don't suppose Casey Ryan had ever looked really scared in his life. His face simply refused to wear so foreign an expression. Therefore, when the spotlight finally revealed him, Casey blinked against it with a half-hearted grin, as if he had been caught at something foolish. The light remained upon him, and Smiling Lou got out of the car and came back to him slowly.

Not even Casey thought of calling Smiling Lou a fool. He couldn't be and play the game he was playing. Smiling Lou said nothing whatever until he had looked the car over carefully (giving the license number a second sharp glance) and had regarded Casey fixedly while he made up his mind.

"Hullo! Where's your pardner?" he demanded then.

"I'm in pardnerships with myself this trip," Casey retorted. He waited while Smiling Lou looked him over again, more carefully this time.

"Where did you get that car?"

"From Kenner-for sixteen-hundred and seventeen dollars and five cents." Casey fumbled in the blankets-Smiling Lou following his movements suspiciously-and got out the makings of a cigarette.

"Got any booze in that car?" Smiling Lou might have been a traffic cop, for all the trace of humanity there was in his voice.

Casey cocked an eye up at him, sent a quick glance toward the Ford, and looked back into Smiling Lou's face. He hunched his shoulders and finished the making of his cigarette.

"I wisht you wouldn't look," he said glumly. "I got half my outfit in there an' I hate to have it tore up."

Smiling Lou continued to look at him, seeming slightly puzzled. But indecision was not one of his characteristics, evidently. He stepped up to the car, pulled a flashlight from his pocket and looked in.

Casey was up and into his clothes by the time Smiling Lou had uncovered a box or two. Smiling Lou turned toward him, his lips twitching.

"Lift this stuff out of here and put it in my car," he commanded, elation creeping into his voice in spite of himself. "My Lord! The chances you fellows take! Think a dab of paint is going to cover up a brand burnt into the wood?"

Casey looked startled, glancing down into the car to where Smiling Lou pointed.

"The boards is turned over on all the rest," he muttered confidentially. "I dunno how that darned Canadian Club sign got right side up."

"What all have you got?" Smiling Lou lowered his voice when he asked the question. Casey tried not to grin when he replied. Smiling Lou gasped,

"Well, get it into my car, and make it snappy."

Casey made it as snappy as he could, and kept his face straight until Smiling Lou spoke to him sharply.

"I won't take you in to-night with me. I want that car. You drive it into headquarters first thing in the morning. And don't think you can beat it, either. I'll have the road posted. You can knock a good deal off your sentence if you crank up and come in right after breakfast. And make it an early breakfast, too."

His manner was stern, his voice perfectly official. But Casey, eyeing him grimly, saw distinctly the left eyelid lower and lift again.

"All right—I'm the goat," he surrendered and sat down again on his canvas-covered bed. He did not immediately crawl between the blankets, however, because interesting things were happening over at Jim Cassidy's car.

Casey watched Jim Cassidy go picking his way amongst the tree roots and camp litter, his back straightened under the load of hootch he was carrying to Smiling Lou's car. With Jim Cassidy also, Smiling Lou was crisply official. When the last of the hootch had been transferred, Casey heard Smiling Lou tell Jim Cassidy to drive in to headquarters after breakfast next morning-but he did not see Smiling Lou wink when he said it.

After that, Smiling Lou started his motor and drove slowly up through the grove, halting to scan each car as he passed. He swung out through the upper driveway, turned sharply there and came back down the highway speeding up on the downhill grade to San Bernardino.

Jim Cassidy came furtively over and settle down for a whispered conference on Casey's bed.

"How much did he get off'n YOU?" he asked inquisitively. "Did he clean yuh out?"

"Clean as a last year's bone in a kioty den," Casey declared, hiding his satisfaction as best he could. "Never got my roll though."

"He wouldn't—not with you workin' on the inside. Guess it must be kinda touchy around here right now. New officers, mebby. He wouldn't a' cleaned us out if we'd a' been safe. He never came into camp before-not when I've been here. Made that same play to you, didn't he-about givin' yourself up in the morning? Uh course yuh know what that means-DON'T!"

"He shore is foxy, all right," Casey commented with absolute sincerity. "You can ask anybody if he didn't pull it off like the pleasure was all his'n. No L. A. traffic cop ever pinched me an I looked like he enjoyed it more."

"Oh, Lou's cute, all right. They don't any of 'em put anything over on Lou. You must be new at the business, ain't yuh?"

"Second trip," Casey informed him with an air of importance-which he really felt, by the way. "What Casey's studyin' on now, is the next move. No use hangin' around here empty. What do YOU figger on doin'?"

"Well, Lou didn't give no tip-not to me, anyway. So I guess it'll be safe to drive on in to the city and load up again. I got a feller with me-he caught a ride in to San Berdoo; left just before you drove in. Know where to go in the city? 'Cause I can ride in with you, an' let him foller."

"That'll suit me fine," Casey declared. And so they left it for the time being, and Cassidy went back to bed.

A great load had dropped from Casey's shoulders, and he was asleep before Jim Cassidy had ceased to turn restlessly in his blankets. Getting the White Mule out of his car and into the car of Smiling Lou had been the task which Nolan had set for him. What was to happen thereafter Casey could only guess, for Nolan had not told him. And such was the Casey Ryan nature that he made no attempt to solve the problems which Mack Nolan had calmly reserved for himself.

He did not dream, for instance, that Mack Nolan had watched him load the stuff into Smiling Lou's car. He did know that an unobtrusive Cadillac roadster was parked at the next campfire. It had come in half an hour behind him, but the driver had not made any move toward camping until after dark. Casey had glanced his way when the car was parked and the driver got out and began fussing around the car, but he had not been struck with any sense of familiarity in the figure.

There was no reason why he should. Thousands and thousands of men are of Mack Nolan's height and general build. This man looked like a doctor or a dentist perhaps. Beyond the matter of size, similarity to Mack Nolan ceased. The Cadillac man wore a vandyke beard and colored glasses, and a panama and light gray business suit. Casey set him down in his mental catalog as "some town feller" and assumed that they had nothing in common.

Yet Mack Nolan heard nearly every word spoken by Smiling Lou, Casey and Jim Cassidy. (Readers are so inquisitive about these things that I felt I ought to tell you-else you'll be worrying as hard as Casey Ryan did later on. I'm soft-hearted, myself; I never like to worry a reader more than is absolutely necessary. So I'm letting you in, hoping you'll get an added kick out of Casey's further maneuvers).

The Cadillac car, I should explain, was only one of Mack Nolan's little secrets. There is a very good garage at Goffs, not many miles from Juniper Wells. A matter of an hour's driving was sufficient at any time for Mack Nolan to make the exchange. And no man at Goffs would think it very strange that the owner of a Cadillac should prefer to drive a Ford over rough, desert trails to his prospect in the mountains. Mack Nolan, as I have told you before, had a way with him.

Chapter XX

With a load of booze in the car and Jim Cassidy by his side, Casey Ryan drove down the long, eucalyptus-shaded avenue that runs past the balloon school at Arcadia and turned into the Foothill Boulevard. Half a mile farther on a Cadillac roadster honked and slid past them, speeding away toward Monrovia. But Casey Ryan was busy talking chummily with Jim Cassidy, and he scarcely knew that a car had passed.

The money he had been given for Smiling Lou had been used to pay for this new load of whisky, and Casey found himself wishing that he could get word of it to Mack Nolan. Still, Nolan's oversight in the matter of arranging for communication between them did not bother Casey much. He was doing his part; if Mack Nolan failed to do his, that was no fault of Casey Ryan's.

At Fontana, where young Kenner had stopped for gas on that eventful first trip of Casey's, Casey slowed down also, for the same purpose, half tempted to call up the Little Woman on long distance while the gas tank was being filled. But presently the matter went clean from his mind-and this was the reason:

A speed cop whose motorcycle stood inconspicuously around the corner of the garage, came forward and eyed the Ford sharply. He drew his little book from his pocket, turned a few leaves, found what he was looking for and eyed again the car. The garage man, slowly turning the crank of the gasoline pump, looked at him inquiringly; but the speed cop ignored the look and turned to Casey.

"Where'd you get this car?" he demanded, in much the same tone which Smiling Lou had used the night before.

"Bought it," Casey told him gruffly.

"Where did you buy it?"

"Over at Goffs, just this side of Needles."

"Got a bill of sale?"

"You got Casey Ryan's word fer it," Casey retorted, with a growing heat inside, where he kept his temper when he wasn't using it.

"Are you Casey Ryan?" The speed cop's eyes hardened just a bit.

"Anybody says I ain't, you send 'em to me-an' then come around in about ten minutes an' look 'em over."

"What's YOUR name?" The officer turned to Jim Cassidy.

"Tom Smith. I was just ketchin' a ride with this feller. Don't go an' mix ME in —I ain't no ways concerned; just ketchin' a ride is all. If I'd 'a' knowed —"

"You can explain that to the judge. Get in there, you, and drive in to San Berdoo. I'll be right with you, so you needn't forget the road!" He stepped back to his motorcycle and pushed it forward.

"Hey! Don't I git paid fer my gas?" the garage man wailed, pulling a dripping nozzle from Casey's gas tank.

"Aw, go tahell!" Casey grunted, and threw a wadded bank note in his direction. "Take that an' shut up. What yuh cryin' around about a gallon uh gas, fer? YOU ain't pinched!"

The money landed near the motorcycle and the officer picked it up, smoothed out the bill, glanced at it and looked through tightened lids at Casey.

"Throwin' money around like a hootch-runner!" he sneered. "I guess you birds need lookn' after, all right. Git goin'!"

Casey "got going." Twice on the way in the officer spurted up alongside and waved him down for speeding. Casey had not intended to speed, either. He was merely keeping pace unconsciously with his thoughts.

He had been told just what he must do if he were arrested for bootlegging, but he was not at all certain that his instructions would cover an arrest for stealing an automobile. Nolan had forgotten about that, he guessed. But Casey's optimism carried him jauntily to jail in San

Bernardino, and while he was secretly a bit uneasy, he was not half so worried as Jim Cassidy appeared to be.

Casey was booked-along with "Tom Smith" —on two charges: theft of one Ford car, motor number so-and-so, serial number this-and-that, model, touring, year, whatever-it-was. And, unlawful transportation of spirituous liquor. He tried to give the judge the wink, but without any happy result. So he eventually found himself locked in a cell with Jim Cassidy.

Just at first, Casey Ryan was proud of the part he was playing. He could look with righteous toleration upon the limpness of his fellow prisoner. He could feel secure in the knowledge that he, Casey Ryan, was an agent of the government engaged in helping to uphold the laws of his country.

He waited for an hour or two, listening with a superior kind of patience to Jim Cassidy's panicky unbraidings of his luck. At first Jim was inclined to blame Casey rather bitterly for the plight he was in. But Casey soon stopped that. Young Kenner was the responsible party in this mishap, as Casey very soon made plain to Jim.

"Well, I dunno but what you're right. It WAS kind of a dirty trick-workin' a stole car off onto you. Why didn't he pick some sucker on the outside? Don't line up with Kenner, somehow. Well, I guess mebby Smilin' Lou can see us out uh this hole all right-only I don't like that car-stealin' charge. Mebby Kenner an' Lou can straighten it up, though."

Casey wondered if they could. He wondered, too, how Nolan was going to find out about Smiling Lou getting the camouflaged White Mule. Nolan had not explained that to Casey-but Casey was not worrying yet. His faith in Mack Nolan was firm.

Came bedtime, however, with no sign of official favor toward Casey Ryan. Casey began to wonder. But probably, he consoled himself with thinking, they meant to wait until Jim Cassidy was asleep before they turned Casey loose. He lay on the hard bunk and waited hopefully, listening to the stertorous breathing of Jim Cassidy, who had forgotten his troubles in sleep.

Chapter XXI

At noon the next day Casey was still waiting-but not hopefully. "Patience on a monument" couldn't have resembled Casey Ryan in any particular whatever. He was mad. By midnight he had begun to wonder if he was not going to be made a goat again. By daylight, he was positive that he was already a goat. By the time the trusty brought his breakfast, Casey was applying to Mack Nolan the identical words and phrases which he had applied to young Kenner when he was the maddest. Don't ask me to tell you what they were.

Jim Cassidy still clung desperately to his faith in Smiling Lou; but Casey's faith hadn't so much as a finger-hold on anything. What kind of a government was it, he asked himself bitterly, that would leave a trusted agent twenty-four hours shut up in a cell with a whining crook like Jim Cassidy? If, he added pessimistically, he were an agent of the government. Casey doubted it. So far as he could see, Casey Ryan wasn't anything but the goat.

His chief desire now was to get out of there as soon as possible so that he could hunt up Mack Nolan and lick the livin' tar wit of him-or worse. He wanted bail and he wanted it immediately. Not a soul bad come near him, save the trusty, in spite of certain mysterious messages which Casey had sent to the office, asking for an interview with the judge or somebody; Casey didn't care who. Locked in a cell, how was he going to do any of the things Nolan had told him to do if he happened to find himself arrested by an honest officer?

When they hauled him before the police judge, Casey hadn't been given the chance to explain anything to anybody. Unless, of course, he wanted to beller out his business before everybody; and that, he told himself fiercely, was not Casey Ryan's idea of the way to keep a secret. More-over, that damned speed cop was standing right there, just waiting for a chance to wind his fingers in Casey's collar and choke him off if he tried to say a word. And how the hell, Casey would like to know, was a man going to explain himself when he couldn't get a word in edgeways?

So Casey wanted bail. There were just two ways of getting it, and it went against the grain of his pride to take either one. That is why Casey waited until noon before his Irish stubbornness yielded a bit and he decided to wire me to come. He had to slip the wire out by the underground method-meaning the good will of the trusty. It cost Casey ten dollars, but he didn't grudge that.

He spent that afternoon and most of the night mentally calling the trusty a liar and a thief because there was no reply to the message. As a matter of fact, the trusty sent the wire through as quickly as possible and the fault was mine if any one's. I was too busy hurrying to the rescue to think about sending Casey word that I was coming. Casey said afterwards that my thoughtlessness would be cured for life if I were ever locked in jail and waiting for news.

As it happened, I wired the Little Woman that Casey was in jail again, and caught the first train to San "Berdoo" —coming down by way of Barstow. I could save two or three hours that way, I found, so I told the Little Woman to meet me there and bring all the money she could get her hands on. Not knowing just what Casey was in for this time, it seemed well to be prepared for a good, stiff bail. She beat me by several hours, and between us we had ten thousand dollars.

At that it was a fool's errand. Casey was out of jail and gone before either of us arrived. So there we were, holding the bag, as you might say, and our ten thousand dollars' bail money.

"It's no use asking questions, Jack," the Little Woman told me pensively when we had finished our salad in the best cafe in town, and were waiting for the fish. "I've asked questions of every uniform in this town, from the district judge down to the courthouse janitor. Nobody knows a thing. I DID find that Casey was booked yesterday for having a stolen car and a load of booze in his possession, but he isn't in jail-or if he is, they're keeping him down in some dungeon and have thrown away the key. It was hinted in the police court that he was dismissed for want of evidence; but they wouldn't SAY anything, and so there you are!"

We finished our fish in a thoughtful silence. Then, when the waiter had removed the plates, the Little Woman looked at me with a twinkle in her eyes.

"Well-sir, there's something I want to tell you, Jack. I believe Casey has put this town on the run. They can't tell ME! Something's happened, over around the courthouse. A lot of the men I talked with had a scared look in their eyes, and they were nervous when doors opened, and looked around when people came walking along. I don't know what he's been doing-but Casey Ryan's been up to something. You can't tell ME! I know how our laundry boy looks when Casey's home."

"And didn't you get any line at all on his whereabouts?" I asked her. Given three hours the start of me, I knew perfectly well that the Little Woman had found out all there was to know about Casey.

"Well-sir —I've got this to go on," the Little Woman drawled and held a telegram across the table. "You'll notice that was sent from Goffs. It's ten days old, but I've been getting ready ever since it arrived. I've put Babe in a boarding-school, and I leased the apartment house. I kept three dressmakers ruining their eyes with nightwork, Jack, making up some nifty sports clothes. If Casey's bound to stay in the desert-well, I'm his wife-and Casey does kind of like to have me around. You can't tell ME.

"So I've got the twin-six packed with the niftiest camp outfit you ever saw, Jack. I've got a yellow and red beach umbrella, and two reclining chairs, and-well-sir, I'm going to rough it de luxe. I don't expect to keep Casey in hand —I happen to know him. But it's just possible, Jack, that I can keep him in sight!"

Of course I told her-as I've told her often enough before-that she was a brick. I added that I would go along, if she liked; which she did. Not even the Little Woman should ever attempt to drive across the Mojave alone.

We started out as soon as we had finished the meal. A Cadillac roadster came up behind us and honked for clear passing as we swung into the long, straight stretch that leads up the Cajon. The Little Woman peered into the rear vision mirror and pressed the toe of her white pump upon the accelerator.

"There's only one man in the world that can pass ME on the road," the Little Woman drawled, "and he doesn't wear a panama!"

As we snapped around the turns of Cajon Grade, I looked back once or twice. The Cadillac roadster was still following pertinaciously, but it was too far back to honk at us. When we slid down to the Victorville garage and stopped for gas, the Cadillac slid by. The driver in the panama gave us one glance through his colored glasses, but I felt, somehow, that the glance was sufficiently comprehensive to fix us firmly in his memory. I inquired at the garage concerning Casey Ryan, taking it for granted he would be driving a Ford. A man of that description had stopped at the garage for gas that forenoon, the boy told me. About nine o'clock, I learned from further questioning.

"Well-sir, that gives him five hours the start," the Little Woman remarked, as she eased in the clutch and slid around the corner into the highway to Barstow. "But you can't tell me I can't run down a Ford with this car. I know to the last inch what a Jawn Henry is good for. I drove one myself, remember. Now we'll see."

Chapter XXII

At Dagget, the big, blue car with a lady driver sounded the warning signal and passed Mack Nolan and the Cadillac roadster. Like Casey Ryan, Nolan is rather proud of his driving, and with sufficient reason. He was already hurrying, not to overhaul Casey, but to arrive soon after him.

Women drivers loved to pass other cars with a sudden spurt of speed, he had found by experience. They were not, however, consistently fast drivers. Mack Nolan was conscious of a slight irritation when the twin-six took the lead. Somewhere ahead-probably in one of the rough, sandy stretches-he would either have to pass that car or lag behind. Your expert driver likes a clear road ahead.

So Mack Nolan drove a bit harder, and succeeded in getting most of the dust kicked up by the big, blue car. He counted on passing before they reached Ludlow, but he could never quite make it. In that ungodly stretch of sand and rocks and chuck-holes that lies between Ludlow and Amboy, Nolan was sure that the woman driver would have to slow down. He swore a little, too, because she would probably slow down just where passing was impossible. They always did.

They went through Amboy like one party, the big, blue car leading by twenty-five yards. It was a long drive for a woman to make; a hard drive to boot. He wondered if the two in the big car ever ate.

Five miles east of Amboy, when a red sunset was darkening to starlight, the blue car, fifty yards in the lead, overhauled a Ford in trouble. In the loose, sandy trail the big car slowed and stopped abreast of the Ford. There was no passing now, unless Mack Nolan wanted to risk smashing his crank-case on a lava rock, millions of which peppered that particular portion of the Mojave Desert. He stopped perforce.

A pair of feet with legs attached to them, protruded from beneath the running board of the Ford. The Little Woman in the big car leaned over the side and studied the feet critically.

"Casey Ryan, are those the best pair of shoes you own?" she drawled at last. "If you wouldn't wear such rundown heels, you know, you wouldn't look so bow-legged. I've told you and TOLD you that your legs aren't so bad when you wear straight heels."

Casey Ryan crawled out and looked up at her grinning sheepishly.

"They was all right when I left home, ma'am," he defended his shoes mildly. "Desert plays hell with shoe leather-you can ask anybody." Then he added, "Hullo, Jack! What you two think you're doin', anyway. Tryin' t' elope?"

"Why, hello, Ryan!" Mack Nolan greeted, coming up from the Cadillac. "Having trouble with your car?" Casey whirled and eyed Nolan dubiously.

"Naw. This ain't no trouble," he granted. "I only been here four hours or so-this is pastime!"

There was an awkward silence. We in the blue car wanted to know (not at that time knowing) who was the man in the Cadillac roadster, and how he happened to know Casey so well. Nolan, no doubt, wanted to know who we were. And there was so much that Casey wanted to know and needed to know that he couldn't seem to think of anything. However, Casey was the hardest to down. He came up to the side of the blue car, reached in with his hands all greasy black, and took the Little Woman's hand from the wheel and kissed it. The Little Woman made a caressing sound and leaned out to him-and Nolan and I felt that we mustn't look. So our eyes met.

He came around to my side of the car and put out his hand.

"I'm pretty good at guessing," he smiled. "I guess you're Jack Gleason. Casey has talked of you to me. I'm right glad to meet you, too. My name is Mack Nolan, and I'm Irish. I'm Casey Ryan's partner. We have a good-prospect."

Casey looked past the Little Woman and me, straight into Mack Nolan's eyes. I felt something of an electric quality in the air while their gaze held.

"I'm just getting back from a trip down in the valley," Nolan observed easily. "You never did see me in town duds, did you, Casey?" His eyes went to the Little Woman's face and then to me. "I suppose you know what this wild Irishman has just pulled off back there," he said, tilting his head toward San Bernardino, many a mile away to the southwest. "You wouldn't think it to look at him, but he surely has thrown a monkey wrench into as pretty a bootlegging machine as there is in the country. It's such confidential stuff, of course, that you may call it absolutely secret. But for once I'm telling the truth about it.

"Your husband, Mrs. Casey Ryan, holds a commission from headquarters as a prohibition officer. A deputy, it is true, —but commissioned nevertheless. He's just getting back from a very pretty piece of work. A crooked officer named Smiling Lou was arrested last night. He had all kinds of liquor cached away in his house. Casey can tell you sometime how he trapped him.

"Of course, I'm just an amateur mining expert on a vacation, myself." His eyes met Casey's straight. "I wasn't with him when he pulled the deal, but I heard about it afterwards, and I knew he was planning something of the sort when he left camp. How I happened to know about the commission," he added, reaching into his pocket, "is because he left it with me for safe keeping. I'm going to let you look at it-just in case he's too proud to let it out of his hands once I give it back.

"Now, of course, I'm talking like an old woman and telling all Casey's secrets-and you'll probably see a real Irish fight when he gets in reach of me. But I knew he hadn't told you exactly what he's doing, and —I personally feel that his wife and his best friend are entitled to know as much as his partner knows about him."

The Little Woman nodded absently her thanks. She was holding Casey's commission under the dash-light to read it.

I saw Casey gulp once or twice while he stared across the car at Mack Nolan. He pushed his dusty, black hat forward over one eyebrow and reached into his pocket.

"Aw, hell," he grunted, grinning queerly. "You come around here oncet, Mr. Nolan, where I can git my hands on yuh!"